DRAGON BONES BOOK I
CONQUEST

CELESTE HARTE

IMMORTAL WORKS

Appropriate for Teens, Intriguing to Adults

Immortal Works LLC
1505 Glenrose Drive
Salt Lake City, Utah 84104
Tel: (385) 202-0116

© 2020 Celeste Harte
https://celesteharte.wordpress.com/

Cover Art by Ashley Literski
http://strangedevotion.wixsite.com/strangedesigns

All rights reserved, including the right to reproduce this book or portions thereof in any form whatsoever. For more information email contact@immortal-works.com or visit http://www.immortal-works.com/contact/.

This book is a work of fiction. Names, characters, businesses, organizations, places, events and incidents either are the product of the author's imagination or are used fictitiously. Any resemblance to actual persons, living or dead, events, or locales is entirely coincidental.

ISBN 978-1-7343866-4-6 (Paperback)
ASIN B083JY95R5 (Kindle Edition)

I want to dedicate this book to my family and friends, who inspired me the entire way through. And to all the black kids that wanted to see themselves as the kings and queens they deserve to be.

BREAKING NEWS

My heels clicked as I stomped the pavement on my way home, the sun beating down hard and making the dry air radiate with heat. Around me, the city buzzed with life—hover cars whizzed through the air above me and crowds of people milled about the street around me.

My eWatch vibrated.

Lora: Jashi, are you all right? What happ

The rest of the text didn't fit on the watch's tiny screen. I swiped at it to get rid of the message, not feeling like explaining how I lost another job. That could come later, after a large scoop of ice cream and several episodes of my favorite crime dramas.

When I finally reached my apartment, I swiped my keycard at the pad so quickly, it didn't even read it properly and a red light declared my access was denied. Another more controlled swipe did the trick. The door opened and I didn't even acknowledge the doorman on my way to the elevator, pushing the heck out of the button to the fifth floor.

I could imagine he saw that as rude. I disagreed. Whatever I might have said to him in my current state of mind would have been much worse than not saying anything at all. In my opinion, I was being remarkably considerate.

The elevator dinged and opened the door to my floor. When I reached my apartment, I kicked off my heels, threw my backpack down on the couch, and swung open the freezer. My ice cream waited for me on the bottom shelf.

I didn't even bother getting out a bowl to scoop it into. I just grabbed a spoon from out the drawer, closed the freezer, and plopped down in front of the HoloScreen to watch crime dramas.

I needed to get involved in a drama that was not my own.

As my mouth filled with the creamy goodness that was strawberry-flavored ice cream, the theme song to "The City of Kohpal: Criminology" started up. The ice cream did me good on a hot day like today.

Actually, every day. Being hot was a fact of life for people living in the desert.

Just as I'd nearly forgotten about my troubles at the diner, Cobolt Falkner—local news broadcaster—replaced the image of the dreamy Detective Asher.

"Hey!" I objected, my protests muffled by the spoon sticking out of my mouth. "Thupid newth channelth interrupting videoth on demand. Thith hath to be thome violathon of righth!"

Colbolt Falkner didn't respond to my accusations. The jerk. "Breaking news. A word from the great Faresh Kahmel of the Omah clan."

I groaned. Not again.

The "great" Faresh appeared on the screen, cameras flashing all around him and his secretary of defense, Arusi Zuwei. The Faresh held himself with definite authority—a dark pair of sunglasses over his eyes, his pronounced jaw set in a firm line, expressionless. Both he and his secretary were of a dark complexion, being native K'sundii, though she was dwarfed in comparison to the Faresh.

The secretary was first to speak. "I'm here to announce that we have successfully claimed another province of the Omani region."

Her dark eyes trained on the camera. "It is now considered part of the Vishra region of K'sundi."

The Faresh spoke, his cold, dark features like stone. "Yes, and my conquest isn't over yet. You can expect new land for the Makril region soon as well. Let the Omanians beware. Stay out of my way or be forced to surrender."

The news broadcast ended abruptly, returning me to my show. Detective Asher had just about wrapped up the case.

If they were going to interrupt video on demand, the least they could do was pause it.

Before I could reach for my remote to rewind my show, my eWatch rang. Groaning, I prepped my finger to swipe away Lora's call when I froze, realizing I was about to deny the wrong person.

Nana.

I took the spoon out my mouth, straightened my back, adjusted the curls in my hair that had been thrown askew by the wind, then answered.

"Hi, Nana," I said as her face hovered in front of me, projected by the Holo emitter on my watch.

"Hey, Jashi. How have you been?" Nana's flawless, brown skin wrinkled as she smiled. I could only hope to age as gracefully as Nana did when the time came for me. Her white, curly hair was still shiny and full. Her skin only showed the slightest wrinkles when she smiled. But the most ageless part of her were her sharp, dark eyes, quick to see through dishonesty and to catch little ones trying to steal cookies from the kitchen. The Holo emitter made her image from the torso up quiver every now and then as the projection glowed before me.

"Fine, fine." I bit my tongue, not feeling very *fine* at all, but no need to worry her. The poor woman put everything into me. She had her own life to be concerned with. Maybe she'd eventually get the message that my moving out meant she didn't have to take care of me anymore. I was eighteen. I didn't need these regular "checkups" to make sure I was all right.

Though, thinking about what happened only a few hours ago at the diner, I had to concede that her "checkups" weren't without reason.

"How have you been, Nana? Have you been keeping up on your medication?" I decided to try to twist the situation into a checkup on *her*. She was an older woman. She was the one that needed taking care of now.

She sighed, shaking her head. "I hate my medication, but yes. Can't rightly own an orphanage if I'm not in good health, so you don't have to worry about that."

Good. I was worrying about *her*, not the other way around. "That's good. How are the kids there?"

"They're just fine. Tobi asks about you, though. I think he misses you."

"Aw, give him a hug for me."

She chuckled. "How's the job?"

"Oh, you know." I couldn't bring myself to lie to Nana, so my mind raced for another topic to talk about so she wouldn't ask any more questions. Anything.

Glancing at the HoloScreen, the news broadcast came to mind. "Did you see what the Faresh said on the news?"

"No, what happened?"

The news always got to her. Nana was an old-fashioned patriot and even went to every ceremony of Prosperity for the nation on weekends. Mentioning the Faresh was sure to deviate her attention.

Careful to hide the smirk that tugged at my lips, I continued, "He's officially conquered more territory for the Vishra region. And he mentioned getting more territory for the Makril region."

"Oh, is that all?"

I frowned at her quicker than I could stop myself. "What do you mean, 'oh, is that all?' This is ridiculous! Faresh Kahmel defended us when the Omanians tried to take over, but once the Omanians surrendered, there was no need for this mission of conquest! How can you just act like this man looking for trouble is fine?"

Her face turned stern, and only then did I realize how high my voice had gotten. "What happened to this nation over the last two years is not to be taken lightly, Jashi," she said. "The Omanians would have destroyed us. Kahmel coming into office was the only thing that saved us from ruin, so don't act like he was unprovoked."

I winced, humbled. Part of me wanted to write off her opinion as just her undying loyalty to K'sundi, but I knew better than that. The Omanians did play foul when they tried to take us over during our weakest hour. "I just don't trust this new Faresh, Nana," I confessed. "I mean, what do we know about him, really? He's from a little-known clan, he has strange politics, and he seems hellbent on taking over Omani for trying to take over us. But other than that, we don't know anything. He has no political background, no deep connections as far as we know. And the Courts, the only people in the nation that have more power than the Faresh, are doing nothing about it."

"Sounds like you have more of a problem with *how* he got in office than his actual campaign. You've always been against the more traditional side of K'sundi."

I bit my lip, once again, exposed. But I was older now and had a firmer understanding of our world, mature enough to have an opinion on it and challenge her thinking.

She was right that I didn't like how Kahmel got into office. Our nation was without a leader for eight years following the assassination of our last Faresh. I still remembered coming home one day from school to find Nana so distraught, she could barely tell me what was wrong with her. She was just shaking, staring at the HoloScreen. The Faresh at that time and his entire family clan had been killed. Even though I was only nine, I was still just as shocked as she was. I'd never heard of it happening before, not even in my history texts.

The case remained unsolved, even to this day. Rebels were suspected to have been involved, though.

The Courts were forced to select a new Faresh from one of the branch families, and the decision-making process took a long time. It seemed like every time the Courts nearly reached a decision, another royal clan family would rise out of nowhere and demand they restart the process in consideration for that clan's right to the throne. Anyone with enough royal blood in their family lineage had a claim. Normally, the Faresh reserved the right to choose an heir from his clan, though he typically chose his first-born. But the whole clan being slaughtered in a mysterious attack that came and went like a thief in the night was unprecedented.

Then came Kahmel and his unexpected claim to the throne.

Nana pegged me. "I don't like our nation's politics," I said. "The rest of the world has *democracy*, Nana, not kings and queens. Their leaders have to work for their positions. And now we have this new Faresh who, for all we know, could be a snake-oil salesman! But because he's blue-blooded and cited some ancient law no one even remembers, he now controls our whole nation."

She shook her head. "You complain that our Fareshes don't earn their positions, so I would think you'd commemorate Kahmel's rise to the throne. He didn't just quote a law and walk into the palace. He unearthed our most ancient traditions, stopped the Omanians from their invasion attempt, and claimed what was rightfully his by law. You're talking out of both sides of your mouth, and I suggest you close both of them if you don't know what you're talking about."

I gritted my teeth, once again put back in my place. Would I always be pushed back into this circle where Nana didn't take me seriously, where I was still being treated like a kid?

But then I realized that maybe this *was* Nana acknowledging my maturity. I forgot that while I was now able to defend my opinions and my ways of thinking, that also meant she could use her sharp tongue to defend hers.

Knowing that made me feel a little better.

And it *was* true that Kahmel had to go through a lot to get to where he was. The Omanians tried to invade us while our nation was submerged in confusion. The Courts weren't made to lead the country, only pass laws. They had no power to militarize the country or set up defenses to protect us from the coming invasion.

Kahmel Omah changed the game when he took a band of men to the borders and overtook one of the major Omanian air fortresses overnight. No one knew how he did it.

Not only that, but he had taken control of the air fortress, slaughtered all of the enemies on it, and had taken all of the data available on its computers to the Courts—a modern-day version of bringing the head of a war general. Kahmel then did the unthinkable, claiming his right to the throne as a hero of war. Eons ago, K'sundi was a country that valued warriors above anything else and, according to the ancient scripts, he had proven his merit as a warrior more than the other clans did by claiming the fortress.

What he was doing was unprecedented, but technically, no one could refuse him. The way I understood it, the laws were so antiquated, no one even remembered they existed. And yet, since there had been no laws made to refute or abolish them, the laws still held. While the other clans had been fighting for years to take the throne, this man had blown all of them out of the water overnight, becoming Faresh in a matter of months.

After that, he proceeded to militarize our armies and defend our territory from the enemy. It didn't take long for them to surrender. But Kahmel didn't accept it. He started two years ago, and he was still claiming their territory as his own today.

I didn't like Kahmel. Everything he did was too mysterious. The rumors about him stated he was ruthless and, above all, paranoid. He had dozens of members of his administration executed for treason against the throne. No one ever saw him out in public unless he made an announcement, like today. And when he was seen, he was always wearing sunglasses. He was just too strange for me.

And potentially dangerous. Defending us from the Omanians was one thing. Destroying them was another.

Seeing that my silence was already admitting she was right, I said, "All right, Nana. But I don't like the idea of warring with Omani just because they did it to us. That's not going to bring peace."

Nana sighed. "I don't blame you. You're young. You have a very modern way of thinking. But when you get to be my age, you learn that you don't get peace by just sitting around waiting for it. You have to fight for it. Kahmel knows that. One day, you'll see." Her eyes drifted off, looking toward me but not at me, and I got the feeling there was more to her words than she was letting on. Just as I was about to say something, she said, "I've got to go. My shows are coming on. I'll talk to you later, Jashi."

Her face disappeared.

Strange. It wasn't like Nana to hide things from me.

Shaking it off, I decided to just watch my show. Pressing rewind on the HoloScreen remote, I continued the show from where I left off, shoving another big scoop of strawberry ice cream in my mouth as I browsed the Internet on my phone for job offers.

EYE CONTACT

The breath from my mouth created little clouds of mist as I walked to my car, rubbing my hands together for warmth as I got inside. I swiped my numb fingers across the touchscreen to access the heat controls, setting it as high as it would go. The fans turned on, and warm air spread throughout the car. I sighed in relief, muttering to myself yet another complaint about living in the desert—ridiculously cold in the early morning and hot in the evening. Never comfortable.

Shaking my head, I activated the HoloControls. A panel of purple screens glowed to life around me, giving me complete control of everything. The rearview screen turned on, and I started up the engine and hover controls. Taking hold of the wheel, I started on my way, joining the hectic traffic above me.

At the last second, I pressed a button, and a light lit up, indicating that the glowing taxi sign below my vehicle was on. I nearly forgot to turn it on. That would have been great. Losing my latest job on my very first day because no one even knew my car was a cab.

The metropolis of Kohpal lay below me—sky-high buildings and flying cars everywhere, the morning sun pinking the sky in the distance, a lonely speckle of clouds drifting by above. Of course, there were never many of those around here. From here, I could just barely make out the peaks that made up the Dharia mountain range from behind the skyscrapers, the natural border between the desert half of K'sundi and the forest half on the other side.

My phone rang, and I glanced at my eWatch. Lora. I tapped on my watch and turned on the speaker phone.

"Hello?"

"Hey, just checking up on you. How's work?"

I clucked my tongue. "By checking up on me, do you mean wondering if I'm still pissed at Dreik? Absolutely."

She sighed, probably knowing I wasn't going to back down on this. She was going to try anyway. Otherwise, she wouldn't be Lora. "I'm sure if you just apologize, he'll let you work at the diner again."

"There's nothing for me to apologize for. Those customers should be apologizing to *me*. They were totally rude, and Dreik refused to stick up for you or me."

"You don't have a degree. You're lucky he hired you at all."

"Yeah, and you have a degree, plus you're working to get your master's and he doesn't stick up for you, either. He's a wuss, and I'm not going back there. Besides, I have a new job now."

"And how long is that going to last before your temper gets ahead of you and you blow up at someone else? I'm just telling you, as a friend, that I think you should at least *try* to cool it sometimes."

I inwardly laughed at the irony of her choice of wording. "If you tried standing up for yourself, I wouldn't have to blow up at people."

She laughed. "They told me you gave him the finger when he talked to you in his office. Should I do that, too?"

"Ha! I'd pay to see that." Just then, my indicator light turned on, a screen showing me someone was trying to flag me down. "I have to go. Technically I'm not supposed to be on the phone, and I've got a fare."

"All right, I'll see you later."

"Bye."

I pulled up the hover car in front of a dark-skinned man in a suit. He hurriedly climbed in but started as soon as he met my eyes. Ignoring his surprise, I asked, "Where are you headed?"

"Th-third—I mean Fourth street. Fourth Street. 3492," he stuttered, seemingly mesmerized by me.

I sighed, setting the car into motion to join the air traffic and bracing myself for the usual questions.

The man seemed antsy. I heard him moving in his seat to scoot forward. "Can you hurry it up? I'm kind of late."

"Yes, sir," I said, attempting to weave through the traffic in the most legal way possible while still acquiescing to his request.

I heard him sigh, scratching his head before deciding to start up conversation—as predicted. "So...you're dragon tribe, then? I-I mean I assume, judging by your eye color."

"Yeeep," I answered, trying to concentrate on getting around the hover cars all around me to avoid getting angry. *At least try to cool it.*

Yeah, I could do that. Cool it. Gotcha.

"Wow, I've never met a real-life person from the dragon tribe."

What, and you've met a real dead one? I wanted to ask. But I didn't. I was keeping my "cool."

"So how does that work?" The guy kept talking like I was actually participating in the conversation. "I've heard that only five percent of the population has roots in the ancient dragon tribe, so for people like you to exist, do both your parents have to be from the tribe, or was it a stray gene from one of them or something?"

"I wouldn't know. I'm an orphan."

That shut him up for a few seconds. "I'm sorry, I didn't know."

"It's fine." *No, it wasn't.*

"Is what the rumors say about the dragon tribe true, then? Like, can you feel when dragons are around? Or communicate with them somehow?"

"No, not really," I said, gritting my teeth.

He tried to play off his nervousness by chuckling. "Oh. I guess a stereotype like that is a little absurd, if you think about it."

"I guess."

My hands gripped the wheel so tight the material was left with indentures from my fingers. Maybe I wasn't capable of following Lora's suggestion of "cooling it."

When we arrived at his destination, I turned to him, watching as he jolted again at my orange-colored eyes. "Here you are."

"Thank you," he said, reaching for his wallet and practically throwing me the money before leaving out the door.

I counted it, then clucked my tongue. All that, and he didn't even tip well.

Starting up my car, I rejoined the traffic in the air, wondering how many people I'd service today who would ask me the exact same questions.

Sometimes I hated the legends saying that those of the dragon tribe were fearsome warriors back in old times. Those stories were nothing but fuel for stereotypes. The tribe wasn't nearly as big as it once was. Most people feared people of the dragon tribe, somehow believing we might be the same savages of legend. But it was a fact of my life that I'd learned to accept.

I frowned as flashing blue and red lights flared behind me. For once, I hadn't done anything wrong. Regardless, I followed protocol and landed my car, pulling over. The policeman came around to meet me, and I realized he wasn't police at all. He was a Zendaalan agent, evident by his sleek, black robotic suit and badge on his chest, sporting the blue, gray, and yellow of the Zendaalan flag.

Equalizers.

His accent was thick over the speaker on the helmet of his suit. "Can you open the trunk of your car?"

My frown deepened in confusion. "Why?"

The man's face was unchanging. "Open the trunk, please."

Grumbling to myself, I hit the button on my car and leaned into my seat as Mr. Winning Personality continued to glare at me with suspicion, his partner rummaging through the trunk.

My Zendaalan wasn't what it used to be when I learned it in school, but I recognized when the partner announced, "Clear," in their native tongue.

Mr. Winning Personality looked to me. "You speak Zendaalan?"

I sighed, switching to his language as best I could. "A little."

He nodded, as if in approval, then continued in Zendaalan. "Please step out the car, ma'am."

Conceding, I did as he asked, racking my brain to translate what I needed to say in his language. "What is this about?" I said in Zendaalan.

His partner approached me. "We're looking for a woman matching your description who was seen fleeing a government office with stolen goods in their car. Allow us a more thorough search of your car and you will be allowed to go."

I had to ask him to repeat what he'd said slower for me to understand. He put it so casually, it almost seemed like an option. "Go ahead," I said, hoping this would be quick. The longer they spent with me, the less money I earned.

The two men proceeded to make a point of making their search as inconvenient as possible, tossing up everything I had in the backseat, pulling up the floor mats, taking an obnoxiously long time to finish. When they finally did, they muttered something between themselves that I didn't quite catch. Then they turned to me, Mr. Personality speaking first. "Your vehicle is clean. But if you ever see anything suspicious, it is your public duty to report it immediately. Zendaalans do not tolerate rebel activity in any country."

I knew the typical lecture. Rebels threaten the peace. The peace is to be upheld by the individual and collectively by the whole. The Equalization could only be upheld with no deviations from Equalized law.

Blah, blah, blah.

Right now, I just wanted to get back to work.

"Yes. Of course, sir."

The second officer corrected my pronunciation of the Zendaalan phrase for "of course." I accepted the correction with chagrin, then silently rejoiced as they climbed in their squad car.

As I got in my car, I groaned at how they left it, messy and upturned. The floor mats thrown haphazardly, my spare jacket strewn across the seat, extra eWatch chargers, earbuds, and the contents of my first-aid kit everywhere. A few choice words came to mind as I set things back in their place.

Really, I shouldn't have complained too much. The Equalizers were tasked with maintaining peace throughout all of the Equalized nations. Our world of Hemorah was once a chaotic planet that was too divided to do its own people any good. But then the Zendaalans, who had mastered the art of peace, spread their doctrine to other nations around the world. By doing so, they created the Equalization, in which all countries surrendered their leadership to them in exchange for the reinforcement of the peace. The Zendaalans allowed the countries under their reign to maintain their kings, presidents, and leaders so long as they maintained the peace the Equalization provided. Otherwise, the Zendaalans had the right to impeach the leader that infringed on Equalized law, or the country risked being labeled a Rebel Country—a fate worse than death, from what I understood.

The Equalization allowed for a lot of freedoms, all in all. They even allowed countries to war with each other, so long as they didn't surpass the allotted war time Equalized law mandated. If that happened, the Zendaalans stepped in and pronounced a victor themselves.

That was another reason I didn't like this Kahmel Omah guy. Part of me feared he would get us in trouble with the Zendaalans. The fear was somewhat unrealistic, seeing as Zendaal seemed to favor K'sundi and its government at the moment. But maybe the Equalizers would get tired of Kahmel's war and put a stop to it. They certainly would if his war took too long. It had been going on for two years so far. He had three to go before the Equalizers got involved.

Or they could do us one better and get rid of Kahmel altogether.

Sighing, I re-calibrated the rear view screens—knocked out of alignment from all of the rummaging the officers did—and hoped I hadn't lost too much time.

I WAS DYING, feeling every last drop of liquid I had retained in my body secreting from my pores as more steam misted the air in the room.

"Why did I let you convince me to come here?" I groaned in agony.

"Because you're stressed and you need it," Lora said. She placed cucumbers on her eyes and reclined on the bench like it was the most natural thing in the world for her, a white, fluffy robe engulfing her thin frame. Her mahogany skin glistened with sweat. Her angular features stood out more as she leaned her head back and sighed placidly.

"When you said it was a spa treatment, you didn't mention a steam room."

"So?"

"So, it's hot! And it's ninety degrees outside!"

Lora only tsked at me, folding her hands over her stomach.

I groaned again. I wasn't kidding about the temperature. By the time it was noon and the sun was up, I'd switched to air conditioning in the cab. Now that it was evening, the heat was unbearable outside, and Lora wanted me dealing with an oven inside?

"It's good for you, I promise," Lora assured me. "Coming here once a month does wonders for my skin."

"I think I'd rather deal with acne."

She tsked again. "Then leave! I'll enjoy my spa on my own, then."

I tsked back and crossed my arms. She was paying for it after all, despite my insisting. She knew I wouldn't have come otherwise. And she really was looking out for my best interests, even though it felt like she was trying to kill me in the process. I had to admit I was pretty stressed these days, especially after losing my job. Besides, I was sure being stopped by those Zendaalan officers formed a knot in my shoulder. "Fine, fine, I'll stay. But only because of the massages," I said, not wanting to admit she was right.

"Then shut up."

Frowning, I took a cucumber from her eye and promptly bit into it.

She sat up so suddenly, the remaining cucumber slice fell to the floor. "Jashi!"

I cackled as she slapped my arm playfully, aware of the other patrons wagging their heads at our ruckus. Not that I cared.

"Oh!" she said, stopping suddenly. "I forgot to tell you. Did you hear? Handi is getting married!"

"Oh?" This was certainly news to me. I knew Handi from elementary school. We weren't close, but she and Lora were.

Lora nodded her head, her short, bouncy curls following the motion. "And guess what? All this time, she was betrothed and didn't tell me."

My eyes widened. "What? I didn't know her parents were old-fashioned. They arranged her marriage since she was little and everything?"

Lora nodded again, sticking out her full lips as she pursed them. "I am so pissed at her. Almost enough to not come to the wedding. I mean, how could she not tell me something this important all this time?"

"Psh. I highly doubt you won't attend the wedding. You don't have it in you."

She crossed her arms, tilting her head up. "You're not the only one who can get angry, you know."

Even pissed and in a steam room, Lora managed to look good. That was just Lora. Her curls fell perfectly around her head, shrunken by the humidity but somehow fuller because of it. Her back was erect, the tilt of her head just so. But while Lora was a professional in the looks department, being angry didn't suit her. What was supposed to be a frown just looked like a pout and wasn't convincing to anyone.

I held in a chuckle. "Maybe she didn't like the guy and didn't want to tell you."

"Maybe," Lora said, shrugging. Then a sadder look touched her eyes. "I wouldn't mind my parents arranging my marriage. I mean, no one loves you like your parents, and I've known parents that searched years for the perfect match for their kid."

"Maybe," I said, hoping to leave it at that.

Lora and I grew up in the same orphanage. She always treated me like a younger sister, but since she was older than I, she left before I did. We related to each other because, unlike the other kids, neither of us knew anything about our parents.

But even then, there was one small difference between us. Her parents died. Mine gave me up.

I knew for her, she wished she had parents who would do things like give her hand in marriage. But I'd always been a skeptic. I felt much more comfortable with my destiny in my own hands rather than trusting anyone else with it. That's why I hated the tradition of arranged marriage. At the same time, I never wanted my skepticism to get in the way of Lora's optimism. That was what made our friendship work. We were polar opposites and balanced each other out.

Mercifully, the timer dinged, and Lora said, "Time's up already? Oh, well. Now we can get our massages."

THE NEXT DAY, I groaned at the red light, silently cursing at it for making me late for my doctor's appointment. Technically, it was me sleeping past my alarm that made me late, but I was going to blame the light.

Rubbing the back of my neck, I had to admit, Lora was right about that spa. It was exactly what I needed. The masseuse did an excellent job of working out the kinks in my back that I didn't even realize were there.

I sighed. I shouldn't have had so many kinks in my back at eighteen years old. Then again, being broke had those tendencies.

Green. Finally.

I hit the pedal and wove through air traffic, only to find myself at another red. I slammed my head against the steering wheel. There was no way I was going to make it in time.

I knew I was going to have to wait for being late, but when they made me wait an hour after my appointment time, it was just cruel and unusual. And it was only so they could draw blood for a stupid, routine test.

"Jashi Anyua?" the nurse finally called.

"About time," I muttered to myself.

Walking into the completely white office, I felt like I was being quarantined. The patient bed hovered above the floor—a white, curvy, hard surface that looked like a coffin to me. I jumped at how cold it was.

The doctor rolled in beside me on a swivel chair.

"So, how are you, Ms. Anyua?"

"Fine," I answered drowsily. All I could think about was after this, I could finally eat and have a coffee. If technology was so advanced, why couldn't they think of a way for people getting blood analysis to be able to eat beforehand?

"That's good. As you know, this is just a routine checkup to check for certain diseases in your blood."

I nodded and stifled a yawn, barely listening. There wasn't much to explain. I'd given blood plenty of times. I just wanted it over with so I could eat.

"You know that the blood analysis after your eighteenth birthday is the most extensive, right?"

"Yes," I answered. Lora had already told me about it. For doctors, they made a big deal about the first blood analysis as an adult, something about it being the prime age for detecting developing illnesses in advance, things like if you were going to get cancer by the time you're fifty or whether you were likely to be infertile. Stuff like that.

"All righty then. Your arm, please."

Rolling up the sleeve to my cardigan, I offered my forearm to him. He took a small plastic square that looked like one of those dishwashing tabs, only empty and with and small needle at the bottom. He placed it on my arm, needle side down, a small pricking sensation flaring there for a moment as the little device filled itself with my blood.

"You haven't noticed anything unusual lately, have you?" the doctor asked as he held my arm still.

Briefly, I wondered what it would be like to actually tell him about the little "incident" I had the other day after I got fired from the diner. But I knew I couldn't do that. I'd never told anybody about my "incidents," not even Lora. Common sense told me nothing good would come out of confessing it anyhow. So I replied with the usual answer.

"No, not at all."

It wasn't a lie. My issues didn't simply arise as of late. They were a burden I'd carried my whole life.

Twitching my fingers, I took a few deep breaths to calm my heart rate as I felt my skin heat up. Now was not the time to get agitated. I had other problems to worry about. Like getting back to work.

846 JESSID STREET

As I hurriedly climbed into my car to escape the cold of the early morning the next day, I decided to check up on what Lora said the other day about Handi. I opened my HoloPhone and the glowing image of Handi's social media page appeared in front of me. I swiped through the images and status updates to find that what Lora said was true. There were several images of her and her new fiancé posing together.

> *I'm getting married!!! My parents introduced me to my fiancé last month. I didn't say anything because I wasn't sure how I was going to feel. I still don't know how to feel, to tell the honest truth, haha. But I think I'm slowly warming up to the idea.*

To further consolidate the post, she had an image of her and her fiancé looking each other in the eye, enthralled with one another.

That explained why she didn't tell Lora. She didn't even find out until last month. I shook my head. Typical Lora, jumping the gun and gossiping about it before getting all the facts first.

But it seemed I might have jumped the gun on my assumptions, as well. I knew people faked happiness on social networks, but as I scanned through the photos, something about the sparkle in their eyes looked...genuine. There were pictures of them messing with each other, pushing one another into a pool, laughing together. It was a very well put-together collage.

It seemed that for her, her parents did a good job of finding someone that really cared for their daughter.

Then I did a double take when I noticed the time. I was supposed to be in the air already.

Flipping the taxi sign on, I flew up into the air, happy to find that traffic was minimal today.

My indication light lit up almost immediately. I frowned. Already? I opened the screen that showed me where someone was trying to flag me down and gasped. Directing the car to meet her, I rolled down the window immediately.

"Nana!"

The woman who raised me was standing next to a man I didn't recognize. He wore a smart-looking suit, carrying a briefcase in his hand.

"Nana, what are you doing here?"

The small-framed woman climbed in the front of the car with me, embracing me in a hug, filling the car with the familiar scent of cinnamon, her favorite tea. Her curly hair was soft as it brushed against the side of my face, and when she pulled away and smiled, her face creased with laugh wrinkles.

But the smile soon faded and turned serious, looking to the man that was climbing in the back, his face humorless as he watched the both of us. "This man was looking for you."

My eyes drifted to the man in question, a frown settling on my brows. "What? Why?"

He flashed a badge I'd never seen in person, one with the seal of the Faresh on it—a dragon's head embedded in its face.

"I was ordered by the great Faresh to find you."

The Faresh? Me?

Nana put a soft hand on my arm. "It's okay. They only want to talk. Take us to the orphanage and they'll explain everything."

My eyes darted between the both of them, half expecting someone to jump out and say it was all a prank. No one did. They weren't laughing.

So I took a shaky breath and said, "Okay."

We drove to 846 Jessid Street.

It had only been a few months since I'd moved from there. The drive to my old home was awkward and nerve-racking, especially with Nana sitting there. I tried to reassure myself that the fact that she'd *led* this person to me meant it had to be for a good reason.

Right?

When we arrived, I got out of the car and followed the man that stepped out as he led me up the steps to the orphanage—a cozy little brick home with blue shutters at the windows. Vibrant varieties of desert flowers grew along the sides of the house. It looked like Nana finally caught on to gardening—or finally decided to hire someone else to do it for her.

I turned to Nana and the man she'd brought with her. "So, what are we doing here?"

She grasped my hands in her small, gently veined ones, taking a deep breath. "There's someone here who wants to speak with you."

"But why here? I don't understand," I said, anxiety rising to my voice.

The strange man answered for her. "Orders from the great Faresh himself."

Nana's lips became a thin line. "Yes. She's here," she said to someone inside the home, and I had to clench my fists at my sides to control my shock as Faresh Kahmel of the Omah clan stepped out of the house.

"Ah, perfect. Good to see you again, Jashi."

⁂

"Zooooom!" a little boy shouted, running across the living room with a little toy spaceship in his hand. "Take that, galactic offender!"

His "attacks" were directed at a light-skinned Zendaalan kid by the name of Tobi. Tobi's golden locks flew around his face as he pretended to get shot and fell to the floor.

Neither of them seemed to care much that the Faresh of K'sundi was sitting in their living room.

Kahmel's huge figure leaned over the arm of the couch, looking at me through the lens of a pair of sleek sunglasses. His chin was covered by a curly dark beard that further concealed his face. But his presence exuded authority. I could *feel* the eyes behind those glasses trained on me, and though the glasses shielded his expression, I felt like I was being analyzed. He was dressed in a shockingly casual manner. A red leather jacket covered his broad shoulders with a T-shirt under that. To top off the laid-back look, he was wearing a pair of *jeans*. Nothing like what I imagined a Faresh would wear.

A bead of sweat slid down the side of my face as I tried to contain my nerves.

I couldn't afford another incident.

I writhed my hands together to keep them busy just as Nana came rushing in. "Tobi, Deme, I told you both you can't be in here!"

She gave a wavering smile to the Faresh as she herded the children behind her back. "I apologize, Your Grace."

"Not at all, Matron Taias."

She bowed her head and backed out of the room while the two boys behind her protested. She took them outside to scold them, but I could hear her voice through the walls.

I directed my attention back to the Faresh, who was still observing me without saying anything. How long was this discussion going to take? I wasn't going to be able to keep my "issues" under control much longer. Anxious situations like these triggered me the most.

The Faresh cocked his head. "I doubt you expected to meet me again like this."

"Or at all," I said, attempting to sound humble. "I thought that as Faresh, you would never visit an insignificant city like Kohpal again."

"Normally, I wouldn't. There are too many issues at the border for me to be able to enjoy a visit to my hometown like this."

"Hmm," I hummed instead of answering. *Issues that you caused.*

Kahmel clasped his large, brown hands together and leaned forward. "How have you been?"

"Fine," I answered, wishing he would just get to the point. My head was spinning in circles trying to figure out how I went from a routine run around the city in a cab to being in a conversation with the Faresh in my old orphanage.

"I remember you were pretty young when my family moved to Hashir. Do you remember me much?"

How could he act like we were old friends or something? I remembered disliking him. He went to my school because he used to live in the district. But he was much older than me, so I didn't take much note of him. I knew his younger brother, Segrid, who was in my class. Segrid and I got along well. I even remembered having a crush on him when I was younger. Lora was the one who liked Kahmel, though she was a junior at the time and he was a senior. I was still in elementary.

But Lora only liked him because she knew he was a royal branch clan, even if it was a lower branch. She eventually changed her mind, claiming he was very cold and distant. I already knew that from playing with Segrid on the street outside the orphanage. Kahmel had monitored us like a hawk. Even then, he always walked around in sunglasses. He was so adamant about wearing them in class as well, the teachers gave up trying to fight him on it.

But then he and his brother moved as soon as the Faresh and his clan were assassinated. The Courts summoned his family to help with the stability of the nation, along with other clan families.

That was it. I was nine when he moved, so I never really got the chance to know him well, especially with our age difference.

I couldn't believe he remembered me.

"Not much, in all truth," I answered. "I remember your brother Segrid."

"I see." Kahmel paused, his expression impossible to read behind those sunglasses. Probably the reason he wore them. "Where are you living now?"

"East Fahar street."

He cocked his head to the side, like he was thinking. "Near where the major hover car dealer is?"

He still remembered the city.

"Yeah, that's it."

Kahmel nodded and paused again. Then I felt his gaze go to my wringing hands before coming back to analyzing my eyes. "You're nervous." The way he said it made it sound like a fact rather than a concern.

"I just don't know why the Faresh of K'sundi would want an audience with me." And in such a nerve-racking way. He was just sitting there, staring at me.

I felt my palms heat up, my body warming like I had a fever, and I knew the tension was becoming too much. This would be disastrous if I gave it even a second more.

"I have to go to the bathroom," I said, jumping up from my seat and darting for the exit. I ran to the bathroom door, but even as my hands touched the handle, flames started to spread across my fingers, blackening the brass.

Opening the door, I slammed it behind me as fast as I could before the flames engulfed my hands completely. It felt like ants were biting across my flesh, the sting of keeping the fire from spreading intense. Sweat beaded down my face as my body heated up, and I strained to keep the heat inside rather than out.

I grunted, the flames on my hands dying down. My heart raced, but I could feel my body cooling now that the initial flare-up was over. When the fire died, my hands were unscathed. They just felt cold now, like something really had died inside me at not being able to use my fire to its full potential.

To make it look like I did go to the bathroom, I flushed the toilet and washed my hands, drying them on the hand towel to the side. I came out of the bathroom and tried to act like nothing happened. I'd dealt with my "incidents" for years and had become pretty good at faking it, but something about Kahmel made me feel like I had to be extra careful with him.

I sat down, feeling his eyes following me once more.

"What is your opinion of my political campaign so far?"

My blood froze. What kind of question was that? And he was so nonchalant, like he already knew I was against it. Did he expect me to lie about it? What would he do if I told the truth?

The man before me was deceptively calculative, coming here dressed in his casual manner, always hiding his eyes, and meticulous about his every word. His initial questions were friendly. This last one was a test, hidden behind a calm face that lacked any traceable hostility.

But I didn't so easily forget that the man before me was a killer. His hands were red with blood.

What kind of answer was he was expecting?

I steeled myself, challenging his gaze right back. "All I've seen is a lot of fighting. Maybe when your campaign begins, I can have something to be impressed with."

We stared at each other in silence.

Then a smile broke his stone face as he laughed, a noise that sounded absolutely humorless.

"Good answer," he said, rising from his seat, his smile still on his face. But then it was gone. "I have a proposition for you."

I stood, eying him skeptically. "Of what nature, Your Grace?"

"It's the reason I needed us to meet here. The house of Omah has formally requested of the house of Matron Taias for your hand in marriage. And she's accepted."

Hiding Out

I lay in my bed, a tub of ice cream at my side and stared at the ceiling. I had no more tears left to cry. At this point, it was no longer grief but shock. And I couldn't figure out who to blame.

I knew Nana was a superstitious woman who strongly believed in the old K'sundii traditions, so her acceptance to the proposal was expected, especially given who was asking. How could she say no to the Faresh, even if she wanted to?

I'd thought about marriage before, and I didn't want to get involved in a relationship, not any time soon. Relationships were messy, and my life was in too much disarray to add one into it.

Sitting up, I decided exactly who to put the blame on.

Kahmel.

Why was he doing this to me? And why me, of all people? I had no degree. I was a high school dropout. I grew up an orphanage. And yet, somehow, he obviously remembered me, and even expected me to remember him!

Not to mention our age difference.

And then there was his proposition, his reason he needed a wife now. As Faresh, he needed to marry someone to carry on his legacy. If he didn't have one, the public would question his security to the throne, and so would the Courts. Everyone would hate to have to go through this hellish ordeal all over again should he face an untimely death.

In exchange for being the wife he needed, he told me the last thing I could have expected.

"I know what you really went running out of here for," he'd told me. "You were anxious. You had to expend your fire. Just like you did all those years ago, when you thought no one was looking. But I saw you. And if you come with me"—I caught my breath as fire danced across his palm as he opened it, then extinguished it as he made a fist—"I can show you how to control it." He took his sunglasses off, revealing his glowing orange eyes. "Because I'm just like you."

I didn't know what to do.

This was the first time I'd ever met someone like me. I thought I was the only one. The first time I discovered my fire, I was six and I had a nightmare about my parents. I'd dreamed that they'd left me in a forest by myself and wouldn't come for me, no matter how loudly I screamed for help. If Nana could have afforded a shrink to examine me, I'm sure they would have found some kind of hidden meaning about abandonment fears linked to it.

I woke up in a bed of flames, but I was unhurt. Nana found me like that, crying in my bed in the midst of flames. She had to evacuate the whole building. If it weren't for her quickness to act, all of the other kids in the orphanage would have died.

The police, firefighters—they all investigated the fire, but none of them could determine the source.

I cried and cried, trying to explain to Nana that it was I who started the fire and to tell the firemen and police that. She looked at me, and I knew she understood I was telling the truth. At the time, I didn't know why she believed me so easily.

But she had taken me by the shoulders. "Don't worry, Jashi, I believe you. But you must promise me never to tell anyone else about it. Do you understand?"

Sniffling, I nodded my head and wiped at my tear-stained face.

She searched my eyes with concern wrinkling her forehead. "Do you know how it happened, Jashi?"

I shook my head, but before I could start crying again, she took me into her bosom and stroked my head. "It's okay. If this ever happens again, the first thing you do is tell me. You understand?"

Again, I nodded.

I had another incident about a year afterward. A few kids at school knocked me over during recess when the teachers weren't looking. I was never good at holding in my temper. I hit the ground hard and started crying tears of anger, and the next thing I knew, my body was heating up. And then everything was on fire. Firefighters came, rescued all of the kids in the school. Everyone was covered in ashes but me. I wasn't even singed.

Again it was investigated, and again they found nothing. The kids who pushed me tried to tell them that I'd started the fire, but no one believed them, and Nana told me not to tell.

It was then that Nana figured out that my fire went out of control when I got emotional. Especially panicked or anxious. She told me it was vitally important that if I felt the fire coming, I had to take myself somewhere no one could get hurt if it went out of control.

I didn't have many more incidents with the fire, not until the day I made her tell me why my parents abandoned me. It was the day Kahmel was talking about. I was nine and depressed and wanted to know why I didn't have parents to come home to. A lot of the other kids at the orphanage were getting adopted, but no one seemed interested in me. I didn't know it at the time, but it was because of my eyes. Most people saw that as a stigma; didn't want a "savage" child. I supposed in some ways, they were right.

I came to Nana and demanded she tell me why my original parents abandoned me. I wasn't planning on leaving her alone until I got some answers, so she told me, and I finally understood why she believed me so quickly after that first fire.

It wasn't the first time I'd started a fire.

She said when the orphanage found me left at their door, a one-year-old baby with a note on the basket, the police were able to trace the note back to the people who wrote it. But when they arrived at the address, they found the house burned to the ground.

They eventually found my parents, but they wanted absolutely nothing to do with me. They called me a demon child and blamed me for their ruin. I ran away from the orphanage that day. Nana tried to stop me, but I needed some time alone. I crawled out of my bedroom window and ran as far as my legs would carry me.

I found an empty lot and sat in the dirt and just cried. I don't know how long I was there. Hours. I felt my fire coming, and I remembered to hide in an alley nearby before it got out of hand.

As I thought back to that day, I realized it had been near where Kahmel lived at the time. But as he said, I didn't think anyone was around. When my fire came, I figured out how to direct it and aimed it at a dumpster.

Since then, I'd slowly learned over the years how to contain it. It was painful to do so, but it protected those around me.

Never in a million years did I think there was ever anyone else like me; let alone someone to teach me.

But could I accept help from the Faresh, whose motives were unclear? Hell, everything about him was unclear. Why did he need a wife so suddenly? This wasn't the Middle Ages. Couldn't he just date someone for the time being to appease the Courts and leave it at that? And again, why me? Was it only because of the day he found out that I was like him?

I shook my head. To hell with tradition. Tradition wasn't worth getting married over.

I put a top on the tub of ice cream and put it in the freezer, then started packing. I was already somewhat of a drifter. Picking up and skipping town was nothing to me. The only thing I cared about were my friends here in Kohpal, but even then, I mainly only had Lora.

Speaking of whom...

Looking at my eWatch, I wondered how to tell her, *what* to tell her. Everything? Most likely so. But would she understand? Or would she try to convince me to stay and marry him? Though Lora was like me in a lot of ways, she was traditional in a lot of ways too. She probably wouldn't approve of my skipping out on everything. I loved my friend, but I couldn't afford her telling anyone about my plans.

I made my decision. I tapped my eWatch and opened up the holographic keyboard that appeared in the air in front of me. I typed a text, then set it on a timer to send in the morning. By that time, I would be long gone.

Now all that was left to do was figure out how to escape the Faresh of all K'sundi.

⸻

Talad was home, I was certain. I rapped on the door more vigorously this time, loud enough to wake his grandmother in her grave.

My breath came out in mist at this time of night. I wore my favorite black coat with the hood over my face, but the cold, dry winds whipped at my face like icy fingers running all along my skin. The night was clear, the stars glittering in their heavenly places. I couldn't help but look over my shoulder every two seconds, as if the Faresh would be standing there, waiting for me.

According to K'sundii law, breaking off an engagement was like breaking the terms of a contract; there were legal repercussions. But for the most part, it involved small things settled in civil court—well, not small for my salary. But if a family really wanted to drag it out, they sued, demanded reparation, things like that. I wondered what the punishment would be for refusing to marry a Faresh. Treason? It wasn't exactly betraying the country as much as was the Faresh's ego, but could it have been seen as more than a civil matter, escalated to a felony?

Before I could sink myself more into that particular fear, the door swung open at that moment. A brown-skinned young man with a frown settled on his brow peered at me through squinted eyes. "Jashi? What do you want at this time of night?"

"I need to disappear. Can you help me?"

That woke him up. Looking from side to side down the empty streets, Talad gestured for me to come in.

I stepped into a house as run down as my apartment. A single lamp lit the room beside an old, worn-out couch. Boxes of takeout cluttered the coffee table, and there was a huge crack on the HoloScreen matrix.

Okay, this was a lot worse than my apartment. It wasn't because of the company Talad kept, but it was because of his questionable connections that I knew he could help me.

"Who do you need to disappear from?" Talad asked me, scratching at his short, puffy hair.

"That's not important." I said stiffly. "The question is, can you help me?"

A sly smile crawled up his imp-like face. "That depends. What are you offering me in exchange?"

"Cash." I flashed three hundred Ramaks in his face before I shoved them back into my purse.

His hungry eyes followed the motion. "All right...I think I know a few buddies who can help you. How soon do you need to leave?"

"Tonight."

Talad's eyes went wide. "Tonight? How do you expect me to help you disappear on such short notice?" He shook his head, seeming to have broken from his money-induced trance. "Okay, hold on. I know you've always been a troublemaker, but I never thought you'd get caught up in anything illegal. Seriously, what's going on here?"

I sighed in exasperation. "All I can tell you is that I desperately need your help, and it absolutely can't wait."

"Does Matron Taias know about this, whatever it is?"

Biting my lip, I nodded. Talad scratched his head again. "All right, all right. If you're that desperate, it must be bad, whatever it is." He paused, rubbing at his goatee. "I don't think I can get you out of town by tonight, but you can stay here until I have things arranged. I know a couple guys who owe me a favor." Then he gave me a smirk that reminded me of the little boy I used to know at the orphanage who ran away all the time. "I'll even do it free of charge."

I grinned. "Thanks, Tad."

"Hey, don't mention it. Come on, I'll show you to my spare room."

THE NEXT MORNING I woke up to find Talad in the kitchen with a bowl of cereal waiting for me. He pushed the bowl to me as he said, "I've arranged for you to meet one of my 'friends.'" He made air quotes. "But I will warn you that my 'friends' are some dangerous people. I can get them to help you with your problem, but I'll advise you that if they ever call you after this, don't pick up the phone."

Scooping up some cereal in my mouth, I nodded.

Talad pursed his lips, then continued eating. "Other than your mysterious secret, how's life treating you? I haven't seen you since I left Taias's place."

"Well enough," I said, chewing vacantly, playing with my hair.

"So where are you headed? If you can tell me."

Good question.

My eWatch buzzed.

I groaned. I'd already forgotten all about Lora.

WHAT? Are you kidding me? This better not be a joke. Where are you? You didn't really leave, did you? JASHI

JASHI, WHERE ARE YOU?

"What's that?" Talad asked as he grabbed the cereal box and poured more in his bowl.

"You remember Lora, right?" I answered absentmindedly, chewing my lip. Reply now? Or wait until I was gone?

"Oh, yeah. Lora's nice." Then Talad looked up from his bowl and frowned. "You mean she doesn't know, either? But aren't you two like sisters?"

I only looked at him, unable to answer.

He held his hands up in surrender. "All right, all right, I get it. No questions." Talad shook his head. "But whatever trouble you're in, I hope you're making the right choice here. Anytime a smart girl like you is with a guy like me..." Instead of completing his sentence, he slurped noisily at the milk in his bowl, which might have made me laugh if he wasn't so right.

I sighed. This was all Kahmel's fault.

Just then, there was a knock at the door.

Talad got up from his seat. "That would be my 'friend.' Remember, be careful around him, all right?"

"Thanks again, Tad."

"Don't mention it. Just promise me you'll be careful, all right?"

I nodded.

Talad opened the door to a tall man wearing black sunglasses, probably of Zendaalan descent, given his pale skin color and light blond hair. His eyes immediately went to me. "Is this the girl you were talking about?"

"Yeah. Jashi, this is Cralan. Cralan, this is Jashi Anyua."

"Not for long, from what Talad tells me." He shook my hand with a cold grip, and a metallic taste went down my throat as I second-guessed my impulsive decision. What was I getting myself into?

Cralan sat down at the kitchen counter, gesturing for me to sit in front of him. As he did, I realized that his other hand was not flesh and bone but gleaming chrome, wires running up it like veins. I resisted the urge to flinch, afraid of being insensitive. I knew that Zendaalans were a race of mainly cyborgs, but it always caught me off guard when I saw their cybernetic parts mingled with their human ones. I remembered the first time I noticed that little Tobi from the orphanage didn't have a chest or stomach, but a shiny metal plated torso that functioned as one instead. It took some getting used to.

"Tell me, what is it that you need?" Cralan said.

"I—" the words were caught in my throat. Where was I going? Where could I go? It had to be somewhere that made it harder for the Faresh to find me, but neither did I want to flee the country.

Then I remembered he said he was preoccupied with the war at the border. Maybe if I hid myself in a small enough town off in the middle of nowhere, under a different name, maybe his other duties would slow his search to find me and he'd eventually give up. After all, he could choose from any other wife on the planet. He didn't necessarily need me. I just needed a town to escape to.

Nana once told me she was from a small town. What was it called?

"I want to go to a town called Gasher. Under a different name."

Cralan raised an eyebrow. "Gasher? You're going through all this trouble just to go to a little place like Gasher?"

"Can you help me?" I insisted.

Cralan shrugged. "Of course I can. Any friend of Talad is a friend of mine," he added with a crooked smile. "Do you have any existing ID I can use as a template?"

Just as I reached for my purse, Talad put a hand on my arm to stop me. "Just use her photo," he said. "I'm sure you have a million other IDs to base hers on."

"Hmm." Cralan chuckled, but it sounded more like a grunt. "All right then. I can have it to you by next week."

"Next week?" I said, rising from my chair. "Can't you do it any sooner than that?"

"Sorry," Cralan responded, shrugging and getting up from the chair, heading for the door. "But it'll take that long to make all of the necessary arrangements. In the meantime, lie low. I'll have the ID to you and take you all the way to Gasher. Sound good?"

I looked to Talad, who nodded. "Fine."

"Great. I look forward to doing further business with you," Cralan said, leaving with another crooked smile on his face.

Talad sighed, sitting where Cralan did a moment ago. "Never let anyone take your ID. That's the first rule of living on the run. Guys like him can sell those on the street for a thousand Ramaks a pop."

"Oh," I said in a small voice, feeling very naive.

Talad patted me on the shoulder. "No big deal. That's why you have me around. You can crash here for another week until Cralan can deliver."

"Thanks again, Tad."

I just hoped that a week wasn't giving the Faresh enough time to find me.

A DEAL WITH A STRANGER

I'd never felt so nervous about going to such a tranquil park.

The Faresh Garr Park, built in honor of its namesake, was, in its own right, beautiful. Built to look like an oasis, palm trees lined the sand, red and yellow desert flowers planted all around. A reflective pond lay in the center of it all, with thick blades of grass growing at its edges. Soft, golden sand offered relief from the asphalt of the city. The park's path went all around the pond, benches flanked all throughout.

Cralan waited at one of those benches, appearing to be deeply engaged in a HoloPaper.

I gripped the straps of my backpack as the full heat of the evening sun warmed my skin. I had the jacket I wore earlier that morning wrapped around my waist, revealing the loose tube top I wore to relieve me of the heat. The long hem of my skirt blew in the wind as Talad and I stepped through the park entrance.

My stomach churned. I'd never done anything like this before. But my resolve stayed the same. If the alternative was marrying the Faresh…

The two of us approached Cralan and sat down beside him.

Without putting down his HoloPaper, Cralan said, "Talad, why don't you go get a cup of coffee for about twenty minutes?"

Talad frowned. "What? No, I'm staying with her. She doesn't—"

"Based on the lady's urgency, I'd say the details regarding her escape are delicate. I need to know why she's leaving if she wants my help."

I shook my head. "I can't. I—"

"Then forget it."

Talad and I looked at each other. We didn't have much of a choice. Talad sighed and walked away with his hands shoved in the pockets of his jeans.

Without his sunglasses on, I could see Cralan's shifty green eyes drift toward me. As soon as Talad was out of earshot, he said, "I hear you want to escape the Faresh."

My eyes widened. "How could you know about that?"

Cralan smirked. "You should have never given me your real name. The Faresh has all of his assets within the secret police out looking for you."

"But then how...?"

"I make it my business to find out about the people I do business with. And I heard it from the grapevine that the Faresh was looking for a Jashi Anyua—short, with long hair, and a round face." He turned to me with about coy smile on his lips. "Sounds like you."

I swallowed, a cold feeling sinking in my gut. "Now that you know, what are you going to do?"

"It's not about what I'm going to do. It's about what I've already done. You see, I've told my boss about you, and he wants to speak with you."

"You told him?" Now I was shaking. This is not how I expected this would go at all. "What does he want with me?"

"In this business, madam, you learn not to ask questions. Come with me."

His cold, metal hand grasped my arm and yanked me out of my seat, dragging me across the sand to where a black hover van was waiting. My sandals filled with grainy particles as I struggled against him.

He swung the back door open and shoved me in, then climbed in behind me, shutting the door and locking it.

I faced another Zendaalan man. A brooding brow framed steel blue eyes, his square jaw covered in stubble. Platinum wispy blond hair fell in a mess over his eyes, trained only on me. His huge hands were clasped together as he sat in his chair, a smirk on his red lips.

"Welcome, Miss Anyua."

I staggered to my feet. "What do you want from me?"

He frowned, like my question offended him. "Why do you look so afraid? As my man has surely told you, all I want to do is talk."

My eyes darted between the two of them, wondering how this spiraled out of control so quickly. "About what?"

"Congratulations on your engagement, by the way," he said, chuckling as he leaned back into his seat. "Only from what Cralan tells me, you're not too happy about it. Unfortunately, we won't be able to help you escape Kahmel. Yet."

"Yet?"

"The Faresh is an arrogant warmonger. He's marched into office just because your ancient policies were based on who were the biggest knuckleheads. No offense. But the attitude of this nation agrees with me. He shouldn't be in office."

Dread crawled up my throat. I had only considered the danger of Kahmel finding me. I didn't even think about his enemies. "And what do you expect me to do?"

He stood and chuckled again. "I think you know what I want from you. But don't think it's not in your best interest. Kahmel is not a man, he's a boy. And this war he's starting is going to do much more damage than he can handle."

My heart thudded against my ribcage. "You want me to convince him to end a war?"

He slapped my cheek. Hard.

Pain flared against the side of my face. "Don't be stupid," he said in an even, cool voice. "You just need to give us information about him. Whatever we tell you to. We'll handle the rest."

My lips were dry, even after I licked them. I tried to keep the tears out of my eyes. "But why? What would Zendaalans care about a K'sundii-Omanian war?"

"We have everything to do with it. Do you know what the Zendaalans have invested into K'sundi?" His face reddened, his tone rising ever so slightly. "We built this country! How dare he destroy everything we've worked to create here? Everything you have is because of us. If he brings K'sundi down in the war, the Zendaalans go down, too."

I fell silent at that, feeling humbled. It made sense that Zendaalans would get involved if they didn't approve of the basis of Kahmel's war. We really did owe everything to them. But then why did they need me to help? Zendaal had the power make Kahmel end it whenever they wanted. There was more to this than this man was willing to tell me, but I wasn't in the position to ask that question.

"Don't think there's nothing in it for you," the man added, his voice calmer. "When we conclude that you've done enough, the Equalizers will help you escape the Faresh and start over fresh, just like you wanted. We'll even offer you protection for a short period, long enough for you to disappear from the radar."

"Protect me?" I said incredulously. "From the Faresh? If I do what you're asking, I'll be guilty of treason!" Panic was creeping into my voice. I thought of all the people he had executed for the crime already. I would easily become one of them.

"Treason?" he frowned. "You've already committed treason by disobeying the Faresh. Running away from your engagement? If we found you this easily, don't you think he's not too far behind? Your only hope at this point is go back to him and pray he has mercy on you."

My heart stopped. I hadn't thought about that.

He continued. "The way I see it, this is your only way out. Either you do what we ask, or we just let the Faresh have you. And if he's slow to accuse you of it, we would gladly corroborate the story of you escaping your contractual agreement with him, as well as scheming against the throne. And you know how he deals with traitors."

I heard a gun cock, and Cralan pushed cold metal against my temple. "I would suggest you decide quickly."

Tears ran down my face as I realized that I'd fallen deeper than what I could get myself out of. I had no choice.

"I'll do what you ask," I said.

"I knew you'd come around," the man said. He yanked at my wrist, opening a screen in my eWatch and typing in a number. "The name's Cromwell, by the way. Attican Cromwell. We'll be in touch."

TIME-HONORED TRADITIONS

Cralan and Attican let me out of the van. The car sped away as soon as I stepped out.

"Jashi!"

Talad ran to me, looking like he'd seen a ghost.

Or maybe I looked like a ghost.

"Jashi, what happened to you? I came back and you were gone! What did they say?"

I was still trying to process that, myself. The whole situation had been ripped from out of my hands. No, that wasn't true. I couldn't even act like any of this was in my hands from the moment the Faresh approached me. I was trapped.

"They said they won't be able to help me," I said numbly.

Talad frowned. "What do you mean? Cralan told me he could."

"Well, he told me he couldn't."

His face was twisted in concern, but he knew I wouldn't say anything more. I wasn't going to risk hurting my situation any further by including anyone else on it. Besides that, I knew Talad. He was a nice kid, but I was worried what he might be willing to divulge if someone waved enough Ramaks in his face. And the stakes were even higher now that the crime was treason.

"I'm sorry, Jashi. I thought they would help you."

I smiled sadly. "I know. And I appreciate it. Can you take me home? I'll put the address in your hover car."

He returned the smile, then nodded. As we started for the car, he stopped me as he took my wrist and looked me in the eye. "If you ever need my help for anything, come and get me. Promise?"

I wasn't sure if his promise would serve for much, but I appreciated the sentiment at the very least. "I promise I'll keep you in mind if it ever comes to that," I said honestly.

Talad dropped me off at my apartment like I asked him to. When he drove off, I looked up at the building I hadn't seen in a week and wondered how I was going to explain myself to everyone I knew. Especially Lora.

I looked at the last message she sent me on my eWatch.

Jashi, where are you? I'm worried sick, and so is Matron Taias. Please be okay.

The message brought unexpected tears to my eyes. Because I absolutely was not okay. I was going to send a reply once I was in Gasher so she could at least know where I was and why I ran off like I did. But now I didn't know what to do.

I swiped my keycard at the pad and heard it ding, stepping into the apartment lobby and seeing the doorman's eyes pop at seeing me.

"M-miss Anyua!" the old man stuttered. "Where have you been? You know the police came around here asking for you? They told me to call as soon as I saw you come in."

I pursed my lips and nodded. "Then do that. Just give me a minute to collect the rest of my things from my room."

Adjusting my backpack on my shoulder, I told myself that at least I would be able to pack more of my things than just what I took to Talad's.

"Miss Anyua!" the doorman shouted behind me, confused. I ignored him and got in the elevator. When I came back down with my luggage, I told the doorman to call the police. I figured it was as good a time as any to turn myself in.

While I waited for them to arrive, I started typing up a response to Lora. Then I stopped, thinking better of it. I would call. The line rang twice before her face appeared on my HoloCaller screen, floating in front of me. "Jashi!" she exclaimed. "What happened to you? Are you okay?"

"I'm fine," I said.

"Where did you disappear to?"

I glanced at the doorman, who was poorly trying to play off his curiosity. I turned back to the screen. "I ran away to avoid the Faresh," I said, hearing the doorman gasp behind me.

"The Faresh?" he was whispering to himself. I supposed the police didn't mention on whose behalf they were looking for me.

"Jashi..." she said sympathetically.

I blinked the tears out of my eyes. "But I changed my mind. I'm going to agree to marry him now and honor my betrothal."

She frowned, her laser eyes seeing right through me. "What happened, Jashi? Did someone threaten to hurt you or something?"

"Look, I have to go," I cut her off. "We'll talk later."

"Jashi, don't you hang up on—"

Her face disappeared just as I saw the police through the glass window of the building.

The Faresh was with them.

I took a deep breath.

He still wore his glasses, but was dressed much more formally in a dark gray suit, a blue striped tie, and a sleek, onyx black eWatch on his wrist. His royal sash draped across his wide chest, a testament to his position. Even behind his sunglasses, the frown on his face was intimidating as he strode toward me even faster than the police.

"Are you all right?" was the first thing he asked, his voice tinged with a dangerous tone.

I diverted my eyes to his shoes, Attican's words echoing in my ears.

"I-I—"

"Were you hurt?"

My mind flashed to Attican, but I didn't dare mention it. "No, I'm fine."

"Thank goodness you're all right. Who brought you here?"

I bit my lip. Talad could get in trouble if I revealed that he helped me escape. "A friend of mine."

"Who are they? I will reward them for bringing you back safe and sound."

"I don't think they want the acclamation, Your Grace," I said, knowing fully well that Talad would love a reward. But I didn't quite trust what Kahmel was saying. He made it seem like I was kidnapped. If he investigated and found out I was staying with Talad for a week, Talad would surely be blamed.

My heart beat at least a hundred times as he paused.

"Very well," he said. "I think your Matron would like to see you. They tell me she's been very concerned."

"Yes, Your Grace," I responded, gritting my teeth at having to be subdued. But I had to play nice now, play Attican's role.

"Then let's go."

He turned to leave. That was it? He wasn't going to question me any further?

Kahmel stopped at the door. "Aren't you coming?"

With few other options, I followed after him.

The city of Kohpal went by in a blur as Kahmel's chauffeur drove us toward the orphanage. It was the nicest-looking car I'd ever been in. The seats were plush brown leather, with plenty of room for more people to sit comfortably.

Kahmel took off his glasses, startling me. I never thought I could get startled by the orange eyes of someone else of the dragon tribe. But in this case, I was scared to death those eyes would see through me. "I was serious when I said I would teach you to use your powers. Have you had any issues lately?"

"No," I answered, feeling strange that he brought it up so

casually, especially since I'd never mentioned it to anyone. I almost had an incident when Attican talked to me, but I managed to get it under control while I was in the car with Talad. Luckily, I was able to suppress the flame from coming at all. Hurt like hell, though.

He nodded, looking out the window. "If you start to have problems, let me know. I can help you."

I didn't say anything after that, hoping we would have the rest of the car ride in silence.

Thankfully, the Faresh didn't say anything after that, either.

▼

"Are you trying to kill me, child?" Nana demanded, a hand on her hip and glaring at me as she turned her back on the soup she had on the stove. "Where did you go?"

Kahmel was waiting for me in the car, so I knew I could talk freely. "I don't want to get him in trouble."

She clucked her tongue. "It was Talad, wasn't it?"

Dang it. "How did you know?"

Nana shook her head and sighed, turning back to the soup. "I knew as soon as you said 'trouble.' That boy is a magnet for it."

I looked down in shame, feeling like I hadn't changed since I was a child and got caught doing something I knew I wasn't supposed to. So much for being an adult. "Are you going to tell anyone?"

"No, not if you don't want me to. But what were you thinking? Why did you leave?"

"I don't want to marry him, Nana."

Nana looked at me and pursed her lips in sympathy. She opened her arms and pulled me into a hug. "Oh, it'll be all right, Jashi. I would have never agreed to this if I didn't think it was the best for you."

"What do you mean?"

"I remember when Kahmel was a young man. He was always stern and mysterious, but he was always very protective of his younger brother. That told me a lot about his character. Most of all, he's always been an intelligent boy. I like the way he sticks to our traditions. Never doubt the importance of our heritage, Jashi. Most people of today do. Kahmel is...different. Even the way he requested the betrothal with the problem of...your parental situation, he found another way of following the tradition of arranged marriage. This is a good thing, Jashi. This is a man of honor."

She stroked my hair gently, and I decided not to argue with her. I already knew she was very orthodox in her beliefs, but for me, just following tradition didn't blot out the fact that he was still a killer. Some part of me couldn't condemn Attican's motives.

LOYALTY

When I opened the door to the car, Kahmel had his sunglasses on again and was talking with someone on the HoloCaller. I froze, not knowing what to do. Did he expect to be able to hold his conversation in privacy?

Reading my expression, Kahmel motioned for me to come in.

Closing the door behind me, I caught the end of the conversation. The person on the screen was the secretary of defense, Arusi Zuwei.

"...they think their information is coming from an inside source," she was saying.

"Then you know what to do with them when you find them."

"Yes, sir."

He then turned off the screen, and I had to hide my shaking hands. Was he ordering the execution of another "traitor"?

I started as he took off his sunglasses again. Why did he keep doing that only around me? It was...disconcerting.

"So," he began, as if nothing happened. Killing seemed nonchalant to him. "I would return you to your home, but though I've done what I could to keep information about you private, I believe the information has been leaked."

My body started to get warm. I needed to calm down, or I would have problems. In spite of his offer to teach me, my anxiety could make me look suspicious.

"So what are you going to do with me?" I said, clenching my fists at my sides and trying to keep my fire under control.

Kahmel said, "I'm torn. I'd like to keep you in proximity of me for your protection, but I would hate to take you away from all of your friends here in Kohpal. On the other hand, I can't stay in Kohpal for too long. I need to manage the battle front." He paused. "But it doesn't look like I have a choice. We'll find a hotel near the city center for us to stay in and place guards all over the building."

Us? My eyes widened. "I don't want to stay in a room with you!" I snapped before remembering that I was already breaking out of my quiet and nice character. Acting really didn't suit me.

The Faresh shook his head. "I'm going to book two rooms."

"Oh." That was a relief. I knew we were supposed to be getting married, but...no. "Will I be able to see my friends?"

"Yes..." he said slowly. "But only inside the hotel, and they'll have to be escorted by security."

It wasn't as bad as it could have been. But it was going to be a bit of a damper to have to treat Lora like a criminal when I saw her next. Or perhaps it was the other way around. Still, it was better than nothing.

My body started to cool down again, pain biting at my palms and shooting up my arms, the fire that rose up unable to exhaust itself anywhere else.

"Are you okay?" he asked.

"Fine," I said, gritting my teeth.

"Hmm," he hummed. Then he turned to open the window the separated us from the driver. "Call the hotel I mentioned earlier and tell them we'll be renting two suites. Take us there."

"Yes sir," the man responded before Kahmel closed the window again. The car left the orphanage, joining the air traffic.

"You know," Kahmel said after a moment, "you don't have to be so formal with me. Just be yourself. I remember the little girl who pushed my little brother to the ground when he tried to ride her bike."

I laughed at the memory, surprised he remembered something like that—and the fact that he hadn't mentioned my little escapade yet. "Well, he shouldn't have tried to ride it without my permission. Nana saved up money for a long time just to buy it."

"Segrid came home crying with a scrape on his knee because of it."

I sniffed. "Served him right."

"That," he said, like he'd caught me doing something that was supposed to be a secret. "That's the way I'd like you to talk to me."

Oops. So much for being nice. Not that he seemed to care. That knowledge calmed me a little. I didn't think I would be able to hold up the pretense for long, anyway.

"All right," I said, reclining more into the seat. "So what now? We stay in Kohpal...and then what? We just get married?"

"Not exactly. I thought I'd give you some time to say goodbye to your friends before we left. Besides, I have to prepare the dowry for the orphanage and I wanted to do it in person."

I blinked. "You're giving the orphanage a dowry?" I knew this was technically an arranged marriage like any other, but still, a rich man giving a poor orphanage a dowry was strange.

"Of course. It's the closest form of following tradition since you have no legal parents."

Ah, yes. Now it made sense. Tradition seemed to be the only thing the man cared about. I was starting to think he and Nana would make a lovelier couple.

But whatever his intentions were, I was grateful the orphanage was getting a well-needed benefactor. At least one good thing would arise out of the situation.

I watched as the city of Kohpal flew by under our car and gazed at the Dharia mountains in the background. I wondered if I was ever going to see my beloved city again.

I might not have liked the circumstances, but I was going to take advantage of the one and only opportunity to stay at a fancy hotel.

When the Faresh said he was booking a suite, he really meant it. My room was bigger than my entire apartment and the apartment across from mine put together. It had a kitchen with a chef droid—a silver ovoid robot that floated around the room with hover technology. There was a bar lined to the brim with glass bottles and shot glasses. The window that stretched from floor to ceiling gave a full view of the Dharia mountains and their beautiful rock face and sharp cliffs, the setting sun giving the cliff side a rich golden hue.

That's when I realized that something was missing.

I pointed at the blank wall directly across from the bed, above the dresser. "Where's the HoloScreen?"

Kahmel walked over to where a black visor sat on top of the dresser. He picked it up and approached me, pushing the glasses over my eyes and pressing a button on the side of my head.

The blackness was replaced by crisp images, a startup screen playing as colorful fireworks revealed text that read, "CyTech Industries."

"Wow," I muttered. And here I thought I was fancy upgrading my Holoscreen to a larger size a month ago.

"What do you want to watch?" Kahmel asked, chuckling.

I didn't have to think about it. "'The City of Kohpal: Criminology.'"

"Then pick 'Video on Demand.'"

At first I didn't understand what he was talking about, but a menu screen came up with various options. Cable, video on demand, movies, theater mode, video games, anything I could think of. But I didn't know how to select any of them. "How?"

"Use your hands."

Frowning, I reached out.

Whoa.

I could grab and drag the screen, select, hold down for options, everything. Choosing 'Video on Demand,' I was brought to a large selection of shows. I scrolled through them until I found my show.

I took off the glasses. "That's amazing."

"If you need anything," Kahmel said, starting for the door, "ask one of the security guards at your door. If you get hungry, go ahead and call for room service." He flipped his glasses back over his eyes.

I was going to be alone. This was a nice hotel, but it didn't dampen the fact that I was saying goodbye to the life I once knew. No more going out with Lora to see a movie or long walks by myself to clear my head. "When can I see my friends?" I figured the least I could do was give them a proper farewell before I left.

Kahmel pursed his lips. "Whenever you like. But not too many people."

I nodded. That was okay. I only wanted to reassure Lora that I was okay. And maybe even Talad.

Just then, my eWatch buzzed.

Unknown number: Meet me at the Stargazer cafe tomorrow at 5. Come alone.

My stomach churned. I tried to mask my expression, turning off my eWatch and turning to Kahmel. "That sounds fine. Could I get some privacy now? I'd like to change and shower. I haven't gotten the chance since I've been back."

Kahmel nodded. "All right, then. I suppose I'll see you in the morning."

I waited until he was at the door before I said, "Oh, and I think I'll meet with one of my friends tomorrow at around five."

He turned to me, frowning. "You can't leave here. I can't risk someone trying to find you. Or any other incidents," he added, giving me a look before dropping his sunglasses over his eyes and closing the door behind him.

I sighed exasperatedly. Stuck dead in between a rock and a hard place.

GOING OUT FOR A SIMPLE COFFEE

It was already ten in the morning, but I still didn't want to get out of bed. It was the bed's fault, really. The water mattress molded itself to fit the shape of my body, no matter what pose I was in. The thick covers swaddled my body in a cocoon that was hard to leave. I was sheltered, away from both Kahmel and Attican.

But it was out of fear of the latter that I got from under my cocoon of protection. I had a couple of hours to figure out how I was going to leave the hotel and meet him.

And it was out of fear of the former that I knew that little endeavor was near impossible.

I tested it last night. The guards outside my door were vigilant. As soon as I opened the door and peeked out, I was facing one of them pointing back at my bed like I was a naughty child trying to stay up all night. The only way I'd be able to get out of this hotel room was if I convinced Kahmel to let me go.

I threw my legs over the side of my bed and sighed. I took my eWatch from my nightstand and scrolled through the rest of my messages. I found one from Lora, expecting it to be full of concern and rebuke. But instead it was a simple one that brought tears to my eyes.

If you need someone to talk to, you know I'm here.

It wasn't much, but it was just what I needed. Kahmel told me that while I couldn't go out and see other people, he would let my friends come see me. I hoped he would make good on that promise.

There was an unread message in my inbox from my doctor, giving me the results from my blood test. I'd completely forgotten about it. Scanning the email, I found that I had a clean bill of health, thankfully, but there was a little note at the end.

> *Dr. Darus Kish: As you can see, everything seems to check clear, but there's something that showed up in our analysis that we need clarification on. At your earliest convenience, please schedule another appointment so we can chat.*

The message didn't worry me much since the rest of it basically said I was going to be fine.

But Kahmel didn't know that.

"No, you can't go to the doctor."

"What?" I asked incredulously.

Kahmel shook his head, raising a glass of orange juice to his lips. We had a breakfast prepared by the kitchen droid—toast, eggs, and bacon.

But not even strawberry jam could cool the heated agitation that rose up in me. I wasn't really sick, but what if I was? Was he really that determined to keep me here? "My doctor says I need to come in right away for further analysis! What if I have something severe?"

He put the glass down. "If you do, you can be examined by the doctors in Hashir when we arrive."

"This doctor has worked with me all my life. Why wait until I can be in the hands of a stranger?"

"I can't risk you being found."

"At the doctor's?"

"The answer is no. We'll have your medical records transferred to Hashir. You should be fine."

I crossed my arms. "*If* I make it to Hashir. Who knows what I have?"

Kahmel scoffed. "Don't exaggerate. If he didn't mention it in the email, it can't be that bad."

Maybe I did oversell it a little.

"You make it seem like there's someone watching my every move. So far, you're the only one who's determined to track me down."

"Am I?" he said, raising an eyebrow.

I stiffened. Perhaps I should have ended the tantrum there. He still hadn't asked me anything about my disappearance. Why? Did he want to hold it over my head that he knew I tried to run away? Was it for moments like this, so he could shut me up by reminding me of it? He was impossible to read, wearing the same expression no matter what. Even though he didn't wear his sunglasses around me, it was almost like his bright orange eyes made him even harder to see through, they were so startling. I was starting to understand the effect my own eyes had on people.

"Who is your doctor, by the way?" he asked.

"Dr. Darus Kish. Why?"

"We're going to need your medical records from him eventually. We might as well obtain them now."

I bit into my toast grumpily. He wasn't going to let me go easily.

Kahmel stood up. "I have to go now. I have several phone calls to make that have to be held discreetly. But I wanted to give you this first."

He reached into his pocket and pulled out a beautiful golden hair clip in the shape of a bejeweled desert flower.

I took it in my hand, staring at it with my eyes wide. I wasn't sure if I'd ever held something so expensive-looking. "Why?" I asked without thinking.

"Think of it as a wedding present." He put on his glasses and started for the door. "When I come back, give me a list of the friends you'd like to have over so we can arrange for them to meet you before we leave."

I clenched my fists at my sides. What gave him the right to tell me when I could and couldn't see my friends? Why did I have to ask him for everything?

Kahmel left, and I sulked around the room.

I had no idea what to do about my dilemma. If there was any window of escape, it was now, while Kahmel was away. But those guards... Nothing would get them to move, and at the first sign of anything, they would call Kahmel right away.

Unless...it was an emergency.

The idea struck me, but it wasn't something I'd ever tried before. I'd always tried to figure out ways to *stop* my fire, not cause it. But Kahmel seemed able to do it, and desperate times called for desperate measures.

Pulling out my clothes from my luggage, I slipped on some jeans and a simple red crop top, then threw on my pink sneakers. I even pushed a few locks of my curly hair back to put the clip in. I saw no point in letting such a nice hair piece go to waste.

I tried to concentrate on the sensations I usually felt when my fire came. Heat, warming, a burning sensation. I closed my eyes and focused, but nothing came. I even tried to open and close my fist the way Kahmel did but came up with nothing.

I sighed and looked to the kitchen. I would just have to start a fire the old-fashioned way.

Turning on the stove to max, I grabbed a kitchen towel from one of the drawers. I really felt bad about having to do this to such a nice hotel, but what had to be done, had to be done. I dropped it on the blue flame on the burner, watching as the flames started to spread across the cloth. It didn't take long.

Then I grabbed the fire extinguisher from the wall and set it down near the door. I didn't want the fire to get too out of hand before someone could stop it. I wasn't an arsonist.

"Help! Fire!" I shouted as loud as I could manage.

The two guards came rushing through the door, and I dashed out of there as quick as a heartbeat.

An open elevator. Pumping my legs, I made it just as the doors began to close, blocking the guards from reaching me. I hit the "L" button and caught my breath as my heart raced.

The Zendaalan couple in the elevator looked at me like I was insane. I gave a smile and a nod. "How do you do?"

When the elevator dinged on their floor, they just stared at me as they left. I waved and hit the "door close" button.

Tourists.

The elevator dinged again, and I was in the hotel lobby.

"It's the Faresh!" someone exclaimed.

I turned to see another elevator opening behind me.

"Jashi!" Kahmel yelled.

Damn.

Sprinting, I charged out the door and started down the streets, hoping to get lost in the crowd while I tried to reach a taxi. Looking back, I saw Kahmel running out of the hotel and looking around for a moment before his eyes fell on me, people all around him gasping and pointing at him.

"Out of my way!" he roared, the people around him parting instantly.

I tapped at my eWatch. "Call a taxi," I told it. A swirling circle appeared to indicate that it was looking, then turned green as one was found.

A car lowered down to where I was, and I swung the door open even before it was completely landed.

"Drive," I ordered.

"Where?"

"Just drive, hurry!"

Thankfully, he took off before he could recognize the Faresh behind him.

I breathed a breath of relief. "Take me to the Stargazer Cafe, please."

The man harrumphed. "Whatever you say, lady,"

I sat back in my seat and wondered why I was congratulating myself.

A CAFÉ RAID

I wrung my hands together, hoping to keep my nerves down before I burned the place to the ground.

When I sent Attican a message saying he had to meet me sooner than five, he answered almost immediately and told me he was on his way. In one sense, it was a relief because I wasn't sure how long I could be away from Kahmel before he found me, especially here near the center of Kohpal. But on the other hand, I was meeting the man who was coercing me into being his spy, so I wasn't thrilled, either.

Already jittery enough, I asked the waiter for a tea when he approached me, hoping it would calm my nerves a little. Attican approached the cafe. He found me almost immediately, that crooked smile crawling up his face.

He approached my table and pulled up a chair. "Look at you. What an obedient little minx you are."

"What do you want?"

"What's your situation right now?"

"In trouble, thanks to you. I had to run away from him again just to meet you. Why couldn't you just call?"

"I wasn't sure if the Faresh had bugged your eWatch already."

Once again, I was presented with an element to the mix I hadn't considered. But I didn't think Kahmel had the opportunity to do anything like that so far. I'd had my eWatch with me this whole time, but the possibility made me a lot more cautious about anything I sent Attican.

The waiter brought me my tea, steaming and smelling like lavender. The scent had a calming effect on my nerves, and after sweetening it with a packet of brown sugar, it proved to be the calmative I needed. "So," I said slowly after a sip. "Kahmel said he's taking me to Hashir in a few days."

"Did he say when the wedding was going to be?"

"No."

Attican nodded in understanding. "All right. From now on, we'll have to talk in encrypted text messages. Give me your wrist."

I took another sip of tea as I offered my eWatch to him. He took out a little tool that looked a little like a dentist drill, tapping on the little device meticulously, activating screens I'd never seen the watch produce. After a second, the watch was back to normal. Attican opened the message screen between me and him. He offered me the little wand he used to tamper with it. "From now on, when you write me a message, send it as though you were talking to a good friend. Then tap it with this."

I took the tool he gave me and gave the eWatch a tap, watching as a dark screen took place of the usual messenger.

"Write what you really need to say here," he went on to explain. "You'll see anything I send you here, as well. This way, if anyone tries to tap into the message and see if it's more than what it appears, all they'll see is lines of code that look like developer information."

I lost some understanding of the concept, but I got the fact that it was a secret message window, and that Kahmel wouldn't be able to tell the difference, which I figured was the important thing.

"Okay," I said, nodding and slipped the tool into my purse.

"I suppose I don't have to tell you not to let that decoder get into anyone else's hands."

No, he didn't. I liked living. "Got it."

"I want a daily report from now on. Make it as detailed as you can, even things you think are unimportant. I want to know about his phone calls, his personal life, anything you can give me."

The thought occurred to me to mention Kahmel's eyes. I didn't think it was publicly known that he was dragon tribe. That kind of thing would be relevant to Attican, but I hesitated to tell him about it. Though I thought Kahmel was a man too cold and callous for my liking, he was still a human being, and I wondered if people knowing about it would compromise his safety. The original Faresh and his entire clan was assassinated, after all. There was probably a reason he wore those glasses to hide his race. It wasn't that the other information Attican was looking for wouldn't endanger the Faresh, but I figured the purpose was more for ending the war than anything else, not specifically for hurting Kahmel.

It could also lead to me revealing my fire, and I suspected that if this man knew about it, he would never leave me alone.

"Very well," I said instead. I wouldn't talk about Kahmel belonging to the dragon tribe until I found out the reason he was hiding that fact. "But what do I do now? I told you, I had to run away from the Faresh to meet you. What if he's angry?"

Attican stood, my irritation rising as he patted me on the cheek like I was his puppy. "With a pretty face like yours, I doubt he'll stay mad. Just—" he stopped, staring out the window, along with every other patron in the restaurant.

With my back to the window, I had to turn to follow his line of sight. I stiffened. A squadron of police cars had pulled up to the cafe, along with a black car. Kahmel stepped out.

Before I could react, the police stormed into the cafe, grabbing Attican by his arms and pulling him away from me. Kahmel was right behind them, his face in a snarl, a dark mass of muscle that scared every customer in the building, myself included.

The Faresh turned my seat from the table to face him, nodding to Attican. "Who is that?" he demanded.

My body started to warm. "I-I-... He's..."

"I'm a friend of hers," Attican said from between the two officers that held him, giving me a look that meant I had better corroborate his story.

"Shut up," Kahmel snapped at him. "I want to hear it from her." he turned back to me. "Who is this man?"

"A friend," I managed to say, clenching my fists, though it was doing little to calm the flames that were coming.

"Why did you run away to see him?"

"Because she's crazy for me," Attican jeered.

The look Kahmel gave him turned murderous. He nodded to the policemen. "Take him away for questioning."

I gestured to the onlooking customers. "Is this really necessary?"

"If you wanted to see this man, you could have seen him at the hotel. Like I said."

"And have us be monitored by you like a prisoner?"

"You're not a prisoner. This is for your protection!"

"Why? *You're* the one who scares me!"

At that, Kahmel stopped completely. The scowl on his face lessened a little, the contracted muscles in his shoulders loosening. His voice came softer after that. "Try to understand. My enemies are many. If you leave my protection, I can't say which of them will find you and kill you."

"Who's the one who put me in this situation?" I challenged. "I wouldn't be in danger if you didn't arrange our marriage!"

"I—" he started, but stopped himself, pausing for a moment before he said. "You don't know that."

Without giving an explanation to his cryptic words, he turned to the policemen and said, "Escort us back to the hotel, please. Have your men ensure that any photos taken here are deleted."

My hands flared with pain. There was no way to let the fire out. The police blocked all the exits and a couple of customers had ducked into the bathrooms.

With no other option, I grabbed Kahmel's arm as he started to walk away, looking to him with urgency. "My fire."

He nodded in understanding. "Come with me to the car. Quickly."

He led me out of the building. We reached his car and got inside just as my hands started to light up, fire spreading across my palms and starting to crawl up my arms. This was going to be a big one. Pain shot through my body as I tried to stop it, because I knew if I let this one out, the results would be combustible.

But then Kahmel grasped my hands in his.

Pain etched in his face as the flames dissipated under his touch. The fire on my arms blew out, and Kahmel's hands were left smoking, a bead of sweat tracing the side of his face.

Relief washed over my body. It was like the fire was absorbed into him, leaving me free from it. "How did you do that?"

"Practice," Kahmel said, grimacing.

"With others like us?"

"With fire." He took a deep breath, taking off his glasses now that we were alone. "What was so important that you had to see this friend of yours?"

"I don't owe you an explanation," I answered, cross. "I leave for half an hour and you have the entire police force after me!"

"You're the one who started a fire in the hotel room."

I stopped. He had a point there. Then I shook my head. "The relationship we have is purely business. You need a wife, and I'm here because you and your family somehow chose me for an arranged marriage and Nana agreed. But my personal life is my business."

He paused, then said, "Very well. But please be careful from now on. Thanks to your little stunt, I don't think I'll be able to keep our engagement a secret for much longer, which means you're in even more danger than you were before."

"Fine," I said, crossing my arms. Hopefully I wouldn't have to see Attican in person anymore, anyway.

"I think we should start for Hashir in about two days. Is that enough time for you to see the rest of your friends?"

I only really wanted to see Lora and maybe Talad, but still, it seemed like awfully short notice to me. Probably to make sure I wasn't going anywhere.

"I suppose."

"All right. When we get to Hashir, I want to start showing you how to keep control of your abilities. Because if you have another accident like this in public, it would be disastrous."

"Are you sure you trust me not to burn down another hotel room?"

"No, but it's not like I have much choice."

WEDDING PLANS

The next day, I waited anxiously for Lora and Talad to be brought to my hotel room.

The room service menu showed that they served strawberry ice cream, so I did the sensible thing and ordered three servings, keeping one with me to eat and storing the other two in the freezer for any late night ice cream emergencies.

Kahmel was able to book two nearly identical rooms at the same hotel, which was good, because I really liked it there. But he increased the security to four guards standing outside my door, and I noticed the distinct lack of a kitchen.

I had already sent Attican a basic overview of what happened after the incident at the cafe. I wasn't sure what good it would do since he was in police custody.

Honestly, I hoped they would arrest him on something. Then I would be free from him. Though I used the decoder to message him, I was going to make sure Kahmel didn't come near my eWatch. I had seen that supposedly friendly facade fall away and reveal the anger he was capable of and shuddered at the thought of it being directed at me.

Then I thought of something. How did he find me at that cafe?

I didn't get to finish thinking about the issue because Kahmel came in through the door, taking his sunglasses off as he came in.

"Your friends are here. But I will warn you that you are not allowed to go with them anywhere outside of this room."

"I already know," I groaned, putting a scoop of ice cream in my mouth.

"I have to go and deliver the dowry to Matron Taias."

"Have a safe journey."

Kahmel gave me an exasperated look before he dropped his glasses back over his eyes and left.

Lora bowed in respect as he exited the room. Before she could approach me, two of the guards came in and started patting her down.

"Is this really necessary?" I asked the guards.

One of them merely looked at me before continuing their pat down. I supposed Kahmel didn't want any incidents with more of my "friends."

As soon as they were finished, Lora came running to me and tackled me in a hug. When she pulled away, she had a finger in my face. "Don't you ever disappear without telling me first again! I was worried sick something might have happened to you!"

Something did. I got involved with Attican. "I'm doing fine," I said instead. "But I'm going to miss you. Kahmel said we're leaving for Hashir in two days."

"Two days?" she said, her features falling. "So soon?"

I nodded. "He's afraid I'm going to run away again."

At that, Lora smacked my arm. "Oh, yeah. I saw you on the news, missy!"

"You did?"

"Yes! All in the news there have been rumors that the Faresh had chosen someone as his bride, but there was nothing confirmed yet. Then they said that someone had started a fire in the hotel where the Faresh was staying, and after investigating, they dismissed it as an accident in the adjacent room, but it raised questions about why he was in Kohpal to begin with. Next thing you know, they have footage of the police surrounding a coffee shop on West Hallo street, and there you were, leaving it with the Faresh!"

I raised an eyebrow at her. "Are you talking about the five o'clock news or the gossip columns?"

Lora tsked. "It doesn't matter! The fire thing did come on the regular news, and so did the footage of you leaving the restaurant with Kahmel. All of the speculating was on the gossip columns, but the rest is still true. And besides, now you can't doubt gossip columns. They were right about you, weren't they?"

One of the guards knocked, then opened the door. "Miss Anyua, there's a Talad here to see you."

"Let him in." I hated all of this security nonsense.

Lora's already wide eyes widened even further. "Talad? When did you start hanging out with Talad?"

"He helped me out with something. I wanted to see him one more time before I left."

She narrowed her eyes. "You went to him to help you escape, didn't you?"

The guards let Talad in, patting him down like they did Lora. When they were done, Talad dropped onto the couch next to me. "Jashi! Man, I'm glad you're all right."

Lora raised an eyebrow, her eyes flicking between Talad and me. "What is he talking about? What did you get yourself into this time, Jashi?"

I sighed, knowing I wouldn't be able to get Lora off my case by just brushing her off. "Listen, I know you're concerned for me, but I don't want you to get involved. I'm in trouble, and I don't want you getting mixed in it, too."

"What kind of trouble?" She spun on Talad. "It was you, wasn't it? I always knew you couldn't be trusted!"

Talad rose his hands up in surrender. "Wait, wait, wait. Look, I didn't mean to get her mixed up in anything. The guys who talked to me said they were going to help her!"

Lora looked between the two of us, then put a hand on her hip.

"All right, somebody better explain to me what's going on or someone's getting hurt."

"Fine," I conceded, then said in a lower voice. "I tried running away to escape my engagement with Kahmel, and I went to Talad so he could help me change my name and move to another town. I was going to tell you," I added quickly as I saw Lora's expression. "But then the guy who was supposed to help me escape told his boss who I was, and they pieced together that I was supposed to marry Kahmel. They want me to give them information on Kahmel and his war with Omani or they'll accuse me of trying to break my contractual agreement with him—because I ran away and am scheming against him."

"Jashi..."

Talad asked, "So, wait. I'm still not quite caught up. How did you get involved with the Faresh? How does he even know you?"

Lora frowned. "You don't remember Kahmel and his brother coming to our school when we were kids?" Her face lit up with understanding. "No, wait. You hadn't moved in to the orphanage at that time. You came later."

"The Faresh lived in our neighborhood?"

"No, dummy. He wasn't the Faresh at that time. In fact, his family is one of the lower royal branch clans. So for the most part, he and his brother were normal kids. Only thing is, I remember their family had weird rules. Like Segrid always had to be home at a certain time, no matter what. And they could never invite people to their house. In order to see them, we had to invite them to ours or hang out some place."

"How long have you guys known him?"

Lora paused. "Me, I've known him for a while. But Jashi's younger. She knew him up until their family moved when she was... how old were you?"

"I was at least nine," I answered.

Lora nodded. "Yeah, that sounds about right."

Talad put his head down, his features crestfallen. "I'm so sorry I got you into this mess, Jashi. I was really just trying to help."

"Wait," Lora said, turning to me. "Why don't you tell the Faresh what happened? He'll have those men arrested for sure!"

I shook my head vigorously. "They'll accuse me along with them. And I've seen what he's like when he's angry. I don't think he'd hesitate for a moment in sending me to death row like the rest of the people he's found guilty of treason."

Talad asked, "Can't you get Matron Taias to break the agreement?"

"How can she? She could get into all kinds of trouble for refusing the Faresh."

Lora said, "Hold on a minute. Despite all of that, I don't think Matron Taias would let you marry this guy if she thought he was as bad as you think he is. Did you talk to her?"

"Yeah," I said. Nana had called him a man of honor. I still felt like her judgment might have been clouded by her nostalgia for the days when traditions like arranged marriages were more common. The custom had all but died except for some rich clan families or among royalty. She must have liked the idea of me being like a story tale princess arranged to be married to a prince, especially since she knew of my humble beginnings, as well as the burden I'd had to bear with my fire. But to me, Kahmel was no fairytale prince, Faresh or not. He was secretive, a master of hiding his emotions, and I was afraid of what he was capable of under his perpetual mask of calm. Because even a glimpse into his other side scared the heck out of me.

Lora pouted, then gave me a small smile. "I'm going to miss you a lot, Jashi, but maybe you can look on the bright side of this, too. You're going to marry the Faresh! You'll have the freedom to do all of the things you've never been able to do. I've always worried about you, going from job to job all the time, never having money."

I smiled, tears stinging at my eyes. I wasn't sure if I was able to see the situation from her point of view, but I was infinitely grateful for the best friend a girl like me could ask for. "Thanks, Lora."

Lora looked to Talad. "And you. You should know better than to help Jashi with whatever crazy scheme she's come up with. The girl acts first and thinks later!"

I smacked her arm. "Hey, I'm right here, you know!"

As we both burst into a fit of laughing and fighting, Talad waved his hands to get our attention. "Can you both please stop acting like idiots? Jashi is still involved with those crazy people trying to turn her into a spy! What is she going to do about that?"

Lora pressed her lips together and narrowed her eyes. "Tell Kahmel! He won't have you executed; you're his fiancée. Then he'll handle them and the two of you can live happily ever after."

If only it was that simple.

But we left the subject at that. Lora knew that if I wanted to talk, we would text each other later. We spent the rest of the afternoon watching movies with two more VR helmets I requested from room service, along with a large pizza with pepperoni. For a couple of hours, it was like the old days, playing and messing around with each other like a bunch of kids. It was nice reliving the days before adulthood kicked in, before Talad started disappearing off the face of the map and I dropped out of high school because of the emotional issues I was dealing with. Before Lora had to leave the orphanage and spend nearly every waking hour of the day working or studying. For a few hours, none of that existed, and we were just a bunch of goofy kids with nothing better to do than act like idiots.

A knock at the door preceded Kahmel's entrance as we were in the middle of a game of truth or dare. He was wearing an ear piece, one I didn't see him wearing when he left.

"I'm sorry, but I need to be alone with Jashi for a moment," he said. There was something different about his expression now. I couldn't place it. Fear? Worry? Anger?

"Why?" I demanded.

"I apologize, but it's important."

Lora gave me a hug, letting it last a couple seconds before she pulled away. "It's okay, Jashi. I know you're okay now, and we got to spend some time together. I have a lot of homework to catch up on, anyway. I'll see you later, I hope."

"Okay, then. See you later."

Talad gave me a quick hug, too. "Thanks for letting me say goodbye, Jashi."

"Stay out of trouble," I said as he and Lora started to leave.

Talad winked at me. "You know how good I am at that."

"So what's this about?" I asked once Kahmel and I were alone. I crossed my arms over my chest.

He took his glasses off, his orange irises startling me again. I hated that. "It turns out we need to move up the wedding. Quickly."

I frowned. "What? Why?"

"There's been a development at the border and I'm needed immediately."

"And what? You have to be married before you leave?"

"It's the best way to ensure your safety." Maybe it was just me, but a touch of fire seemed to ignite in those eyes of his when he said, "Nobody will touch the Faresha of my country while I'm gone."

THE FARESH OF K'SUNDI

Kahmel Axon Kai of the Omah clan, Faresh of K'sundi

Jashi slept soundly as we flew in my private jet on our way to Hashir, her breath even and soft. We flew past the Dharia mountain range, the cliff formations looking like paper creases from this distance. Already, we were far away from the city of Kohpal. I hated having to rip her away from her everyday life like this, but the situation left me with little option.

I let a little fire light up in the palm of my hand and watched it dance for a moment, a little flicker of life that used to control me until I learned how to be the master of it. Once, I resented my fire. I didn't understand it, and it made me have to distance myself from having a normal life just to keep it secret. That is, until I learned to become one with it. I clenched my fist again, extinguishing the flame. I turned my attention back to Jashi, noticing the way her features smoothed out when she was at peace like this. Even now, I still couldn't believe she was actually here with me; someone who shared this strange ability I lived with my entire life, a kindred spirit whom I'd never found before or since the day I saw her.

I was determined to make sure nothing happened to her like what was attempted on my life after my first adult blood examination. What did she say her doctor's name was? Dr. Darus Kish?

Sighing, I took off my sunglasses and kneaded my temples. I came just in time. Jashi just didn't know how much she scared me when she said her doctor wanted to bring her in for "further analysis." Like hell I was going to let her go after that.

Only she started a fire and ran away anyway. Though, thankfully, not to her doctor.

Taking another look at the girl who was fiery in every sense of the word, I realized that my mission to protect her would be even more complicated than I already expected. I expected most of the opposition would come from the people who were after her, not from Jashi herself.

I hoped she would see things my way once I was able to finally explain everything to her. It put me a lot more at ease to know we would be married soon. As Faresha of the country, she would be virtually untouchable, at least for as long as it took for me to handle what was going on at the border and come back.

I just hoped Rand was doing okay.

My eWatch rang. Answering it quickly, I stole a glance at Jashi but found that her sleep was undisturbed. "Hello?" I whispered as Arusi's face appeared in front of me.

"The investigators couldn't hold anything on Attican. They had to let him go."

Damn.

Taking a deep breath, I calmed the heat that rose to my palms, feeling it disperse as I let it go. "All right."

"There's always next time."

"I was hoping there wouldn't have to be a next time," I said, clenching my jaw. "There's nothing we can do about that."

"In other news, Rand's condition isn't critical anymore."

I breathed a sigh of relief. "Good. I needed to hear that."

"You should be able to see him soon. Should I put that in your schedule?"

"No. You may as well scrap my schedule with Jashi around. I can't take my eyes off her for two seconds before she's throwing herself in the face of danger again."

"Does she know?"

"Not yet. I'm hoping to be able to tell her soon, but first things first. There's the wedding, the border, and teaching her to control her fire. All are equally important and need to be addressed before we can even talk about that."

"Yeah..." she said, pursing her lips. "Are you sure this is really going to work, Your Grace?"

"Jashi is the best chance we've got, Arusi. The way she comes up with a new way to get into trouble, I don't doubt she lacks wit, at the very least."

Arusi chuckled. "If you say so."

"All right; bye."

"Oh, and sir?" she added a split second before I was about to hang up.

"Yes?"

"Congratulations on the wedding."

DRAGON NEST CAVES

Jashi Anyua

I squinted as light fell on me, accompanied by the sound of shutters being raised. Still, I kept my eyes closed and was drifting back toward blissful sleep when a gentle nudging kept me from the gates.

"Jashi, we're landing in Hashir now."

Frowning at the disturbance, I turned over, sleepily drifting away again, only to be coaxed back toward the land of the waking.

"Jashi, you have to wake up."

I opened my eyes at a slit. Kahmel sat beside me, his chiseled features close to my face as he nudged me again. Annoyed at the prodding, I sat up and yawned. "I'm up, I'm up," I said groggily.

"We're in Hashir."

"I heard you the first time."

Wiping the sleep out of my eyes, the drowsy fog cleared. We were in the nation's capital, a city I'd wanted to travel to for years, with gorgeous and tall buildings I was dying to see. Turning to the window to look, I screamed as soon as I did, drawing away from it and clutching Kahmel's arm. "What is that?" I said pointing at the flock of creatures flying in the air, trembling as if they'd sense I was watching them and start flying toward us.

"Dragons," he said, as though it were the most simple thing in the world.

My eyes couldn't have opened any wider. The reptilian creatures flew in circles around each other, serpentine animals that flew without wings. From this distance, all I could see were their forms, like a swarm of black snakes slithering through the air above the skyscrapers of Hashir.

"Are wild dragons common here?"

"Ah, I forgot. The dragons haven't spread as far as Kohpal yet. See, the reason Hashir has dragons"— he took me by my shoulder and held me against his chest, pointing his finger and directing my line of sight in alignment with his—"is because of those."

He pointed at the mountains, the same range that cropped the background of Kohpal. But these mountain cliffs had pockets, little holes sporadically dotted along the rock.

I frowned. "What are those?"

"Their nesting ground."

The idea of living in Hashir was starting to seem less and less pleasant. "Why don't you get rid of them? They're a threat to everyone, living in the wild like that."

"That's what everyone keeps telling me. But I veto any motion to fill their caves with land. I like them living here."

I looked at him like he was stark-raving mad. "Why?"

He shrugged. "They remind me of myself."

Raising an eyebrow, I settled within myself that I would never understand this man because I couldn't help but agree with what everyone else thought. Dragons were violent creatures by nature. Historians spent centuries studying them, and more modern research showed that of all of the animals that inhabited this world, dragons were among those of the lowest amount of brain function, defining them as creatures of pure instinct with no sense of morality or sympathy for other forms of life. Normal animals, when tested, showed signs of having some form of conscience, things that their brains were capable of categorizing as right or wrong. Dragons didn't even remember their young. The babies they bore fed from the scraps the mother left by accident.

That was why in ancient times, those of the dragon tribe were so revered in K'sundi. They were ruthless savages, notorious for having the conscience of a dragon. In a nation that elevated clans to royal status based on military prowess and the wits of a warrior, the dragon tribe ruled with an iron fist, respected by the fear they instilled.

In all of the world of Hemorah, only the Zendaalans were able to create a means of taming the creatures, opening a whole new way of living with them. Or, rather, the only way.

It figured Kahmel related to dragons, of all things.

Then he added, "I own a few, actually. It took a lot to get them, too. They're the first dragons I ever tamed on my own. When I was younger, I found them at this Zendaalan dragon trade unit I was visiting. They were going to put them down because the electric collars weren't working on them. They'd adapted to the pain. A couple friends and I found out where they were being held and broke them out. We decided to try to train them ourselves."

I couldn't believe what I was hearing. "You tried to control an untamed dragon without collars? Is that legal?"

He smirked. "Sort of. And there were three. Anyway, that was all before I became Faresh, and it was the last time I pulled something like that. I was able to use them to take the Omanian air fortress with my group, and all that power made a huge difference in the battle." A smile crept up his face. "The Omanians didn't know what hit them."

"Wait, your group? Group of who?"

"Group of...friends." The way he said the last word made me narrow my eyes at him, dubious.

"And you and your friends tamed dragons without electric collars?"

"Got them relatively tame, yeah. I could show you when we get to the palace, if you'd like."

I shuddered. "No, thanks." Turning back to the window, I wondered what in the world Nana could have possibly seen in this man.

When we arrived at the Hashir airport, my mouth dropped. I had never seen so many races in one place. There were Zendaalans, Omanians, and every other race in all of Hemorah—Udish, Vahdelans, Lokidians—all in their different styles of clothing. I saw robes, wraps, army uniforms, clothes I would consider normal, like jeans and tops, and then there were even people that wore little more than beads and jewelry. I jumped when I saw someone with tentacles coming from their head, their skin a palish gray.

Behind me, Kahmel said, "Don't tell me you've never seen an alien."

I shook my head in wonder, trying not to stare at the person walking by, but finding it impossible. "What race is he?"

"*She* is an Isoran."

"Oh," I said in a small voice, my eyes following the person as they walked by. This was why I'd always fantasized about coming here to Hashir one day. There was so much more to the world, and I knew I could find people from every corner of it right here in the capital.

"Stay close to me from here on out."

I groaned. "Why?"

But my question was answered when I saw a flock of reporters armed with cameras and flashing lights making a beeline toward us.

"That's why."

Kahmel's bodyguards surrounded us as we started on our way for the exit. Heeding his advice, I got closer to Kahmel as we moved into the midst of the chaos. Flashing lights blinded me, making me blink so fast I could barely see ahead of myself. Kahmel took my hand in his big, rough one as his bodyguards made a path for the two of us.

"Is this the rumored bride-to-be?"

"Who is this at your side, Your Grace?"

"Would you like to make a comment about the current status of the war with Omani?"

"Do you have an opinion on it, miss?"

Kahmel's voice boomed above them all. "No comment," he said, his tone with an edge to it that even made the reporters think twice.

They changed the strategy to their questions. "Please, great Faresh, can we get a statement?"

"What about you, miss? Any statements?"

"Please, just give us one statement, Your Grace."

Kahmel ignored them as we set them behind us. We caught the stares of every eye in the airport, and the attention made me squirm. This was definitely going to take some getting used to.

My eWatch buzzed, but I didn't recognize the name. Derill Shaad? Tapping on the message, I understood immediately.

I'm out. We'll talk later.

I didn't think I needed the decoder to understand it. Suddenly conscious, I glanced to the Faresh to see if he noticed me looking at my eWatch. Thankfully, he was focused on us getting to the exit.

As we left the airport, Kahmel had a limousine pull around front for us. If I'd thought there were a lot of reporters in the airport, outside looked like a personal parade. The bodyguards opened the car for us, and Kahmel shepherded me in before getting in himself.

"Take us home," he told the driver, then closed the window between us and him. He turned to me. "Today you'll be meeting my family, and then you can give my people a list of the friends you'd like to invite to the wedding."

I gritted my teeth. Great. Inviting all my friends to a wedding I didn't want to attend—and I was the bride. Not to mention I was planning on getting the heck out of there once Attican was done with me.

Then again, Lora would kill me if I didn't invite her.

I decided the list would be extremely limited. This arrangement was like I'd already said: business. But for the first time, it sunk in how much attention this wedding would draw. People I knew from the orphanage, school, all the jobs I've had...all of them would know that I was marrying the Faresh. What would happen when I disappeared from everything without a word? It would be an embarrassment to Kahmel, for sure, but I didn't care much about that.

I did care about how it affected Nana.

I sighed. There wasn't much I could do about it, though.

What Kahmel said next threw me completely off of my train of thought. "Don't trust any of my family members."

"Wait, what? Why not?" I couldn't imagine what family members I would have to worry about. I didn't know much about them, or how many he had outside of his parents since they were extremely closed off, from what I remembered. But Segrid was much more pleasant than Kahmel ever was; I knew that.

He looked at me, and I saw that steel in his eyes again—the kind that reminded me very much like that of a dragon. But he laughed, the noise sounding dark. "They want me dead." While I was left speechless, he went on to say, "Just stay close to me when I introduce you. We won't stay long."

"No, no, no, you can't just say something like that and move on like it's nothing. Why do your parents want you dead?"

"Not just my parents. My brothers, too."

"But you only have one brother."

He shook his head. "There's a lot I'm going to have to explain about my family. First, Segrid isn't my only brother."

"He's not?"

"I have four."

My mouth dropped. "How can you have four brothers I've never met?"

"When have you ever seen me with anyone other than Segrid? My parents always made us keep our friends distant so they wouldn't know anything about our family dynamics. They sent Segrid and me to one school and my other brothers to another in a different zone."

"But what's the point? What does it matter if people know you have four brothers?"

"Because we're a royal branch clan. I'm not sure how much you know about how royal branch families live, but there's a lot of secrecy involved. They usually don't let people outside of their own know much about their family."

I whistled, leaning back into my seat. "That's not a family, that's a cult."

He shrugged. "I'm not going to argue with you. I've always thought it was ridiculous. Especially since it separated me from the brother I was always closest to."

"And who was that?"

"The only person in my family you're allowed to be around. My twin brother, Rand."

I threw my hands up. Of course he had a twin brother. Why not?

"Rand and I are the eldest," he went on to say. "But Rand won't be able to attend. He's been feeling unwell. Then there's Sokir, Jahl, and you already know Segrid. He's younger than you by about a year, I think."

"And your parents?"

"Kolin and Mira. They're both scholars."

Frowning, I crossed my arms again. "And how are they going to feel about you marrying a high school dropout?"

Kahmel shook his head and waved the subject away. "It doesn't matter how they feel. They'll have to get used to it. Anyway, meeting my family is just a formality. After that, we're going to the palace so you can get settled in. Relax," he added as he saw my face. "The estate has multiple houses. I wouldn't go against tradition like that."

I looked out the window to hide rolling my eyes. Like I would do *that* with him because of tradition. But typical that the only thing that seemed to bother the guy was anything that had to do with precious "tradition."

Oh, yeah. And dragon nest caves.

PRINCIPLES

Despite the hour and a half car ride where Kahmel described his family to me, I felt like he had prepared me for nothing when I arrived at the palace home.

The palace was grander than anything I could have imagined. I'd seen pictures of it online, but seeing it in person was far different. The structure had been passed down from generation to generation for centuries. It was huge, with little towers that peaked throughout the structure. The roofs were shaped like orbs, like the buildings K'sundi used to have hundreds of years ago. The deep orange-gold walls glittered in the light of the setting sun. A reflective pool stretched out in front of it, mirroring the building and the pink skies behind it.

Kahmel told me a little about their history—which school his other brothers went to, how his parents worked as scholars together investigating ancient K'sundii history, the names of a few of his closest cousins, things like that.

What he didn't prepare me for was the fact that these people were almost worse psychopaths than their son.

"So, Jashi, what makes you think you're good enough to marry our son?"

Kahmel's mother looked at me from across the dinner table with black eyes that analyzed my entire person from top to bottom. Her hair was straightened—an onyx bob streaked with white, cropped around her face at angles, bringing more attention to her heightened cheekbones and wrinkled pursed lips. Glittery green dusted her eyelids, and her lips were painted a deep rouge. Thick false lashes hooded her beady eyes, fanning me as she blinked quickly, waiting for my answer.

We sat at a long table with Kahmel at the head. I sat on the opposite end. His parents sat next to each other, and their sons filled up either side. The table was full of food of all kinds, a banquet I was itching to dig into, but Kahmel's parents stared at me like this was an interrogation rather than a meal. Before we arrived, Kahmel had arranged for me to have someone dress me up for the occasion, so I was wearing a blush pink dress that flowed to my feet, a patterned sash around my waist like a belt with a bow in the back. My hair was pushed back by a headband, and I was wearing gold earrings and bangle bracelets that clanged against the table as I picked up my fork.

I still felt out of place.

But I didn't care whether they interrogated me. I was going to eat.

Before I could come up with an answer, Kahmel spoke for me, and I took the cue to dive into the roast chicken that taunted me on my plate. "Mother, please."

Her eyes widened, making her lashes touch her eyebrows. "Don't you 'Mother, please' me! You show up telling us you're ready to get married and you come back with her?"

I frowned, looking at him. "Wait, you went to the orphanage representing the 'house of Omah,' and your parents didn't know who you were marrying?"

Kahmel merely sipped his wine nonchalantly. "They told me they didn't care whom I chose to marry. I was free to decide on my own."

Oh, well, it was nice at least *he* had a say in the arrangement.

"This is ridiculous!" his mother snapped, and I wondered how she managed to make her hand into such a tight fist with her long, navy blue acrylic nails on. "It was your idea that we go through the process of arranged marriage to find yourself a bride! And we went along with it thinking you would do so the traditional way, like you said, which meant finding a proper wife. Why would you even remember this girl? She doesn't even have an education or a proper family! I can't imagine who you made the proposal to."

I munched on some piece of toast to bite down a few choice comments that came to mind. Frankly, I didn't understand why he chose me, either. That didn't mean I liked being belittled, though.

"Actually," Kahmel said, "traditionally, a wife was chosen based on having virtue and a strong spirit that she could pass on, to give a warrior children with hearts like steel. Only modern-day interpretation has turned that custom into a fox hunt for a stupid girl with a lot of money."

"Son." His father spoke up, a smile spreading across his smooth caramel face to reveal a set of perfect teeth. But it was a smile absolutely devoid of emotion or anything trustworthy. I was starting to see where Kahmel got his personality from. His father had salt-and-pepper hair that was cut short and a white, low-trimmed beard covering his chin. "You spout useless babble all day about traditions that have all but died—and for what? You've decided yourself to revive customs as old as the first Neanderthals."

Again, I turned to Kahmel, only to find that he seemed apathetic to what either of them were saying, and it was only then that I realized that he wasn't wearing his glasses. This was the first time I'd seen him without them in public. I supposed he didn't have to hide himself among his family, but I noticed none of the rest of them had eyes like his or mine. Could it be that the dragon tribe gene was somehow only prominent in him?

He calmly looked over to his father. "Weren't you the ones who taught me about those *Neanderthals* all my life? You made it your career to research them, and now you're upset because I've chosen to respect their ways? *Our* old ways, mind you."

The friendly smile on his father's face fell away, a dangerous edge to his eyes. "You know that's not what I mean."

"Then please, explain. Explain why you didn't reproach me for following old traditions to become Faresh and secure your positions in various branches of the government, not to mention raising your social standing from being one of the lowest royal clans to being the very highest. Why wasn't it wrong to consult the ancient traditions to become the Faresh and bring this nation out of chaos, but it was wrong for me to choose to marry Jashi based on the same principles?"

His parents said nothing. The two of them didn't seem much interested in their meals after all of that, but I was. And thankfully, without the heated conversation, the roast chicken tasted all the better.

After an hour or so, Kahmel's mother complained of feeling sick and excused herself from the table. Kahmel's father followed after her to drive her home. The other three brothers finished eating dinner with Kahmel and me, but the meal was mainly held in silence.

As dessert was being served, I felt my eWatch buzz and looked to see "Derill Shaad" had sent me a message.

I heard you were getting married. Congrats!

"I have to go to the bathroom. If you'll excuse me."

Kahmel touched my arm to stop me. "Are you all right?" he asked.

He must have thought it was my fire. "I'm fine," I said. "I'll be right back."

Letting me go, he pointed and said, "Down that hall and to the left."

Going down the way he indicated, I stepped into the bathroom and pulled out the decoder from my purse. Opening the message again, I tapped on it to reveal the black screen that was the secret messenger.

Attican: The questioning didn't last too long before they had to

let me out on lack of evidence. Good news, right? So, I saw you on the news. You're in Hashir already? When's the wedding?
Me: I don't know. Kahmel hasn't told me yet.
Attican: Find out. Let me know by tonight.
Me: Fine.

Just before I deactivated the screen, he said,

Attican: Write a response on the regular messenger. It makes our interaction look more natural. I promise you the Faresh will be monitoring your eWatch, so don't mess up.
Attican: I have people everywhere, so don't think I can't reach you in Hashir.

I put a hand through my hair, trying to control the shaking in my hands. He didn't have to keep threatening to keep me scared. Between Attican and the threat of Kahmel discovering me, I had plenty to worry about.

Writing a quick message to make our correspondence look natural, I flushed the toilet and ran the sink water before I left the room.

I was just about to turn back into the dining room when I heard one of Kahmel's brothers saying, "Are you trying to make a mockery of our family?"

Discreetly, I peeked around the corner to see who was talking. It was the one who introduced himself as Sokir, third oldest and just younger than Kahmel and his twin. All the brothers had features in common, but Sokir was the leanest of them, with a long, serious face and a prominent jawline. "I know you better than this. What's the real reason you're marrying her?"

"You think there's some mystery as to why I chose Jashi?"

"You can play those games with Mom and Dad, but I'm not stupid. Just get rid of her before this becomes an embarrassment for all of us. Don't you see that you've been slowly going mad? First this war with Omani, now this ridiculous marriage."

"It's like you're trying to run this family to the ground," added Jahl, who was slightly thicker than Kahmel and Sokir.

Kahmel laughed, the kind of dark laughter that made my skin crawl. "Look who's talking. You don't think I know what you talk about behind my back?"

"Kahmel," Segrid started, the youngest and shortest of all of them. "Don't be paranoid. We just want what's best for the family name."

"What a lie," Kahmel bit back. Then he turned back to Sokir. "And you can tell your Zendaalan 'friends' that you're not getting anything out of me about Jashi. I will find every one of the spies they've slipped into my administration to keep an eye on us and have them executed one by one."

As I felt my hands start to burn, I rushed back into the bathroom, my heart pounding. Flames raced up my arms, and I hate to bite my tongue to keep from crying out. The taste of metal filled my mouth.

Finally, the flames died down, and I had to take a moment to breath. Taking some tissue in my hand, I wiped the sweat from my face and took a deep breath.

I'm not even doing anything big. It's just text messages, I thought. But what could Kahmel have been talking about? What were his brothers trying to find out about me? And were they somehow involved with Zendaalans, too?

As I left the bathroom a second time, I found that Sokir, Jahl, and Segrid were all getting up to leave.

Kahmel turned to me. "My brothers have to leave early. Just as well; I wanted to talk to you."

The three men gave me a smile and a curt nod before saying their goodbyes and leaving. The Faresh and I were left alone.

I sat down next to him, trying to resist the tears that threatened to fall. This crazy mess was entangling me deeper and deeper in by the day, the notion of ever escaping seeming more and more outside of my reach.

"What did you want to talk to me about?" I asked him.

"Our wedding. Who will you invite to it?"

"Just my friends, Lora and Talad." I'd decided. I didn't want anyone else to have to attend.

Kahmel blinked, but he didn't comment on it. "Matron Taias also told me she'd want to come when I gave her the dowry," he added instead. "I think we should hold the wedding within a week. I told you Rand wasn't well, but I didn't tell you why. He was hurt on the battlefield. I'm going to have to leave to go down there. We're in a crucial stage at this point in the war, and I can't afford not having someone I can trust to lead the battle."

"You don't trust many people, do you?"

He shook his head, sighing, the look in his eye distant, like he was talking more to himself than me. "I can't. Everywhere I look, there are more spies, traitors, someone else who questions my claim to the throne. I can't even trust my own family."

He looked to me like he'd only just realized that he'd said that in front of me. "I'm sorry," he said, the fire in his eyes calming. But I had already seen another face of his. The rumors were true; he was extremely paranoid. "Anyway, I can only be with you a few days after the wedding. After that, I'll have to go."

I chuckled, but the sound was humorless. "It makes no difference to me. As far as I'm concerned, we're just business partners."

I wasn't proud of it, but I wanted those words to hurt him. He'd ruined my life, made me resort to having to change my name to escape my obligation, got me tangled up with gangsters. So, yes, I wanted it to sting. I wanted to give him a taste of what he was putting me through. But I didn't really think my words would have much bite. This was probably just business for him, too. But, oh, how I wished I could make him feel how I felt.

Then I realized that in a way, I could. I didn't like Attican at all, but maybe what he was doing would work in my favor, for all of

K'sundi. I didn't want Kahmel for a husband. K'sundi didn't need him for a Faresh. The way Attican put it, if I succeeded in his mission, not only would I be able to start fresh, but I could even help dethrone the Faresh.

Thinking about it, Kahmel already told me something important. His brother was injured and he was about to go in his stead. And they were in a crucial stage in the war right now. I was sure Attican could put all that information to good use.

"If there's nothing else, I'd like to go to my room."

Kahmel nodded, and for a split second, something flashed in his eyes. But as he stood up, it disappeared again. "I'll walk you to your new home. It's just next door. Tomorrow I want to come over and teach you how to finally control your fire."

We walked away from the dining room, and for some reason, the look that flashed across his face stuck with me. If I didn't know any better, I would have said there had been pain in his eyes at what I said.

No, it couldn't have been. It must have just been my imagination.

Dragons didn't feel pain.

FIRE

When someone knocked at my door the next morning, I was so absorbed in my own thoughts, I almost didn't notice. All I could think about was the response I woke up to when I checked the messenger. I had sent my message last night.

> *Kahmel and I are to be married in a week. His twin brother, Rand, was injured on the battlefield, so he's going down to the border to reestablish order. He's horribly paranoid; it doesn't look like he has many people he can trust. According to him, he's at a critical point in the war at the moment. Not sure what that means, but that's what he told me was why he urgently needed to be down there.*

His reply came while I was still asleep.

> *This is good. Real good, minx. But it isn't enough. You need to ask him for details. Specifically:*
> - *Where will he be stationed?*
> - *What condition is his brother in?*
> - *Where are his army bases stationed?*
> - *Where is the battle most "critical?"*
> - *Why is he at war with Omani?*
> *Find out.*

The message confused me on multiple levels, especially with the last request. Didn't the Zendaalans already know why Kahmel was at war with Omani? And if they didn't, why couldn't they find out themselves? Was Kahmel keeping his politics hidden, even from the Zendaalans? The more I learned about Kahmel, the more I feared for this nation's safety.

The repeated knocking at the door brought me back to reality. The first time I heard it, part of me forgot that I was the one supposed to open it. Having this open home all to myself made me feel like I didn't really belong.

You don't, common sense reminded me.

I shuffled toward the door in my house-shoes, opening the door to see Kahmel standing there, dressed in gym clothes, complete with a gray sweatshirt, pants, and gym shoes—and of course, his black sunglasses.

"Are you ready to train?"

My interests lay conflicted. I wanted so desperately to learn to control my fire like he could. However, I also was tired of seeing him every day. But I sighed. At least after the wedding, he would be away for who knew how long with the war.

"Sure," I said, letting him inside. "Give me a moment to change."

Kahmel nodded and sat down on the sofa.

As I went into my room and pulled open my enormous closet, I found it was not only packed with my things, but enough clothes for at least a dozen more outfits, not to mention cocktail dresses and heels. Checking the tags on all of them, I found they were all my size.

The sight made me stop. I didn't understand Kahmel. There were times he didn't seem like such a bad guy, like filling my closet with clothes, making sure I was comfortable, training me to use my fire. But then there were times he seemed like a maniac bent on using his power to satisfy his paranoia of everyone being out to get him. And then there was that angry side that showed its head every so often that scared the heck out of me.

I didn't think I could love him as a husband or that I would ever agree with his politics, but maybe I could persuade him out of this war. After that, Attican would be satisfied enough to let me go, and he could sneak me out of the palace estate to let me live somewhere in Gasher. Of course, there was the chance the Faresh wouldn't give a damn about what I had to say. It was worth giving a shot later down the line, as he came to trust me more.

If he could.

I picked out a yellow tank top and some simple gray shorts. Seeing a nice pair of pink and black gym shoes, I slipped those on, too.

When I came back into the living room, I found he had already removed his glasses and was stroking his beard in thought.

The thought occurred to me that I could use this training session to my advantage and ask those questions Attican wanted answered.

"Let's go outside," Kahmel said. "We don't want you burning anything down if something goes wrong."

"I thought the point was not to be seen."

"My entire estate is extremely private. I've instructed most of the staff working the grounds not to enter your private living space. We'll be fine."

Shrugging, I followed him toward the sliding glass door that led to the backyard. Then he kicked off his shoes and sat on the ground with his legs crossed.

"Please, sit down," he invited, gesturing to the ground in front of him. "And take off your shoes."

It seemed I didn't need gym shoes after all. Kicking them off, I sat down and mimicked his pose.

"What do I do first?"

Kahmel closed his eyes, resting his palms on his kneecaps. "You will learn meditation."

I resisted rolling my eyes. "And how exactly does one learn to meditate? It's just thinking with your eyes closed."

Without opening his eyes, Kahmel said, "If that's what you think meditation is, it only proves how much more you need to learn it."

I mockingly mimicked what he said with my mouth. "All right," I said out loud.

"Close your eyes," the Faresh said, opening his. "And put your hands on your knees, palms facing down."

I followed his instructions, wondering what exactly this had to do with controlling my fire.

"When you breathe, concentrate on self-awareness. Feel the air as it enters your lungs and concentrate on it as it leaves."

"That doesn't make any sense."

"Just try."

Sighing, I did as I was told. Breathe in, breathe out. I heard Kahmel breathing in front of me, long deep breaths. So I adjusted mine to match his. His breathing was much farther spaced apart, with deep exhalations that I strained to keep up with.

It took only a couple of minutes for me to get bored. I wasn't very good at doing nothing for too long.

Deciding now was as good a time as any, I said, "How's your brother?"

"Meditation is supposed to be held in silence."

I opened my eyes, resting my aching back as I leaned forward and propped my elbow on my knee, resting my head on my fist. "Meditation is boring."

Kahmel sighed, opening his eyes. "Jashi, please. If you want to control your fire, this has to be the first step."

"Are the other steps more interesting than this?"

"And what exactly do you consider interesting?"

I shrugged. "For starters, what you showed me earlier. I thought I would be learning that."

"You will. With time. Now, please close your eyes. And get back into the proper pose."

Reluctantly, I obeyed, and soon I heard Kahmel breathing again.

Keeping my eyes closed, I asked, "So, how's your brother?"

Kahmel sighed again. "He's doing better."

"How did he get hurt?"

"Omani sent an attack that caught us off-guard. They fired on our dragon-fliers viciously, and Rand got hurt. If it wasn't for his dragon veering in the air instead of spiraling to the ground, Rand wouldn't be here."

"Rand is a dragon-flier?" I exclaimed, my eyes widening.

"Jashi..."

I closed my eyes. "So...Rand is a dragon-flier?"

"Yes."

Then something connected. "Wait, so if you're going to be filling his shoes, doesn't that mean you're a dragon-flier, too?"

"Yep."

"That must be so amazing! I've only seen dragons on the HoloScreen. To actually ride one must be a dream."

"It seems I'm not the only one who likes dragons."

I stopped, glaring at him. If he was trying to make me seem more like him, he would be sorely disappointed. "No, the kind of dragons I like are the tame ones. And that isn't possible if they're allowed to live in the wild."

"Jashi, if you're going to talk through your meditation, at least do so with your eyes closed."

I figured that was a good trade-off. Closing my eyes again, I said, "Anyway, as I was saying—dogs don't live in the wild. They're domesticated to control the spread of disease and everything else they can carry. The same applies to dragons, and even more so. They shouldn't be allowed to live in the wild. They're too dangerous."

"I didn't see those dragons we flew by yesterday hurting anybody."

I tsked, curling pieces of my hair around my finger. "It doesn't matter. Their only nature is to kill and destroy. If not now, later."

"So you think that the only way to stop that is to domesticate them all?"

"Yes. That's why we get our dragons from the Zendaalans. They're the only ones who know how to train them properly."

"And do you know how that training is done?"

I hesitated. "Yeah, I remember seeing a documentary about it once. The only way to get them to release their killing nature is to teach them through the electrocution collars used to control them. I don't necessarily like that part, but the dragons aren't like other animals. They said in the documentary that their minds function more like machines than beasts. It's...it's like taking into consideration the suffering of a fly—something too simple to understand it."

"Flies wouldn't learn anything if you electrocuted them."

I paused, tugging at the ends of my shirt. He was right. But when the alternative was letting them free and making people live with the threat of being attacked... "Well, if you're so against the way dragons are tamed, why use them in your army?" I countered. "Hardly any other Faresh before you have tried to use dragons in warfare like this. Why be the only one?"

I heard Kahmel chuckle. "Who said my dragons were tame?"

Once again, he decided to leave me in mystery rather than explain himself. I heard him get up, so I opened my eyes.

"That's it for today," he said.

"What?" I said, standing. "That's it? But I didn't learn anything!"

"Yes, you did. You know how to meditate now. Though I recommend it with less talking. At least you have the concept. Next time you get upset, I still prefer you to come find me, but if I'm not around, try the breathing exercise."

I crossed my arms. "Now what? You go off to do whatever Fareshes do, and I'll do what, exactly?"

Kahmel scratched his beard. "I wanted you to get to know Arusi, but that probably won't happen until after the wedding. She's busy handling some important business right now."

I frowned. "The secretary of defense?"

"So you've heard of her."

"Yeah. But I don't know much about her."

"I think you'll like her. You'll be spending a lot of time with her and Rand while I'm away."

"Why them?"

"Like I said, I've instructed all of my personnel that they're not to interact with you. If and when you leave the estate, you're to go with bodyguards and either Arusi or Rand present."

I raised an eyebrow. "So I suppose when you say I'll like her, you're saying I have to like her because I'll be spending every waking moment with her. And your brother Rand. Great."

"Arusi's nice and gets along with anyone. I don't think you'll have any problems."

It was a brush-off. "Fine, whatever."

Kahmel put his shoes and sunglasses back on. "I'll be back tomorrow to continue our training. By the way, you're free to communicate with any of your friends on your eWatch, in case you were wondering."

"I can barely contain my excitement."

"Can I see your eWatch, by the way? I'll put Arusi's, Rand's, and my contact information on it."

I remembered what Attican said about Kahmel bugging my eWatch. But I figured he would eventually find a way to do it anyway. I was going to be living in his own home pretty soon. And besides, I had my decoder.

I shuddered. I still hadn't wrapped my head around the idea of living with Kahmel. But one issue at a time.

He took the eWatch when I handed it to him, punching in the numbers quickly and handing it back. "One other thing. Please limit your excursions to once a day if you go, and you have to come back home if your security guard tells you to." He pointed to one of the contacts on the list. "That's his number. If you want to leave, ask him to take you."

"But I have to wait until Rand or Arusi can take me?"

"Yep. And Rand is still in the hospital. He should be okay in time for the wedding, though."

"So what am I supposed to do in the meantime?"

Kahmel started for the door. "Sorry. As I said, you can call your friends."

"It's only ten o'clock. Lora's still in class."

"Sorry," he repeated. "It's for your safety." Then he left.

I sighed, plopping down on the sofa in the living room. Back to my prisoner status.

DEARLY BELOVED...

The week before the wedding passed surprisingly quickly. Talking to Lora helped me a lot. She made sure to call me every day as soon as she got out of class, talking to me much longer than she was supposed to. I had to make sure she hung up with me before too long, or she would forget about her studies. I wouldn't let that happen on my account. When Lora was busy, I even called Talad a few times, and we reminisced about the good old days before he used to get in trouble with the law.

I only saw Kahmel when he came to do more meditation sessions with me. It made it hard to find out much information about the war. In some way, I felt like he was doing it on purpose. Every time I would ask, he would give me short answers that I could have learned from the news, or he would discreetly redirect the conversation to another subject.

The only other time I left the house was for wedding preparations. At Kahmel's house, I met with a seamstress for the dress, a choreographer for the dance, and a ceremony director so I would know the proper conduct for the wedding. It was hectic.

The situation allowed for no questions about the war.

Why was he avoiding me? I didn't think he suspected me of anything, otherwise he wouldn't have tolerated me being so close to his home. Though I couldn't leave the grounds, I could go down to his house every so often when he wasn't busy. I only did so when I needed something from him, like when I couldn't get the HoloScreen working.

Obviously, an emergency.

But while I was there, I noticed how vacant his home felt. He didn't entertain any guests and didn't invite family. He just attended meetings and had phone calls all day. At least, from what I could see.

If he had suspicions about me, I didn't think he would keep me around for long. So why did he avoid my questions like he did? Was I nothing but an obligation to him? He was probably receiving a lot of pressure from the Courts to get married. And what better wife to appease them than an intimidating girl of the dragon tribe to reinforce his standing as a "warrior"? His lessons with me were likely only to ensure his house didn't burn down while he was away. He didn't answer my questions because he had no reason to.

It wasn't like he was marrying out of love.

The night before our wedding, Kahmel texted me, saying that he wanted me to have dinner with him so we could talk.

I didn't spend long picking something to wear, deciding on a basic yellow dress and some white flats. I let my hair curl wildly around my head in an afro and put on a little lip gloss.

When I arrived at his door, I rang the doorbell and waited. The cold of the night nipped at my bare shoulders. Since his house was right across from mine, I didn't bring anything to stave off the cold. I rubbed at my arms until he finally opened the door.

"Why aren't you wearing a jacket?" he said, gesturing for me to come in. "It's freezing out." He'd chosen to wear a smart suit for the evening, along with a green satin tie and what looked like a brand new pair of black leather shoes. The edges of his hair had been lined up quite evenly, and his beard had taken a significant trimming.

I suddenly felt underdressed, but I shrugged off the feeling. It wasn't like I was trying to impress anyone. "That wouldn't make much sense. We're neighbors."

He reached out his hand. "Shall I take your purse?"

I nearly handed it off to him, but stopped when I remembered that I needed the decoder if Attican contacted me. "I'm fine. I prefer to have it on me," I said instead.

Kahmel shrugged. "As you wish."

He guided me back to the dining room where I had met his family. On the table was a meal for two—steak, baked potatoes, and a colorful mixed vegetable dish. Freshly baked loaves of bread complemented the setup on the table, along with a bottle of champagne on ice.

Always the gentleman, Kahmel pulled out my chair for me. I gave him a small smile, sitting down as he pushed me into my place at the table before he moved around the table and sat down as well.

Kahmel took a deep breath, wringing his big hands together. "Thank you for coming."

He was looking at me strangely this evening. As a matter of fact, he was acting strangely, too. His demeanor was almost...fervent, nervous, even.

Was he anxious about the marriage?

I didn't know quite what to say. You're welcome?

"Thanks for having me," I decided was the polite answer.

Seeing that I was waiting for him, Kahmel gestured to the food. "Please, dig in. Don't let me stop you."

Taking his advice, I picked up my fork and knife and cut through the tender meat of the steak, finding it to be just as good as it looked. But I didn't enjoy it as much, knowing he hadn't revealed his reasons for calling me here.

He sighed. "I know I've put you in a difficult position by arranging this marriage. But I hope you know that I plan to make this arrangement as comfortable as possible for you. Other than what I feel is necessary for your safety, you'll be able to do as you wish. Even go back to Kohpal to visit your friends."

My fork clanked against the plate as I set it down. "Oh, really?" I said, sarcasm dripping from my tone. "Then I can go back home? Can

I live like a normal person after we're married? Not having you chase me down like an animal whenever I leave your sight? Here's an idea: You could free me of our arrangement, and maybe I'll marry someone of my choosing. Or not. That should have been my decision, not yours. So I hope you forgive me if I don't say thank you for this leash you've tied around my neck, as slack as it may be."

Kahmel looked away, the hand that held his fork clenching into a fist. "I asked your Matron Taias for your hand in marriage, and she agreed. I've done everything as per tradition mandates—"

"I don't give a damn about tradition!" I was so tired of all his justifications over tradition. "Tradition died a long time ago, and for a reason. Nowadays girls like having a choice in who they get to marry. Because this is barbaric."

His eyes returned to mine, his ember-colored stare smoldering. "I don't understand. If this is how you feel, why did you turn yourself in after you disappeared for a week?"

"Be-because," I stuttered, catching myself before I misspoke. I took up the fork and poked at the vegetables. "I was afraid. I thought you would wind up finding me anyway, and if I turned myself in, you wouldn't accuse me of disobedience."

Kahmel frowned. "Why would you think that?" Then understanding dawned on his face. "It's because of the rumors about me, isn't it? You think I'm some kind of ruthless tyrant."

"That's because you are. I mean, what kind of man waltzes in on an orphanage for some girl's hand in marriage without getting her consent first?"

"I would have, but I didn't have time." He huffed. "I wanted to."

I shook my head, laughing. "You act like any amount of convincing would have made me want to be with you willingly. I told you from the beginning—even if you somehow convinced Nana that this was a good idea, for me this is nothing more than a business arrangement. Don't ask anything more of me."

Kahmel opened his mouth to say something but then closed it again, clenching his jaw. "Very well," he said finally.

I stood from the table. "Suddenly, I'm not hungry anymore."

Before he could say anything, I marched away from the table and slammed the door closed behind me.

Tears slid down my cheeks as the cold whipped at my face. When I entered my home, I closed the door behind me, leaning against the door and sliding to the floor. My tears fell freely.

This time tomorrow, I would be that man's wife.

※

I FELT like a princess in my wedding ensemble. My dress folded and fit my curves like a glove. My draping sleeves reached the floor, blending along with the train of my bright red dress. My makeup was flawless—a maroon-rouge color painted on my lips, my eyes dusted with a gentle smoky color.

Ceremonies filled the morning. From the time I woke up until the actual Binding Ceremony, I either knelt, stood, or bowed my head in homage to another time-honored tradition dedicated to the Great Spirits.

It wasn't like I didn't respect the Great Spirits or anything, but Lora and Nana were always more into it than I was. Did I attend the dragon festivals every new year? Sure. Did I attend every Ceremony of Thanks? No. Did I believe that by dishonoring my agreement with Kahmel that the Great Spirits would bring shame to my family name? Not really.

If I still had family out there, I believed they caused too much shame of their own to notice any I might have brought on.

But being wife to the Faresh, we had to follow through with all of the typical customs of newlyweds: the ceremony of good wishes, the ceremony of fertility, the dedication of our lives to the Great Spirits.

Most of the ceremonies for that morning were held in private, as they were considered private affairs between the bride, the groom, and the ceremony director. It wasn't until I was taken to the palace court did it really settle in for the first time that I was marrying *the* Faresh of K'sundi.

A crowd roared as our limo entered the courtyard. All around us, people screamed and cheered at us, throwing roses at the car as we pulled up. When the door was opened for me, I walked into a sea of flashing lights, feeling like a celebrity as countless news broadcasters announced my appearance.

Kahmel had made our engagement as secretive as he could manage, so the reporters and news crew were in a frenzy as we walked the velvet rug leading up to the palace.

As soon as we set foot inside, a trio consisting of a piano, harp, and a flute starting playing. We walked down the aisle stiffly and slowly, as I was taught during our rehearsals. There were so many eyes on us, I didn't think I'd be able to find Lora, Nana, or Talad if I wanted to.

We approached the ceremony director, who held in his hands the red tie of Binding, one that he would soon tie the both of our hands and officially declare us husband and wife.

As we turned to each other, one set of eyes in the audience stood out more than the others. Turning my head as slightly as I could manage, I saw Attican sitting near the front row, and my heart rate doubled.

I never invited him.

Seeing that he'd caught my eye, Attican waved, a curl on his lips.

He was there to remind me what I was here for. This was a mission, nothing more.

Not that I needed the reminder.

"Dearly beloved, we are gathered here today..." the ceremony director started, segueing to his speech and good wishes for our marriage. The proceedings took a long time, and I tried to hide how my hands shook throughout the entire time.

Then Kahmel took me to be his lawfully wedded wife, and I took him. When we kissed, for a moment I regretted that he was marrying someone who held absolutely no regard for him and who was ultimately going to sell out every secret possible to end his reign over K'sundi.

But he chose this, and the feeling of regret didn't last.

MOONLIT DANCE

After the Binding Ceremony, the rest of the day went by in a blur. Flashing cameras, a lot of posing and fake smiles, so many words of congratulations—too many to count. Kahmel introduced me to what seemed like thousands of people from nations all over the world and even other planets, along with hundreds of his distant family members. So-and-so of this family clan, so-and-so of that family clan. I came to appreciate the fact that my family was too ordinary to belong to any clan because remembering family members was a headache.

I finally spied Lora, Talad, and Nana at the banquet. With so many people there, all I could do was smile and wave at them while they gave thumbs up in support. But I also saw Attican multiple times, which soured any encouragement I got from my friends.

We approached an enormous banquet table lined with colorful fruits, cakes, pies, cupcakes, and every manner of brightly colored desserts I could imagine. Strangely, it wasn't Kahmel's family members seated at our sides. They were placed at a table somewhere else in the room.

I was stunned when I saw an exact replica of Kahmel sitting near the middle of the table, directly beside where Kahmel was supposed to sit. The duplicate had his arm in a cast and a sling, a bandage wrapped around his head. That was the only difference I could discern between the two of them. They had the same dark complexion, chiseled jawline, and thick build. It wasn't until I noticed that the intense, orange eyes were absent on the duplicate did I realize the true difference between them. Since Kahmel always wore sunglasses, no one would be able to know the sole discrepancy between him and his twin.

"Jashi, this is my brother, Rand. Rand, I've told you about my wife, Jashi."

Rand stood and grinned, marking the second stark difference I noticed between the two. I hadn't seen Kahmel smile once, but his twin had a smile that reached his eyes. He took my hand and shook it. "I've heard a lot about you, Jashi. Nice to finally meet you. Would have come to see you sooner, but..." He shrugged the arm with the cast. "I was busy."

"Nice to meet you," I said, the phrase feeling stale in my mouth after having to repeat it so many times tonight.

A woman I recognized from the HoloScreen stood as well. Kahmel reached his arm out toward her. "Jashi, this is Arusi Zuwei, my secretary of defense."

Arusi was a lot shorter in person than she looked on screen. Long, curly locks of hair framed her heart-shaped face. Her honey-colored skin was flawless, and she revealed a perfect set of teeth when she smiled. To be honest, she looked too pretty to be the secretary of defense of K'sundi. This was the one who helped Kahmel make decisions of warfare and battle?

"Pleased to meet you, Faresha," she said in a small voice.

I smiled politely, but no matter how many times people said it this evening, I couldn't get used to people calling me that—probably because I knew it couldn't last. The title wasn't mine to claim, after all.

From the corner of the room, Attican maintained his constant visual of me. He drank from a champagne flute, a smirk on his pallid features.

Kahmel and I sat as festivities continued all around us. I was too distracted to be engaged in any of it, though I smiled and nodded when required, ate the food before me, and held a few short conversations. My mind was preoccupied with what I'd been trying to avoid thinking about all week long.

I was married to Kahmel now. What would he expect when we went home? As one who had insisted on remaining chaste, I had no experience in matters of the bedroom.

I was so immersed in my own thoughts, I didn't even notice Kahmel had said something.

"Jashi," he repeated.

My attention was whisked back to reality as I realized he was standing and holding out his hand. "Are you ready to dance?"

The dance. I'd completely forgotten about it.

My heart pounded against my chest as I placed my hand in his. Kahmel helped me from my chair and guided me away from the table. It felt like I was gliding toward the outer courtyard in a trance, every eye on us as we led the party outside. There, a band started playing an upbeat rhythm, candles and lights all around us to banish the darkness of the night and illuminate the court. The sky glittered with stars, a full moon standing testament to the occasion.

It would have been a beautiful wedding.

If it weren't for the groom.

Kahmel slipped his hand around my waist and clutched my hand in his. I panicked as my body started to warm, oblivious to the nippy cold of the desert night. Our cue was coming up, the piano and percussion climaxing to a tender refrain. As nervous as I was, the heat quickly spread to my hands, and I knew I didn't have much time.

"Kahmel, my fire," I hissed, my breath misting in his face.

His eyes met with mine behind his dark glasses, and as close as I was, I could see the bright orange tint that hid underneath them. "Remember your meditation exercises."

"How is that going to help? We have to dance, and I can't remember the moves!" I whisper shouted.

Our cue was mere seconds away.

"Concentrate on your breath. Any fire that leaks out, let me handle. As far as the dance, don't worry. Just follow my lead."

I highly doubted I could, but we had no more time to debate. Our dance had started. Kahmel started circling me like a lion with his eyes trained on a gazelle that strayed too far from the herd. With no other choice, I did as he told me and followed his motions, taking deep breaths as I did.

Breathe in.

Breathe out.

Breathe in.

Breathe out.

The beat changed, and Kahmel followed the cue seamlessly, taking me in his arms, dipping me to the tune of the song.

Between our hands, flames flickered to life, and the way my body continued to heat up, I knew there was more where that came from.

Kahmel grunted as his body absorbed the flames, sweat beading down his forehead. "Concentrate. I have to let go of your hand. Just keep breathing. When I let go, you have to follow after me."

"No, no. Please don't."

"Now."

I exhaled as he released my hand, feeling the air that left my lungs hot like fire. Embers flew from my mouth, and my body was washed over with the feeling of cool relief. My eyes widened. The fire left me...and it didn't hurt? The only time I got this kind of relief was when the fire was free to exit like it wanted or when Kahmel absorbed it from me.

I didn't have time to celebrate my victory.

The song continued. Kahmel's eyes stayed trained on mine as he took more steps around me, his hands trailing around my hips before he began stepping backward in rhythm to the song, taking me with him.

Now that I was free of worry about the fire, the moves of the dance started to come back to me. I swayed my hips and shoulders as

I followed Kahmel's steps, then let him take my hands again, twirl me, then dip, our faces within a hair of each other.

A smile broke his face. "I knew you could do it. Do you remember the next part?"

Seeing him smile at me for the first time caught me off guard. What was with him? "Just barely," I stuttered.

"Okay. Then let me lead you."

He moved behind me, holding my back flush against his chest, swaying with me for a few beats. Then he guided my arms to move with his, a few gestures in sync with the melody. I felt his foot slide mine to make the sweeping movements we were supposed to be doing at this part. Remembering the sequence, I fell into alignment with him, then turned back toward him when it was time.

"You got it now?" he asked.

I nodded.

From there, we both moved in accord, with the song, with the choreography, with each other. As the tune started to die down, we moved apart, then walked back toward each other and finished with one more dip.

The song ended.

The roar of applause erupted all around us as we just stood there, catching our breath, our faces close together. A rush of heat flew in my face, and I realized it was coming from Kahmel, embers flying from his mouth.

Was he nervous, too?

I didn't have time to ask, because he lifted me from the dip, and the rest of the partygoers were permitted into the court.

Kahmel turned to me. "Is there anyone you wanted to talk to before we go?"

Just like that, I was whisked away from my illusion of security, reminded that it was time to go home now.

Home to Kahmel.

TWENTY QUESTIONS

We would be having no honeymoon. Kahmel took me to his private living quarters, and I bit my lip as he escorted me through the palace. Behind us, fireworks burst as the party continued.

Walking through the castle was like being transported back in time. It truly looked like it hadn't changed in the hundreds of years housing the Fareshes of K'sundi. Beside the courtyard where Kahmel and I danced, there was another courtyard in the middle of the building, where countless halls led to all corners of the palace. A fountain graced the center of the courtyard, with colored lights illuminating the pillars of water and revealing the mosaic tile at the bottom of it. We walked past this little paradise to turn down the hall, where old-fashioned sconces lit the way to his bedroom.

Kahmel opened the door, ushered me in, and closed the violet curtains to his window.

I opened my mouth to say something when Kahmel said, "You can take the bed. I'll sleep on the floor."

I blinked. "What?"

But he was already taking a blanket from his walk-in closet. He pulled out a spare pillow and threw it on the floor next to the mattress. He straightened out his "bed," then he went into his closet and closed the door. "I'm only making you sleep here so there's no rumors spread about our sleeping apart," he said from in the closet. "That's why I closed the curtains."

"But aren't your servants sworn to secrecy or something?" I said, frowning.

Kahmel stepped back out in a plain white shirt and his underwear, his sunglasses now off. He sighed. "They're supposed to be, yes. But I have spies all throughout my palace, watching my every move."

My stomach dropped, hearing that. Little did he know I was one of them.

"How do you know?" I said instead.

He sat on the floor on top of his covers. "No one wants me as Faresh. Or haven't you noticed?" He said it with a humorous smirk on his face as though he thought it was funny. "I've known for a while that my courts were plagued with traitors. I can only prove the existence of a few of them. The rest are protected."

"By who?"

"The Courts themselves. They hate me. They can't get rid of me because they don't know how to. I followed some of the most ancient traditions in our culture to become Faresh, and now they're scrambling to find an interpretation of the law they can use to kick me out. But it's hard when they dismissed the old laws as archaic and no one studies them anymore."

This was the first I'd heard of anything like this. I knew the Courts were uncomfortable with him, but to try to sabotage his reign, having to spend years searching for a Faresh again? "So the Courts hired spies to find a reason to impeach you?"

He shook his head. "I said the Courts protected the spies. They didn't send them. Zendaal hires them. The K'sundii Courts protect them."

I bit the inside of my lip as dread slid down my throat. "Why Zendaal?"

"They hate that I'm winning this war. They're afraid of what I'll do when I get what I want."

"And what do you want?"

Kahmel pinched his lips together as he fluffed his pillow and lay against it, leaning his head on his hand. "I told you my parents were scholars, right?"

I nodded.

"They specialized in researching the history of our nation. And they always taught me a lot about the forgotten past of this country. We've changed a lot over the past couple centuries." He stared up at the ceiling. "I suppose you could say I'm just bringing things back to the way they were."

As usual, Kahmel's explanation only left me more confused. But it did make me realize that whatever motives Attican had were a lot more complicated than I'd first assumed. I felt like a pawn in a game much bigger than I could understand, and I was being very, very used.

I fought the tears that stung at my eyes. I just wanted out of all of this. How much information would Attican need before he let me go?

Suddenly, I was very uncomfortable in my wedding dress. "Where are my clothes?"

"The servants already moved them all to my closet."

Much like he did, I entered the closet, closed the door, and peeled off my dress, feeling like I was swimming in fabric when it fell off my body. My eWatch buzzed, and I cursed under my breath.

I took the decoder out from one of the folds of the gown and tapped at the phony message that hid the real one.

Meet me whenever you can. I'm staying in Hashir for the time being. Be quick about it, minx.

I sighed. But at least meeting him didn't require running away this time.

Then I cursed again. My entourage. Somehow, I'd have to lose them before I met with Attican, but of course that was my problem, not his.

Fine.

I wrote a message in the regular chat to disguise the hidden message, then tucked the decoder away in one of my purses that was hanging in the closet. I picked out some random pajamas from one of the shelves and put them on.

Opening the door, I found that Kahmel was already lying down under his covers, and I thought he was sleep until he turned his head to me. "Can you turn off the light?"

I did as he asked and flicked the switch, then crawled into bed feeling very awkward. That was it? No...nothing?

The more I got to know Kahmel, the more he confused me.

"Jashi," Kahmel said, turning over to face me.

"Yes?"

"I know you see this as a business arrangement more than a marriage, but still, I doubt you want to live with a stranger, and neither do I."

"So what are you suggesting?"

"Want to play Twenty Questions? Ask me anything about myself, and I'll ask you. There are no rules about the questions you can ask, but we have to promise to be absolutely honest about every answer. And there's no skipping questions."

Interested, I sat up, turning on the lamp beside me to see him better. I could get Attican's information this way. "All right," I said. "You go first."

Kahmel sat up and crossed his legs, pausing for a while. "Have you ever dated anyone before?"

That was his first question? I shrugged. "No. Never."

His eyebrows raised. "Never?"

"Relationships are a lot of drama I don't have time for. Now it's my turn." I paused, deciding not to be so direct with my questions about the war. I wanted it to look natural when I asked. So I tried to think of a different question first. Then I thought of one I honestly did want the answer to. "How old are you?"

Kahmel chuckled. He tilted his head up. "How old do I look?"

"Old. I'm only eighteen."

"I'm twenty-eight."

My mouth dropped. "You're joking."

Kahmel shook his head. "I turn twenty-nine this year."

"That's a ten-year difference."

He shrugged. "What does it matter either way? There are people who marry with a much wider age gap."

"Wait, wait, wait, okay, but if you—"

"No, wait, it's my turn."

I sighed. "Fine. Go."

"Where did you run away to after I arranged our betrothal with Matron Taias?"

Pausing, I tried to decide on the safest way to answer the question without getting Talad in potential trouble. I still wasn't sure if Kahmel was willing to have anyone killed over that. "I hid out with a friend."

Kahmel nodded, as if he was processing the information. "All right. What was your question?"

"If you were marrying for love, would you care about how old she was? I mean, what if she was my age?"

Again, he laughed, and for the first time I noticed the mirth in his eyes looked genuine. "Don't you think that's a strange question for my wife to ask me?"

I tsked. "You said I could ask any question."

"Yeah, I did. Well, the answer is no, I wouldn't care either way."

"Why not?"

"It's one question each turn. Stop trying to cheat."

I crossed my arms. "Fine, ask your question."

"What's the name of the friend who hid you?"

My stomach started twisting itself in knots. Was he just playing this game so he could find Talad and punish him? Kahmel couldn't be trusted. I couldn't let my guard down around him. He could trick me into the sense of comfort, make it seem like wanted to protect me, look out for me. But it was nothing more than that—an act.

I made up a name off the top of my head. "Niah Parid."

He raised an eyebrow. "Really? And a certain individual by the name of Talad Grimes wouldn't have anything to do with it, would he?"

I tried not to let my shock show. "One question at a time."

He held up his hands in surrender. "Go ahead."

Deciding to start to angle my questions toward the war, I said, "I don't understand much about politics. Why did you continue the war with Omani when they had already surrendered? Why go after their land?"

"I already told you," he said.

I frowned. "What do you mean?"

"I'm restoring things to the way they were."

Now I was really confused. "What do you mean by that? The way what was?"

"Hmm," he hummed. "I suppose I'll allow this one since your first question was already answered before. You remember learning in history class that K'sundi used to be a lot bigger than it is now?"

I racked my brain. Vaguely, I remembered failing such a class. It was just such ancient history, the subject didn't hold my interest much. That was a time before the Zendaalans created the Equalization, helping the K'sundii reject their barbaric ways and live in accordance to the Common Law. I wasn't that excited to hear stories about savages who thought it was normal to kidnap wives and burn down villages with the dragons they had no idea how to tame.

"Sure, maybe a thousand years ago," I said.

As if reading my mind, Kahmel said, "Just because it was a time before the Equalization doesn't mean that era is obsolete. Before the Zendaalans came along, we owned what's now West Omani. But when the Zendaalans passed the Common Law among all of Hemorah in recent centuries, they demilitarized K'sundi and left them vulnerable to Omani, who seized the opportunity to start a takeover. They would have conquered all of K'sundi if it weren't for the rebel army that rose up and fought the Omanians off to protect what they had left."

I resisted the urge to roll my eyes. I wasn't here for a history lesson. "So...now you want revenge a couple hundred years overdue?"

"The word isn't revenge. I want to set things right, the way they should have been all along."

"If that's the case, you may as well sever K'sundi from the Equalization. It sounds like your problem..." I saw the look in his eyes as the pieces fell together in my head. "is more with the Zendaalans than it is with the Omanians."

Kahmel cleared his throat. "All right, you've asked your fair share of questions, well past the maximum of one. My turn already."

I was merely a pawn in a much bigger game. The Zendaalans were after Kahmel just as much as he was after them. But why was he so against them? What did he care about a dispute several centuries old?

"I don't know if this is a sensitive question for you, but I've always been curious. Are your birth parents still alive, to the best of your knowledge?"

Again, his question took me completely by surprise. "As far as I know, they are."

Kahmel stroked his beard in thought. "All right, you can go now."

I was suspicious about the nature of his question, but I wouldn't waste my turn asking. I had to stay focused on Attican's questions. "You'll be leaving for war in a few days, but you haven't told me anything about it. I don't even know where you'll be stationed. Where are you going?"

He chuckled. "Sneaky, asking me questions about the war now. I'm not normally allowed to answer any question about that. But for the purposes of this game..." He paused. "I'll say this: One of the places I'll be stationed is north of the Dragon's Heart river basin. My goal is to reclaim K'sundii territory at least far enough to take the basin."

I was about to ask why but remembered that I had already run out of questions. "Your turn."

"I know you don't trust me, Jashi."

I raised an eyebrow. He was right. I didn't.

"And I know I can't ask you to love me," he continued. "But I'm hoping that during your time here, you can see that there's more to me than what the media wants you to believe I am. If I can prove to you that I know what I'm doing to protect this country, can you promise me that you'll consider being someone to stand by me? There are only five people I know I can trust—Rand, Arusi, my ambassador, my army general, and now you. All I'm asking is that you give me a chance. Will you let me earn your trust?" He was looking at me directly in the eye with a smoldering stare that could instill fear just as much as it could captivate. He reminded me of fire in that moment—something that could destroy anything its path if it chose to, but could also be the difference between life and death.

This game had evolved far beyond being a casual round of Twenty Questions. I nodded, rather numbly, as I wondered why this man continued to mystify me.

"Thank you. It's your turn."

I shook my head and turned over. "No thanks. I'm tired. Goodnight, Kahmel."

I would continue my investigation in the morning. Right now, I had enough answers to keep Attican off my back a little. That should be good enough. I wasn't sure how many more of Kahmel's questions I could take.

"All right, then. Good night, Jashi."

ARCHAIC TECHNOLOGY

I drifted in a cloud. Surrounded by the bright tones of a pastel blue and pink sky and clouds tinted with gold, I had not a care in the world. The clouds swaddled me in a protective layer that shielded me from the petty fretting of the world below me, safe in my fluffy paradise.

The wind stirred. Something disturbed the air in paradise.

I turned to see a dragon, black as tar, slithering toward me, flames lighting the inside of his mouth. His inky form came closer, and the clouds that once comforted now restrained, confining me to my place as the dragon neared. My body started to warm.

It was on top of me, its black form eclipsing the sun. The glistening scales that lined its body seemed to be the last light I would ever see again. Its huge face came closer to mine, but the flames turned to vapor as it breathed out over me a warm steam, its whiskers floating in the air around me, tickling my skin.

"Will you let me earn your trust?" it said in Kahmel's voice.

Panicked, I finally broke from the confines of the cloud.

Only it wasn't a cloud. It was the covers of my bed.

I shot up. My heart was racing, and my hands were already pricking with heat. I threw off the covers, but my hands were already on fire. Flames ignited where my hands touched the material.

Before I could react, a strong hand gripped mine, a grunt leaving his mouth as the flames dissipated. Kahmel took my other hand, the fabric of the sheets still in my grip as the fire was extinguished. With his head this close to mine, I watched as beads of sweat collected at his temples.

He turned to me, grunting. "Are you all right?" His arms trembled.

"Does it hurt when you do this?" I asked, my face twisting to see him in pain like this.

Exhaling, Kahmel let go of my hands and backed away, leaving smoke where there were flames. "I take it you had a bad dream."

"Yeah," I said, scratching my head. Some part of me wondered which was scarier—my dream or my reality.

Kahmel briefly closed his eyes and took a deep breath. When he opened his eyes again, a steely mien erased any evidence of pain as if it was never there. "I want to take you around the palace and a few other places. I'll introduce you to the few people I do trust."

Sighing, I shook off the panic still left over from my dream and the fire. "Ah, the ever-shrinking VIP list."

"We'll eat breakfast together and then we'll go," he continued. "I'm going to take a shower now."

Kahmel got up and went into his closet, coming out with a fresh change of clothes in his hands. Before he went into the bathroom, he looked at me over his shoulder. "Please don't leave here without an escort."

I scoffed as the door closed and I heard the shower start. Was he still thinking I might run away? Rightfully so. But I didn't like having to play the obedient wife just because he asked me to. I seriously considered roaming around the palace on my own just to show him I could do as I liked.

However, I was here on a mission, not to prove a point. Of the questions Attican wanted answered, I had one left. I already knew how Rand was doing, and I knew that one of the places Kahmel would be stationed would be near the Dragon's Heart river basin. I also knew his supposed reasoning for going to war with Omani, though I still didn't understand it. All that remained was finding out where his army bases would be stationed, which would be a much more difficult task. It didn't look like Kahmel wanted me knowing much about the war, and he definitely wouldn't answer any direct questions about it like that.

Maybe it was good enough I knew where Kahmel would be stationed. If he was going to be at the Dragon's Heart river basin, his army bases shouldn't be too far from him, right?

I wasn't sure what information would be relevant to Attican. I figured I might as well try and see where it led me.

Then I remembered that he wanted me to meet him. How would I pull that off?

I glanced at the door to our bedroom. It would be easier to figure out how to leave if I took a tiny look around, right? Now that it seemed Kahmel wasn't looking to accuse me of treason, I decided to give myself a little more freedom. If I was going to be his wife, Kahmel would have to learn that this wife wasn't planning on sitting around the house knitting all day.

Sliding out of bed, I inched toward the closet and changed into something quickly. It was still a little nippy this early in the morning, but I knew it would warm up quickly, so I chose a loose orange skirt that reached my ankles and a red wrap top along with a simple cardigan that would shield me from the cold of the morning until it moved on to warm up in the afternoon. Putting on a plain pair of sandals and throwing my hair up in an up-do, I stepped out of the closet. Kahmel was still in the shower.

I walked out into the hallway and made my way for the center courtyard we passed by the night before. The glowing colors of the fountain were much less pronounced now that it was morning, but I could see the pattern of the mosaic at the bottom clearly—pretty colors of blue, yellow, and orange.

People darted about this way and that. Chefs, cleaning ladies, gardeners, servants. Some of them glanced uncertainly toward me, but most of them went about their business. They almost looked... afraid of me?

Then I remembered that I was the Faresh's wife, not to mention dragon tribe. Of course they were afraid. They thought the man would accuse them of treason if they so much as glanced at me. And from what I could tell, it was with good reason. The man was definitely paranoid.

Choosing a path at random, I started down the halls of the palace. The way it was so well preserved, I felt like I was in a time capsule, like every crack in the stone wall or chip in the ivory floor boards or dent in the golden sconces, had been there a hundred years.

Ancient weapons hung in display in various positions along the walls—a machete, a sword, a bronze shield, a dagger. A testament to the warriors that wielded them. Occasionally, I stumbled on a painting of a past Faresh hanging in the halls, each with a plaque under it giving the years they reigned. Most of them I recognized from my history texts; others were literally thousands of years old.

They said the history of K'sundi ran eons long, but I had never been sure if it was true. Reading about our ancient history was one thing. It was another thing to see physical evidence of it. Even the quality of the paintings differed greatly from one painting to the other. Some were executed with great detail, while others were what was now considered primitive, though I was sure they had been masterpieces in their day.

Then I remembered reading in a paper one time about a room in the palace that held all of the recorded history of K'sundi that only the royals had access to.

Turning down the hall that I remembered had the most paintings, I wondered if I could find it. I was a royal now, right?

I walked down a corridor that ran along the outside of the palace with an ivory balustrade lining the edge, pillars interrupting the banister and framing the scene behind it like it was a painting. From here, I could see the flying traffic of Hashir and the transit system that snaked around the skyscrapers that skewered the heavens. Looking to the mountains to the east, I saw more dragons going in and out of the caves. A shiver rippled down my spine. From here, they almost looked like insects, not at all like the vicious predators the whole world knew they were.

Just like Kahmel.

Remembering my dream, I tore myself from the scene and moved on. I didn't want to think about it anymore.

I had argued with him on our way here, wondering who would protect the people from the dragons. But I considered that perhaps a worse threat than the dragons that presided over the mountains was the dragon king himself.

Who would protect us from him?

I found myself at the end of the hall in front of a door that, after giving the knob a twist, turned out to be locked.

I tsked. I was really looking forward to getting a look inside. Kahmel might have been willing to take me back later, I supposed. It was presumptuous to assume I would have been able to get in so easily.

"Would you like to come inside with me?"

I jumped, spinning to see a Zendaalan man in front of me. Dressed in a smart suit with several colored pins on the collar, he held the air of importance. His brown hair was slicked back, one green eye flecked with gold and the other a bright red, the pupil shrinking and growing as he focused in on me—a mechanical eye, no doubt. He wore a pair of glasses, glinting in the soft light of the cloudy sky. With a pleasant smile on his face, he reached for a key from his pocket and unlocked the door with a resounding click. I tried not to stare at his metal hands, which were a much more human-looking version than the ones I'd typically seen. All the wires were hidden away, the creases in the metal so thin they appeared nonexistent. It was just a smooth, shiny metal that caught light and let it dance all over its surface.

He gestured inside. "Ladies first."

Following in after him warily, I wondered just how I got myself into a situation every time I strayed away from Kahmel. Was he the magnet for trouble? Or was I?

Every worry I had about the Zendaalan disappeared as soon as I got a good look at where I was. We were surrounded by books, the smell of aged paper and ink wafting between the shelves. There were just as many books lining the shelves as there were scrolls. It was like stepping into a painting.

I ran my finger along the spine of a tome, just to know what it felt like. I'd heard about books before, and I'd seen models of ones in museums. But this one was real, with pages and everything.

"Can I?" I asked, looking to the man that brought me in.

"By all means," he answered, taking a seat at a desk in the center of the room, turning his chair so he could watch me, waiting to see my reaction.

Taking the book in my hand, it was a lot heavier than I thought it would be. My finger traced the edge of it, and I marveled at the fact it was able to last so long. It wasn't even made of metal like modern-day eReaders. What kept the pages together?

Since the only way to find out was to open it, I pried my nail between the sheets of paper, peeling it open carefully, feeling like it might fall apart in my hands. I almost dropped it as it flipped open, but managed to keep the book securely in my hands.

The pages didn't glow; there were no settings to adjust the font size, offer a dictionary, or anything. The words were simply there, printed on the page. A number at the bottom the only other thing it offered. I leafed through it only to find that was all there was. No wonder it was so heavy. Each page was another sheet of paper, and there had to be a couple hundred.

"This is amazing," I muttered as I continued my examination. "When I heard that there was a room in the palace that kept the history of K'sundi, I expected a huge database. Not...this."

"Yes, I find that the K'sundii practice of preserving your history like this to be a very quaint quality of your people. We Zendaalans don't see the point in going through such pains to preserve something so fragile, but it's through reading tomes like the one you're reading now that Kahmel discovered the law that qualified him to become Faresh, so there must be some logic to it. Now he has members of the Court poring through the very books we dismissed to remember what it was like when they were written."

I stopped. We? Was he one of the people trying to get rid of Kahmel? But how was a Zendaalan a member of the K'sundii Court? I suppose he could have been a K'sundii citizen, but what interest did he have in the old laws and our most ancient history? From the way he talked, he wasn't very impressed with our people. Suddenly, the polite tone of the man in front of me now seemed condescending.

"Is that what you're doing now?" I asked, observing the books set out before him on the desk with a newfound curiosity.

He nodded, turning to one of the books in question. "Little other choice now." He adjusted his glasses and opened the novel. "Your husband isn't supposed to be here, great Faresha. He's quite lucky to have made it thus far. But I wouldn't expect this to last much longer." He glanced at me with a new cold edge to his green eyes. "Enjoy your fifteen minutes of fame while it lasts."

"Faresha?" I started as I heard Kahmel's voice.

When I turned around, it took me a second to realize that it wasn't him. He wasn't wearing sunglasses, and his eyes were a deep brown, not bright orange like Kahmel.

Rand put himself between me and the man at the desk, taking a defensive pose. He looked at me. "What are you doing in here?"

"I just wanted to see the books," I said sheepishly, still trying to make my brain register that he wasn't Kahmel. When I was introduced to him the night before, his persona was more mirthful, which made him look completely different from his twin. But now that his tone was more serious, they were identical, both of them reminding me of the dragon from my dream.

"Please, don't blame her," the Zendalaan man said. "I'm the one who let her in."

"I can see that. But what are you doing here, Dralus?"

"Research. Isn't that what your leader, Faresh Kahmel, promotes?" Dralus said, tilting his head back. "That's the only reason he's here, after all."

Rand only eyed him, and though I could only see him from behind, the way the muscles in his back contracted, I didn't want to be the one that stare was directed at.

Dralus didn't flinch. He adjusted his glasses and returned to his reading. "Remember what I said, Faresha. Now, if you'll excuse me, I'd like to be left to my studies."

"Let's go," Rand said, taking my hand and leading me out the room. He locked the door behind him before turning to me, the intense look on his face disappearing. "What were you doing with him? Kahmel's been looking all over for you."

"I was just trying to get a look around. I wanted to know what the history room looked like. Did you see all those books? It was amazing!"

"Never talk to any members of the Court," Rand insisted.

"How was I supposed to know he was a member of the Court? All I know is he let me in."

He chuckled nervously, running a hand through his hair. "Kahmel told me you were a handful, but gosh..."

I put my hands on my hips. "What do you mean by that? He's the one always trying to lock me up somewhere."

"I wonder why." At the sour look I gave him, he said, "Let's get you back to Kahmel. He's been turning the palace upside down."

I sighed.

However, as Rand lead me back down the halls, Dralus's words echoed in my head. It seemed like Kahmel's fears about the Courts trying to overthrow him were very real.

But was their reasoning unfounded?

THIS MAN AND DRAGONS

"Can't I leave you for five minutes without you disappearing somewhere?"

Kahmel held his face in his hand as we sat across from each other at the breakfast table.

I took a piece of toast from the table and slathered strawberry jam on it, giving him a shrug as an answer.

Sighing, he took a fork and started on his own breakfast. "I'm trying to give you the freedom you're asking for, but then you run away again. What am I supposed to do? Tie a bell around your neck so you ring when you run?"

I gave another helpful shrug, biting into my toast and enjoying the crunch that followed after, accompanied by the sweet taste of strawberries.

Rand sat down next to me, getting a plate from the table and heaping on sausages and eggs from the trays, moving awkwardly with that cast still on his arm. "She talked with Dralus."

"What?" Kahmel said, his head snapping up.

"In the history archives, just before I brought her here."

I groaned, shooting Rand another sour look. "Tattletale."

Kahmel sighed. He took a piece of toast for himself and spread a little butter on it. His voice was strained. "Listen, Jashi. I know you don't understand it, but trust me. Stay away from anyone outside of the people I'm trying to tell you are trustworthy, especially members of the Court. If they'll do everything they can to get me out of the way, the same applies to you."

"Nothing happened! We were talking about the books in there, that's all." Taking a sip of the orange juice, I remembered my conversation with that Dralus person. "By the way, is it true you studied *books* to find out about the laws that allowed you to become Faresh?"

Kahmel waved the subject away. "That's beside the point. Who was talking more? You or him?"

"Him," I answered, frowning. "Why?"

"I told you everyone is a spy. They'll do anything for information. I'm afraid they'll try to use you to get to me."

I supposed he might have been right, especially given Dralus's veiled threat. But it was more directed at Kahmel than me. I tsked. "What do I know that could possibly do you any harm? You won't even tell me anything about the war," I said, a sad attempt at hinting. It was worth a shot.

Kahmel looked around, then tilted his glasses down to show the bright orange color underneath before pushing them back in place. "You already know more than anyone outside of my family."

Oh. Yeah. I'd forgotten that I was the only one who knew about that. But what good would that do anyone?

Now that he mentioned it, I never did find out the reason he wanted to keep that hidden. And with Attican wanting to meet with me, I questioned my resolve to keep that secret for the moment. I still didn't understand why he kept the fact he was dragon tribe hidden. What did it matter? There were a lot of stereotypes about us, but with all the other rumors about him going around, being dragon tribe should have been the least of his worries.

Would I continue to keep his secret from Attican?

Perhaps I still didn't have enough information about the subject to make a decision. Maybe now was a good time to ask.

"Why do you keep...uh, that hidden?" I said, taking his cue and not mentioning it in public. "I mean, you never asked me to keep my eyes hidden."

"Our parents have kept it hidden ever since he was young," Rand answered, taking a big bite out of his sausage. "At first, it was to keep unnecessary attention away. Being a royal branch clan, appearance is everything."

"At first?" I repeated.

Kahmel cleared his throat, sending Rand a look as he sipped at a cup of water. When he finished, he said, "Maintaining a certain look in front of the people is even more important now than it was before. My parents, if you didn't notice, are somewhat delusional. They had more importance in their own heads than they did in their bloodline. But as it turns out, all of the hiding they did when I was younger helps me now that I'm Faresh."

Yeah, right, I thought. That little coverup was about as graceful as an elephant on ice skates.

But it inspired an idea. When Kahmel was gone, I'd be able to get Rand alone without his brother to shut him up. I could re-ask the question then. There was definitely something more to the dragon tribe thing than he was letting on. That was for sure.

Did it have anything to do with his fire?

It occurred to me that I didn't know if his family knew about his fire. I assumed they did. My parents knew. That was why they abandoned me. When it came by accident so often, I presumed it was impossible for them not to know. I inwardly sighed. Whatever he had to say about his parents, at least they tried to protect their son and keep him hidden from unnecessary attention. And he obviously kept his fire extremely well hidden. Better than to leave him altogether.

"So," Kahmel said, stirring me from my thoughts. "When you finish eating, I want to introduce you to my people. I have to attend an event and make a short speech. You can meet them just before then. You'll be expected to show as well, but you won't have to say anything. It's just for appearances."

"All right," I said. Not like I had much choice in the matter.

At my side, Rand sighed. "Straight to business right after your wedding? You guys didn't even have a honeymoon."

"I don't want one," I said directly, ending the matter at that.

Rand shrugged. "There are better things to do than attend boring conferences with this stiff."

"Like?" Kahmel prompted.

"Like dinner. Like movies. You know, normal stuff."

An idea came to me. "Like going to the mall," I suggested.

"You want to go shopping?" Kahmel asked. "You know you'll have to be escorted, right?"

"Of course." I batted my eyes. "But I'd like to get a few outfits that better suit my tastes."

"You don't like what the servants picked out for you in your closet?"

"She's obviously telling you that she doesn't," Rand objected. "I, for one, think it's a great idea. Maybe if you let her do what she wants every once in a while, she won't have to run away from you so much."

Kahmel pursed his lips, pensive. "Fine. But it will have to be tomorrow. Today will be too busy with preparations for the speech."

Smiling, I nodded to Rand appreciatively, though I very much liked what I had in my closet and I had every intention of escaping again, anyway.

I made a mental note to message Attican the first chance I got to be alone.

❦

IT WAS GETTING HARDER and harder to imagine going back to living from check to check in a rundown apartment when all of this was over. My version of dressing up was wearing a flimsy dress I got for fourteen Ramaks from EK Fashion at the mall, nothing like the baby blue blouse I wore that was buttoned down the middle with cuffed sleeves. The material was so soft, it felt like I was wearing a bedspread. A tight pencil skirt hugged my legs together in a white and gold floral print, complemented by a pair of black peep-toe heels. A professional styled my hair in cornrows and lightly dusted my face with a natural-looking makeup. Matching gold earrings and a necklace finished off the look, along with the royal sash that marked me as Faresha. Lora would have been proud.

Kahmel came in the room. "Wow."

The way he looked at me made me squirm. Strangely, I never considered whether or not Kahmel thought I was attractive. He never did explain why he wanted to marry *me* in particular, so I didn't think it was ever a physical attraction.

I guess I was wrong.

"Are you ready to go?" he asked, his expression difficult to read.

"As I'll ever be."

Kahmel led me out of our room. "It's not going to be so bad. It's nothing in comparison with the longer speeches I'm usually required to give. It touches on what we were talking about earlier."

"About what?"

He smirked. "The dragon caves."

What was with this man and dragons?

Big beefy bodyguards flanked either side of the limo waiting for us out front, along with Arusi, Rand, and two other people I didn't recognize.

"Jashi, you already know Arusi." Arusi wore a pretty white dress that came past her knees. Her dark hair was tied up in a bun, two pieces of hair in the front allowed to dangle and curl freely. She gave a small smile and bowed, along with the others in turn. "This is Khes Chukan and Asan Mur. Khes is a very important general in my army fighting at the border and one of my most trusted comrades."

Khes was huge. His tall muscular body made Arusi and me look like dwarves in comparison. Three scars traced his left eye like claw marks, the iris a milky gray while the other eye was dark brown. When he smiled, it was hard not to stare at the scars that moved with it. "You flatter me."

"Asan is a politician whom I allow to represent me on occasion."

The man in question laughed mockingly. "And by that, he means cleaning up after him while he's busy playing soldier boy at the border or starting trouble in the Court." Asan was a lean man with almost completely black skin. A short beard and sideburns framed his angular face, and he had a pleasant smile that showed perfectly white teeth. He came off to me as a lot more easy-going than I expected of a politician, especially working under such a hard man as Kahmel.

"That's what you're paid for," Kahmel said.

Asan shrugged. "I'm not complaining. There are rumors that you send me out in your place to hide how ugly you are. That's why you wear sunglasses everywhere you go, which makes me better-looking in comparison."

Kahmel scoffed as Asan laughed. Did he just call the Faresh ugly? And Kahmel let him?

Then again, Kahmel let me say all kinds of things to him, now that I thought about it. I just assumed he didn't care how I felt one way or another.

His words echoed in my mind.

I'm hoping that during your time here, you can see that there's more to me than what the media wants you to believe I am.

Will you let me earn your trust?

Part of me wondered if this was what he was talking about, if maybe there was more to Kahmel than met the eye. But I dismissed it. If that was the case, he wouldn't have made me marry him. And he wouldn't have assumed that his life of glamour would be a good enough substitution for a meaningful relationship.

"That's enough fussing," Arusi said. "Let's go before you make us late."

※

I STOOD behind Kahmel as flashing cameras blinded us from all angles, Arusi, Rand, Khes, and Asan at my side. We stood on a stage above a sea of people of all ethnicities.

All fell silent as Kahmel stepped to the podium and started speaking.

"I've been asked on multiple occasions to destroy the caves on the side of the Dharia mountains because the dragons in the area use them as nests. My response, as it's been on multiple occasions, is still no."

The crowd stirred in discontent but was silenced immediately as Kahmel raised a hand to stop them. There was a dangerous edge to his voice when he said, "The public assumes that the threat of a dragon attack is the worst of their troubles. I assure you that it isn't. The Omanians have tried to snuff us out at our weakest, after the Faresh before me was assassinated, and you believe that this is over? The wolf that's come after our sheep hasn't run away. He just knows how to hide very quietly.

"My people are doing what they can to keep control of the dragons, and, as I've said before, the creatures are closely monitored at all times. Questions?"

He pointed to someone that had raised their hand.

"Your Grace, isn't it true that you refuse to use the standardized form of taming them? How can you say that you're keeping control of them if they aren't tame?"

There was a nodding of heads throughout the audience. It seemed to be a popular question. I rather agreed.

"Do we tame the lions that reside in the west? Or the bears that occupy the forest of Lisdan? I don't see why we should treat the dragons any differently if they haven't caused any problems. Just because Zendaal has declared one way of taming the dragons as 'standard' doesn't mean it's the only way to do it."

Another person raised their hand.

"But isn't it really because you want to use them in the war with Omani? Is it true that you want to keep them wild so they do more damage in battle?"

"I am using dragons in the war with Omani, yes. However, my dragons have never caused any unnecessary harm."

I narrowed my eyes at him. A sneaky way to answer the question without revealing the fact that the dragons he used in war were completely untamed. He used an interesting choice of words. So what *necessary* harm had his dragons caused that he wasn't mentioning?

Someone else raised their hand.

"They say that the dragons have been spreading their nests to more areas toward the east and west. Are you going to discourage their movements?"

Kahmel shook his head. "I don't see why. I find it funny how a nation that used to be known as the people of dragons now wants their dragons either dead or with a clip on their wings and a tag on their necks. Have we so utterly lost the gumption to deal with them? I'm keeping the dragons wild to remind you of who we used to be. Don't just give yourselves over to the Zendaalans and let them tell you what to do with them. We are an independent state-country. And I feel that most K'sundii forget that." He glanced at me, smiling in a way that crawled under my skin. I grinned back at him, like he knew I had to in front of the cameras. Sly move.

"I have no further comments."

NOTHING IS AS IT SEEMS

Kahmel had other business to attend to, so I retired to my bedroom to relax, alone at last—but not before he advised me that if I wanted to leave, I was supposed to send a message to Rand or Arusi on my eWatch. I felt like he wished he could go back to setting guards at my door, but thankfully he didn't. Not that anything would have hindered me if I wanted to leave.

This time, I didn't. After unwinding a while by watching a few episodes of "The City of Kohpal: Criminology," I realized that being involved between Attican and Kahmel had all but severed me from my social life. I wanted to at least let the people who knew me know that I hadn't dropped off the face of the map.

Turning on my eWatch, the screen that glowed in the air in front of me showed hundreds of unread messages. People I hadn't talked to in ages were now checking up on me and seeing how I was doing. I sighed. Was our society so vain that all it took was a little clout to make people that thought you were invisible to suddenly have your best interest at heart?

Of course it was.

Seeing that Lora was online, I skipped all the other unread messages and started a conversation with her. Thankfully, she wasn't doing homework or anything—so she said— and we talked like nothing changed. Soon, we were sending each other messages so quickly, it became apparent a HoloCall was in order.

Her face appeared in front of me on the holographic screen. "How's the life of a queen treating you?"

I was hoping she wouldn't start with that. Shrugging it off, I said, "It's all right. But being guarded twenty-four-seven isn't fun."

"Couldn't you just order them away to give you some space?"

I shook my head. "The Faresh wouldn't allow it. Frankly, I don't know *who* I'm allowed to order around at this point." Wanting to talk about something outside of my own problems, I decided to change subjects. "So, anything new with you? How's school?"

Lora sighed deeply. "The Zendaalans announced another rebel country," she said in a low voice. "Did you hear about it?"

I shook my head. "I haven't been keeping up with the news recently. Which country?"

"Vahdel."

"Oh." I knew the Zendaalan International Officials warned that Vahdel might fall out of the Equalization soon. They'd been warning the country for a while. Apparently the recent lawmakers who were voted in didn't agree with Equalized law, and Zendaal warned that refusal to hold another vote might result in a severance. "It finally happened?"

"Jashi, it was horrible. A lot of my friends at school are Vahdelan. They were being hauled away right in front of us. Couldn't even pack their things," she snapped.

I pursed my lips, solemn. The reality was depressing but ever-present when you belonged to a country that decided not to abide by Equalized law. Thankfully, K'sundi was a country that had been dutiful in its obedience to the Equalizers for centuries, unlike other nations such as Vahdel, Ud, Midsonia, and the three quarters of Hemorah that didn't take seriously the privilege to be a part of such an all-inclusive unification. They took it for granted, and their people had to suffer because of it.

Still, I didn't like the way the Zendaalans handled it, forcibly exiling the natives of any rebel country from non-rebel territory. The matter was treated as seriously as harboring a traitor. Zendaalans didn't tolerate any hint of rebellion, deporting foreigners to their home countries. There, they would have to live in the rough circumstances that inevitably came out of living in a rebel country, cut off from all contact and trade with Equalized nations, with all Equalized countries as their enemy.

"Sometimes I hate the Equalization."

"Lora, hush up!" I hissed, as though a Zendaalan official could be behind me as we spoke. "Don't let anyone hear you say that kind of thing. Someone might think you support one of those rebel groups you hear about on the news!"

"Oh, please. Nobody's really as scared of the rebels as they claim. They're only mad because they ask questions."

I frowned. "If I didn't know any better, I'd say you support them."

"I'm not against them," Lora put plainly. "I don't think it's right that if the whole world doesn't conform to certain rules, one nation gets to decide to treat them as outcasts and doom them to poverty and starvation. Zendaalans go around the world with soldier-trons, aiming to destroy all nations outside of their system, and you think that's okay?"

"Well, the rebels certainly aren't making the situation any better by raiding the government offices or threatening to release information if they don't meet their demands. We're lucky Zendaal has so far ruled that the actions of K'sundii rebels are separate from the opinion of the government, otherwise we might have been doomed to the same fate as Vahdel."

Lora sighed, looking at me exasperatedly through the HoloCaller. "At least they're doing something. I mean, I get that it's dangerous, the possibility of being declared a rebel country, but..." She shook her head. "Never mind. Forget I said anything."

She spoke quickly, and I got the feeling she was somewhat irritated with me. The Zendaalans may not have been right in everything they did, but certainly the strength our nations had in our unity was better than the barbaric squander rebel nations resorted to when they were separate from it.

Before I could respond, Lora said, "Anyway, I have to go do my homework. I'll talk to you later."

"See you," I said, feeling more than a little guilty. I realized I hadn't said much about her fellow students being taken away, something I was sure was traumatizing for her. "Sorry about your friends. I hope they're okay," I added before she could hang up.

Then she paused. "Thanks, Jashi," she said, softer now. "I'll talk to you later."

"See you."

Just as I hung up, I saw another message from "Derill Shaad." Sighing, I took out the decoder and tapped on the phony message.

Good job on the information. I'd still like to know where his army bases are, but I won't push it for the moment. Let's do what you said and meet at the mall. Find a way to lose your entourage and I'll be waiting for you at Ronnie's Burgers.

Groaning, I felt like throwing my eWatch against the wall. I hated living like this.

A knock at the door startled me. I switched off my eWatch and stowed the decoder under my pillow just before Kahmel opened the door.

"Ah, you're in here."

"And I didn't run away," I drawled, rolling over and getting out of bed. Today had been a long day, and the shower was calling me.

"For once," he remarked. As he took off his glasses, I noticed his eyes looked more sunken in than they had this morning.

"What happened to you?" I started picking up towels from the closet on the side. "You look like a train wreck."

He shrugged, kneading the space between his eyes. "I've been in meetings with the Courts all day. They disapprove of my speech this morning and are still trying to talk me out of going down to the battlefield myself. I was hoping to have a lighter workload to spend more time with you before I have to leave, but I guess they had other plans."

I rolled my eyes, stepping into the bathroom and closing the door behind me, calling through the wall. "Not a big deal."

"It is to me."

Surprised by the change in tone, I shook it off and started the shower, half expecting him to laugh, make some indication it was a joke.

But he didn't.

"I made you a promise to teach you how to control your fire," he said through the door as I peeled off my clothes. "I plan to stick to it. And I meant it when I said I wanted to get to know you."

I ground my teeth as I thought about that particular promise, stepping into the shower and letting the warm water calm the tension in my shoulders. Did he *honestly* think any amount of time getting to know each other would make me like him more? That it would fix this situation he got us both in?

"Did it ever occur to you that I don't want to get to know you?" I snapped. There was a pause, and I hoped it was because I'd finally shut him up. "If the only reason you're here is to fulfill some obligation you feel toward me, don't bother. I'm here because that's what an arranged marriage is. It's other people deciding on another person's happiness and telling them to live with it. So I'm living with it. But I'm not happy about it."

He didn't say anything, so I finished taking my shower, running my fingers through the curls of my hair as I gave it a quick wash and conditioning with the products I found in the stall. The towels proved to be soft and plush as I wrapped one around me like embracing a teddy bear.

Wrapping a smaller one around my hair, I stepped out of the bathroom thinking Kahmel had left.

Instead, he was sitting at the edge of my bed, waiting for me.

Rather than acknowledge him, I went into the closet to collect my clothes, not in the mood to care that I was half-naked.

"This is why I'd like us to get to know each other better. I don't want to be your enemy, Jashi," he said. "I don't want it to be like this all the time."

Why was he so upset about this? We both understood from the beginning that this was only an obligation.

"It's a little late for that."

I closed the door partly to give me privacy to change and partly hoping it would end the conversation. This was why I didn't want to get involved in a relationship in the first place. Too much drama for my taste.

After a moment, he said, "You had a bad dream this morning. Do you always trigger your fire when you have a nightmare?"

"Not always," I sighed, grateful for the change in subject. I pulled my pajamas over my head, then reached for the hair products I'd brought from my apartment when I moved. "Every once in a while. I got used to leaving a fire extinguisher close to my bed."

With my hair products and a comb in tow, I came back into the bedroom and sat on the other end of the bed, taking off the hair towel and beginning to apply my hair creams and detanglers.

Kahmel shook his head. "That shouldn't be necessary. I want you to know how to put out a fire with your hands as a last resort. If you can stop the fire from getting out of hand in the first place, you won't have to put it out yourself."

"What's the difference between just using the fire extinguisher and doing what you do?"

But his eyes were on the hair products, straying to my hands and hair as I distributed the creams through the strands with my fingers. He blinked, as though he just remembered what he was talking about. "Fire extinguishers make a lot of noise. So does running for a bucket and filling it with water. To keep our secret hidden, we have to leave as little evidence as possible that we even have it. Now that you're in the public eye, you'll have to be even more careful with your fire than you were before."

I nodded, seeing how that would be useful, even after I left him and this lifestyle behind. The last thing I'd want to do is to draw attention. "What do I have to do?"

"Follow me." He stood. "I'll take you somewhere we can be alone."

"Hold on," I said, finishing up with the creams and combing through my hair—a quick process now that it was treated—then did a braid on either side of my head so that I wouldn't have it dripping everywhere. "Now let's go."

Kahmel grabbed his sunglasses and led me out of his room and down the now darkened halls of the palace, lit by the artificial candlelight of the sconces. We went down a path I'd stumbled upon earlier that morning but found that it was nothing more than a dead end.

"Why are we going down here?" I objected. "There's nothing there."

Kahmel laughed as he looked at me, and if I didn't know any better, I would have said that those tangerine eyes behind his sunglasses were dancing despite his obvious fatigue.

No, it must have been the candlelight.

"You really did give yourself a tour of the palace. But that's why you should have waited for me to be your tour guide. Because then I could have explained to you."

We reached the end of the hall, where a painting of a previous Faresh stared at the both of us. Beside it, on the other walls of the corridor, more ancient weapons lined the surface. Kahmel took a sword from its display and slid it into a slot on the side of the painting's frame. I heard a click.

"In this palace," he said softly, "nothing is as it seems."

The wall slid silently to the side as he pushed it, revealing the entrance to a little private garden. I stepped inside with my breath taken away. It was a quiet little secret with brick walls that closed it off from the outside. In the middle, a wood bench faced angelic white statues. We stepped on cobblestone, surrounded by brightly colored flowers tinged with silver light from the moon. Kahmel closed the door behind us. Above us, no windows graced side of the palace to see this little garden. We were completely hidden.

"This is beautiful," I breathed, feeling like the word was an understatement. It was funny how such simplicity was so enchanting to me. There wasn't much to this place, and yet that was the beauty about it; it didn't have to be complicated to be magical.

"The palace has a dozen other hiding places and secret tunnels. The Fareshes of long ago created them to hide the royal family in case of an attack."

I shook my head, tsking. "Do you have to be a walking history lesson all the time?" It *was* interesting, though. Too bad it didn't help the previous Faresh or his family.

I shivered. That was another reason not to stay here. Who knew if whoever killed the last Faresh would come back to kill Kahmel and his entire family, too? Especially given his reputation of not being particularly liked by anybody.

Kahmel said, "We can practice here and no one will see us." He held out his hand and opened his fist, a fire igniting in his palm. "Starting a fire is somewhat difficult." Waving his fingers, the fire danced to the right and to the left. "But learning to control it is what I want you to practice. That way, if your fire ignites out of your control, you can stop it before it gets too out of hand."

I was enthralled as I watched the fire flicker in his palm.

"Focus on the flame."

Concentrating, I centered my attention to the flame and watched as it moved. I wasn't sure what I was supposed to be looking for, but it certainly was beautiful, free to breath and dance in his palm like it was meant to be there.

"What do I do now?"

"Will it to move."

Right. "Will it to move," as if it was just that simple. It was a beautiful flame, but I felt no different in its presence. "It's not my fire. This is yours. How can I do anything to it?"

"It doesn't matter," he insisted. "All fire is yours. Though the one that comes from you is the one that listens to you best, all fire is a part of you. Now, focus and try to move it."

My brow furrowed as I tried to imagine it moving, like Kahmel made it do a second ago. But it didn't do anything. I shook my head. "I can't."

"That's because you're afraid. You can't control the fire if you fear it. For anyone else, fire is a thing to be feared." Kahmel let the fire grow in his palm, licking towards the sky before settling back down to size. "But you're a dragon. You can't afford to fear it because you can't live without it. Accept the fire as part of you and you'll be able to control it like an extension of yourself." He smiled, and for once it reached his eyes. "Only we can dance in the flames and not get burned. Don't hate that part of you."

Something clicked in my mind.

I *was* connected to my fire. Every time I stopped my fire from flaring up in me, it was like something inside of me died. There was no distinction between it and me. It wanted freedom as much as I did. Never had I imagined my fire as an extension of myself, but that's what it was.

The fire in front of me somehow felt...tangible. The sensation was difficult to put in words. The flame was like a living thing, and we spoke the same language. It took a moment to make the connection, but I could *feel* the fire. It wasn't mine, but it responded to me all the same. We understood each other.

I didn't need to will it to move. It moved with me, just as easily as I moved my arm or my leg.

The flame moved across Kahmel's hand in accordance with my thoughts—left, then right, even up and down. Kahmel lowered his hand and let me hold it in the air. My heart raced, heat coursing down my arms but not hurting me this time. Instead, the feeling was exhilarating, warmth coursing through my body and rushing to my hands as I moved with the fire. There was no longer a distinction between us. We were one.

But I suddenly felt strain. Without Kahmel there to hold it up, the effort to maintain it airborne became taxing. It was like lifting heavy weights, and a bead of sweat slid down my face.

I felt my control slip, the heat in my body dissipating. I exclaimed as the fire fell to the ground in a burst of flames.

Just before it landed, Kahmel extended his hand, and the flame stopped an inch above ground, returning to its candle-sized form before it disappeared with the clenching of his fist.

"I wanted you to see that, despite the amount of power you hold," he said, straightening himself, "you can still lose control. It takes a lot of time and practice to strengthen yourself to the point where you can control it with little to no effort."

I was panting, but I had never felt so alive. I had unlocked a part of me that I'd never had the freedom to explore. I understood myself better. That rush of heat. I was still hot from it, my fingers twitching like my body ached to do it again, free to release all that potential. But I knew it was probably best to follow Kahmel's advice and pace myself.

"If you decide to practice on your own," Kahmel continued. "I would suggest somewhere private and without anything flammable in case you lose control. I'd prefer you not to try it when I'm not around to help you, but I doubt I could stop you if you decided to do it anyway." He reached into his suit pocket and pulled out a red lighter. "You can use this for practice until you can bring your own fire forward at will."

I took the little lighter, pressing the trigger to watch the flame that it spurred on. The feeling was the same. I was aware of it and it was aware of me. I knew I was probably too drained to try to control it, but I just wanted to watch it, as if I had discovered fire for the first time. And in a sense, I felt like I had.

"Thank you," I said. It was more than I deserved, especially after arguing with him like I had.

But Kahmel didn't complain. He turned to reopen the door. "No problem."

QUEEN

Kahmel was gone when I woke, his bedding put away with no evidence it had been on the floor next to the bed.

I threw on some clothes and threw open the door, eager to explore the palace unsupervised. Arusi stood on the other side, her hand frozen mid-air in a knocking position.

"Faresha," she said, bowing. I hadn't seen her outside of the formal settings we'd met in so far. Today she was dressed in an emerald green blouse and white skirt, a thin red sash over her shoulders that marked her position. "The Faresh has asked me to be your escort for today and apologizes for not being available. Urgent matters have called him away. He will return as soon as he is able."

I should have known it wasn't going to be that easy.

"I would suggest getting used to dressing more formally around the palace." Her eyes went over my outfit, and I had to admit there was much to be desired from the simple red top and pants I'd chosen. "There's an array of clothes laid out for you in your closet."

Muttering to myself, I changed into the clothes she was referring to, complete with accessories. This time I came out in burgundy colored wraps that felt a good deal more traditional and regal. A patterned sash that expressed my title as Faresha wrapped around one shoulder and around my waist. Jewels bedecked my fingers, bracelets and circlets adorning my arms, and a large golden necklace that sat on my chest like a bronze plate made me feel like a museum exhibit. When I looked in the mirror, I barely recognized who was looking back at me. This girl looked regal, majestic, maybe a little intimidating, my fire-like eyes glittering among the golden baubles I wore.

Except the girl in front of me was no Faresha. She was an orphan playing dress up.

A good deal more sobered, I joined Arusi for breakfast.

"So," Arusi started after a while, breaking the silence we had so far maintained since we started eating, the only noise to be heard the clinking of my jewelry as I moved. "What do you want to do? The Faresh tells me you'd like to go out. Is there anywhere that grabs your interest?"

In other words, Kahmel told her I had a knack for getting away and to try to keep me busy. I groaned inwardly, once again feeling the tug on my invisible leash. There wasn't anywhere I wanted to go in Hashir with a complete stranger. If Lora and I were going out, that would be a different story, but even though Kahmel said I could send for her, she had her studies to worry about.

Arusi set her fork down and dabbed her mouth with her napkin, setting it to the side of her plate. "How about a tour of the palace? Kahmel tells me you took an interest in it."

How much had Kahmel told her about me? I nodded and downed the last contents of my cup of juice. "Let's go."

The sounds of our footsteps bounced off the richly colored wall of the palace.

She led me into a banquet hall with a long table that looked like it could feed a hundred people. Golden sconces adorned the walls, but they seemed almost dull in comparison to the gleaming silver chandeliers that lined the ceiling above the table, with topaz-colored crystals dangling from the metal rods, showering the table and floors in sparkling honey light.

I felt like I was in a story book and any minute the gorgeous K'sundii princess would come down the halls and take a seat at the table with royal clan families from all over the country—the Faresh and Faresha at the head of the table, toasting to the prosperity of the nation.

"This is amazing," I breathed, drifting toward the table and fingering the groves on the silverware, watching my face warp in the reflection of the metal.

"They say Fareshes have dined here for hundreds of years and that this table has seen hundreds of lords from dozens of nations gathered in the name of making peace."

I huffed. "Kind of like a crude Equalization, huh?"

"Hmm." She crossed her arms. "You could say that."

Before I could ask what she meant, she said, "Let's move on, shall we?"

More grand halls paved the way through the palace, the walls decorated with paintings, modern and old. We entered a huge room that was empty except for the ruby red rug leading up the stairs to a raised platform, where two thrones demanded precedence in the lonely space.

"This is the throne room?" My voice echoed through the room.

"Yes. This is where the Faresh conducts a lot of his business, but not all. Days like today, he has to meet with the Courts at the Legislation House."

"Huh. Why haven't I seen him doing anything here, then?"

Arusi folded her hands behind her back, very business-like. "He's lightened his workload for the time being to get you used to life in the palace. As much as he can, that is."

A guard rushed into the room, saluting and giving a slight bow before saying, "Ms. Zuwei, uh, there's a Dralus Comer to see the Faresha, on official business for Zendaal."

Arusi clenched her hands at her sides. There was a chilly tone to her voice as she said, "Send him in. We're already in the throne room." Arusi turned to me and added, "As should any formal meeting with the Faresha be. This will be good practice for her to get used to this kind of thing."

Arusi took my side quickly, and it left me wondering if I was the only person against my taking the throne.

Other than the Zendaalans, that is.

Arusi gestured to the imposing chair in the center of the room. "Faresha."

I did as requested, though it felt like the seat would swallow me whole. Even dressed as I was, sitting where I was, I didn't feel like Faresha. I felt like an impostor. Because I was.

I hadn't noticed Arusi taking position beside the throne until her commanding voice shook me from my thoughts. "Send the chancellor in."

The guard nodded. The Zendaalan man that let me into the palace library strode in, head held high. His glasses glinted in the cool light of the windows behind me, hiding his eyes, giving him all the friendliness of a snake.

"Good afternoon, Faresha. I apologize for such an abrupt meeting. Official business, you understand. How did you enjoy the library the other day?"

"Fine," I said, swallowing. I still felt quite gullible for not questioning a man letting me into a locked room, only to learn he was one of Kahmel's enemies.

Or did that make him my ally?

My alliances were confusing.

"What have you come for, Chancellor?" Arusi said coldly, her expression hard as steel.

Dralus regarded her like a dead bug on a windshield. "Though I have personally made an acquaintance with Her Majesty, the Zendaalan government would like to know a little more about the mysterious new Faresha. Faresh Kahmel Omah has said very little about her, and we're curious. Your sudden marriage is more than a little scandalous."

Tell me about it, I agreed silently. "What do you want to know?"

With a flourishing bow, Dralus said, "Naturally, everything, Your Majesty. As peace enforcers throughout the world, it is our job to be concerned with any new leadership of any country within the Equalization."

I stiffened, not sure how I was supposed to answer that. Surely if Kahmel's parents disapproved of my background, the Zendaalans would be furious. But then again, that was a matter for Kahmel to be concerned with. If he didn't think far enough to consider the Zendaalans' approval, that was his problem.

I opened my mouth to answer, but Arusi put a hand on my shoulder. "The Zendaalan Consulate are meeting with His Grace the Faresh, as we speak. If you have any objections about his wife's position, you can ask him at the Legislation House. But the Faresha's royal abode is neither the time nor the place to do it. This is a form of disrespect toward Her Majesty's honor, sir, and her husband will hear of it."

Dralus stiffened, but plastered a smile on his face, narrowing his eyes to slits behind his glasses, one of them gleaming red underneath as he did. "Very well. Then perhaps rather than talking about what got her here, whatever that may be, we can discuss her politics. For example, can the Zendaalans trust her to uphold the peace as an individual and help the collective as a whole? It is, after all, the only way to keep the Equality we all share."

"Yes," I said quickly. I didn't care about making Kahmel look bad, but I did care about getting the nation in trouble with the Zendaalans. How could Kahmel leave and not prepare me for something like this? I didn't know what I was doing.

"There's your answer." Arusi tilted her head up. "Will there be anything else, Chancellor?"

A sly smile crawled up his face as he exaggerated another bow. "That was the most important. I shall take my leave." His eyes connected with mine as he said, "It's good to know the Zendaalans can depend on your loyalty, Faresha. For what it's worth," he added lowly before exiting the room.

What the hell was that?

"Hmph," Arusi grunted beside me. "Don't worry, Faresha," she said, placing a hand on my shoulder again, like she could read my mind. "When the Faresh hears of this, he'll be furious. He'll handle it, believe me."

Her sentiment might have been meant to comfort me, but it didn't. Despite what the Zendaalans' motives were, and whether I liked it or not, I was on their side, not Kahmel's.

IT'S BY DESIGN

When Kahmel got back at around lunchtime, Arusi pulled him aside and spoke to him in whispered tones, probably about what happened earlier.

Rand came with him. He sat with me while Kahmel and Arusi talked. "I suppose I'll have to bring you with me shopping today," I said. "You or Arusi, I suppose."

He grimaced, messing with the tassels at the end of the tablecloth. "Yep. Sorry to be so intrusive, but the life of the Faresh and his family can be dangerous."

"So I hear. But don't you think your brother"—I looked to Kahmel, who was still deeply engaged in his conversation with Arusi. —"is a little paranoid?" I said in a low voice. "He seems to think everyone is his enemy. Why does he wear those sunglasses all the time?"

Rand's eyes narrowed at me, like he knew exactly what I was trying to do. Just as he'd opened his mouth to speak, Kahmel spoke up.

"Arusi just told me what happened while I was gone." He pulled up a chair and sat facing me. "I'm sorry that the Zendaalans spoke to you in this way. They weren't supposed to do that."

Rand's eyes went wide. "Wait, the Zendaalans were here?"

I dropped my gaze, playing with the end of my hair. "Well, it was just one official. And he only had a few questions about my loyalty to the Equalization, that's all. I don't see what the big deal is."

Kahmel stroked his chin. "Still, it's improper not to follow procedure."

He nodded to Arusi and she excused herself. Kahmel was outwardly even-faced, but I noticed the slight throbbing in his temple and how his jaw was set. And by the way he glanced at Arusi as she left, I got the feeling Arusi was about to do something about it.

I had bigger things to worry about. "We should be leaving soon, right? How long does it take to get to the mall?"

"Actually," Rand started. "Kahmel can't come. He has more meetings with—"

"I'm coming," Kahmel cut him off suddenly, to my chagrin.

Rand frowned. "Asan's going to be mad."

"Screw him." Checking his watch, he started typing something. "There are more important things than being at the Courts' beck and call every waking hour of the day. Jashi and I are supposed to be getting to know each other."

His twin brother sighed, wagging his head. "Why hire someone to help manage your PR if you're not going to listen to him?"

"Shut up." Kahmel finished writing the message on his eWatch. "I'm canceling now. As far as they're concerned, I'm unavailable."

Rand shrugged. "Your funeral."

More like mine, I thought, still trying to figure out how I'd get around Kahmel during our little excursion.

I HAD FORGOTTEN this was Hashir—K'sundi's leading capital of modern technology. Being in a palace whose structure had barely changed at all within the five hundred years of its existence sort of detached me from that fact.

The Azure Blue Mall of Hashir brought me crashing back to that reality.

Despite the fact that I had to meet Attican, I really did want to visit this mall at least once before I left. I'd read about this place in magazines, but seeing it in person was larger than life.

We passed several entrances—including the tenth floor through entryways accessible to hoverboards or hoverpacks—as well as parking for those who owned dragons.

The dragons here had a much more calming effect on me than the ones I saw with Kahmel. Like machines, they all stared forward blankly with black metal collars on their necks. Remotes connected to the electric collars gave the riders complete control of their dragons as easily as one controlled a toy car. A lot more sensible than the nonsense Kahmel was talking about.

Kahmel tensed as we drove by them.

The limo dropped us off through the VIP garage access, so Kahmel, Rand, and I walked through a parking garage full of expensive cars toward the elevator. I didn't know model names, but I recognized several of them from movies or magazines, the kind that could be set on autopilot and were virtually noiseless in the air.

We were dressed in street clothes—Kahmel in a gray tank top, khaki shorts, and a baseball cap which, combined with his dark glasses, made him difficult to recognize. Rand wore a striped T-shirt and blue jeans. My own disguise included a thin scarf that covered half my face along with a yellow top and matching skirt that flowed around my legs as I walked. Instead of my usual thick, long curls, I wore a braided wig, the synthetic braids long enough to reach my elbows, twirling around me with every move I made.

The disguises were the trade-off I'd made with Kahmel. It was either this or come with a legion of guards, which would have made my escape impossible. Besides, I much preferred anonymity. I regretted ever being jealous of celebrities. Fame was annoying.

We reached the elevator—a round pad that hovered above the floor and had a HoloScreen displaying a panel of buttons.

Kahmel moved to push one.

"No!" I exclaimed. "I want to do it. I've heard the elevators here are special."

"Oh, yeah, they are." He backed up from the panel of shiny buttons. "Have at it."

There was the typical list of floors, but there were also customized experience options with a set path that gave you a tour of the mall depending on your interests. There were buttons with their descriptions beside them, accompanied with a screen shot of the stores you would visit on that path—"High End Fashion," "Casual Fashion," "Prom/Special Events," "Sportswear/Equipment," "Electronics," "Toys and Games," and even "Holiday Shopping." I figured events like Kahmel's speeches qualified under "Prom/Special Events" but also could have been "High End Fashion." After a moment of contemplating, I decided on the former.

The pad under us started and sent us into a hole in the ceiling, and the display of buttons switched to a red "STOP" button.

When we emerged from the garage, we were surrounded by a sleek white environment, a trending hip-hop song playing in the background. Patrons walked or rode other elevators. A gentle female voice announced a sale or a special at one store or the other, ending each message with, "At the Azure Blue Mall, we cater to the needs of the individual. Finding the perfect purchase here is never by accident. It's by design."

Our elevator slowed as we passed a boutique displaying gorgeous gowns of every description.

"Want to stop here?" the female voice said. "At Ellie's, you'll find dresses perfect for your prom experience. You'll shine like a star in one of their galaxy collection dresses, inspired by fashion from the planet Carixx."

The "STOP" button moved aside to make room for a green check mark and a red X. Beside it was a timer that counted down from thirty to give me time to decide before the elevator moved on.

"This is so cool," I said.

Kahmel chuckled. "You like this kind of thing? It's like a flashy advertisement. Only you choose to watch it."

Rand said, "So you want to stop here? Look, if you slide on the screen, you can preview the stuff they have inside."

Moving around me to show me what he meant, Rand slid his finger across the display, revealing a screen of dresses and their prices.

My jaw dropped. "Two thousand Ramaks for a dress?"

"That's a good price," Kahmel said. "The outfit you wore yesterday cost more."

With that newfound perspective, I looked over the dresses again. But despite the beautiful presentation, none of the clothes were actually my taste. So I pressed on the X, and soon we were gliding through the mall again, passing by stores and patrons with ease.

As the elevator slowed again, I immediately pressed the check button when I recognized the store. The elevator had barely come to a stop before I jumped off.

"Hey, wait up!" Rand exclaimed behind me.

But I was already in the store. True to its reputation, E-Ternal had rows and rows of high-end fashion, ranging from business chic to dresses fit for red carpet events. Lora and I had fantasized about coming here for years. I grinned. Just because I was here with other motives in mind didn't mean I couldn't enjoy myself.

Kahmel and Rand caught up with me. "I assume you want to start here," Kahmel said.

"Give me a minute," I said, turning on my eWatch and calling Lora. It was a little after four on a Friday, so I was hoping she'd be free.

Her face appeared on my eWatch, and I pressed the button to transfer the image of her face to appear on a HoloScreen in front of me.

"Hey, Jashi! How are you doing?" she asked.

"You'll never believe where I am."

Her eyes were already taking in the scene behind me. "No..."

"Yes!"

"Oh my gosh, you're at E-Ternal! That is so awesome. Girl, whatever you buy, buy two—one for ya girl down here!" she laughed. "I'm just kidding. But have fun!"

"No, wait, I can get you stuff." I looked to Kahmel. "Right?"

He nodded. "Of course. It's no problem."

Lora's already wide eyes widened even further. "Is the Faresh there?"

I turned myself around so she could see Kahmel and his brother. "Yep, I'm here with Kahmel and Rand."

Her brows furrowed. "Oh my gosh, he has a twin?"

"Yeah, I didn't know either," I said, turning back to her. "But he was at the speech, too. Remember, the one from yesterday?"

"Oh, yeah." She nodded, taking a sip of a water bottle she must have had to her side. "Now I remember seeing you standing next to someone. But I didn't even notice he looked just like the Faresh. How come I never see him in the news or anything?"

Rand came closer to the screen to answer. "Well, I'm usually out on the battlefield. I don't have time to get all the fame and glory like Kahmel. You know, fighting for our nation's freedom apparently isn't important enough to be on the news."

Kahmel scoffed. "You don't even like the spotlight."

"The question isn't whether or not I like the spotlight," Rand said, crossing his arms. "The question is if I *deserve* it."

The two continued to bicker, and I marveled at how rigid Kahmel looked on the exterior and yet gave no objections to any of the people closest to him teasing him. Even with me, he never complained.

So why did someone like him have such a frightening, angry side?

I turned back to Lora. "I wanted to 'bring' you on my shopping trip so you can help me out. Shopping's just not as fun without you around."

Kahmel turned from his argument with Rand. "You know, if you want to invite her to visit, I can arrange for that to happen."

Lora's mouth dropped. "Oh, well, sir...I mean Your Grace, I can't. You see, I'm studying for my finals. I wouldn't have time to make the trip. But thanks so much for the offer and for taking great care of my friend. Maybe another time. And there isn't any need to get me anything, I was just playing, really."

Kahmel nodded. "All right. Another time."

After gathering more than a few things to try on, I took my eWatch with me to the dressing room so Lora could tell me if it worked or not. When it came to fashion, Lora was my superior in every way. She knew how to look for things that worked well for me, and helped me experiment with styles I never would have thought could look good on me.

Knowing I was short on time and wanting to try out the other stores in the mall, we left E-Ternal and tried rode the elevator to other shops and boutiques, leaving each with more bags. Not all of it was for me, though I wouldn't tell Lora that. There was no way I was going to be here at Azure Blue Mall with no set budget and not get her anything. While I hoped to be able to come back here, I had no idea what Attican wanted to talk about. He might have been ready to get me out of here soon. So just in case this was my last chance to show how much I appreciated her for coming through for me when I needed her most, I was going to get her something nice at the very least.

Five o'clock came far too soon. I didn't want to make my getaway too obvious, so I decided the oldest trick in the book would be the best course of action.

"Ooh, can you hold my bags for a second? I have to go to the bathroom."

"Now? We're about to go home, you can go there."

"Sorry, it can't wait. I'll be right back, promise. Literally, two minutes."

He sighed. "Fine. We'll load your bags in the car."

"Thanks."

Turning away from him, I got back on the elevator and let him watch me press the button to the restrooms.

As soon as the elevator was out of sight, I pressed "STOP," then hit "Food and Dining." The elevator took me to a food court, and I identified Ronnie's Burgers almost as soon as it arrived.

Stepping off the pad, I hurried inside and quickly found Attican. He smiled, gesturing to the man sitting across from him and waving me over.

"Jashi, I'd like to introduce you to my business partner. I hear you're already acquainted with Mr. Sokir Omah, one of your husband's younger brothers."

TUBS OF STRAWBERRY ICE CREAM

Sokir and Attican dragged me outside the mall, behind the dumpsters in the back. I tried to control my panic as I realized that I'd be alone with them this time. A deep breath pushed hot air from my lungs, and the fire dissipated.

"I'll make this brief," Sokir started. "Mr. Cromwell has told me everything you've done for him so far, which has been a fantastic help, by the way. My brother is annoyingly elusive, which makes finding any useful information about him almost impossible. But what we need from you now is something slightly more dangerous than anything you've done so far."

"Why are you doing this?" I said without thinking. Kahmel tried to tell me this could happen. Why hadn't I listened?

Sokir's dark eyes flickered with a dangerous edge to them, but his voice remained calm. "Kahmel is an embarrassment to this family. The way he claimed the throne has no honor, and the Zendaalans don't want him here. The Courts are entertaining him while he pretends to be something to save face. But he will never truly be Faresh. Not in the real sense."

I tried to remember what Kahmel told me about Sokir. He was the next oldest besides Kahmel and Rand. Like most families to the Faresh, he had a comfortable position high in the government. He had also tried to talk Kahmel out of marrying me when he thought I was in the bathroom.

"But why—"

Attican grabbed my arm and yanked me closer to him. "You're in no position to ask questions, minx. You do as you're told and you shut up. Understood?"

Sokir held up a hand to abate him. "No, wait, I will answer her."

Attican released me after a moment's pause.

"All of Hemorah is a better place because of Zendaal," Sokir said. "All any country has to do is understand that the freedom that Zendaal allows us is given with the expectancy of compliance when they ask for it. And they don't tolerate any deviance from that compliance, or everything would fall into chaos. My loyalty to my country comes before my loyalty to my brother, Ms. Anyua. And so should yours. He should not be fighting this war."

I shook my head. "Zendaal has no real reason to oppose the war. There has to be another reason they don't want him there."

Sokir grabbed my jaw, squeezing hard on my cheeks as he pushed me against the wall. "Even a girl as slow as you can understand that this situation is a lot bigger than you. You couldn't get Kahmel's army base positions. I'm sure he has information on it stored in his eWatch. While he's sleeping, you need to put this chip into it." He held up two black devices on his finger, each smaller than a centimeter. "One for your eWatch and one for his. It will crack his password and activate an instant data transfer to your eWatch for you to examine. You have to find and send to Attican the relevant information quickly because you only have a few minutes after the password is broken before your device will be detected. Wait until the right moment to access his information from your eWatch. Once Attican gets the message, one of our people will come to take you away. After that, you can forget any of this ever happened and live out the rest of your life in Gasher under an assumed name."

He released me with a sneer, and I rubbed at my sore cheeks. My body began to heat up rapidly, like I was struck with a sudden fever.

If I did this, I would be cementing my alliance Kahmel's enemies, and I wasn't sure I wanted to do that anymore. People would die. Their deaths and potentially even Kahmel's would be on my head.

At this point, I didn't know why Kahmel was at war with Omani like this, or why he wanted to make K'sundi "like it used to be," but he hadn't been wrong so far. Not about his family or the conspiracies against him.

I was the one who was wrong.

Sokir placed the two chips into a small plastic bag, zipping it closed. He placed it into my hand. "Do I have your word?"

I swallowed. "Yes."

A smirk crawled up his face. "Good girl."

Attican said, "Someone's coming."

"Damn it." Sokir looked back to me. "We'll be in touch." Then they both ran for one of the back doors to the mall and disappeared inside.

Kahmel and Rand rounded the corner.

"Jashi! There you are!" Rand exclaimed. "What are you doing here?"

Kahmel faced me directly, taking off his sunglasses and staring me in the eye, his tangerine glow piercing. "Who brought you here?"

"I got lost on the way back from the bathroom."

He took me by my arms, his grip gentle, and his eyes searched mine unrelentingly. "Who brought you here?" he repeated.

My body started to heat like I was struck by a sudden fever. Breathing out made embers fly, but that release only relieved a portion of the fire within. I wanted to cry. I didn't want to be Kahmel's enemy anymore, but the people who controlled me were much higher up than I could have ever imagined. Not even Kahmel could protect me from my fate.

I was a traitor, and there was nothing I could do about it.

Shaking my head, I took another breath, the hot air finally releasing the heat from my body. "I came here on my own. Really. Sorry to have made you worry."

Kahmel looked to Rand. "Meet me at the car."

Rand nodded and did ask he was asked, disappearing around the corner.

We were left alone, and Kahmel still hadn't let go of my arms. "I'll protect you, Jashi. But you have to tell me who brought you here. I don't know what they told you, but—"

"'They' didn't tell me anything! I'm okay, all right?" I snapped, trying to keep tears from my eyes. "Now, let me go already."

Sighing, Kahmel heeded my request, and I promptly put him behind me as I stalked toward the waiting limo.

We didn't say a word to each other on the way home, but Rand and Kahmel sent each other several worried glances that didn't escape my notice.

When we got back, I didn't say anything as I marched straight to Kahmel's room, closing the door behind me. I climbed into bed, buried my head in his pillow and cried.

I had no idea what I was going to do.

THE NEXT FEW days passed in a blur. Kahmel tried talking to me. I got a couple worried messages from Lora and even Talad, but I became a recluse. I went along with Kahmel to a few events he had to attend, but I didn't say much to him or anyone else. I just didn't have it in me. The fantasy was over. It was time to say goodbye.

Every night, I stared at where Kahmel kept his eWatch, holding the chips in my hand. Every night, I said I would do it. But I never did. I didn't want to do this to him. We may not have been in love, and I was still unclear on his motives for both this relationship and the war, but I was starting to think there was more to him than met the eye. He was surrounded by traitors, and I was one of them. All this, and yet no explanation why.

I kept telling Attican that I hadn't found the opportune moment to plant the device, but he was starting to get antsy. I wasn't sure how much more I could stall.

That question was answered one night as Kahmel came back from some meetings with the Courts. I was in bed, a carton of ice cream in my hands.

"I have to leave tomorrow."

And just like that, I was out of time.

"Oh," I said in a small voice, putting another spoonful in my mouth.

"I don't know when I'll be back." Kahmel put his sunglasses on the dresser beside him. "It could be anywhere between a few months and a year, depending on how things turn out."

"Oh," I repeated. Tonight really was my only chance. But how could I do it, knowing I was helping make sure he never came back at all?

An awkward silence followed, until Kahmel broke it. "I hope you don't think I'm assuming, but I've noticed that you've seemed somewhat depressed lately."

"Me? Depressed?" I tried to sound surprised enough to make it believable, but even I thought I was overselling it.

Kahmel gestured to the tub of strawberry ice cream I clutched in one hand with a big spoon in the other. "You eat a lot of ice cream when you're stressed." Kahmel continued. "I haven't noticed you talking to your Matron Taias at all, and I remember her specifically asking me to make sure you checked up on her every once in a while. I feel bad leaving you all alone without anyone to talk to other than my people. Maybe you could send for the Matron to come visit you. Just talk to Rand or Arusi and they'll arrange it."

I avoided Kahmel's eye contact. There was a reason I hadn't reached out to Nana yet. For one, I couldn't help but feel like if she hadn't agreed to my marriage to Kahmel, I wouldn't be in this situation in the first place. I didn't hold it against her; I knew how traditional she was. But it didn't make it any less awkward to start a conversation with her. Another reason was that I knew I was going to leave. I didn't want to bring her under suspicion of anything when I disappeared, so it was best I kept her as far from my situation as I possibly could.

But still, I couldn't help but admit there was a certain truth to Kahmel's words. I did miss her a lot.

"Why are you so nice to me?" The question sounded a lot more accusing than I intended it to be. But at this point, I was in a sea of confusion. No matter which way I looked at it, I couldn't find any reason he would ever choose to marry me, of all people. Before this situation went either way, I wanted to finally know why.

But to my surprise, this time it was Kahmel who was avoiding eye contact with me. "This marriage isn't a punishment. You're the one doing me the favor. Why would I treat you any other way?"

I refused to be dismissed that easily. "I'm doing you the favor? I mean, in comparison to you, I'm a nobody. I'm not even part of a royal clan family. My idea of a successful life was getting a managerial position at EK Fashion, and I was perfectly content with that. But then you, the Faresh of K'sundi—reputed for being a heartless, murderous leader—you arrange with Nana to marry me. Me! Then, on top of that, you surround yourself with mystery, never answer a direct question, and never explain anything. And you do weird things like offering to sleep on the floor the night of our wedding!"

Kahmel was silent, and I knew I was on to something.

"There's more to why you married me than what you're telling me," I realized. "Something that makes you handle me with kid gloves. It doesn't make sense any other way you spin it." Frowning, what Kahmel said the night I met his parents came to mind. That traditionally, women were chosen for wives based on the strong children they could produce. "It's because of my fire!"

He shook his head vigorously. "No!"

"Then it's because I'm dragon tribe. I heard you tell your parents that it's traditional to marry strong women that can make strong children."

This time, he laughed, infuriating me further. "No."

"Yeah, right! You study tradition all the time in those books! Like you would marry someone for any reason other than some ancient custom. What, was there an old rule about marrying within your race, or something? Or better yet, dragon tribe women made better warriors. Is that it?"

Why did my questions suddenly feel like an interrogation, even to my own ears? I was trying to find holes in a theory I had already considered but didn't want to have to acknowledge out loud. Maybe if I didn't utter the thought, I could prevent it from materializing into reality.

"No!" he shook his head. "Look, I have to leave in the morning. Why don't we talk about this when I get back?"

"That could be months from now! Just because you're the Faresh doesn't mean this isn't dangerous." I resisted the tears that stung at my eyes as I felt a pang of guilt. "There's no guarantee you're coming back."

Kahmel sat on the edge of my bed and took my hand, looking me in the eye. "If the Great Spirits help me, I'm coming back, Jashi. We have the Omanians cornered. That's why it's so essential that I leave now. I'm already late staying with you as long as I have."

I summoned the strength to ask the question that I'd been avoiding since day one. "Do you have feelings for me?"

He bit his lip, turning away from me, but keeping his gentle hold on my hand. "I didn't want to have to bring this up right before I had to leave. I didn't think it was fair to you."

My eyes widened. "You do?"

Kahmel looked at me, almost apologetically. "Yes."

THEY WANT TO BURY THE FIRE BUGS

I yanked my hand from his. "So there was more to the story than just pleasing the Courts."

"That was part of the reason..."

I scoffed. "So because you're Faresh and can have any woman whenever you like, you decided to arrange our marriage so I wouldn't have a choice!"

He shook his head. "No. I regret having to do this to you. But we had to get married quickly so I could protect you. No one would be able to touch you if you were Faresha of the nation."

"Protect me from what? Did someone somehow know about your feelings? Like your family?" I stopped, realizing that I should stop talking about his family before I revealed what I knew about Sokir.

"No, I never told my family about how I felt toward you. The danger that surrounds you has nothing to do with me. It never has. I had to marry you as soon as you became of age because it was the only way I could think of to protect you."

"From who?"

He sighed. "Zendaal."

A sinking feeling slid down my gut. "What do you mean?"

"Do you read the HoloPaper?"

Frowning, I said, "Not much, why?"

Kahmel opened a screen on his eWatch, bringing up an article on the Internet. I gasped as I recognized the face of my doctor. I'd forgotten all about the follow up appointment he'd asked for. Then I read the title of the article, and my eyes darted back to Kahmel.

"You arrested my doctor for treason?"

"When you turned eighteen, you went in for an extensive blood examination. So did I, when I was your age, only at the time, the age for the examination was twenty-one. It's the first time in your life that they do an examination of that degree. So a few years after my family moved to Hashir, I had to come in for my blood test. The day after, they asked me to come in for a follow up, just like they asked you, remember?" He showed me his arm, and I noticed for the first time a scar on his forearm that looked like a needle mark, but it was much thicker than any ordinary needle. It almost looked like a bullet wound.

"When I went in, they strapped me to a bed and hooked me up to a machine I'd never seen before, and the doctor was dressed in a fireproof suit. I was injected with something that started my fire all over my body and hurt like hell. As the needle emptied into me, I started seeing dots. I knew they were trying to kill me. But they had no idea that I already knew how to control my fire. I blasted the guy that was working on me in the face, broke out of my confines, and took the needle out. It was the first time I ever used my fire in a fight before.

"After that, I went to my parents. They knew about my fire and helped me cover it up all my life. But..." His jaw clenched. "They turned on me, too. I came home to find men in suits waiting for me. My *parents* had turned me in. Or at least, they'd tried to. With Rand's help, we both took the men down before they could overtake me, and we both left home. Rand and I lived alone together after that for a few years. We realized that my fire was no longer secret, and it was because of that blood test.

"Agents sent by either Zendaal or K'sundi came after me constantly, but because of the chaos of the government at the time with the assassination of the Faresh and his family, they were too uncoordinated to make a successful attempt to apprehend me, so we were able to fend them off."

He paused, chuckling. "I know it sounds strange. At the time, you were all I could think about."

I frowned. "Me? Why?"

"Because of that day I saw you with your fire when you were younger. I was rejected by my family because they were afraid of how having a freak son would tarnish their name. It was the only thing that made me feel like I wasn't alone, even when my parents and family sold information about me every chance they could for a couple thousand Ramaks. Because I knew there was someone out there who was just like me. And it gave me something to fight for. I didn't want you to have to go through the hell I did."

My face warmed. I was confused by how someone who barely knew me would be so fixated on saving me from a fate I couldn't possibly know about. And my gut twisted at what I was doing to him in return.

"So Rand and I came up with a plan," he continued, "to break into the doctor's office where they tried to kill me and to use my abilities to take any information we could find on the business they handled there to finally get some answers on why they did what they did to me.

"In the official government documents, they call people like you and me Fire Bugs."

My fists clenched in my lap. There *were* people who knew exactly who I was. Kahmel and I were never alone. My mind went back to my doctor, all those times I was tempted to tell him what was really bothering me, wishing someone could help me. And all that would have done was seal my fate.

Kahmel gestured with his hand. "I'm sure the original naming was lost thousands of years ago. Fire Bugs are only found within members of the dragon tribe, which you already know is a minuscule percentage of the population of this country as it is. Within that small percentage, only two percent have our abilities. They kill us off when they discover us with the blood analysis, and they extract something during the procedure that I still haven't figured out what they need it for.

"All I know is, after I learned that, I knew I had to learn more and protect other people like me." The Faresh set his jaw. "Based on the reports I found in the doctor's office, I didn't think the existence of the 'Fire Bugs' was a recent thing. So I dug into my parents' old contacts to conduct my research into the origin of people like myself.

"I found out that the dragon tribe is a small percentage now because they died off, and the modern-day people of the tribe are those whose gene pool bears a prominent enough gene to produce our eye color. But it doesn't happen in all families, even when they have dragon tribe blood, which is why they make up such a small percentage. That's why I'm the only one in my family with the trait. But every passage I found, even in books, gave very limited information. And the data I found only dated as far as the Equalization.

"The most I found about the Fire Bugs were fairy tales of people that were said to be one with the dragons back in K'sundi's ancient times. Our existence was not only much more deeply rooted than I first assumed, but our existence was even documented during the K'sundii prehistoric period, eons ago.

"I knew that the only way for me to get the answers I was looking for was to go higher up in the government and discover the secrets myself. So I gathered a group of my closest friends, people who I knew had a problem with the Equalization as much as I did."

I held a hand up, putting my ice cream aside. At this point it was nothing more than melted sludge anyway. "Wait, what does the Equalization have to do with this?"

He stood up. "It has *everything* to do with it. You should take a good look at the 'banned' list that the Zendaalans put in place. Documents detailing too much information about the dragon tribe were banned. The reasons behind their dying off is banned. Most K'sundii history before the Equalization was banned. Why?"

"Because ancient K'sundii were barbarians," I said in a small voice. "Being part of the Equalization came with a price, and that meant giving up our violent past."

Kahmel laughed. "You sound like a history text. They stripped us of who we used to be and justified it by painting us as the bad guys. What if that isn't true at all? Then what did we need the Equalization for? They enforce their control all over the world, pretending to do it in the name of kindness so they have the right to be just as violent as the people they're supposedly saving. What they did to K'sundi is no different. The order to kill the Fire Bugs didn't come from K'sundi. The K'sundii followed orders from Zendaal without even knowing why. My friends and I formed a sort of resistance."

"You mean like the rebels?" I exclaimed.

Kahmel put his hand over my mouth. "Shh...not so loud. Yes. We raided government offices to find information, but we never did anything violent. Our main goal was to find the ancient books—the physical ones, not the digitized. The Zendaalans could easily control any and all digitized information about our history. But the books, they couldn't quite get rid of those. They made the mistake of dismissing them as obsolete."

"Where did you get rebels?" I said, taking his hand away. My head was spinning. I couldn't believe Kahmel could be serious.

He chuckled. "Arusi, Khes, Rand, and Asan were my best men."

My jaw dropped. "This nation's trusted officials...are secret rebels."

He gestured to himself with a smirk. "Don't forget, I'm the rebel king. I became Faresh in order to access what we couldn't with the resources we had."

All of the strange news reports about him were starting to make sense. "So when you over took an Omanian airbase..."

"That was with my men." He grinned, a proud twinkle in his eye. "The rebels, as you call them. We used the situation to our advantage.

Through all of our findings and research, I found the old laws that permitted me to rise to the throne."

My mouth fell open. "But becoming Faresh just for information? Isn't that a little extreme? What about the nation? What about the other royal clans that had the right to reign as much as you do?"

"You act like I have no regard for my title." He threw his head back. "I take my position very seriously. The only downside is the fact that my family is now the main royal family clan. At least until I can build a case against them to have them thrown out. But this country was in utter chaos before I came to take the throne. I was the best candidate for the throne because I'm the only one who isn't in the Zendaalans' pockets. Besides, becoming Faresh was the only way to save you in time."

"Me?"

Kahmel sat back down beside me. "I only had a few years before you turned eighteen. And if I didn't come up with a way to save you, they would have killed you."

I could barely see him through the tears the blurred my eyes. "Why? Why were you so determined to save me? Why did you even remember me?"

A smile spread across his features. "How could I forget? The spunky neighborhood girl who made my little brother cry when he tried to take her bike ended up to be the only other person on the planet I've ever known who was just like me. I've been looking, Jashi. We're the only ones I've been able to find. I couldn't stop thinking about the beautiful woman you would become one day, and the fact was that if I didn't do something, that beautiful woman would die at a very young age without ever having have a chance at a future." Pursing his lips, he added, "I wish I had the opportunity to get to know you first, before we got married, but the situation forced my hand. So to protect you..." He paused before saying, "I've had my people watch over you since I created the resistance."

"You've been watching me?"

"I know how it looks, but it was for your safety."

"How extensive was your search into my 'safety?'"

He looked away, taking off his eWatch and handing it to me, making my stomach turn with guilt. "It's all there. You dropped out of school when you were rejected by a potential adopted family. Your friend Lora is getting her doctorate in gastronomy. Before I arranged our marriage, you were working a taxi job, which was directly after being fired from a diner you and Lora worked in together."

My hands felt clammy. "You've been stalking me for years?"

"Jashi, it's not like that."

This time I stood, backing away from him. "And what, you just decided you could define my destiny for me, huh? Behind my back with Nana?"

"I believe in fate," he said, getting up and taking my hands. "I knew I'd seen you in that alley that day for a reason. And now that I see the kind of woman you grew into, I know I was right. As I said, I wish we had the opportunity to get to know each other, but I was out of time. But think of what we could be together. We can fight this, whatever this is that's trying to kill us off. We're stronger as one than we are individually."

I didn't know how to process what I was hearing. Kahmel had developed feelings for me at some point. He'd been stalking me—not to mention he was the leader of a group of rebels.

I was never someone who questioned the Equalization. There were people I knew who had, like Lora, but I never associated myself with the movement. I thought it was reckless and pointless. But now I didn't know what to think. Was it reckless and pointless to fight against the Peace-Bringers when they were ordering the deaths of people like me and Kahmel? With such a miniscule percentage of people who could possibly have the trait, it wouldn't surprise me if we were the only ones left in K'sundi.

With nausea rising up in my gut, I realized that I didn't have a choice left in this situation at all. However Kahmel felt about me, he was Faresh of K'sundi, and I was a traitor. I'd sent Attican information every day since I'd been here. It didn't matter if I felt justified at the time, or if I was forced, Kahmel would have to deal with me as a traitor.

And traitors were executed.

As a storm of emotions raged in my head, Kahmel tilted my chin so I looked up at him. "I know you don't return my feelings toward you. I couldn't ask you to. All I ask is the same that I asked on our wedding night. Let me earn your trust. Stand by me while I fight for this nation's freedom. I don't have all the specifics yet, but I'm going to need your help to free K'sundi from Zendaal. And other nations like us."

My eyes widened. "Me? How?"

"There's a reason they're after what they call Fire Bugs. We threaten them somehow. And I believe their greatest fear is our meeting, which has happened with you and me. Whatever they're trying to keep hidden, it has to do with a time before the Equalization. We're the last living traces of our nation's history. That is, us and Omani."

Suddenly the pieces of the puzzle fell together in my head. "Their territory used to be part of K'sundi."

"It's the only other place where I can get any answers. I figure the best way to piece together this nation's story is to put the nation back together again. I have nothing against the Omanians, and I'm only interested in the land that used to be K'sundi. Figuring out what the Zendaalans are keeping from us is the first step toward getting out from under their grip. That's why I have to go, and I don't want to come back until K'sundi's size is restored to the way it used to be three hundred years ago. I won't ask you to love me, but I'm asking you to let me protect you and to love K'sundi enough to help me save it."

A TEXT GOODBYE

Kahmel had long since fallen sleep. It was 4:08 in the morning, and I was still awake. The shadows of the night fell over me completely, but my eyes had adjusted to the dark, and his eWatch remained where he left it, in my hands. Tears streamed down my cold cheeks as I knew what my fate would be, whatever Kahmel might have wanted.

I was a traitor. As Faresh, he had to arrest me if he found out, regardless of how he felt. And if I decided to stop helping Attican and Sokir, they would call me out as a traitor, resulting in the same.

There was no way out for me.

But I didn't want to hurt Kahmel. I now knew the reason behind that rough exterior of his. He was a warrior misplaced in time. In a day when bravery was a commodity and courage was hard to find, he didn't belong. His thoughts were constantly toward those he meant to protect. His family left him for dead a long time ago, a testament I could relate to.

I couldn't do this thing to him, even if it was the only way I could save myself from this mire.

Taking a deep breath, I finalized the plans that were brewing in my head. I knew Kahmel was going to get hurt either way, in an emotional sense. But, as he said, I couldn't love him the way he loved me. Perhaps this would help him move on a little easier.

Or maybe not.

On my eWatch, I finished the text message, then saved it for later. Then I used the bluish light that came from my eWatch to illuminate Kahmel's. I slipped the little black chip into his eWatch, then did the same to mine.

Climbing out of bed, I silently packed a bag with nothing but the clothes I came here with; none of the things Kahmel bought me. Guilt gnawed at me too much to take anything else from him. Lastly, I put on a hoodie that would cloak my face well.

Instinctively, I reached for the hair clip Kahmel gave me before we got married, realizing I'd worn it every day since.

If I had the right to take one souvenir of my time here, the hair clip would be the one I wanted most. It was simple, but like the secret garden he showed me, that's what made it special to me.

After a moment's hesitation, I slipped the hair clip into the curls of my hair. It was a small thing. I doubted Kahmel thought much of it, anyway.

Putting the bag down by the door, I tiptoed over to where Kahmel was sleeping on the floor, crouching while I held my breath to replace his eWatch beside him.

I froze as his eyes flew open.

For a painful moment, I thought it was all over. But as his eyelids fluttered and he shifted positions, I realized he was still half-sleep and didn't know what I was doing.

"Go back to sleep," I whispered, grateful for the shadows that hid the tears that dripped onto the floor beside him. "I was just returning your eWatch, is all."

That, and stabbing you in the back, I didn't mention.

"Okay," he said groggily, and I knew he didn't really register what I'd said. "Be sure to let Rand know."

I chuckled, wondering if he'd even remember this conversation when he woke up. "I'll do that."

"And you have Arusi's number if you need it, too."

"Yes, I know," I said, nudging the covers over him a little more to help lull him back to the world of dreams.

"Okay, good."

Just as I turned to leave, his arm wrapped around my torso, pulling me in closer to him with startling strength. I lay with my back flush against his chest, his arm resting on my stomach. He breathed out contentedly.

"I love you, Jashi."

My tears spilled onto his pillow, and I didn't know how to reply. But it turned out that I didn't have to. The way his breath evened out, I knew he was asleep again. Struggling to keep my sobs quiet, I decided I'd have to wait a few moments to make sure he was good and sleep before I slipped from his hold. For a few seconds, I just felt him breathing peacefully against my hair.

Once I felt he wasn't going to wake up, I carefully picked up his arm from my abdomen and slid my pillow from my bed to put it in my place. His arm closed around the pillow, and he stirred for a few excruciating seconds but settled back to even breathing.

Then I crept back toward the door, picked up my bag, and walked out.

With my hoodie concealing my features, I walked down the same hall Kahmel took me down, arriving at the dead end with the painting of the Faresh staring at me. Ignoring his portrait's judging looks, I took the sword from its display on the wall and plunged it into the side of the frame, hearing a click.

The wall slid to the side when I nudged it, and I passed through to the secret garden Kahmel took me to before. Closing the wall behind me, I examined the brick walls of the garden.

Kahmel told me before that there were all kinds of secret passages that the Fareshes before him used in case they had to escape. This little secret area wouldn't make any sense if it didn't have an exit. I suspected there were hidden cameras all over the palace, so I didn't want to leave through the exit and risk Kahmel finding me too quickly. If he trusted the secrecy of this place enough to practice our fire here, it was probably secure enough for me to make my exit as well.

The night wasn't as bright as our wedding night, when the full moon was in place. But the gibbous moon served well enough to illuminate the wall. My fingers traced the surface meticulously. I didn't want to miss even the slightest detail.

Then I felt a niche in the surface, like a thin line carved into the brick. Stepping back, I noticed the brick pattern was interrupted there, ever so slightly. The door was definitely here. But how would I activate it? Touching on the brick and pushing against it served for naught. Looking around, I figured there had to be some sort of trigger like the sword with the painting.

The angelic statues.

There were three of them, dancing in a circle around each other. Studying them and prodding their forms, I tried to figure out a way to activate the exit. Coming up empty, I frowned. There was nothing else about this little garden that was of enough note to be the way out. It had to be the angel statues, but how?

Perhaps something about them hinted to the answer. They were children with feathery wings and textured hair. It seemed like they were either dancing or playing a game of tag, because they were looking to each other in turn as they formed a circle of chase.

No, one of them wasn't looking to the child in front of him, he was looking to the one behind him.

My frown deepening, I realized that the child in question looked a bit strange, now that I thought about it. Something about his head position looked unnatural in comparison to the direction of his body.

His head was twisted too far.

Taking the head in my hand, I twisted it in the direction he was supposed to be looking in, hearing a click as the ivory bust followed my motion. Behind me, the false wall moved aside.

I was out.

DRAGONS: PART 2

CAN WE TRUST HER

Kahmel Axon Kai of the Omah clan, Faresh of K'sundi

I clutched something when I woke up, something that smelled like Jashi. The smell of spiced perfume was faint, but I recognized it. She smelled like that when I kissed her on our wedding day, and so did my bed, now that Jashi slept in it. Frowning, I opened my eyes, a split second before my alarm buzzed at my side.

Why was I holding a pillow?

Dread crawling up my throat, I turned to find that Jashi wasn't in her bed and that the pillow that was in my hands was, in fact, missing from it.

I shot out of my sheets, turning off my alarm and cursing when I stepped on something in my hurry. My eWatch.

Didn't I leave that with Jashi last night?

All grogginess left as I hoped the situation wasn't what I thought it was.

"Jashi?" I called, on the off chance she was in the bathroom or the closet.

Still not willing to accept that she'd run away just before I left for war, I opened the bathroom door, looked down the hall, went into the closet. It was by the time that I checked the closet that I had to acknowledge that Jashi ran away again. Clothes were tossed everywhere, and one of her suitcases was gone.

But why did she leave me with my eWatch and her pillow?

Vaguely, I remembered dreaming about her. I couldn't remember much, though, just the memory of holding her, the smell of spice on her hair. It was a blissful thought, but far from reality at the moment. She wasn't in my arms, far from it.

Slapping my eWatch on, I called Rand.

"What is it, man? Do you know how early it is?" said his tired holographic face.

"Come to my room. Quick."

"Why?"

"Jashi ran away again."

He scoffed. "Doesn't she do that at least once a week?"

"Rand, I'm serious. Her suitcase is gone and some of her clothes are missing. I think she might be gone for good this time." I paused before adding, "I told her how I felt last night. And just about everything else."

Rand was more awake now. "Here I come."

In a few moments, I heard a knock on my door, and Rand came in, dressed in a t-shirt and sweatpants. He probably threw on the pants just to get here.

"Okay, so..." he started, taking a seat on Jashi's bed. "How much is everything?"

"I told her everything about the Fire Bug files and the resistance."

Rand paused. "I thought the plan was to tell her when she could be trusted."

"I couldn't put her off any longer. Didn't *want* to put her off any longer."

He sighed. "And I'm assuming by her disappearance this morning you don't suspect she's on our side? You know I usually trust your judgment, Kahmel, but are you sure that was the best way to handle the situation? I mean, now everything you said to her could be repeated into the ears of any number of Zendaalan spies as we speak!"

"Then it's up to us to make sure she doesn't have the chance to. Have the guards tear up the entire palace if they have to. And alert the secret police."

"I already sent out the order. But Kahmel, be honest with me. Do you really think we can trust Jashi?"

Pursing my lips, I said, "I believe in her."

"Do you believe in *her* or what you've imagined her to be for all these years? I know you say you're okay with Jashi feeling nothing for you, but I don't believe you're unaffected by the fact that things didn't turn out the way you hoped they would with her. She doesn't want to be with you, and it doesn't look like she was very convinced by your heartwarming speech last night. You can't tell me you're not the least bit disappointed about it."

"Of course I'm disappointed!" I snapped, a little louder than I intended.

Rand flinched, looking down at his arm cast before he looked back up and said, "Look, I'm sorry, I—"

"What I'm more concerned about is the fact that her life is in danger." I looked at the eWatch on my arm. "Let's not forget that that's our top priority. Not my feelings. We have to find her before the Zendaalans do, because you know she's dead if we don't."

My twin nodded his head solemnly. "You're right."

Sighing, I slumped into the armchair beside the window, mentally and physically exhausted. It killed me that Jashi didn't trust me yet. What more did I need to do?

"I need to know I can leave this in your hands," I said. "If it were up to me, I wouldn't leave. If we're right, everything we've done so far depends on her. Tell me I can trust you to look after her."

Rand looked at me a few moments, then back at his cast, the shadow of shame eclipsing his features for a moment. He nodded firmly. "You can trust me to take care of her, Kahmel. I won't let you down."

Getting up, I patted my brother on the back. "I know."

It was time to go.

"I'll leave this up to you now," I said, turning for the door. "I'll see you when I get back."

Rand jumped up from his seat. "Wait, Kahmel. Did you check the things Jashi took with her when she left?"

I frowned. "Not really. I just took a glance at the closet and knew she was gone. She definitely didn't take everything; there were clothes everywhere."

Without explaining himself, he went into our closet for a moment, then came out. "She took the hair clip."

For the first time that morning, relief relaxed the tension in my shoulders, if only by a little. "Then we've got her."

Having a tracking device embedded in Jashi's hair clip was a necessary evil. Part of me hated it. I didn't want to do it, but the alternative was letting her fall into the Zendaalans' hands.

***

WITH A FEW TAPS to my eWatch, Khes soon appeared on the holographic display screen, his one milky eye and his one brown one looking at me strangely. "Your Grace. I heard about the Faresha."

I leaned over and took a few nuts from a dish on the table in front of me, glancing out the window of my jet.

Ah, that's what that was. The look of sympathy. "Yes, I'm working on the situation as we speak," I said, turning back to him. "But that's not—"

"Do you have any idea where she went? Have you heard from her?"

With a deep breath, I told myself not to get angry with Khes for sympathizing. I wasn't used to people having the emotion directed toward me, and frankly I didn't want it. Sympathy didn't get things done. Action did.

"The situation is under control," I assured him. "In the battle at the southern border, a lot of dragons and dragon riders went down. So where are we on the dragon count?"

Khes grimaced, scratching at his stubbled sideburns. "Not good. And you already know that with the pains it takes just to break one in..."

"I'll take care of that. Let the armies know that my arrival will be a little delayed, but they can expect another squadron of dragons in return."

"Yes, sir. And by the way, about the dragons..."

"Yes?"

"There was another accident."

I put my face in my hand, kneading the skin between my brows. Damn. "How bad is it?"

"Not as bad as it could been, but what with the results of the last battle and the fact that you're coming late, the men and lieutenant generals alike are losing their resolve to use them. They feel like they're fighting with an enemy from within and without by either Omanian soldiers or their own dragons."

I knew I would have to be hard. When it came to those I knew before I became Faresh, it was easier to handle them and know they trusted my judgment. But outside that select few, people obeyed me out of obligation, without any sense of loyalty. Winning over the trust of my nation was going to be an uphill battle.

However, there were more important things at stake than looking kind in the public eye.

"Send all of the lieutenant generals a message. They are to leave the dragons alone. In the case of that one individual, have him taken off of dragon rider duty, and assign his dragon to someone else."

"They want the dragon put down."

"I don't give a damn what they want. The dragons are too valuable. We need them to take the Dragon's Heart river basin."

"Yes sir. If that's the case, then—"

"No, wait," I said, pausing to think a moment. "Assign me to the dragon. I'll take it."

Khes looked hesitant. "I'm not sure if that's the best idea, Your Grace. From what I hear, this particular dragon is wild enough, for sure. It's a wonder the rider was able to do anything with it."

"That's okay. I want the dragon. As a matter of fact, send it to meet me."

My army general frowned, the scars around his blind eye creasing. "Where are you going?"

"To get more dragons. I'll be at the caves of the Dharia mountains."

Khes chuckled. "You've got a lot of guts, I'll say that. Very well, sir. Will there be anything else?"

"Keep me up to date with anything you hear about Jashi."

"Yes, sir."

With that, I hung up the eWatch and looked out the window of the plane, looking out at the mountains in question. The very dragons I mentioned were flying closer to the city than I liked, past the boundary my Dragon Watchers set. I checked my eWatch and saw that, indeed, there was a warning from the Watchers that the dragons were beyond the boundary and that they were in the middle of getting the situation under control. With Jashi having gone missing, I hadn't checked any alerts on my eWatch at all.

I typed a quick message to the head of the Dragon Watchers to let him know that I would be arriving shortly to help with the situation and that I needed all of his best men to help me deliver the dragons to the army.

Tapping on the button beside my armrest, I spoke to the pilot. "Change of plans. I need to get to the dragon caves."

His voice came back with a dubious tone. "Are you sure, Your Grace?"

"Do it."

The pilot's voice was a good deal more respectful this time. "Yes, sir. I mean, Your Grace."

Good.

Taking my hand off the button, I looked through the messages on my eWatch, replying to some and completely ignoring others. Even as I flipped through the messages, more were being sent to me. Already busy enough with this situation with the dragons, I decided not to respond to anything new. That was my first priority at the moment.

Until I saw one come in, sent by Jashi.

Clicking on the unread message as quickly as it appeared, I read the text and frowned.

I'm sorry I have to do this, but by the time you read this, I will already be gone. What I'm about to do will send an alert to your eWatch within a few minutes. But I'm sending you this message first so you know ahead of time. The Zendaalans are about to find out where your army bases are, your battle tactics for taking Omani, everything.

I'm hoping that by letting you know I'm giving you a better chance of changing your tactics before the Zendaalans use the information to take your armies by storm. But in actuality, I have no idea if what I'm doing will even help.

The Zendaalans and your brother Sokir have been using me as a spy. I didn't have a choice in the matter, but it doesn't make me any less of a traitor to you and to this country.

Thank you for letting me learn more about who I am. I could have never dreamed to know that much about myself and my abilities. I wish I could have stayed long enough to learn more. But I know that what I've done is worthy of the death penalty.

Now you see why I had to leave.

Sokir. My fist clenched, and my body soared in temperature as I wished that between my hands was my brother's neck. I didn't suppress the flames. Fire came out of my nostrils with every exhalation.

Quickly, I wrote a reply.

I already knew that the Zendaalans were manipulating you. If you come back, I can explain. You're not worthy of death, Jashi.

With another fiery breath, I added to the message.

Sokir is.

DISCONNECTED

Jashi Anyua, Faresha of K'sundi

As the scenery of Hashir whizzed by my window, I saw that Kahmel had written a message back, but I couldn't stand to bring myself to read it.

Instead, I finalized the process of the data transfer, and my eWatch flooded with thousands of files. I wasn't sure I would even have enough room for the transfer to finish, but within a few moments, a pop-up appeared, telling me that the transfer was complete. Checking on the storage, I found that the files made it in with only a couple of megabytes to spare.

I quickly sorted through them to find the ones Attican described and sent those to him first. Then I chose a bunch of files that looked miscellaneous enough to not be of much importance. Enough things to make Attican feel like he received all of the data.

I deleted the rest of the files—*FirebugResearch.txt, AncientKsundi.pdf, BookFindings.jpg*. I didn't want Attican to have his hands on anything like those.

As I scanned the files that went into the trash, I stopped at one named *MatronTaiasLetter.txt*. Curious, I tapped the file open.

The letter was simple, nothing more than a few lines.

"You couldn't have thought of a better gift as a dowry. I can see that you are a very thoughtful man, and I don't doubt that you will take good care of my dear Jashi.

"With kind regards, Taias."

I chuckled at such an old-fashioned ending to the letter, but typical of Nana to do everything old school. But what was she talking about, dowry? I knew Kahmel gave one...

Then I realized that there was an image attached to the file, but with such a huge data send and deletion in progress, the eWatch was slow to bring it up. When it did, I gasped.

Nana stood at the door of a house I didn't recognize with all of the kids staying with the orphanage all posing around her. The house was huge—enough to fit double the amount of kids she had. A front lawn and the houses on either side indicated it was in a very well-to-do neighborhood.

He'd bought Nana a new house for the orphanage as part of the dowry.

I quickly blinked away the tears that threatened to fall. Nana had complained about that old house for years. She always said it wasn't good enough to keep the kids that passed through there all the time, and that if she had the money, she would give us the very best the market had available. And unknowingly, or perhaps knowingly, Kahmel made that dream a reality.

A message flashed in red on my eWatch, cutting off all access I had to the files I was looking at before.

UNAUTHORIZED PRESENCE DETECTED. ACCESS TO FILES HEREBY DENIED.

I was out of time. And according to Attican, my location was being sent to Kahmel's eWatch now. I slipped into the bathroom—a room that was little more than a toilet and a sink. Taking the lighter Kahmel gave me, I held it under my eWatch for a few seconds, jumping as sparks flew. The device caught fire. Breathing deep, I concentrated on the flames, and felt them respond to my attention. Reaching out my palm, I inched the fire toward my hand, smiling as it left the watch and followed my direction. Once it was sitting in my grip, I closed my fist, like I'd seen Kahmel do.

The fire extinguished, leaving only a charred eWatch in its wake. I tossed the now useless device into the garbage can nearby and returned to my seat with a surge of accomplishment. Judging by the scenery, I wasn't far from my destination.

As if in confirmation, a voice came on the speakers.

"Ladies and gentlemen, we are now arriving in Odarlan. Please don't forget your baggage and personal belongings..."

The message droned on.

Taking my suitcase, I got up from my seat again and waited at the exit to get off the train. I cursed. Forgot my other ticket. Hurrying back to my seat, I picked up my one-way airline ticket to Omani, then joined the other people waiting to get off the train.

THINGS THAT CAN'T BE TAMED

Kahmel Axon Kai of the Omah clan, Faresh of K'sundi

"We tried to trace the signal, but it was cut off almost as quickly as it appeared. I think she destroyed her eWatch."

"And what about the hair clip? Can't we trace her with that?" I demanded.

"We *could*," Rand replied over the HoloCaller. "Emphasis on the past tense. We tracked her location as far as the airport in Odarlan. We think she took a train there by the way her signal moved. But she had a couple hours' head start. By the time we collected the data from her tracker, she was already in the airport. I tried to mobilize the secret police in that area, but by that time, the signal had already cut off. I think she's on a plane now."

My fists clenched. "Find her."

"Look, man, we're doing our best. If you had tied that bell around her neck like you said, none of us would be in this mess."

I forced myself to relax. Taking out my frustrations on Rand wasn't going to bring Jashi back any sooner.

Some part of me wondered if I could have handled the situation with Jashi better. Maybe if I told her that I knew about Attican, she would have trusted me sooner.

When she ran away the first time, I sent the special police to put an APB out on Jashi, telling them to keep an eye out for her for all of the black market networks. If her blood was already in the system, I wouldn't be the only one looking for her. The Zendaalans found her first and told her contact to threaten her. That was the reason she even came back in the first place.

I knew all of this. But I didn't tell her because, as Faresha, no one could easily get to her. It wasn't impossible, as the last Faresh proved, but it would stall the Zendaalans at the very least.

So I let her be my spy. It was crazy and stupid, but I thought if I showed her that I trusted her, she would trust me in turn.

Maybe telling her what I did last night was premature. But at the same time, I was tired of keeping everything secret from her.

No. That wasn't it. I was too eager at the idea of having her seeing me as more than some—what did she call me?—a heartless, murderous leader.

It didn't matter either way now. Despite my precautions, she still ran away. She still didn't trust me.

Taking a deep breath, I said, "Send the investigators to try and figure out what flight she took. I have to go."

"Will do."

Hanging up my eWatch, I turned back to the men who were waiting for me. The Dharia mountains loomed above us, a steep winding path carved into the surface. A sign that read, "BEWARE—DRAGON NESTING GROUNDS AHEAD" marked the side.

A shriek went out, bringing my attention to the shadow that passed over me and the men I was with. The serpentine form of a dragon covered the sun, the wind that followed whipping at our clothes as it passed. Another shriek pierced my ears with a reminder that every other time I'd come to this cave, it was with a completely clear mind. It was the only way to deal with dragons. They could sense weakness, vulnerability. Even the slightest of deviation of attention could get someone killed.

And today, my attention definitely deviated.

I shook myself. Rand would handle the situation with Jashi. I could protect her by making sure I won this war. Especially when we took over the river basin and surrounding area. And the only way to do that was to ensure my army had the dragons we needed.

The dragon above us didn't engage. Instead, it flew up high above our heads and into a cave. But looking back down the path where we came, I saw a lot more lurking around the city limits.

In other words, very bad news.

I turned to the Dragon Watchers. "How the hell did the dragons get so far beyond the boundaries you set?"

The men were dressed in the most modern Dragon Watch uniforms, clad in black suits that had padding on the shins, forearms, and midsection, as well as a sleek helmet with a red visor, but they looked at me as though I was the beast they were worried about.

Honnar, a bulky man who looked to be in his forties, stepped forward. "The dragons aren't responding to the way you ordered us to handle them anymore. They've adapted."

"And what steps have you taken to handle them, if any? They're halfway to Hashir already!"

"Every step your new legislation allows, Your Grace," Honnar said, a retort iced with feigned respect. I couldn't blame him. According to the rest of the world, the only way to handle dragons was with electric torture devices. Doing anything else was unprecedented. I couldn't expect them to trust the methods I was asking them to use. Given the circumstances, I supposed I couldn't expect anything more than that.

The dragons in the distance slowly, but surely, made their way toward the city. *Is it so hard to stay outside of the city limits?* I griped to them inwardly. All it would take was one serious incident for the Courts to have the right to order the use of electric collars.

Flying in the face of my mental supplications, the dragons continued their advancement toward Hashir.

Neither Jashi nor the dragons could be tamed, no matter how hard I tried.

"Very well. Let's go up to the Tower and see what we can do."

"With all due respect, sir," Honnar said, his face hard. "We were in the process of handling the situation before you came here. We can do this."

I smirked, knowing full and well how Honnar was planning on solving the problem had I not showed up. If things were looking this desperate, there could have only been one solution on his mind that would keep his job position, at least from his perspective. "Today's your lucky day. With me here, we can solve the problem twice as fast."

Honnar's jaw clenched, and I saw him bite back what he wanted to say before he said, "And the new dragon you had sent here? What are we to do with that?"

Ah, yes. I'd nearly forgotten. "We'll use it to help us with the current problem."

I hoped that I was killing two birds with one stone by using this unruly dragon to help me with the others rather than serving us up as an easy lunch.

DRAGONS DIE FIGHTING

Dragons, I found, were most dangerous not when they were hungry, but when they were bored.

Even as we climbed toward the Dragon Watch Tower and I heard the roaring inside rip through the air, I somehow knew the sound was different from a hungry roar. It was a taunt—a challenge to be opposed rather than the need to kill. The feeling was baseless since I hadn't even seen the dragon yet, but somehow I knew. The roar of this dragon was one that was guilty of having nothing better to do than be destructive.

Why did that remind me of Jashi?

Shaking myself, I centered my mind. This beast wouldn't hesitate to kill me if I didn't have complete control over myself.

The sun seared every part of bare skin it could find, blazing across the nape of my neck, my black suit absorbing every ray of light and baking me with it. Outside of the bustle of Hashir, it was easier to remember that K'sundi was really a desert country. Our shoes crunched on a dirt road that was nothing more than an etching on the dry, rocky surface of the mountain. Desert plants drew along the cracks of the rock and dust, including several varieties of spiny cacti and some kind of dried grass that crackled when we stepped in it. Occasionally, a lizard or snake darted across our path and broke the monotone of the lengthy trek.

That, and the occasional roar of a dragon that was loud enough to hear from Hashir.

Even with the sound-proof earpieces that we communicated with, the roars reverberated through my skull. The screeches of a disgruntled dragon could easily deafen the unprepared.

Of course, dragons were in a permanent state of disgruntled.

The seven men with me looked more scared of me than they were of the dragons. Their captain, however, didn't echo that fear. In fact, he looked like he wanted me gone for a completely different reason. But I couldn't be sure. The looks of hate, fear, and intimidation all blurred together at a certain point.

A huge shadow crossed over us and a shriek filled the sky. An azure dragon fixed its wild black eyes on us, scales glistening like sapphire in the sun and starting to glow dangerously bright. It circled above us, wide nostrils flared and bat-like wings spread like a cloak that shadowed its body. Brandished onyx talons, a snarl revealed teeth like knives, the look in its eyes decided. It took less than a second for it to start descending, falling from the sky at a dive for us.

The Dragon Watchers had armed me before we started climbing. Reaching for the metallic cylinder at my side, I activated the laser whip with one hand, activating the mobile shield emitter with the other. The Watchers acted first. A tendril of light slashed at the dragon right in the snout, extracting another tremendous cry that would have shattered our eardrums if it weren't for our ear pieces.

The dragon recovered quickly. It landed on the ground in front of us and charged, fire lining the insides of its mouth.

Damn. The creature wasn't dumb. It was directly blocking our path, and without our flying vehicles, it was going to be hard to escape the flames.

For the other Dragon Watchers, at least.

Someone grabbed me by the arm and pulled me in line with the other Watchers, forming a line at either side.

"Sir, raise your shield emitter," Honnar instructed to me, his voice coming in from my ear piece.

I did as he asked, raising the device that looked like nothing more than a black brick. Entering the dimensions of the shield in a quick second, I hit the button on the side, watching as a glowing forcefield went out before me. The golden rectangular shape interlocked with the forcefields of the other Dragon Watchers, forming a long wall in front of us.

The dragon spewed fire, a pillar of flames hungrily slamming against our shielding. The frustrated reptilian beast rammed into the wall we created, trembling as volts of small electric shocks went out from the humming forcefield to keep it back. The dragon retracted, pacing the ground beyond the shield and staring at us with a look that could only be described as hatred, assuming an animal was capable of such a thing. If it wasn't convinced that it wanted to kill us before, our audacity to keep it back seemed to confirm its resolve more than ever.

"All right, men," Honnar called out. "Let's convince him he's got better things to do than to be here bothering us. Advance."

The shielding went down on two points of our wall as the corresponding Watchers rushed forward. They lashed at the dragon with their laser whips, bloody lacerations carved into the skin wherever they made contact. The dragon recoiled every time it was hit, trying to shield its head under the cover of its wings.

Honnar joined in on the onslaught, brandishing his whip and attacking with rapid cracks toward the face. The dragon roared, breathing down fire on Honnar, but Honnar raised his shield in time to block it, then continued his attack.

None of them saw the dark look that crossed the dragon's eyes as it flinched back.

"That's enough," I said into the ear piece. "It will back off if you leave it alone now."

The two Watchers at either side of the dragon hesitated, looking to their leader to see how he would react.

Honnar continued, looking at me over his shoulder with a glance. "No offense, sir, but we know what we're doing. Men, keep going."

The men hesitated for a second before the two Dragon Watchers at his sides obeyed his request and kept whipping. I reacted before the other Dragon Watchers could stop me. Taking down my shield, I rushed toward the dragon and tapped my laser whip to switch to a lower mode.

The dragon moved before I did, lurching forward and tackling Honnar. The Dragon Watchers at his side whipped at the dragon, but it proceeded to gouge its talons into Honnar's shoulder, unflinching at the trails of red that now covered its body.

With my whip taken off burn mode, I flicked it at the dragon's neck, wrapping the whip around its neck and yanking its head away a second before it tried to sink its teeth into Honnar. With crazed eyes, the dragon focused on pulling away from the laser whip that now acted as a leash, its actions jerky and uncontrolled. The creature didn't act from strategy or planning but from the dire need to be loosed from constraint.

"Kill it!" Honnar screamed.

My soles dug into the ground as the dragon pulled me with him, the two of us entering a match of tug-of-war. The Dragon Watchers circled, their whips at the ready. They brought on a barrage of lashes, but it only served to enrage the creature. It tossed its head from side to side to shake itself from my hold, jerking me around, threatening to make me lose my footing. It was immune to the fiery cuts that covered its whole body.

Finally, one of the Dragon Watchers pulled out a gun, and shot the creature square in the head. The dragon shrieked, lashing out for a few seconds as it bled from the hole in its forehead, this time completely knocking me down. With another two shots, the creature was silenced, a gory mess of blood and cuts, mottling the sapphire scales that served as its armor, now a strange purple where the blood dripped down its body.

The Dragon Watchers all ran to Honnar's aid, and I picked myself off the ground, cursing inwardly as I ran to his side. His shoulder and chest were gashed thoroughly, his uniform ripped to shreds. Blood stained his clothes and the ground beneath him, and his face was a sickly color.

"You," I directed to some young-looking Watcher, his orange eyes throwing me off guard for a moment. He must have been one of the men who was following me because I would have noticed otherwise. "Call the Watch Tower for assistance."

The young man nodded, turning on his eWatch just as I heard a grunt from under me.

"The dragons are becoming more and more unruly," Honnar croaked, his face twisted in pain. "Your new laws insist that we use this antiquated form of taming them, and it's not enough." He looked down at his crumpled body and twisted his lips twisted. "You see what it's doing to us. If you want these dragons under control, use the electric collars, Your Grace. Or use a more lethal degree of laser whips."

"You forget your place, Honnar," I said, fighting to keep sympathy at bay. I had to hold strong, set an example. "You have no right to question me or the law. The Dragon Watchers will continue as they have." Honnar glared at me through his pain. I ignored it. "How much longer until help arrives?"

The young dragon tribe boy took a second to realize I was talking to him. He started, then looked down at his eWatch. "They're saying they're almost here."

The men surrounding us looked between Honnar and me in fearful silence.

"Your new dragon laws won't last," Honnar grunted, his eyes hard. "I hear the Courts are working to appeal your decision."

"So did I," I replied sardonically. "If and when they succeed, perhaps we can have that discussion." My eyes narrowed at him. "Watch your tongue if you don't want trouble, Dragon Watcher. Understood?"

Fear finally eclipsed Honnar's features, and I was certain he had ideas of me having him executed for such a slip of the tongue.

Fear, I found, worked faster than having to explain myself.

Honnar opened his mouth to say something, but I held up a hand to stop him. A group of Dragon Watchers ran toward us, med kits in hand. I breathed a sigh of relief. Honnar would live.

Looking over at the butchered dragon on the ground in front of us, it didn't look like capturing one of the beasts would be an option. Dragons would rather die fighting than be constrained.

I once again thought of Jashi. Once Rand found her, I would have to figure out some other way to protect her other than keeping her under constant supervision. If all restraining her did was encourage her to leave again, I had to take my chances and allow her to do as she wished. I just had to figure out how to keep her safe.

Just as I would have to figure out how to get these dragons in line without killing them or us in the process.

"I PREFER UNORTHODOX"

Thankfully, despite my concerns, we had no other dragon encounters on the way to the Dragon Watch Tower. Using vehicles around dragon nest caves was dangerous, as they made too much noise and attracted attention. That was why protocol for Dragon Watchers was to only use aircraft when confronting dragons that were getting out of line but not to travel about the mountains themselves.

We approached the Watch Tower on foot, two men carrying Honnar on a stretcher. One of the Watchers flashed a pass card to give us entrance. We stepped onto a wide platform that hovered above the floor, blue light glowing from the bottom of it. The Watchers hit a button, and we went up. The Tower was mostly an empty expanse here on the bottom floor, but the top floor proved busy and cluttered with commotion. A team of men in uniform marched around a circular room, addressing various glowing screens with a birds-eye-view camera display of different viewpoints of the mountain, mainly around the caves.

A lean man in his thirties approached us briskly, his eyes going straight to Honnar. "We got your distress call. What happened?"

"Well—" the dragon tribe boy started to answer.

"Your commander failed to follow orders and endangered his entire squad as a result. That's what happened." I lifted my chin and folded my arms across my chest. "I came here for dragons, and now I have to clean up after all of you because you can't keep the dragons in line and away from the city limits? With Honnar's form of taking charge, it's no wonder."

The lean man clenched his jaw and swallowed but wisely kept his mouth shut. Good. Maybe now they'd work harder at coming up with a solution.

"What's your name and rank?" I asked the man.

His face taut with indignation, he said, "Tillian Deroh, second in command."

"Good. I'm going to take a group of Watchers to meet with the dragons nearing the city limits to show you how it's done."

His hands balled into fists, but he spoke with a level tone. "I didn't know you knew how to do that sort of thing."

"There's a lot you don't know about me," I spat, daring him to challenge me.

Whatever response passed through Tillian's mind, he responded with respect due my position. "Then let me show you our best team." He pushed a button on the forearm of his uniform. "Jemmorah, Kent, Ashed, come to the main Watch room at once." Then he looked to the dragon tribe boy that came with my escort. "You, too."

The boy's bright eyes lit up. "Really?"

"Of course," he said with a sly dose of contempt underneath. "I'm sure that whatever the Faresh has to teach will be invaluable to your studies. All of you."

I frowned as he gestured to three other Watchers who had entered after his call, all around the age of the dragon tribe boy.

Suddenly, I understood what Tillian meant.

College interns.

Of course.

Turning back to him, I asked, "Is the dragon I had sent here already?"

"Ah, yes. I'm sure you heard it roaring on your way up here. An unruly thing, though I say that as if they all aren't. As a matter of fact,

T'shan, why don't you take him to it? Get him a suit and then to his dragon. Wouldn't want another incident."

The eager dragon tribe boy saluted me. "Right away, sir. Uh, please, Your Grace, come with me."

As T'shan led me and the other interns away, I sent Tillian a glare—one he would feel, even if he couldn't see it through the dark lenses of my sunglasses.

Even set up to fail, I was going to get my point across. I could even teach these teens a thing or two about the right way to handle a dragon, and then it would be Honnar and Tillian looking like fools.

"Wow," the teens breathed, and even I had to admit the dragon before us was awe-inspiring. But he was equally deadly, which I needed to make sure the trainees kept in mind.

The dragon was black like night, snake-like with no wings. It bared its teeth at us, a row of white knives dripping with saliva. Glossy scales like porcelain plated the creature with an impenetrable-looking armor, its talons fixed to the ground with laser ropes. The inky body whipped and jerked to be free of its constraints, rage in every movement. It was much bigger than the dragon that approached us on the mountain side. It shook the entire building with its thrashing. The whiskers reached out at us like tentacles but couldn't quite reach, and the dragon screamed in frustration.

"What are your names?" I wanted to know.

The heavy-set boy answered first. "I'm Kent."

"Jemmorah," the girl answered.

One that hadn't said anything so far said, "Ashed."

The dragon tribe boy spoke up last. "T'shan, sir."

I nodded, trying to commit them all to memory. "Then let's head out, team."

The four of them nodded and gave a simultaneous, "Yes, sir!"

I strode toward the creature.

"What are you doing?" T'shan shouted to me but didn't dare come forward to stop me. Whether he was afraid of the dragon or me, I appreciated it, regardless.

Keeping my eyes on that of the Wingless, I asked, "So, I take it you're a college student, right, T'shan?"

"High school, sir. I'm only 17."

A high school intern? What kind of Watch Tower was this?

"My dad is a Dragon Watcher," he said, his words rushed and nearly breathless. "He wants me to be able to start college already having some experience on the field."

The explanation was a sound one, albeit unordinary.

The dragon roared, trying everything it could to free itself from its restraints. Desperately, it reached for me now that I was within range of its whiskers, but I dodged them, ducking between its legs so I would be hard for it to reach. Then, in a fluid motion, I used the bend in the talon to give myself a boost up to its back.

"Where did you learn that?" a girl about Jashi's age asked.

"Practice!" I had to shout as the dragon beneath me roared and tried to jerk me off. But I lurched forward, reaching across the scales to grasp a whisker on one side. The dragon screamed again, but when I pulled on the whisker, it stopped abruptly. Careful not to lose my balance, I reached for the other whisker, taking it in my hand. I yanked on both, seating myself better on its back as the dragon stiffened, its movements limited by its tender whiskers, now under my control.

"Bet they don't teach you this kind of thing at the schools you go to. Draconology courses only teach you about the study of the ZST. And the Zendaalan Standardized Technique only teaches you how to torture a dragon into submission, not how to deal with one with its mind intact."

"Are you saying that what you're doing is...illegal?" Jemmorah asked, tugging at her sleeves.

I considered the question. "Not illegal. Unorthodox. All of my practices are founded on research. Only the information is so old, no one remembers it."

Jemmorah cocked her head. "But I heard that the dragons used in the war aren't being tamed the standardized way. Does that mean all of the dragon riders are...unorthodox too? Couldn't that put them in danger?" She spoke quickly but then shut her mouth, as if realizing that perhaps she shouldn't have said it.

I didn't mind the question, though. "If I felt my people were in any real danger, I would put a stop to it at once."

No need mentioning that this dragon was guilty of the very concern she was expressing. It wasn't like what I said wasn't true—not that she, or anyone else, needed to know that.

At a final attempt to assert its discontent, the dragon flung itself to either side, but I tightened my gripped on its whiskers for stability, exacting a pain-filled shriek from the creature. It finally settled down.

But I knew better than to trust it. As soon as I let my guard down, I would be catapulted into the wall—or along the side of the mountain, if we were flying. I had to be careful.

I turned to the Watch team. "Get to your fliers, then meet me outside the Tower. We're going to approach the dragons nearest the city and try to stop them. Set your weapons set to stun or a lower setting. We're not trying to kill these dragons. We want to capture them."

One of them frowned, a tall, heavy set guy with a low cut hairstyle. "Capture them? I thought the objective was to reset the boundary and kill if necessary."

The way the girl shot him a look, I figured he wasn't supposed to let that slip, but I already knew the Dragon Watch Towers were making unnecessary kills. Without being allowed to use the collars, they felt it was the only way to protect the populous. I didn't like it, but at the same time, I knew that was why I needed to set an example. There were better methods than torture.

A PRESENT FOR JASHI

The red-tinted visor—part of the Dragon Watch uniform I now wore—protected my eyes from the air that whipped around my body as the dragon and I riding soared through the air, allowing me to nudge the dragon to go even faster than I normally allowed. The feeling was exhilarating, racing through the sky as the desert below me passed by like a HoloScreen movie on fast-forward.

Beside me, the four Dragon Watchers hovered in flying vehicles shaped like mini-jets. The fliers were only big enough to fit one passenger, a tinted black window to top its sleek design. Built for speed, the vehicles were made to be as thin and small as possible.

I preferred dragon riding to using a flier any day.

The dragon grumbled under me, vibrating his whole body. And then he lurched, hurtling toward the ground.

I pulled at the whiskers, hearing it scream in pain. But it didn't halt its descent.

"We're coming, Your Grace!" Jemmorah called over the interlink.

"No need," I said, already maneuvering my position on the dragon's back.

"But..."

"I'll just be a second."

If only this dragon would stop trying to kill us.

Since the dragon's whiskers weren't helping me get it under

control, I pulled out the laser whip, setting it to medium. It wouldn't kill, but it certainly wasn't going to be comfortable. I cracked down on the dragon's side, just to show that I meant business. The dragon wailed, trying to jerk me off before it remembered that I still had its two whiskers in my other hand. Every whip of its head would only result in a painful backlash on one of its most tender parts.

The dragon's descent was slower, but it still wasn't ready to stop yet. The ground hurtled toward us. I had to act quickly.

Flipping the whip's setting a notch higher, I cracked on the dragon's side again, this time seeing red marks where I made contact. The dragon straightened, once again taking to the skies and flying level with the Dragon Watch fliers.

I cringed at the marks I'd left in its side. Dragons were notoriously stubborn creatures. The problem was their remarkably high tolerance for pain. A dragon would rather die than concede to anything it didn't want. How did the dragon fliers of the past teach their dragons how to trust them, how to listen? A good flier had to somehow teach his dragon that they were to be respected. Dragons didn't seem to respond well to anyone they didn't respect.

How to earn that respect was anyone's guess.

But if I didn't learn how to get earn this dragon's respect, it was going to be put down, and I couldn't afford to lose any dragons right now.

Especially after what Jashi told me. The Zendaalans now knew our strategies, and they were going to give those secrets straight to the Omanians. If the idea I had developing in my head ever since I saw her message was to work, everything would depend on having dragons. I couldn't afford not to get them now.

"What did you do?" asked Ashed, wonder filling his voice.

"There," T'shan said, saving me from having to respond. "To the southeast, sir. There's a bunch of dragons trying to get past the backup barriers. If they get through those, we only have one backup left before they get to the city."

I looked to where he indicated. A group of five dragons slammed themselves against the holographic barrier that barred them from the city.

"It's time. Follow me."

"Are you going to be okay on that crazy dragon, Your Grace?" asked Kent.

"I'll be fine," I said, tightening my grip on the dragon's whiskers. I had to be.

Soaring down the mountain-side and flying across the desert expanse, we neared the first barrier, now nothing more than a broken machine hovering in the air, the forcefield it was supposed to be projecting flickering in and out, though mostly out.

I watched as Ashed approached it in his flier, lowering the hood and leaning out to hit a few buttons on the device, a low whine going out as it shut down, the flicker stopping. "Man," he said, a touch of awe tingeing his voice, "these things must be strong to break through the shielding like this. I mean, it must have hurt like the devil just to reach the projector."

Kent said, "Yeah, so why exactly are we trying to catch them?"

"Kent, shut up," remanded Jemmorah hurriedly. "He didn't mean to question you, Your Grace."

We soared beyond the first barrier, and ahead, the dragons had spotted us.

"Ashed, I'll take the right; you take the left," Kent said.

"On it." Ashed hopped back into his flier, lowering the glass cover of his flier again and taking off with Kent. The two fell into line, the two fliers taking opposite positions as the dragons came flying toward us.

"Sir," Jemmorah said, "I'm not sure how you plan to capture the ones you want, but we're going to try the typical aversion strategy. Is that all right?"

Curious how they would handle the situation on their own, I said, "By all means. Follow your typical procedure and I'll come in to make the capture afterward."

"You don't have any tactical suggestions?"

"No, I won't get in your way. I'm only here to help."

There was a pause over the interlink, which might have been a nervous swallow from Jemmorah before she said, "Yes, sir."

Then she and T'shan raced toward the dragons.

Deciding that my presence would be best served taking a backseat for the moment, I pulled on my dragon's whiskers to direct it toward a sand dune. We landed in a position that gave me clear view of what was happening, but I was ready to take off if one of those dragons took an interest in me instead.

There were two Wingless that I counted, the rest being the typical Draconian—less serpentine in form and more saurian, with a bulky, muscular body. Much shorter than that of the Wingless.

Two of the fliers activated the whip modes on their vehicles, glowing tendrils of dangerous light snaking out of their machines. They engaged the three Draconians, cracking whips on their backs and forcing them to fly away from the group.

The remaining two fliers erected shielding layers in front of them, coming around the Wingless and then ramming into them from behind, sending the Wingless back toward the mountains, away from the city.

I chuckled, now thoroughly impressed. Despite whatever the second in command's intentions were, these teens were well-organized.

But the dragons weren't keen on being deterred from their goals so easily. The Draconians that Kent and Ashed chased flew up at a steep angle, making an arc in the air before lowering again, now behind the fliers and reversing the order of the chase. Two of the dragons blew pillars of fire toward the Dragon Watchers, knocking the mini-jets off course.

"Kent, Ashed, are you guys all right?" T'shan yelled over the interlink.

"Shields are down thirty percent, but we're all right," Ashed responded. "Concentrate on herding your dragons back toward the mountains. We got this."

"Roger that," Jemmorah's voice came back.

Ashed and Kent's fliers realigned their positions, then split up, making the Draconians have to divide to chase them. Their flight patterns were erratic and didn't make sense to me at first, but then I watched as the dragons started getting confused trying to mimic the movements, becoming frustrated and all the more determined, flapping hard to fly even faster. All the while, they were being lured farther away from the barrier, keeping interest in the pursuit by the difficulty of it. A clever strategy.

Meanwhile, the Wingless that had been pushed away from the city were getting restless. They snaked through the air in a zigzag pattern to get around their pursuers, but Jemmorah and T'shan were persistent, blocking off the dragons' movements whenever they tried to get back toward the city.

My dragon snapped its head up, sniffing the wind, unbothered by the sand that blew across its face. It snarled. What had spurred its interest?

It shot up to its feet and took flight almost frantically, darting for the barrier to the city.

"Your Majesty!" T'shan yelled.

"Don't break off your pursuit; I'm fine," I said, pulling on the whiskers, trying to get it back under control. But the dragon didn't react. I tried lashing at the sides of the beast with my whip, but it had no effect at all. The dragon dashed through the hot air of the desert as if its life depended on reaching the city.

Putting the whip back in its holster, I tried with the whiskers again, the muscles in my arms contracting as I fought to pull the dragon's head to the side and divert its flight path. The dragon strained under my hold, snarling and growling in protest, but it finally gave in, curving in its path a couple hundred meters from the barrier.

We landed roughly in the sand as the dragon continued to fight, but it eventually grumbled into submission. I checked to see if we had caught the attention of the dragons the Watchers were trying to divert, but it looked like those dragons were too busy with their pursuers to care about what we were doing.

Damned if I knew what set the thing off. Unless it was interested in cacti, I couldn't see anything that could have possibly disturbed it so much.

"Team, we have a problem!" Kent yelled over the interlink.

I took a closer look at the contention in the air. The Draconians and the Wingless were getting crazed, too. The dragons chasing Kent and Ashed had decided they weren't interested anymore, turning around and going right back for the barrier at startling speeds. Kent and Ashed pursued, matching them in velocity, but the dragons reached the barrier first, slamming their bodies against it, causing a shudder in the air as the forcefield hummed against them. It was obvious that the constant barraging was wearing on the shielding interface. One of the three dragons blew fire at it, the intensity of the flames warming the air, even from where I stood.

My dragon was getting antsy, obviously wanting to join in the action but apparently aware that I wasn't about to allow it.

I frowned. Dragons didn't act this way for no reason. There had to have been something making them *need* to get beyond the barrier.

A second dragon started breathing more flames on the forcefield, the third one continuing its bodily barrage. The two fliers cracked whips on their backs, but it just made the dragons seem to throw any rationality aside, ignoring the lashes and blood now covering their bodies, throwing themselves at the wall and breathing on it wildly.

Jemmorah screamed, the sound almost muted over the interlink. I spun in her direction. The Wingless had started attacking the fliers, ramming into them, biting at the hull with crushing jaw strength. One of them had bit into Jemmorah's flier and was trying to take her away.

"Jem!" T'shan yelled.

"I got her," I assured him.

Pulling at my dragon, we took to the air toward Jemmorah's flier as the dragon that held her tried to take her behind a dune of sand. It saw us and started flying faster.

"Hang in there, Jemmorah."

"Just hurry!" Her voice shook.

My dragon was an unruly one, but I hoped that it at least had enough army training with its original flier to know a few basic commands.

"*K'mhet!*" I yelled.

My dragon reacted immediately, opening its mouth and breathing fire on the dragon in front of us.

The Wingless wailed. It landed on the ground, dropping Jemmorah's flier and coming at us with vengeance. I lashed at it across the face, giving it a good reason to believe I wasn't to be messed with. The dragon snarled, then darted from us to join the others at the wall.

"Kent, Ashed, the Wingless is coming for the force field. I'm going to make sure Jemmorah's okay."

"No," Jemmorah objected. "I'm fine. My flier's shields took quite a bit of damage, but I'm all right, just a little shaken. Go for the Wingless. Uh, Your Grace," she added quickly.

"All right," I accepted reluctantly, but seeing her step out of the vehicle and begin examining it confirmed her statement. I guided my dragon to pursue the Wingless that had escaped us. It wasn't alone. The dragon that T'shan was handling had slipped past him, coming toward the wall with gusto.

We had all five dragons right back at the barrier, and it was obvious by the flickering of the force field that the shielding wasn't going to last much longer. Something had to be done soon or we might very well have to evacuate the city of Hashir.

"Sir, if they get past this barrier, it won't be much longer before they reach the next one and get to the city," Kent pointed out. He paused before saying, "Should we kill them?"

"No," I said, gritting my teeth. "We're not going to kill them."

But that meant I was going to have to come up with a plan, and fast. I cursed under my breath. Dragons were unpredictable, but the way they were acting was nothing short of crazed. Something must have set them off, but from what I could tell, there didn't seem to be anything disturbing them. At least nothing I could see from this side of the wall.

I made a mental note to have someone investigate later.

"How would you all like to become dragon fliers?" The idea was ludicrous, but it was the only one I had.

"Are you serious?" Ashed asked nervously. "I mean, are we even allowed?"

I chuckled. "As far as I'm concerned. Wait for my signal. I'll tell you all what to do. Jemmorah, can you fly?"

"Well enough, sir."

"Good. Hold your positions until I say otherwise."

Leading my dragon toward the five rampaging ones, I stood up, precariously balancing myself on my Wingless's back. We approached them as the Watchers' fliers stayed idle in the air around us. Clenching my jaw, I forced myself to concentrate. I couldn't fail here.

Somehow, that brought Jashi to mind, and it occurred to me that she might not have ever seen a dragon in person before. At least, not close up. I knew she showed apprehension when we talked about the subject, and while I knew dragons could be unpredictable, they were simply creatures that were misunderstood.

Maybe I should give her one as a gift.

The thought refocused me, and suddenly, failing wasn't even a possibility anymore. I was going to get Jashi's present to her. And that was that.

THE CALL OF DUTY

Pulling the Wingless around to fly alongside the wall, I shouted, "*K'mhet!*"

The dragon breathed flames on the creatures flocking the shield generator. They scattered momentarily, refocusing their attention on me with murderous looks. But that was exactly what I wanted.

"Kent, I want you to eject from your flier and land on the dragon closest to you. Now!"

The Watcher did as I asked, leaping out of his vehicle. He landed on the back of a Draconian, the dragon taken by surprise and instinctively taking off with Kent on its back.

I heard Kent yelling in a combination of awe and fear, but he had a good grip on the beast. He was going to be all right. In the meantime, I had to keep the other dragons' attention to make sure the shielding stayed intact. "*K'mhet!*" I shouted, pulling my Wingless to fly off to the side of the other dragons as it spewed fire at them. It got their attention, drawing them away from the shield generators.

As I took off, I said, "Kent, stay on your dragon. Reach for his ears and hold on. They're the most sensitive part of a Draconian, like the whiskers are on a Wingless."

"Use them like reins?"

"Exactly."

"I'll try, sir."

Kent sounded unsure, but I believed he could do it. I believed they all could.

Hearing a screech, I turned to see a Wingless drawing in its breath. I steered my dragon to the side to dodge a pillar of fire as it blazed through the air above my head.

"T'shan, get ready to claim your dragon," I said. "Start your flier again and go for the Wingless that's on my tail."

"Sir, I don't know if I can—"

"Just do it."

T'shan's flier leveled up with the dragon that pursued me. T'shan jumped from out of his flier, falling shakily on the Wingless, much to the dragon's chagrin. It snarled and snapped, but its assailant was safe from its reach and had reached around its face to snatch two whiskers in his hands, claiming control of the Wingless's flight direction. T'shan turned the dragon away from me and back toward the mountains.

"Wooooooohooo!" T'shan's yelling was nearly loud enough to burst eardrums.

"You're not leaving me out," Jemmorah said, and I turned to see her flier was already in pursuit of the remaining Wingless that was chasing me, breaking off its pursuit of me to run like its life depended on it. But the girl was determined, her flier matching the dragon's speed in moments. Soon, she jumped from the vehicle, grasping the dragon's form and seizing its whiskers like she'd done it her whole life.

"Yaaahooo!" she shrilled as she forced it back toward the mountains.

Two dragons left, both of them Draconians.

"You're up, Ashed," I said.

"I don't know about this, Your Grace. I'm not as experienced as the others."

"Listen, Ashed," I started, swerving as another burst of flames burned the air to my left. "You need to understand two things about dragons—they can smell fear, and they love hesitation. Just do what you need to do, and do it with authority. Take this dragon. Now."

I heard him take a deep breath from over the interlink.

Another pillar of flames was cut short as Ashed landed on the dragon's back. It wailed, bucked, and screamed, but Ashed stayed firmly where he was. Taking hold of the Draconian's ears, he struggled against it until it was heading back toward the mountain.

I smiled to myself, imagining the look on the face of the second-in-command when the rookie interns he sent to come with me came back with dragons they'd tamed themselves. That would teach him a thing or two. Anyone complaining that the dragons were impossible to manage without torture or killing would have a hard time proving their point now, not when a bunch of college students just showed them up.

The lone Draconian still pursuing me growled in frustration. It soared in speed, chasing my dragon's tail hard. It snapped at the air, trying to take a bite out of my Wingless's hide. To say the dragon was angered would have been an understatement.

As it drew a breath, I tugged on my Wingless's whiskers. The dragon swooped downward just as an arc of lightning shot from the Draconian's mouth, the dragon flying right over my head as it overcame us in speed.

Damn. An Elemental.

I should have noticed its scales were bright yellow in color, not like the more muted tones of green, gray, and red that the other dragons were. And it hadn't tried breathing fire when the others had. All tell-tale signs of an Elemental.

I smirked. It would be perfect for Jashi.

Taking out my whip, I lashed at the neon yellow dragon as it passed through the air above me. Nudging my dragon to follow, I made sure to stay behind it to avoid any more attacks.

A jerk almost knocked me off my dragon's back.

My dragon was trying to throw me, the sneaky bastard. It had waited for the perfect time to rebel again. It lurched and buckled, screeching loud enough to pierce eardrums.

I could see why the original rider had trouble with it. Being in the midst of battle, the dragon probably took advantage of every opportunity it had to toss the poor guy. It was a wonder he lasted as long as he did.

I changed strategies. I didn't have time to have to deal with this Elemental dragon and the Wingless I was riding at the same time. Taking the whiskers that were in my hand, I reached down, pressing my body to the dragon's back as I, with some difficulty, was able to fasten one to my ankle on one side, then the other. It wouldn't be able to get rid of me without losing one of its whiskers in the process.

The Elemental dragon was circling, coming around to face us again, its mouth open and ready to fire on us.

I was tempted to set my whip to a higher setting to force my Wingless in line. But I shook the idea off almost as soon as it came. I did the opposite instead, setting the whip to the lowest setting possible and deciding to kill two birds with one stone. I flicked the device and watched as it wrapped around the neck of my dragon, giving me sort of reins. Pulling it taut, I forced the dragon to fly higher, feeling the beast's resistance strain against my hold, but I kept my grip. We flew over the Elemental as another arc of lightning blazed through the air below us.

"Hyah!" I yelled, pulling the whip so that the Wingless curved in the air and sent us back down, this time directly on top of the Elemental.

Both of these dragons were going to learn who their master was.

I directed my dragon to continue his downward spiral toward the Elemental.

"Sir, what are you doing?" came T'shan's voice. "Aren't you coming with us?"

"Yeah, just a minute."

There was a jerk as the two beasts crashed into each other, my Wingless on top. With the Elemental's flight pattern interrupted, we all went down. Pressure in my stomach rose up to my throat as we free fell. The Dragon Watchers screamed something in my ear, but I couldn't tell what they were saying. I didn't have time to find out. I pulled my whip to the right, toward a mound of dunes to the east.

The Wingless followed the motion, sending us crashing into an explosion of sand. My body jerked as gritty grains filled my mouth, along with the taste of metal. I bit tongue in the landing, but that seemed to be the worst of it. I untied the Wingless's whiskers from my ankles and hurried to climb off of it, sliding off the Elemental as I went. The two monsters were on top of each other, and the Elemental wasn't about to go anywhere with that heavy Wingless on its back. And I figured my dragon had the wind knocked out of it and wouldn't be flying anywhere, at least not for the time being.

"I need someone to come back with a flier and a towing device for me. I have two slightly injured dragons. They're all right. They'll just need some help making it back to the Watch Tower."

"As you wish, Your Grace," T'shan answered.

WARTIME

My dreams were filled with images of holding Jashi in my arms, only to have her ripped away by a dragon that took her out the window to hide her away. I spent the rest of my dreams searching fervently for her, ordering a search party to find her by any means necessary.

I woke up in a cold sweat, the crippling fear of never finding her clinging to me.

Groggily, I reached for my eWatch. But there was no update from Rand about her. Clenching my jaw, I told myself that my brother was doing all he could and that I should focus my efforts on the war, as I promised.

Despite that, I still held the eWatch in my hand a few moments more, half hoping a message would come in any minute. Last Rand talked to me, it sounded like she was flying, which was why we couldn't track her yet. Wherever she went, she must have landed by now, right?

I had to force my fists to unclench, the images from my dreams still flashing through my mind.

If those Zendaalans so much as laid a hand on her…

A call came through as I entertained brutal thoughts of what I would do to any Zendaalan who gave me just cause. I nearly groaned when I saw it wasn't Rand.

"Hello?" I said as Khes's face appeared in front of me.

"Your Majesty, I have urgent news. One of our hidden bases in the recently claimed territory has been raided."

My stomach twisted. The information leak had produced its first fruits. How would I handle it without getting Jashi in trouble?

Running a hand through my hair, I said, "What is their current status?"

"They're still under attack. We've sent support, but their prospects don't look good. The attack took us completely by surprise. Especially with Rand away."

I nodded. "I'm leaving to join you now. In the meantime, tell all of the soldiers at the other secret bases in the new Vishra region to evacuate the bases and support the ones under attack."

His eyes widened. "But that would leave the region vulnerable to being retaken, sir."

"I know that," I snapped, then forced myself to continue in a calmer voice. "The bases are vulnerable anyway."

Narrowing his eyes, Khes opened his mouth to say something, but I cut him off. "I'll explain more when I get there. Meet me at Base 0189."

He shrugged, still eying me doubtfully, but conceded, "Yes, sir."

With that, I hung up and breathed out, wondering exactly what explanation I would give.

And once again, my thoughts drifted to ways I would deal with Sokir as soon as Jashi was found. I eventually arrived at imprisonment after a long speculation at other, less legal—but oh, so satisfying—methods of handling the situation.

In any case, every moment I spent here at the Tower was another moment that could have been spent toward defending my armies, finding Jashi, or planning Sokir's arrest. If I had shown up to meet the army yesterday, could the loss of life at the secret bases been avoided?

I growled. There wasn't enough of me—or anyone else on my side, for that matter—to go around. I had five more dragons to add to the ranks, which would be invaluable to our cause, but was it worth the precious time lost?

There was no answer to that. But I did know what I was going to do.

There was one thing I wanted done here at the Watch Tower before I left. I called up Arusi. It didn't take long before her holographic image appeared before me. "Sir? I thought you were at the border already."

"Change of plans. Look, I don't have much time to explain, but I need you to send your team of private investigators out here."

"What for?"

I scratched my chin. "You hear about the dragons causing trouble at the boundaries?"

"Yes, of course."

The dragons had become crazed, determined. Almost beyond control. There had to have been something on the other end of that field to make them lose it like that, something they desperately had to get to.

"I need them to check out the area just inside the boundary."

"Okay...for what?"

A good question. I shook my head. "Anything strange. And report back."

"All right, then."

Hanging up with her, I took a quick shower and got dressed to leave, putting on the usual suit that I wore around the public. I somewhat missed the Dragon Watch suit I wore yesterday, when I got to be directly involved in the action rather than just sit around and direct it. But that didn't matter nearly as much as the safety of my people, so the thought was fleeting.

As I opened the door to leave, T'shan stood there. His bright orange eyes were wide with anxiety, his mouth gaping like a fish out of water.

I raised an eyebrow at him, aware that the action would only make him more nervous but not having the luxury to be pleasant with anybody right now. "Whatever this is about, be quick."

He slammed his mouth shut, then gave a short, but deep bow. "Your Majesty. I want to learn more about dragon flying. The way you do it." He rose from his bow, his bright orange eyes intense. "You were right yesterday—the only form anyone ever learns is the ZST. I'll never have the opportunity to learn if I stay here." T'shan bowed again. "I beg you to let me learn from you. Or someone like you, Your Majesty."

The boy spoke so quickly, I didn't really grasp what he was trying to say at first, or perhaps I was too distracted to pay much attention. "That isn't possible."

I moved around T'shan, thinking that he'd given up, but he moved in front of me. "You come here," he said, "complaining that no one knows how to manage a dragon like you do, then refuse to train me. Yesterday wasn't nearly enough to actually learn anything. You'll never get what you want unless you have someone else to train others. Otherwise, Watch Towers like this one and others will always use excessive force to restrain the dragons."

"I see."

T'shan didn't waver from my stare. "Fifty-four dragons were killed by this Tower this year alone. The people who are in control don't know what they're doing. It's not right for you to complain about the way things are done if you don't do what it takes to change it."

T'shan was right.

"You really want to learn how to fly a dragon?"

He nodded firmly. "My parents sent me here to learn to be the very best of my class. I'm willing to do whatever it takes."

"I can't afford to waste time staying here, I'm..." I looked around before I continued in a lower voice. "I'm going to the border. Unofficially." T'shan nodded to affirm he got the message. "I'm taking the dragons with me. If you're really determined to learn from me right now, come with me. After the war, I'll keep you on as a sort of protege. What do you say?"

T'shan hesitated. "But I'm still in school."

I shrugged. "Consider yourself drafted."

A grin spread across his face. "You won't regret it, sir."

I already was. If the Courts weren't breathing down my neck enough already, wait until they caught wind of this. But it didn't matter. T'shan was right. I needed to bring on someone I could trust to handle the managing of the dragons. He may have been young, but he and his friends had proven to be more than capable.

As a matter of fact...

"Do you think you could convince your friends to come with us?"

APPRENTICES

The four new dragon fliers gawked as we stepped into the corridor of the air-fortress base 0189. Their awe and amazement reminded me of my first time coming here, fighting to reinforce my authority in such an intimidating space.

Vaulted ceilings rose a couple dozen feet high. Lines and lines of fighter jets gleamed under the cool lighting, fully armored men directing them to be moved from one end of the fortress to the other, many fliers in the process of being deployed.

Khes approached us, frowning as he laid eyes on my four guests. They shuffled awkwardly as he neared, probably startled by the way the scar on his eye looked when he furrowed his brow.

"I'll explain later," I told him. "For the moment, have someone take them somewhere they can use as their rooms so they can leave their things."

Khes shrugged, flagging some soldier down and repeating my instruction to him.

"I'll be right with you," I told them.

"Yes, sir," Jemmorah said dutifully.

"Follow me," the soldier told them.

They obeyed, walking around like awe-struck zombies—almost like when I took Jashi to the mall.

I shook my head. Why did everything remind me of Jashi?

"Should we talk in my office?" Khes asked, refocusing my attention to the issues at hand. I nodded. We both went up the steps to the catwalk, going through the door to his room.

He closed the door behind us. "If you don't mind my asking," he started, which meant he was going to speak his mind, whether I minded or not. "What the hell is going on here? When I told you the secret base was raided, you didn't look the least bit surprised. And who're these four teenagers you've brought up? This is a place of war, not a high school field trip!"

I sat at one of the chairs in front of Khes's desk. "Are you done?"

He huffed as he sat down in front of me. "Yes."

I paused, deciding on the vaguest explanation I had planned, speaking in a low voice. "There's been a leak. A big one."

Khes's eyes widened, then he sighed, leaning back into his chair and covering his face. "Great Spirits...how big a leak?"

"Big. That's all you need to know." I stopped him with a hand as he opened his mouth to object. "And the kids are with me. I have a plan to handle the Omanians fronting the attack, as well as how to prepare for what they plan to do with the information they gained from the leak."

Khes frowned as I explained my idea to him, interrupting several times to ask a question before he finally nodded in acceptance. He put up his hands in surrender. "If you're going to keep the source of this leak to yourself, will you at least let me know if it's patched up yet? Or can we expect even more leaks from this mysterious source?"

That was a good question. But the way Jashi just disappeared, I didn't think she was still in contact with the Zendaalans controlling her. "As far as I know, it is."

"'As far as you know'?" My army general shrugged. "If that's good enough for you, it's good enough for me. This plan of yours might work a great deal better if I had an idea what it is you're trying to keep secret. We've seen a lot together, sir. And I don't see why I would be any less loyal to you now than I have before."

It was only after he finished speaking that I realized his eyes were touched with a degree of hurt, and it occurred to me that I never considered the possibility that any of my closest men would actually be hurt if they thought I couldn't trust them.

The situation with Jashi made me feel incredibly, frustratingly, and infuriatingly helpless—an emotion I was never comfortable with. Even with the best of my abilities to protect Jashi, she still slipped away from my grip.... It made me want to shield her even more. I felt like I'd already let enough happen to her as it was, not preventing her from getting caught up with those Zendaalans in the first place. The last thing I was going to do was let someone blame her for something I should have prevented from the start.

"Jashi was being threatened into giving up the information to agents of Zendaal."

Khes drew a sharp breath. "How long has this been going on?"

"Probably as soon as we met the second time. The only other person I told about it was Rand. Of course, I couldn't tell her that I knew or..."

"You'd have to tell her the real reason she's at the palace."

I nodded.

Khes breathed out, leaning back into his seat again. "Don't you think she ought to know by now?"

Throwing up my hands, I said, "Well, now, of course. But it was complicated. She didn't trust me not to execute her for running away the first time I met her, not to mention all the times she'd run away since. If I told her everything at once, I may as well have kissed her goodbye, and the Zendaalans would have gotten to her for sure! You know she had a doctor's appointment the week after I arranged our marriage? She's been this close"— I held my thumb and index finger within a hair of each other—"to getting captured by the people waiting to get their hands on her since the day we met."

Khes cackled. "You have quite the lady there, Your Grace. I don't think I've ever seen you this riled up. You must love this girl, because if I didn't know any better, I'd say you were more afraid of Jashi than you are of taming the wildest, fiercest dragon out there."

There was a certain truth to his words. Taming a dragon, I knew how to do. But getting Jashi to listen to me...that was another beast altogether.

THE FOUR DRAGON Watchers assembled themselves into a line and stood at attention as I entered the room.

"At ease," I assured them, wondering how I could get them to relax around me. It would be improper for them to act casually, but surely there was an alternative to this "yes sir" response. "You'll accompany me as I go on various tasks with my dragons. From my experience, the only way to learn is through practice, so that's exactly what you'll have. You'll each be assigned a dragon..."

Their eyes lit up simultaneously.

"Are you serious?" T'shan asked.

"But not today."

As quickly as the light came into their eyes, it disappeared.

"There are extenuating circumstances that I have to handle, which means your training will have to wait." They deflated at that, but it couldn't be helped. This battle took top priority. "However," I added. "When this battle is over, I'll personally see to your training sessions. By the time my campaign here is over, you'll be as good as my best dragon fliers here."

Kent raised his hand.

I inwardly sighed. There had to be a way to get these kids to loosen up. I wished Rand was here; he was much better at getting people to open up than I was.

"This isn't a classroom."

He chuckled nervously and lowered his hand. "Can we pick the dragons we tamed?"

"Absolutely not."

T'shan frowned. I understood his excitement, but I couldn't risk them all getting themselves killed riding unruly dragons. I knew that

that sort of thing could get ugly fast. "They're untrained and have never had riders before. Your little joyride from before was a one-time thing. From now on, you'll be using fairly tame dragons, but don't forget what I said earlier. Just because they're relatively calmer doesn't mean they aren't clever creatures, especially when you're a new flier."

Jemmorah asked, "So what do we do in the meantime?"

"Someone will show you where you're allowed and where you're not. There's a recreational room you have access to, as well as a cafeteria if you get hungry."

T'shan's bright eyes were like balls of eager fire. "Thank you for this amazing opportunity, sir. We won't let you down."

Jemmorah nodded in agreement. "Taming and riding a dragon was the most thrilling experience I've had in my life."

"I didn't even know dragon taming like that was possible," Kent added. "I mean, I'd heard of it, especially when the debates about it on the HoloScreen all the time. But to find out the that the Faresh himself knows how to do it?"

"We are truly honored, sir," Ashed said.

A wave of gratitude washed over me, and I smiled, something I wasn't used to doing in public. My tinted glasses helped me create a barrier between me and the world that I'd simply gotten used to.

Composing myself, I replied, "You're welcome," before leaving the room.

Khes's voice came on my communicator. "Your Majesty, we're ready to ship out."

"Understood. I'm on my way."

My shoulders squared, I made my way to where my not-so-agreeable dragon waited for me. The time for niceties was over. It was time for war.

My eWatch buzzed. Rand had sent a message, and with three words, nothing else existed anymore.

We found Jashi.

Before I could compose a response, he had sent a second that crushed whatever flicker of hope the first ignited.

But she's at the one place on Hemorah we can't reach her.
   Ambush

My presence on the battlefield made a lot of people nervous. It wasn't that a Faresh couldn't be on the battlefield. They just never were. Well, 'never' wasn't exactly accurate, but the only documents of it ever happening, like the inspiration for most of the things I did, were ancient. I used that to my advantage. When the men knew that Rand or I were watching, they made a point to be on their best performance.

My dragon was clad with armor, the latest in dragon-riding technology. Black plating lined its inky back, making it look like a metallic black snake curled up on a hill. The saddle boasted a protective dome that shielded the rider from any gunfire, wrapping me in a gleaming shell of hard plastic and glowing panels that kept me in contact with the army, a display of their positions represented by an array of red lights on a grid of the battle ground in front of me.

But I wasn't flying yet. I was waiting. We all were. The red lights on my grid all held their positions as planned, surrounding what was supposed to be a top secret army base. On this side of the Dharia mountains, a forest teemed with life—the canopy of trees leaving a pattern of leaves on the forest floor where the light broke through. Cloaked in a special camouflaging technology, the army base didn't seem to interrupt the wildlife in the slightest, but the illusion was ruined by the fighter jets that took off from seemingly nowhere as they engaged the Omanian airships firing down on them. I could see the whole battle playing out from where I was stationed on an upward slope. The Omanian airships swarmed the air like angered bees, closing in on the base every second. The angled K'sundii fighter jets took to the skies to stave them off, but the fat, rounded Omanian airships severely outnumbered them.

I had to let out fiery breaths of air several times from within the protective dome atop my dragon to avoid blowing myself up.

I kept losing focus on the battle itself. My thoughts kept drifting back to Jashi.

Sokir, my own brother, put Jashi into this situation. It was because of him that she exiled herself and went to the one country on the planet I couldn't reach her. And the Omanians were using the information she'd been forced to steal to undertake what they believed to be the perfect sneak attack.

Well, unfortunately for the Omanians, Sokir, and the whole damn lot of Zendaalans, Jashi was just as clever as she was beautiful. Her quick thinking had provided me the key I needed to face this attack.

Now if only I could out-think that quick-witted mind of hers enough to tell her.

Rand was alerted as soon as Jashi's tracking device came back online—in Omani. Anyone I would send might put Jashi in more jeopardy, especially if she tried running from them, as she always did. Though she drove me crazy every time she escaped, I had to admit she thought her plan through to the letter. She'd eluded me despite the tracking device in her hair comb.

I sighed, fire flaring from my nostrils. She'd risked so much to try to save me and my men. I would prove to her that she was the reason behind our victory, not our downfall. I would make sure of it.

This was not going to be a day of defeat for K'sundi.

"We're awaiting your word, sir," came Khes's voice over the communicator.

"Hold position," I assured him. It wasn't time yet.

The battle raged on, the Omanians closing in and forming a tight circle around the army base. The timing would have to be perfect. If I let them get too close, they would start dropping bombs on the forest floor and it would be over. But making my men start too soon might ruin our chances.

As the number of K'sundii fighter jets continued to dwindle, I had to clench my fists to control my emotions. Jets were dropping from the sky like flies, landing in a wreckage of dented metal and broken glass. Fighting the urge to give the cue to the general, I had to remind myself that though those men were dead, many more would die if we did this wrong.

I counted the number of fighter jets left. It still wasn't time. There weren't enough Omanian airships on the field yet—they still had backup.

As if confirming my thoughts, another wave of airships came from behind the treetops, plenteous as the first. As they closed in on the first wave, I said, "Now, commander! Retreat!"

"Roger that."

The K'sundii air jets abandoned the invisible army base, leaving their defensive positions in the air and engaging in escape maneuvers to weave through the air fleet that surrounded them. The Omanian airships tried to block off their exodus, but being faster and smaller, the air jets were able to evade their attempts.

My dragon stretched its neck upward, straining as it tried to roar, stamping its feet impatiently. The noise-absorbing muzzle on its mouth swallowed what surely would have been a bellowing roar. Dragons loved the heat of battle. Perhaps forgetting its hatred for me at the moment, it whiffed hungrily at the air, itching to join the ranks in the sky.

I ached to go as well. But as I had to do for myself, I pulled the reins that now bridled the dragon, connecting to the inside of my dome to give me control of the beast, calming it down.

"Not yet, boy," I said, more to myself than to the dragon.

Realizing that I had nothing to call the dragon by, I wondered what its name was.

While we both waited for our chance to join the battle, I pulled up the dragon's file on my eWatch, finding that there was little more information than I already knew—just that it was a Wingless, was known for rebellious behavior, and that it had injured its previous rider. It had no name. Raising an eyebrow at one particular line of text, I added, "Sorry. I meant 'girl,' I suppose."

I looked up at the sky. It still wasn't time. The Omanians were being cocky, circling their newly claimed base like a bunch of vultures, a few scattered members of their fleets lazily pursuing my fighter jets. They were tomcats toying with a couple of mice.

Fine. Let them think that. "Well, I guess we don't have anything to do yet, so why don't I come up with a name for you? Calling you 'dragon' all day doesn't suit me much."

The dragon, if she cared, didn't show it as she curled her head under her arm, apparently disappointed that she couldn't join the fight yet.

I stroked at my beard in thought. She was definitely free-spirited, if somewhat unruly. But what dragon wasn't? Still, behind the look of apathy toward anything that didn't excite her, I felt like there was a gleam of intelligence that shone through, which was the reason she surprised her first rider and myself the other day, pretending to be submissive and accepting while we were flying when all along she was awaiting her opportunity to act out.

"How does Huntress sound?"

The dragon rose her head from under her arm, tilting her head toward me, almost like she understood me and liked the name. Somehow, she seemed almost...calmer, like her muscles had relaxed under me as soon as I'd said it.

"Huntress suits you. Now if only I could teach you to hunt the enemy, not your rider."

Huntress's gaze snapped up to the sky, and I followed her stare. The Omanians had finished gloating and were heading straight toward us.

"Okay, Khes. It's time. Don't hold back."

"Yes, sir."

I flicked my reins, and Huntress eagerly leaped into the air. Other dragon riders left their stationary positions, along with the fighter jets we'd hidden throughout the forest. The K'sundii jets that were once being chased swiveled around to fire on their pursuers, now backed by the jets and dragons. From the sides, more jets and dragons rose from under the cover of the trees, leaving the Omanian airships completely surrounded.

I turned off the muffle on Huntress's mouthpiece, letting me catch the end of a vicious roar of excitement. Around us, other riders did the same, the air vibrating with the collective shrieks of dragons and the blaze of gunfire.

The Omanians broke off from their pursuit, engaging in a retreat that looked clumsy and confused, having to break off from their high speeds and throw themselves into reverse, a fact we'd anticipated and would be using to our advantage.

"Sir, we're initiating the Delta position," the general said on my communicator.

"Do it."

Mixed groups of four, five, and six started forming among our ranks, mixed with dragons and fighter jets alike. A group of three jets and a dragon joined me. It was a practiced strategy, so no communication was necessary. The small groups engaged the Omanians at various positions, nudging them with gunfire and dragon fire to make them break off from their retreat formation.

My group closed in on a couple of Omanian airships, laser fire raining down from the back ports on the ships. Huntress ducked and dodged on her own, not needing encouragement to do what was already in her to do. I was surprised how little effort I had to put into guiding her. It seemed she finally decided to do as she was told. Then again, I'd been fooled by her before. I just hoped she would behave well enough to finish this battle.

"*K'mhet!*" I yelled, and she breathed a pillar of flames on an airship with gusto, the heat palpable even from within my dome. Guiding her around the first ship, I directed her toward a second.

"*K'mhet!*"

More flames licked up the metal plating of the airships, warping the metal wherever the fire touched. The fighter jets fired at the weakened metal, sending the airships hurtling toward the ground.

The battle significantly changed in tone. The other Omanian airships were either scattering, broken off from their group by the small groups of K'sundii, or going down. Fire painted the heavens red as airships burned and dragons blew flames. The enemy was more concerned with getting away than fighting back, and with good reason. Our jets fired with enthusiasm, breaking off Omanians into smaller, more easily taken groups, shooting them down and going back for more.

I led the front of the battle, slowly driving a wedge between the Omanian airships. Soon, the enemy was in full retreat, not even bothering to try firing back. They were too busy focusing on putting as much power toward their retreat as possible.

"They're heading back toward the border, Your Grace," Khes said. "The other hidden bases are reporting similar results. Do you want our men to give chase?"

I chuckled, the noise sounding dark even to my own ears. The happiness I felt was bitterly mingled with anger. This victory was going to be dedicated to Jashi, and I wanted to end the day on a high note. I wasn't sure how far we could get, but I had a good feeling about this. The Great Spirits were on my side, and I could feel it. "Tell the men that they are to keep going and not to stop until something stops them. This is a day of victory, of conquest for K'sundi, and I want it to go down in history texts."

WORKING AT A DINER AGAIN

Jashi Anyua, Faresha of K'sundi
A few weeks later...

The setting sun poured light through the dirty windows of the restaurant, but not even its golden hues could give the place lighting that made it look flattering. The dirt and grime seemed cemented to the floor in various places, so stuck not even vigorous scrubbing with my mop could remove them. But as the boss had insisted plenty of times, he cared more about speed than efficiency, so the specks of crud would stay where they were, mocking me every time I passed my mop over them.

The bulbs in the few lighting fixtures in the room were spotted with some kind of grimy black substance on the inside, a couple of them blinking in and out throughout the day. The restaurant smelled like a vague mix of bleach and grease, but bleach did nothing to deter the roaches I saw scuttling across the floor. The boss instructed me to kill them when possible and dispose of the bodies outside. It couldn't be said that the boss didn't care about the fly problem, since he proceeded to swat them with his flyswatter every time he saw one, leaving the splattered remains right there on the counter, wall, or wherever he killed them. No amount of "cleaning" could make the place feel clean, but I worked until it resembled something close to it.

Just as I was almost finished, Mr. Vitya barked something at me in Omanian from outside the restaurant. I didn't understand any of it. "Janna" was the only word I understood, as it was the name I told him was mine. He made a lot of angry gestures, pointing to the clock and acting exasperated, so I assumed it to be the same complaint as yesterday.

Clean faster.

Stifling a sigh, I cradled the handle to my mop and put my hands together in an apologetic gesture, even giving a slight bow to get my point across. "I'm sorry, sir. I'll do better next time."

Mr. Vitya sighed, muttering to himself as he reached into his pocket and counted out my pay for the day.

I finished up the rest of the floor, threw out the water from the mop bucket, and put my cleaning materials in the janitor's closet. Then I waited as Mr. Vitya finished counting up my pay.

He dropped a few Jeels—the standard currency in Omani—in my hand and some change. The pocket change he handed me was well below the minimum wage here, but despite the language barrier, Mr. Vitya and I had an understanding. I was here illegally and needed money, and he wanted cheap labor to keep his dingy little restaurant running.

Thankfully, the other person I cleaned for paid much better, though Mrs. Maresh was much more demanding, expecting cleaning as well as cooking and tending to her two boys.

Before I walked away, Mr. Vitya stuck a thick finger in my face, speaking slow and broken K'sundii. "You need learn Omanian, *hasra*."

"Yes, sir," I replied, moving around him and biting back the other comments that came to mind, afraid he might understand them. After all, I didn't know what *hasra* meant, but as many times I'd seen him say it with a sour look on his face, I'd pretty much guessed.

I crossed the street, hugging my jacket closer to my body as the wind whipped at me. The nights weren't nearly as cold as they were in the K'sundi deserts, but fall was approaching quickly, and with it a brisker cold in the wind. I hoped it would stay warm a little longer. I couldn't even think about trying to pay a heating bill.

I needed to pick up a few groceries now while I was near one of the cheaper stores in the city. A curse fell from my lips as the bus lowered from the sky and paused at the stop. If I missed it, I'd be walking. Again. Or I'd have to wait for the next bus, whenever that would be. But I desperately needed eggs and something for dinner tonight.

I walked into the convenience store that was barely a block from where I stood.

"Hello, Janna," said the man at the corner.

I smiled at Kravya, a younger man with light bronze skin and wispy curls in his hair. He had been kind to me since I arrived in Omani. And helpful, as it turned out he spoke K'sundii pretty well. "Hey, Krav."

"We have a sale going on right now. Two yogurts, price of one." He pointed to a sign that I assumed stated as much in Omanian.

I considered the deal. So far, I'd avoided buying anything other than absolute necessities to save money, but I supposed I could afford myself a guilty pleasure if it came at a low price. And if I closed my eyes, I could pretend it was ice cream instead.

"Thanks, I'll take a look."

"Right over there," he said, pointing and smiling.

I picked up two yogurts, then collected the other few items I would need—eggs, a few cans of soup for dinner today and tomorrow, and a small carton of milk. As I came back to the counter, I found Kravya engaged with the cheap HoloScreen he was watching beside the counter. He didn't even notice me approach until I cleared my throat.

"I'm sorry," he said, returning his attention to me and scanning the products I'd brought to him. "I was watching the news. About the war."

"Oh?" I said, my attention suddenly on the screen, guilt twisting my gut. I tried following the news as best I could, but it proved difficult without understanding Omanian. I had no idea how Kahmel was doing or whether my traitorous actions had damaged his campaign.

Kravya nodded grimly. "It doesn't look good. They say K'sundii troops are advancing quickly. Much too quickly." He made a face of disgust. "This new leader, he is telling his troops to keep conquering, conquering. Where will they end? Do they want all of Omani?"

I tried to contain my enthusiasm. I couldn't look like I was on my country's side. Not here. But this was the first I'd heard of anything to do with K'sundi since I'd came to Omani.

Kahmel and his men were okay?

"Wow," I said, accepting my items as Kravya handed them back to me in a bag, and I handed him the money. "He certainly is bold, the newest Faresh of K'sundi."

Kravya shook his head, frowning. "I hate him." He gave me my change, then pointed to the HoloScreen, an angry-looking Omanian speaking behind a podium. "He is saying that this Faresh, Kahmel of Omah, he is telling us his terms, *his* terms! As if we are to surrender after we have *already* offered surrender before this big fuss he make over nothing! Now he want to discuss terms!" Kravya huffed. "I say no. We lose, we lose. But with dignity, understand?"

I nodded in agreement, trying to look as concerned as he was while I inwardly rejoiced. "I have to go now. Thanks for telling me about the yogurt."

"Thank you for the interesting conversation."

With a smile, I turned away and walked out the door, groaning inwardly as I remembered that I'd have to wait for another bus to pass. While I waited, I tried to calculate how long it would take before I could afford a new eWatch so I could keep up with the news by logging into K'sundii news websites. But with the cold coming, I would have to save up for a heater instead. As far as clothes went, I was fine with what I brought with me, so I wouldn't have to worry about that. But there was also rent.

My hand went up to the hair clip I still wore every day. I knew it would be worth a pretty penny, but every time I thought about selling it, I couldn't bring myself to do it. I unclipped the hair pin, examining it. It was good quality, for certain. The kinds I usually bought had rhinestones that popped out after a few weeks. But this was the real thing—the tan gems that formed the desert flower shape twinkled bright in any kind of light, the surrounding white stones looking like stars encased in silver. I polished it every day, and the silver looked impeccable because of it. My gut twisted at the sight of it, and my eyes started to sting.

I put it back in my hair. I wouldn't be selling it anytime soon.

Pushing those thoughts of the past out of my mind, I glanced back at the restaurant as Mr. Vitya started talking with two men outside the door, wondering if he would be willing to let me work a few extra hours for a while so I could afford both an eWatch and a heater. I could make it work, so long as Mrs. Maresh was willing to—

Wait.

Those men were in suits.

Zendaalan men. And they were showing Mr. Vitya a HoloPhoto. Of me.

His eyes made contact with mine, and I started running.

"Hey, stop!" I heard one of the men calling behind me.

Yeah, like I was going to do that.

Instead, I ran toward the downtown area. Their footsteps didn't sound too far, and I knew they would catch up if I didn't do something. Turning down a smaller street, I tried to keep myself oriented so I wouldn't get lost.

I pulled out the lighter Kahmel gave me.

Seeing a trash bin on the side of the street, I turned, picked it up, and threw it at them. As discreetly as I could, I lit the lighter, pulled the flame from the little device, and launched it at the trash can, watching it go up in flames as soon as I did. Then I bolted as fast as I could and smirked as I arrived exactly where I'd intended.

The marketplace of this city was always bustling with activity, vendors and buyers alike filling the streets, shouting out prices and making offers. Ducking low, I pushed between the people, stealing a glance backward to see where the Zendaalan men were. As I'd hoped, they were scanning over the crowd in complete confusion and patting out the little flames that had caught on parts of their clothes.

I continued down the street, weaving through the crowd. There were branching roads to this market, so I turned down a road and then looked back toward the Zendaalans, watching as they continued down the wrong path.

My heart rate finally slowed, and I turned down the street and found a bus stop that would take me home. Thankfully, the bus didn't take long to arrive.

I'd forgotten about the eggs in my bag until I returned to my apartment and found the mess in the plastic bag. It looked like a yellow blood bath in there.

But that was the least of my worries.

This wasn't the first time I had to escape Zendaalans on my tail. The first week in Omani, I stayed in a hotel with the money I'd brought with me for the journey so I could look for a place to stay. I had no choice but to use my actual ID to stay there, which was probably how they found me so quickly. Fortunately, I had already found a place by then, and after I escaped them, I moved in to my current living space. I knew it was only a matter of time before they found me again. I certainly stood out around here—a K'sundii foreigner who didn't speak a word of the language. But what could I do about it? I couldn't go back to Mr. Vitya, that was for sure. But just because they knew about that job didn't mean they knew about Mrs. Maresh across town, or that they knew where I lived. It took giving the landlord here some extra Ramaks along with the cash for the first few months' rent, but he accepted letting me stay without knowing more than the name I gave him.

And I never told Mr. Vitya where I lived since he paid me in cash after each shift.

Hopefully, I would be safe staying here a little longer, and so long as I asked Mrs. Maresh if I could work extra hours, I could still pay the rent. She was a *hasra*, but she paid well and always wanted extra help around the house. Plus, she spoke some K'sundii.

Taking a rag and wiping down the rest of my groceries, I opened one of the yogurt cups, took out a spoon, and sat on the couch, feeling the dirty cushion dip low under my weight. Then I shoveled a big scoop in my mouth, telling myself it was ice cream.

I almost fooled myself into believing it was.

It had been two days since my run-in with the Zendaalan agents. Since then, Mrs. Maresh had kindly taken me on for more hours, but she used that to call me in for extra hours that I wouldn't be paid for. Like today.

Wiping the sleep from my eyes, I put the caller on mute so I could finish my cereal while she barked on the other end. She needed me to come a few hours earlier than usual today and I was late.

After I finished downing the milk, I took the caller off mute. "Yes, Mrs. Maresh, I'm coming right away."

"Good! And I want the house spotless by the time I get back, understood?"

"Yes, Mrs. Maresh." I threw the bowl into the sink and started pulling my shoes on. By her tone, you would think the school calling and saying her son was sick was my fault somehow. However, she did pay for the crude eWatch that could do little more than receive calls. It had no connection to the Internet, though. Technology only advanced for those who could afford it.

"And you are to make sure my son is taken care of. Do anything he asks for. Make him something to eat."

"Yes, Mrs. Maresh."

"And be quick about it! Don't arrive late like you did yesterday!"

Once again, I wished I had a motorcycle so I wouldn't have to depend on the bus. Frowning, I paused at something that was playing on the HoloScreen. I recognized Kahmel's name on the news announcement, and that of the president of Omani. But I couldn't understand what was going on. I knew it was a big deal because it looked like the same thing I saw all the newspapers talking about. But now that I was avoiding the neighborhood around Mr. Vitya's restaurant, I didn't have Kravya to keep me up to date with what was going on.

"Are you even listening?" Mrs. Maresh's shrill voice demanded.

"I'm sorry. Yes, I am. I was just looking at the news. Do you know what's going on with the Faresh of K'sundi? I've been seeing him all over the place lately."

She sighed exasperatedly, but I couldn't tell if it was at me or the political situation. "It's about Faresh Kahmel of Omah's terms to our country. Our ridiculous president is talking about agreeing to his terms. If you spoke Omanian, you would not need me to explain! This is why you should learn!"

I supposed I wasn't going to get anymore explanations out of her. "Yes, Mrs. Maresh."

"By the way, when you arrive at my house, call me every once and a while and tell me how Rhis is doing."

Throwing on my jacket and grabbing some money for the bus, I started for the door. "Yes, Mrs. Mar—"

My door flung open, the lock flying across the room as two men barged in. One grabbed me, keeping me in a lock hold as the other snatched my eWatch from off my wrist and threw it to the ground, grinding the device underneath his foot, silencing Mrs. Maresh's questioning voice on the other end.

"We've gone through a lot of trouble to find you, Ms. Anyua," the first one seethed.

"Or should we say Janna Anessi?" the other taunted.

"Why won't you people just leave me alone?" I begged, my eyes stinging.

The one that crushed my eWatch sneered. "Because we have people in the Zendaalan government who would love to talk to you. Let's go."

My hands heated up, and I was about to use the opportunity to my advantage, but I was interrupted.

"Is that so?"

The two Zendaalan men froze, and so did my lungs.

That voice.

"Release the girl and put your hands up," said another voice. It was followed by the clicking of guns with their safeties being removed.

The man before me paled, slowly putting his hands behind his head, the man holding me grunting as he did the same.

"Stand against the wall," the second voice commanded. The Zendaalans obeyed, leaving me free to turn and face who was at the door.

"Do I have to get you out of some kind of trouble every time we see each other?" Kahmel said. His voice was level, but I could hear the tinge of outrage in his tone, and I thought it was directed at me until I realized he was looking over my shoulder at the Zendaalan thugs behind me. "Whatever the Zendaalan government wants to discuss with my wife will have to go through me first."

GOING HOME

Kahmel pulled me aside as the two officers who were with him handcuffed the two Zendaalan men. I breathed out the remaining heat building up in my chest, realizing I didn't need to use my fire anymore.

Unless I did.

Kahmel's eyes were hidden from me by his sunglasses since we were in public, but his worry was clear in his body language, with his jaw taut and his shoulders completely squared. I wasn't sure if he was aware of how closely he held me, his hands on my arms. He had trimmed his beard short, and I didn't dislike it. From this close, he smelled like a mixture of pine and...campfire smoke. Was that how laser residue smelled?

"Jashi, are you okay?"

My heart tried to flutter out of my chest. I didn't know how to feel. Part of me was afraid he was here to arrest me, have me executed for my crimes against K'sundi. But at the same time, I couldn't deny the feeling of safety he exuded, standing here in front of me, hauling away the "bad guys." No one—other than Nana—had ever taken care of me like Kahmel did. He'd traveled all this way just to find me.

Or he was here to punish me. Despite his own feelings, he was still Faresh.

I pulled away from him. "I'm fine."

"Is this your wife, Your Grace?"

Someone I hadn't noticed stood in the hallway. It was a guy my age with piercing orange eyes that clearly marked him as dragon tribe. He was tall, with close cropped hair, cleanly shaven at the edges. His demeanor was as serious as ever, his stare never wavering from the Zendaalans who were being taken away.

"Yes, this is," Kahmel answered. Then he looked to him and the other officers. "Wait for us out front."

The dragon tribe boy nodded. "Yes, sir." Then he gave a short bow to me. "Faresha."

Kahmel closed the door, facing me as he said, "We need to talk."

The tears that spilled down my cheeks startled me. I didn't expect that seeing him like this would bring so many emotions all at once, but it did, dredging up all of the dirty feelings I had to keep secret all this time. He was standing here alive *in spite* of everything I'd done.

I turned away from his gaze. "Kahmel, I'm so sorry—"

"I knew about the Zendaalans controlling you all along."

I whipped around to face him. "What?"

Taking off his sunglasses, he took me back with those startling eyes of his again.

"When you ran away that first day and you tried to get a fake ID, you came up on every radar in the black market. The Zendaalans got to you before I could stop them. I found out about them the day they approached you with their little deal."

"Why didn't you tell me?" I demanded.

"Because I knew you would have run away again, thinking I would have you arrested. And I couldn't afford you being off on your own before we were married and you had your title to protect you from the people who were after you."

My eyes narrowed at him as I subconsciously took a step back. "Yeah? Then what about after we were married? Why didn't you tell me then?"

"Because—" he stopped himself as the exclamation left his lips, pursing his lips and slowing down. "You still weren't convinced that you were on my side. Even you said you thought I was a murderous tyrant. Nothing I said would have convinced you otherwise. That's why I wanted to wait for the right moment, when I had returned from the war and…maybe you would see all of the blind faith I put into you, even knowing that you were being used."

"A lot of good it did us now!" my voice cracked as the tears continued to flow.

Kahmel frowned. "What are you talking about?"

"I could have had you and all of your men killed," I squeaked, all of the bravery and fire gone now. Nothing I did was justified. Treason was still treason.

He shook his head. "When you sent me that message and warned me, I was able to turn the entire battle around."

This time, I frowned, remembering for the first time that he shouldn't even be here. Wasn't he at war with Omani? "How are you here now?"

He smirked. "Don't you keep up with the news? Omani has agreed to my terms, and I'm here to finalize the agreement. They've agreed to give over the land that I've specified. Everything that used to be K'sundi's. The day they tried to invade my secret army bases was the day we started winning this war. And now, because of that advantage, because of you, it's almost over."

I couldn't believe what I was hearing. "That's what all those news channels was broadcasting? News about this?"

He nodded.

"So what do we do now?" I asked.

"We go home. There's still a lot I want to talk to you about, but not here. I'll feel better once we're back in K'sundi."

"And then what?"

"What do you mean, 'and then what?'"

I sighed exasperatedly, frustrated that he wouldn't get to the point. "Will I have to stand trial? Go in for questioning?"

"For what?"

Now I was getting angry. "For treason!"

Kahmel broke into a fit of laughs. "Not in a million years. My brother on the other hand, I plan to handle personally. But you..." His fiery eyes were smoldering. "All I plan to do with you is take you home. To me."

Flabbergasted, I stuttered with my mouth flapping open. "But I committed a crime."

He raised an eyebrow. "Can you prove it? Do you have the eWatch you used to receive the data, maybe?" At my silence, he remarked, "I didn't think so."

"But...this isn't fair!"

"Fair to whom?"

"T-to..." I stammered. "To other criminals! You're only sparing me because I'm your wife."

"You're not a traitor. You were being used," he said firmly.

I scowled at him. Here I was, thinking he was going to do his job as a responsible leader and have me arrested like everyone else who did the kind of thing I was forced to do.

Silly me.

"So what about Attican and Sokir?" I asked, still wanting to believe he cared at least a little about looking impartial. "If we go back to K'sundi, they'll accuse me of treason for sure. Then you'd have to imprison me."

Kahmel sighed. "It's like you *want* to go to jail or something. You're going to give my men all the information they need about Sokir and his goons, and by the time we're done with them, they won't be able to raise any accusation against you. Believe me. Now can I bring my wife home, please?"

He extended his hand to me, and I realized how much I actually wanted to take him up on his offer this time. I sniffed, wiping at tears. "There is one more thing, though."

"What now?" he groaned.

"I have to call Mrs. Maresh. She was kind of expecting me."

KAHMEL SAT NEXT to me in his private plane. I looked over at him, not quite sure what to make of him. He was a man of contradictions. With a bulking form and perpetually dark mien, he gave the appearance of being cold, unapproachable—certainly not friendly or anything close to it. Nothing he did would ever convince anyone otherwise, until they realized that he surrounded himself with people who were his opposite in every way. Arusi, Rand, Asan, Khes...me. He opposed no one with anything they had to say about him, didn't back down at being challenged. It was nothing you would ever expect from a man with a hard, unapproachable exterior. With his sunglasses a constant shield from the rest of the world, no one could ever see the other side of him. And I felt a part of him preferred it that way.

The one thing about him that remained was his determination as a leader, and the slow-burning anger that was always present in his demeanor—only now I knew that it wasn't without reason. He was surrounded by enemies; everyone was his traitor.

But I wasn't one of them anymore.

I wasn't sure if I could ever see myself really falling in love with him, though. A lump formed in my throat as I remembered our unfinished conversation. He had confessed his love to me last time we spoke. Did he expect an answer now? I wasn't sure if I had one. We were technically married, but I wasn't sure if I was still angry at him for taking the option of being able to choose away from me.

I picked at my nails, not sure how to break the silence that had so fair remained untouched since we boarded the plane.

"Kahmel..."

"Jashi..."

He gestured to me. "Go ahead, you first."

Regaining my composure, I said, "About our last conversation..."

"No need." He beat me to it. "I know you don't feel the same way

I feel about you. I don't expect that to change overnight. We'll continue business as usual."

In part, what he said relieved me. I was glad there was no animosity between us, or expectations outside of what we already had. But at the same time, I was married for all intents and purposes. I realized that even if I liked someone else, there was nothing I could do about it, especially being in the public eye as Faresha. Though Kahmel was nice, and I now knew he wasn't a heartless dictator, and he obviously had feelings for me, he wasn't my type. What if I one day became interested in someone else?

Before I could continue my train of thought, Kahmel was saying, "I was going to ask you a question, too."

"Go ahead," I allowed.

He put his hand through his hair. "Before we get back to K'sundi, I have some final business to take care of at the army base. It won't take more than a few hours. It's just some finalization things that have to do with the terms of agreement I set for Omani in exchange for peace. But while we're there, I want to show you the present I got you."

My ears perked up. "What kind of present?"

"You'll see," he said, smirking, his fire-colored eyes staring deeply into mine, like he was still taking me in, as though I was a mirage that would vanish from his fingertips in a second.

I couldn't quite blame him, either.

"That's not fair. At least give me a hint," I insisted.

Kahmel considered it, stroking his shortened beard. "No matter what I tell you, I think you'll find the surprise to be pretty *shocking* either way."

I blinked. Was that supposed to be a hint? Something to do with the word *shocking*?

Deciding not to give him the gratification of being asked for details, I went on to change the subject. "So how does this work, anyway?" I said bluntly. "I mean, you married me for my protection and all, but does that make us really married? I mean, what if we meet other people? Then what do we do?"

"What other people?" He asked, then narrowed his eyes. "Who have you met?"

I shrugged. "No one in particular. I'm just saying 'what if.' There's millions of people in this world and on others. Who's to say one of us doesn't find a perfect match with one of them?"

"Wow," he chuckled. "No sooner than I find you, you start looking for someone else!"

"I'm not!" I insisted, irritation prickling at me. "I'm just asking."

He raised his hands in surrender, but I could sense the veiled anger that simmered underneath. "All right, all right." Then the anger disappeared as his eyes gleamed with something else. "Well, I guess if there was someone you were interested in, there would be nothing I could do about that."

I waited, expecting he would add something else, raising an eyebrow when he didn't. "Really?"

"I can't control your feelings." He shrugged, then gave me a mischievous look. "But don't forget I'm still the Faresh. And should something...unfortunate happen to this person, I can't say I would have any control over that either."

Narrowing my eyes at him, I couldn't tell if he was just messing around, or if the glint in his eye was now almost welcoming the idea, like he was itching to oppose anyone that challenged his claim to his wife.

Either way, I was ready to change the subject again. "So what's my present?"

"You'll have to wait."

Damn it.

KAHMEL'S PRESENT

I expected the army base to be in K'sundi, but as the plane started to land long before we crossed over, I realized what it meant for Kahmel to be on a conquest. It felt strange to acknowledge for the first time that Kahmel was, in truth, a conqueror. This had been Omanian land. But it now belonged to K'sundi.

To my husband.

Though I'd heard that some of K'sundi's army bases were located in the air, this one was on the ground, and it wasn't camouflaged like I'd heard they could be. Men marched around a long expanse of pitched tents, dressed in robotic fighter suits. This part of Omani—or rather, Southern K'sundi now, or again—was steamier, a sticky warmness in the air, defiant against the approaching fall months. All around me the jungle expanse, trees, vines, and brush all tangled together.

But what knocked me off my feet were the dragons.

The air quivered with movement as they arced through the sky and shook the trees, streaks of crimson, black, forest green, and violet. There was a mix of Draconians and Wingless, some being ridden by fliers, others not at all. My hand went to Kahmel's firm bicep, and I shrank into his shadow in a shameless display of eat-him-first.

"It's all right," he tried to assure me.

My feet froze to the ground, and I could only stare wordlessly at the reptilian monsters that passed through the air. My eyes darted between them and Kahmel, who looked at me like it was the most normal thing in the world. *Nuh uh.* Whatever the gift was, it was no longer worth it.

"I think I'll wait for you in the plane," I managed to say, turning to run back to the car that took us there, only to be stopped by Kahmel's immoveable arm, as I refused to let go.

"Jashi, I wouldn't bring you here if it wasn't safe."

"But don't accidents with dragons happen all the time?"

He grimaced. "I'm not saying it doesn't happen, but that's just what I want you to see, Jashi. The dragons aren't as bad as you think when they're treated properly. Every day my men and I are learning more ways to keep them in line without using Zendaalan electric collars." He practically glowed with pride the more he spoke. "I want to show you what we've done. Please."

Another glance at the creatures flying through the air almost sent me bolting back toward the car, but Kahmel's calm presence encouraged me to stay. I supposed that he wouldn't have come to get me all the way from Omani and then willingly put me in the way of danger. Besides, I had never seen a dragon this close before, and I couldn't deny that as much as I was afraid of them, they also fascinated me.

Slowly, I pried my fingernails from the indentations they left in Kahmel's skin and followed after him into the base.

Khes met us inside. I was getting used to the scar over his eye now. The way it creased when he smiled was somehow endearing. "Ah, if it isn't her Highness the Faresha. Do you know the trouble you cause us all running off to who-knows-where all the time?"

"All right, all right, Khes," Kahmel said. "That's enough. Is it here?"

Khes nodded. "Yes sir. Waiting for you in the tent right over there." He pointed to the largest of all of the tents at the base.

I hated feeling out of the loop. "What is?"

Kahmel smirked at me. "Your present."

Before I could inquire, four people my age came running toward us. One of them was the dragon tribe boy who accompanied Kahmel when he came to get me. They gave slight bows before the both of us.

"Faresh, Faresha," the dragon tribe boy said, rising again with a big grin on his face.

Kahmel said, "Jashi, I wanted to introduce you. This is T'shan, Ashed, Kent, and Jemmorah. They're not so much soldiers as trainees. They've been learning with me over the last few weeks on how to properly care for dragons and train them for themselves."

They all bowed to me in turn, making me feel awkward all over again. I didn't feel like anyone should have to bow to me when just yesterday I was eating soup out of a can.

The one Kahmel introduced as T'shan said, "Oh! Your Grace, Asan told me to let you know that the Omanian councilor has arrived."

Kahmel waved the matter away. "Tell Asan to entertain him until I get there. I'll be right there."

T'shan looked a little unsure, like he wasn't certain what Kahmel was asking for was even allowed, but he nodded and bowed again. "All right, then. Um..."

"Yes?" Kahmel raised an eyebrow.

Jemmorah spoke up, her eyes lighting up. "Do we have time to go dragon riding before we leave again?"

Kahmel laughed. "Try to make it quick. We won't be here long. Tell Asan what I said first, though."

"Yes, sir!" Kent said, pumping his fist, then ran off with the others. "Let's go guys!"

Ashed pumped his legs until he was running ahead of all of them. "Last one there has to clean up the stables."

Jemmorah laughed. "You're on!"

I chuckled, turning to Kahmel as they all sprinted, surprised. "Since when do you laugh around other people?"

He shrugged. "They're good kids. Surprisingly open-minded." In a lower voice, he added, "I think they could eventually be trusted. Especially if I train them myself."

Frowning, I asked, "Train them? For what?"

He held my gaze, pursing his lips before saying, "You really need to see your gift."

⁂

I HAD no idea what possessed Kahmel to make him think I would ever want this as a gift. Not in a million years. Not in a billion.

Just...*no*.

We were in the biggest tent at the army base and had to climb some stairs to reach the entrance several flights high. I should have taken that as a sign. What gift required stairs to reach?

A yellow Draconian snarled and snapped at the air, pacing around the stake that kept it chained to the ground.

"How is this a gift?" I said as I debated whether I wanted to hide behind Kahmel again or shove him over the railing.

His sunglasses were off since we were alone, and the look in his eyes told me he was enjoying this way too much. He slapped a hand over his chest as though he was insulted. "I think you might have hurt his feelings."

I stared at him incredulously. "Hurt *his* feelings?"

He shrugged. "Or hers. We haven't really checked yet." As I made a face at him, he added, "It's still a little spirited, but I wouldn't bring you close if it wasn't safe. It's contained in a forcefield, see?"

Squinting my eyes, I noticed the air shimmering around the beast, a translucent dome of protection. I cautiously released Kahmel's arm from my death-grip. "Fine," I said finally. "I still don't understand why you would give this to me as a gift. It's a monster."

"That's what you thought about me. Have you changed your mind about that?"

I picked at my fingernails as my cheeks warmed. No, Kahmel wasn't a monster at all. "I suppose."

Kahmel's eyes danced, then he offered his hand. "Can I take you down to meet it?"

Now he had me fighting between my stone-cold fear and the creeping curiosity I also couldn't deny was there, too. "All right," I found myself saying, taking his hand and letting him lead me down the staircase.

It opened its mouth, and I jumped as an arc of electricity buzzed through the air inside the forcefield.

"What was that?" I breathed.

"I forgot to mention. It's an Elemental."

For a moment I forgot to be afraid. "What's that?"

He stroked his chin. "There are several types of dragons. You know the difference between Draconian and Wingless, don't you?"

I nodded. "Draconians are the ones like this. They have wings, and look more like lizards than the Wingless do. The Wingless look more like snakes, but they can fly through the air without wings. No one really knows how, do they?"

Kahmel shook his head. "Not really, no. There a lot of theories about anti-gravitational energies exuded from their scales, but there are also a lot of studies that deny it. It just proves that there's still a lot about dragons that no one understands. At least not the way things are now."

"Like yourself?" I challenged, earning a smile and a chuckle from Kahmel in response. Something about him seemed different now from when I left, like a burden was lifted from his shoulders. He was much looser now. Was he really that burdened with worrying about me before? Did my agreeing to stay with him give him that much relief?

"Anyway, an Elemental is a kind of dragon that doesn't breathe fire. Instead, it has special abilities that vary based upon the kind of dragon it is."

Suddenly his riddle from earlier made sense.

"I want to teach you to train a dragon to listen to you."

I shook my head, stepping away from him. "Me? Train a dragon?"

Kahmel's reassuring arm pulled me closer.

"I know you can do it, Jashi. I believe now more than ever that the dragons are essential to the way of life for K'sundii. And it has to start with us."

I found my hand seeking after his, letting his grip pump encouragement into me as he reaffirmed his grip on my waist. My heart pounded, but I wasn't unsure like in the beginning. Kahmel was a man with a cause. But that didn't mean he confused me any less, or that that determined fire in his eyes didn't scare me a little. Not because I feared for my safety, but for his, I realized. "But why us, Kahmel? Are you trying to change the foundation of Hemorah? Redefine the use of dragons, expand the borders of K'sundi, dig into history so old no one remembers it? Haven't you considered..." I paused, biting my lip, almost afraid that even speaking it would somehow materialize my fears into reality.

"What?" he prompted, then pursed his lips. "You mean you're afraid Zendaal will announce K'sundi a rebel country because of me?"

I stared at him, the unspoken seal broken. But it was exactly what I was thinking. "Isn't this dangerous? I mean, I know there are some downsides to the Equalization, but what's the point in changing what's been in place for centuries and risking putting our people in danger? So we go on like we have before. What difference does it make?"

"It makes all the difference in the world." I pulled away from Kahmel's arms and spun to face the one who spoke.

"Jashi," Kahmel murmured. "I think you know Matron Taias Morred. She's the owner of an orphanage in Kohpal. And a longstanding member of the rebels of K'sundi."

Nana crossed her arms, making a disapproving face. She shook her head. "Jashi, Jashi, Jashi. You've always been a good girl, but always so stubborn when I tried to teach you about your people's more ancient ways. Squirming and twiddling your thumbs at every

Ceremony of Thanks I dragged you to. Now you'll have to listen to my—what did you used to call them? Old people stories?" She gave me a knowing look. "But I think you're ready to listen now, aren't you?"

Dumbfounded, I nodded numbly.

THE TALE OF THE DRAGON KING

"You're a rebel?" I said, still not willing to believe what I was hearing.

She hushed me. "Not so loud, child. Do you want all of Hemorah to know?"

I slammed my mouth closed. How could my sweet old Nana be involved with rebels? The same woman who spent years preaching to me "the old ways"? And now she wanted to do away with a system that had existed for centuries?

"How did you get involved with *rebels,* Nana?" I blurted. "When did this happen?"

She chuckled. "I've been a member longer than Kahmel. Much longer. I helped him and his brother escape the K'sundi government when they were younger. And I told him to marry you." She laughed, shaking her head and giving Kahmel a knowing look. "Not that he needed much encouragement."

Kahmel looked away, scratching his neck. I turned back to Nana. "But...why?"

Nana cocked her head, her face touched with sympathy. "Your generation is so separated from your roots. Every generation is slowly erasing our history with each passing era." It was as if she were immersing herself in yesterdays long past even as she spoke. "In my day, we were detaching from our past as well, but while the

Zendaalans did everything in their power to erase the days before the Equalization, they couldn't silence the power of word of mouth. My grandmother told me stories passed down to her by her grandmother of a day when Zendaal didn't get to decide whether a nation survived or starved. When the dragons reigned the skies, unholstered. When the K'sundii were the mightiest warriors in Hemorah, and the most revered. Not the barbarians they'd have you believe we were." Nana sighed. "I didn't know about what they call the Fire Bug at the time, and you were the first time I'd seen anything like it. But after Kahmel moved away all those years ago, my connections informed me that a young man was seeking our help with a problem identical to yours. That's how Kahmel, his brother, and I got involved. Kahmel was the best thing that ever happened to the resistance. As son of a scholar, he had access to documents of the past we could only dream of seeing. And as a royal clan member, no one could blatantly oppose him. When he proposed the idea of becoming Faresh, it created an opportunity like we've never had before to make the biggest impact we've ever been able to make within the rebels. So together with the members of the resistance, we helped him find out everything he could about what they were doing to people like you and him."

"But to what end?"

"To find out what went wrong. All the rebels want is to find out what the world was like before the Equalizers." Her tone turned hard. "So we can know how to eradicate them."

The gravity of what Nana and Kahmel were planning sunk in, and suddenly I felt cold.

I shook my head, wanting to go back a few points. "Wait, wait, wait. You participated in all of these criminal activities this whole time? How have I never known?"

Nana's eyes danced with mischief. "Oh, I found ways. To be sure, I was a much more active member in my youth, breaking into buildings to find books on behalf of the resistance, helping immigrants get here from rebel countries, that sort of thing. But by the time I settled down and opened my orphanage, I was mainly doing administrative and management work. You know, sending rebels work here and there. Every once in a while I did hide an ally or two." She winked. "You remember how you used to be afraid of going into the basement because you said you heard voices behind the wall?"

My eyes widened. "You're kidding."

"I always felt bad for never being able to tell you." She tilted her chin up, grinning. "But yes, I hid people behind a false wall in the basement." Then she shrugged. "What? You thought I was just a little old lady who knitted all day? I hate knitting. I much prefer the action, but..." she looked down on herself and shrugged again. "This old body isn't made for that kind of thing anymore."

Kahmel placed a hand on my shoulder and pulled me close. "Matron Taias was responsible for most of the help the rebellion sent my way. They helped protect Rand and me when we needed it most. That's how I was introduced to Khes, Asan, and Arusi. They were assigned to me by Matron Taias."

Nana nodded. "When Kahmel and his team started to uncover more about the Fire Bugs, I knew they'd come for you, too. Arranging your marriage did several things at once. In the immediate sense, it protected you from what almost befell him. But I also knew he would help you connect to the dragons as easily as he did."

This was a lot to handle all at once, but I was slowly starting to understand. "Why do we keep going back to talking about dragons? What do they have to do with anything?"

Nana wrapped her arms around herself, adjusting her wrap dress as she did. "Everything, dear. Many dismissed my grandmother's tales as fiction, but I always felt there was some truth to them. I never would have guessed her stories were more factual than most history texts. She told of dragons that weren't as raucous or ravenous as today's. They were spiritual beasts that were the secret to the success of K'sundi's mightiest warriors." A slow smile crept up her mouth, the twinkling in her eyes sharp and knowing. "But one part of her stories always baffled me. She never took it back, though. She told the stories exactly as she was told, and I'm going to do the same as I tell it to you.

"The dragons of today are disregarded, seen as mindless animals, treated more lowly than a pet. And those of centuries ago were not seen too differently—until one day, a select few warriors of a mighty tribe took interest in them. This tribe held such high regard for the dragons, they even named their tribe after them, used them as a symbol of their power.

"The dragons were so astounded by these humans, they took up the matter with their King, who presided in the Great River basin. The River King knew these humans would be the best way to form a connection between his kind and the humans. They would be their bridge. So he ordered the dragons to send for these humans of the dragon tribe, this tribe of brightly colored eyes.

"But when the humans arrived, they found they could not pass to the realm of dragons where the King resided. Only dragons could go. So the Dragon King bestowed upon them the Ethereal Fire, which made them what the dragons came to call Half-Dracs. As they were only half dragon kind, it took at least two to enter the Realm of Dragons.

"For their honor and respect, the dragons would forever be an ally to the K'sundii, and especially to the dragon tribe. The Dragon King then made an agreement with those the dragons called the Half-Dracs, one that only the Half-Dracs were allowed to know. After that day, the K'sundii became one of the most revered nations in Hemorah because of their powerful fleets of dragons and dragon riders—this in a day when man scarcely knew a dragon could be ridden.

"Other nations were jealous of their power. Who could blame them? The connection the dragon tribe had to the dragons was incomparable, and it was said that the Ethereal Fire that the Dragon King bestowed on those people was passed down inherently. The lineage of Half-Dracs communed on behalf of the Dragon King and his people from their realm to the K'sundii directly for generations.

"But they say that one nation figured out the K'sundii's weakness, the only way to sever their relation to the dragons. Somehow, this unknown country learned the secret terms of the agreement between the dragons and Half-Dracs and found a way to trick the Half-Dracs into breaking it.

"From that day on, K'sundi, the great country of warriors, was never the same again. All of the knowledge they'd attained—how the dragons worked, how to befriend one, even a few utterances in the dragons' language to use as command words for riders—none of that seemed to matter anymore. Their mightiest warriors and dragons lost their strength, their powerful connection weakened, and K'sundi did not fare well. The dragons began dying off to mysterious circumstances, and so did those the dragons called Half-Dracs, connected even to the end.

"No one really knows what happened to K'sundi that brought it from mighty to fallible, but they say the Dragon King knows how to restore us by teaching the K'sundii how to restore the terms of their agreement once more. Two of those the dragons called Half-Dracs would have to consult him, as they did before, and find out what went wrong.

"As you're probably doing now, I too thought my grandmother's tales were nothing more than that—a tale. But when Kahmel told me that the code for people like him and you was Fire Bug, it reminded me of another part of my grandmother' stories.

"You see, she always said that with their ember-colored eyes and *fiery* countenance, those that the dragons called Half-Dracs were called Fire Bred by the humans—which to me just sounds like an altered form of Fire Bug."

The conclusion hit me like a ton of bricks. *That's* where the stories of the Fire Bred came from? All I knew them to be were fiery mascots of the Light Festival, portrayed as dancing fire characters that traveled up the mountain and brought down enlightenment to the people of K'sundi. But I always thought it was just a story, no more real than the story of the pixie that stole children's socks and shoes, or the tales of spider spirits, responsible for the weaving of dreams. I would have never related the tale of the Fire Bred to myself. In current stories, they weren't even human. Little fire creatures, rather, more friendly monster than anything human.

"But don't you think this is a little far-fetched?" I said, finally. "You're not seriously considering Kahmel and I go up to the River Basin looking for some kind of Dragon King, are you?"

Nana nodded. "It's no more far-fetched than believing you're a girl with fire powers who, instead of wetting the sheets when she was younger, burned them."

Behind me, Kahmel chuckled, and I narrowed my eyes at him. Somehow, I felt like he was enjoying my complete and utter confusion. "Don't you have a meeting to attend?" I said, suddenly remembering the Omanian councilor who was supposed to be waiting for him—and wanting him to leave.

Kahmel shrugged. "He can wait."

Nana grasped my hand in her wrinkled ones, but her grip was firm and unshaken. "I know this is all hard for you to believe, Jashi, but you must believe. This is the forgotten history of your people, of your legacy, and you and Kahmel have to find out what needs to be done to right a wrong that sent all of Hemorah spiraling toward these dark times, allowing one country to gain dominance over all, with the power to make or destroy a nation in a day. I believe the Zendaalans are the ones responsible for the loss of our connection to the dragons, which is why they claimed the power of the dragons for themselves and tortured them into submission so that no one would ever remember what our people were. They knew that out of the K'sundii could rise the Fire Bred, the only people on Hemorah powerful enough to challenge their rule. That's why they started looking for people like you and killing them. And that's why it was so important for Kahmel to marry you and save you, or all would have been lost. I don't know what's going to happen when you arrive at the Dragon's Heart, but I do know that whatever you find is what the Zendaalans have tried to prevent us from knowing since the day their dominion started."

A small smile touched her face. "I told you that Kahmel was a man of honor, and I meant it. I wouldn't have allowed him to marry you if I didn't feel like he was the best person for you. Not only do I believe he loves you, but I believe that what you are to each other will change nations, both being one of the few remaining members of the dragon tribe and Fire Bred. Your unity will bring the world together in a way it's never been mended before, and not in the name of 'Equalizing.' You'll prove what a true unity is when you come against the Zendaalan rule and restore things to the way it should have been a long time ago, both on Hemorah and in K'sundii. Your fates were woven together in the book of destinies."

I wasn't sure why Nana's words brought tears to my eyes. It was all so overwhelming and confusing. I wanted to believe it was real. I wanted to believe there was a reason I was born like this. The idea of having a purpose for all these years I'd spent in hiding, ashamed of who I was, and suffering in silence...it was tantalizing.

"So, what now?" I asked in a small voice.

"Now you decide," said Kahmel. "I've fought hard to reclaim what belongs to K'sundi, and now the Dragon's Heart river basin is ours again. Will you come with me to find whatever we can about the Dragon King?"

"If you want to turn back, this is the moment to do so," Nana said. "Kahmel will do whatever it takes to protect you wherever you decide to go, but now is the time to say something if you don't want to be a part of this. What are you going to do, Jashi?"

I swallowed, wiping at the tears that determinedly continued to stream down my face. "I want answers." Looking to Kahmel, I said, "Let's go to the River Basin. Let's find the Dragon King."

THE DRAGON'S HEART RIVER BASIN

Kahmel left to attend his meeting with the Omanian councilor, and I asked Nana to wait for me in the car. I was alone with Kahmel's 'gift'—a restless dragon that shot bolts of lightning from its mouth.

I'd never entertained the notion of owning a dragon. It'd never even occurred to me. I didn't feel particularly connected to the unruly Draconian. I didn't feel any special tingling, and I didn't start hearing its thoughts. I did feel a sense of responsibility, though, and that was heavier than any other sensation I could have been feeling at that moment. I felt responsible for using these abilities I was born with for something useful, and for being part of something bigger than me. Having expensive dresses, watching people bow to me, even being married to the Faresh...none of those things made me feel royal. But this awesome burden made the feeling undeniable.

I was the Faresha of K'sundi.

And for the first time, I liked the feeling. No one was forcing me to do it. Kahmel, the Zendaalans, Sokir—none of them were influencing my choice this time. The decision was mine, and I was confident that I made the right one.

Finally.

The dragon paced around its confines, and I wondered what it was like when they were free to live with K'sundii. Was owning a dragon common? Were they as dangerous to come near as they were today? I had so many questions, and I especially wanted to know how they would help us loosen Zendaal's grip on the world.

I took a deep breath. I was agreeing to help disband the Equalization—a system of peace that had been in place for centuries. What would be the cost of this freedom we were fighting for? Could our freedom more deadly than our bondage?

The answer to that question scared me. Still, I felt Kahmel and Nana and the others were right. What the rebels proposed was going to be far from easy, even for the Faresh of the nation. But I was convinced that it was necessary. It was time to see how the world fared on its own, without a dictating nation to decide their fate.

"You're still here?" Kahmel came down the stairs to join me standing on the outside of the forcefield containing my dragon.

I nodded. "I've been thinking."

"Understandable," he said, stroking his chin. His eyes were covered by his sunglasses, but in a second, he had flipped them up again.

"Why do you always do that?" I wanted to know.

Kahmel frowned. "Do what?"

"Take off your glasses around me. You've done it since the day you came to get me at the orphanage."

He hooked his thumbs in his pockets, considering it. "I don't really know, to tell the truth. I've always worn them so people wouldn't know that I'm dragon tribe. At first, it was because of my parents, but then it helped keep people from knowing they had a man of the dragon tribe as Faresh. I guess I don't like having that barrier with you."

I made a face at him. "You like the intimidation it gives when people can't see your eyes, don't you?"

Kahmel slipped his arm around my shoulders. "Yeah, that too, I suppose." He jerked his head toward the exit. "Are you ready to go? Matron Taias is waiting for you in the car."

"All right," I said, giving a lingering glance toward the angry dragon behind the field of light before turning around.

He walked with me, smirking. "You're beginning to like it, aren't you?"

"That's not it," I said quickly, turning away from him before he could see my grin. "I just don't like how it has to be confined here like this. Must be miserable."

"Oh, is that it, then? Well, as soon as it's properly trained to, you know, not eat you, it'll be free to roam around as it pleases."

I frowned at him. "It has to be *trained* to not eat me?"

Kahmel nodded sadly, pursing his lips. "Dragons have been trained by electrocution for centuries, and I think that's why they act so crazed now. So far, we've been able to stabilize dozens of dragons, at least to a certain extent, without the collars. Accidents have happened, but nothing too bad. Now, we may not be able to ride your dragon to the River Basin instead of taking the plane, but my dragon, on the other hand is raring to go. Oh, wait," he said, evidently enjoying himself, "you don't like dragons. Forget I said anything."

"All right, all right!" I said. "I want to ride a dragon. Can we really ride it to the River Basin?"

He grinned. "Absolutely. I think she'd love the exercise. She's been getting restless."

Flying on a dragon? It sounded amazing. But having to admit it?

I punched Kahmel's arm as we walked up the stairs.

"Hey!" he exclaimed, rubbing his arm as if I'd actually hurt him.

Laughing, I was about to do it again, but stopped myself before I did. Was I actually hitting the Faresh? Since when were we even close? As my cheeks warmed, I realized how close I allowed him to get before Nana showed up. Did I want him that close? Was I ready for that? Would I ever be ready for that?

I dropped my hand to my side again.

As we approached the door leading out, Kahmel stopped. "You can't mention anything we've talked about here. You can't tell anyone where we're going or where we've been from this moment on unless I tell you it's okay. You're officially a rebel now, and you know what will happen if you're found out."

I nodded, and he smiled. "Good to have you aboard, Jashi. Welcome to the rebellion."

WHATEVER I MIGHT HAVE IMAGINED RIDING a dragon would be like, the actual experience was exponentially more *majestic*. We rode bareback. Kahmel insisted on it, and I was glad he did. As we soared through the heavens, the dragon's body churned beneath us as it slithered through the air, fluid and elegantly. Wind blew my curls from my face, clawing at my clothes. My arms wrapped around Kahmel for stability while he conducted the dragon, leaving me free to gaze at the heavens above and at Hemorah below.

"This is amazing," I muttered.

"What?" Kahmel shouted over the wind.

"You do this kind of thing all the time?" I asked instead, louder this time.

"All the time." I could feel his smirk even from behind him. "You like it, don't you?"

I breathed in the cool, fresh air. "I could be up here for hours."

He turned to me, laughing. "I told you dragons weren't so bad. Now, your dragon will take some time to train, especially being an Elemental, but when it's ready, you should be able to fly it as often as you'd like."

The idea was certainly attractive. "Kahmel, do you really think the dragons will make a difference in the rebellion's efforts against Zendaal? I mean, we're pretty outnumbered, aren't we?"

Kahmel breathed deeply. "It's definitely a long shot. But I think we have a fighting chance. Especially when we find more of the Fire Bugs. Or Fire Bred, however you prefer to say it."

"You think we'll find more people like us?"

"I'm sure of it," he said as I rested my head against his back.

"We're not alone, Jashi. Otherwise, they wouldn't be searching for us with blood tests. There are definitely more Fire Bugs out there. They're just all under the age of eighteen."

As the scenery beneath us changed from forest to city, I looked over at what was once Omani, and a question occurred to me. "What will happen to the Omanians now that they're surrendering part of their country to K'sundi? Will you have to kick them out?"

"No," Kahmel said quickly. "I would never. There's a lot of political headache to handle, but as far as I'm concerned, the Omanians can stay where they are. Zendaal might have a problem with it, though."

"Why would the Zendaalans have a problem? What do they care?"

Kahmel sighed. "As I said, political headaches. From my two years of experience being Faresh, I've found that Zendaal is usually the underlying cause of most of our problems. They always talk about peace, but they're usually only concerned with the peace they allow. We'll have to see how this plays out."

My hands started to heat up. I tried to calm the fire, but couldn't find the peace I needed. Just as I was about to breathe out embers, Kahmel took my hand off his stomach and gripped it in his. I let the flames come, and Kahmel tightened his grip as the fire was absorbed into him.

"It'll be all right," he said, giving my hand another squeeze.

I slipped my hand from his hold and replaced it around his waist, raising my head from off of him. I tried not to think about the twisting and turbulent emotions within. I cleared my throat. "How much longer until we reach the river basin?"

"Not long. See the river Dihmus?" He pointed.

A river snaked through the ground, like a silver vein in the light of the sun. "Oh, wow," I breathed.

"That's one of the branches of the river. We're following it to the Heart, where the other three branches converge."

I could see where he was talking about, but I didn't see anything that indicated where a dragon king might be hiding. There were just several winding veins of river crossing each other. The once-Omanian city had already passed behind us, giving way to a more jungle-like terrain, with rugged cliffs all between.

"Let's land," Kahmel said, tugging on the reins of his dragon to guide it downward.

We descended and landed on a cliff that overlooked the rushing river beneath it, the jungle behind us. Kahmel slid off the dragon, then helped me down. He stroked the Wingless behind the ears, and the dragon purred in pleasure. "Good girl. We'll be back. *Hat sud*."

The dragon blinked, as in response to the strange word, then assumed a resting position, curling up on the ground and tucking her head beneath her arm.

I frowned. "Hat sood? What does that mean?"

"*Hat sud*. It's a dragon command word. They say Zendaalans were the first to discover the ancient language the dragons seem to understand. I don't believe that, especially knowing what I do now. Whatever the origins, there are a few words dragons somehow understand and respond to when you speak them. *Hat sud* is a command word to make a dragon stay where you left it. I can teach you all about commands when you learn to ride your dragon, but for now, let's stick to the task at hand."

"Which is what, exactly?" I said, crossing my arms and looking around, not seeing anything that stood out to me as somewhere a Dragon King might hide.

"We find out where the Dragon King is supposed to reside, like in the legends."

I nodded. "How do you expect us to do that? This isn't exactly a natural park with signs pointing out where the Dragon King lives."

Kahmel tapped at his eWatch, pulling up a holographic screen with an image of a book, like the ones I'd seen in his library. "I didn't bring us all the way out here without a plan. I have a few points of reference. Look."

Coming to his side, I got a better look at the screen. This book looked even older than the ones at the library. Much older. The written K'sundii was medieval and used so many obsolete terms, it was nearly illegible to me. Kahmel swiped at the screen, passing by photos of other pages to the same book, as well as several passages of others.

"These are all books that describe legends pertaining to the Dragon King. None of them go so far as to mention how to access his realm—"

"*If* such a realm exists," I pointed out.

He shrugged. "They do tell stories warning children not to go up what's called the 'winding way' leading to the 'Trembling One's' cave. The other members of the rebellion and I have cross referenced a lot of books mentioning a 'winding way' leading to the 'Trembling One' here at the River Basin, which we've come to assume is another name for Dragon King."

"Or just a bedtime story."

"Look at it like an adventure." He gently nudged my arm with his. "I didn't see you object like this with Matron Taias around."

I chuckled, crossing my arms. "Of course. It's tradition to respect your elders, you know."

"Ah, I see," he said, nodding with a half-smile. "And it was out of respect for her that you rode my dragon with me, then?"

Instead of answering, I gestured for him to lead the way. Kahmel walked ahead of me as we trailed a rough path along the lip of the cliff side. He took me down, the both of us stepping carefully to find firm footing along the jagged rock face. Though the view and scenery were amazing, the thrill soon wore off. It felt like we were on a childish scavenger hunt rather than anything to be taken seriously, climbing down rocks and hopping over cracks in the canyon's surface like children. The only thing missing from the scene were the cardboard swords, and we would have been no different than the games I used to play with Talad.

We approached an eerie crevice in the cliff side. I was about to voice my concerns when a shriek froze me to the ground. I spun to see a dragon arcing in the air above us, circle for a moment, then fly away.

Kahmel took my hand in his and squeezed reassuringly. "I think it's gone."

I shook him off. "Was that a *wild* dragon? I thought they didn't have those in Omani."

Kahmel scanned the skies. "I thought so, too."

"Why don't we just go?" I hugged myself to steady my shaking hands. "This has been fun and all, but do you really think we're going to find the entrance to the realm of the Dragon King?"

He pursed his lips. "Whatever the reason for the dragon being here, we'll be safer hiding in this crevice than going—" Kahmel stopped, his eyes widening. A pair of reptilian eyes stared back at us. The creature climbed down the side of the cliff, coming toward us.

It was on the ground in an instant, blocking the entrance to the very crevice Kahmel was about to suggest we duck into. Its eyes were trained on us, a snarl rumbling from its mouth.

I inched toward Kahmel. "What do we do?"

But he was already stepping in front of me, lighting both hands aflame with more fire than I'd ever seen him use. He snarled right back at the dragon, and it recoiled, but the skinny Draconian maintained its position in front of the crevice, emerald scales glistening in red light from Kahmel's fire. It wasn't a large dragon, especially in comparison to the ones Kahmel's people were riding, but I knew even small dragons were devastatingly powerful and ruthless with their kills.

Without turning away from the beast, Kahmel spoke slowly and through his teeth. "Start heading toward Huntress."

"Who?"

"My dragon. Don't run, walk. I'll join you in a second."

I hesitated, not wanting to leave him alone, but he was much more experienced in dealing with dragons than I was, and being difficult could just make the situation worse. I started away from Kahmel, then screamed as I was face-to-face with a light blue

Wingless, sauntering toward us from the side, whiskers waving in the air around its face. Behind us, small dragons the size of dogs came flying from the canyon in flocks, darting all around us. Then the Wingless took flight as well, dancing in the air in figure-8's around us. More dragons came crawling from the crevices, either circling us like lions with their sights on a kill or taking flight with the rest.

"What are they doing?" I had to shout to Kahmel above the screeches and growls that filled the air.

He shook his head, confused. "I have no idea. I've never seen anything like this before. There's not even supposed to be wild dragons in this area, much less babies."

The smallest ones must have been newly hatched, and the one blocking our way to the cave was an adolescent. But none of them had so far even touched us. They only circled endlessly, barring our escape.

Something tingled in me, a premonition I couldn't shake. I knew I would back out if I thought about it too much. I took a deep breath and stepped toward the cave.

Kahmel grabbed my arm, the fire on his hand extinguished. "Jashi, are you crazy?"

"I know what I'm doing," I told him, deciding not to add the "*I think*" that almost slipped from my mouth.

Giving me one more wary glance, he released me, and I continued toward the cave. The dragons around me snarled and growled even louder, but they parted when I approached them, slinking around as though they disapproved of my presence but were somehow hindered from opposing it.

I approached the dragon that barred our access to the crevice Kahmel mentioned earlier, receiving a vicious growl in response, the noise still piercing. My heart throbbing against my chest, and with shaking hands, I touched the cool snout of the dragon, feeling the creature stiffen under my touch.

Then, it exhaled, a long breath that warmed my face as it calmed.

As though we'd shared some secret between us, some sacred rite, the dragon stepped aside.

I turned to Kahmel, who was staring at me in shock. "I think... they somehow know who we are. The dragons call us Half-Dracs, remember? The Dragon King—" I looked into the cave, dark and unwelcoming, but I was sure that I was right. "He's in there. These are his dragons, his family. They were trying to protect the entrance to his realm."

DEEPER INTO THE CAVES

Once past the tiny entrance, the huge interior of the cave became came into view, large enough to be one of those sanctuaries Nana took me to every Ceremony of Thanks. Stalactites and stalagmites protruded from the ceiling and floor like teeth, making the cave truly look like the mouth of a dragon. But a path corkscrewed its way through the middle of the room and between the teeth, running deeper into the dank cavity.

"I think this is the 'winding way' you mentioned earlier."

"Yeah," Kahmel breathed incredulously, his voice bouncing off the walls. "Nice job, Jashi. And look."

He nudged me and pointed to the opening where we came from. The dragons stared at us from outside. The crevice wasn't big enough for them to fit through, but they seemed content with watching us expectantly from outside.

"Doesn't look like they're leaving us more choice than to keep going, then," I said.

"Then, let's—"

The ground shook and rumbled, a low growl emerging from the depths of the cave. I clutched the wet surface of a stalagmite for stability until the quaking stopped. Kahmel and I looked at each other.

The Trembling One?

Without any other options, we moved on, our footsteps echoing off of the walls and filling the silence. The air felt a few degrees cooler, the formations in the walls making it already look like another world. Stones glistened with moisture, and there was the pitter-patter of dripping water in the background adding to the eerie feeling within the cave. The path we followed looked to be groomed—neat and level, like it was man-made. If the dragons were unable to enter the cavern, who had maintained it all these years?

The quaking increased in frequency the farther we went, the low growl getting louder and louder, seeming to be coming from everywhere. But somehow, I wasn't afraid anymore. I was ready. Kahmel and Nana had been right about everything so far, and if this meant that I could finally use my fire for something useful, that I didn't have to hide anymore, it was worth it.

Our journey took us into narrower chambers, where we had to crouch in a few areas or twist sideways to get around the rock formations. Then the passage opened again, and Kahmel and I stopped as we found ourselves in a small room. Two podiums stood in the middle of the room, marbled white stone with gold gilding wrapped around the base of a bowl that made up the top. A velvet rug led up to the podiums, and behind it all a tattered banner hung on the wall. It was once probably a royal violet but was now a dirty gray, matted with dust, with bronze trimmings around the edges that flickered with the gold it used to be. In the middle was the silver symbol of a dragon holding a shield. The image sparked a memory in me, but I couldn't remember where I'd seen it until Kahmel spoke up.

"It's the old flag of K'sundi. Before the Equalization."

He was right. If the tattered cloth was thoroughly cleaned, it would look just like the images I'd seen in history texts of our flag before the Equalizers. They had removed the image of the dragon, leaving only the shield in our current banner.

"I guess back then they didn't have spray cans to write 'K'sundi waz here,' huh?"

Kahmel gave me a look. I shrugged at him. He might as well learn early that his wife was many things, but a history buff I was not.

"We need to figure out how to get the Dragon King's attention."

"And how do we do that?" I said, approaching the podiums tentatively, crinkling my nose at the thick layer of dust that lined it. I touched the cool outside of the bowl. "I don't suppose it activates with fingerprint analysis, either."

He gave me another look as he came over to examine the bowl as well, and he earned another shrug.

"I think we have to use our fire," he said.

I frowned. "What makes you say that?"

Kahmel reached a finger into the middle of the bowl and slid it along the surface, pulling back what I thought was dirt and dust.

"It's soot. There's been fire here before."

Putting my hands on my hips, I said, "And you thought my ideas were dumb. If that's what sends you to the Dragon King, why doesn't anyone just light a match and set the thing on fire?"

Kahmel shrugged. "The dragons outside seemed to know who we were. Maybe the podiums do, too. Just try standing on the other end over there and lighting your fire in the middle."

With a final shrug, I said, "My fingerprint idea makes more sense. But if you say so..."

I came around to the second podium and pulled out the lighter Kahmel gave me. "Do you think I could light it with this? I can't force my fire to come like you can."

"Maybe? Just try it."

I ignited the lighter, then coaxed the flame into my palm, my heart leaping at feeling its response. With a little more effort, I willed the fire to lift above my hands, feeling the strain like I was lifting weights. Finally, and a little clumsily, I let the fire fall into the stone bowl of the podium, then jumped back as it erupted from a small flame to a roaring fire, washing the room in a blood red.

On the other side, Kahmel did the same, lighting a flame across his fingers, then throwing it down into the bowl.

The ground heaved, knocking us off our feet. Rocks fell from the ceiling, crashing into the floor. The fire in the podiums shot upward, two blazing-hot pillars that pulsed against the top of the cave.

A cry shot out from the depths of the caverns, echoing off the walls. The rumbling intensified, chunks of the ceiling falling to the ground.

A glowing white dragon emerged from the way we came. Bright like a bolt of lightning and just as quick, it darted through the air and grabbed me in one clawed hand, and then Kahmel.

With another shriek, the dragon took us up into the ceiling. The last thing I saw was craggy rock and my own arms bracing for impact as my blood-curdling screams filled the cave. I squeezed my eyes shut. Seconds passed, and I felt no impact. Stranger still, I felt cool air against my face, with gentle winds caressing my hair and skin. I reasoned that I probably wasn't dead, which was good.

Cautiously, I opened my eyes, and gasped.

The dark caves of the river basin had been replaced by an astral world of wonder where stars glittered across the heavens in a smattering of light that looked like diamond dust. Swirling colors painted the black sky hues of pink, blue, and purple with accents of orange, green, and yellow all in between. This celestial ceiling was not dark; it was an obsidian background stirred with dazzling lights that made it seem like day and night at the same time.

I screamed as I looked down. There was no ground. We flew through empty space that held no landing point, no destination to be seen.

"Jashi," Kahmel said to my side, in the other claw of the dragon, his eyes glazed over in wonder. "This is the Dragon Realm. We made it."

But what exactly was "it?" There was nothing here.

No, wait. There was something here other than stars—a black slab against the colorful environment. As we got closer, the features became clearer, and it was apparent that the thing we were nearing was a rock, floating in space. Atop it sat a castle with towers that pointed like needles into the boundless skies. Stone walls came into view, lined with battlements, an intimidating gateway serving as the entrance.

The glowing dragon dropped us unceremoniously on a patch of grass next to the impressive structure, then roared as it flew away, a glowing strip of white disappearing into the starry background.

Kahmel got up, craning his neck as he gazed at the castle. "I guess we go in."

I took his hand as he offered it to help me up, nodding numbly.

We approached the gates, and the portcullis rose, the groaning replaced by absolute silence when it stopped.

The courtyard looked like a thing of dreams. The floors were tiled, and in the center was a reflective pond that stretched across the entire pavilion, mirroring the galaxies above with a perfect duplicate, giving the entire court an otherworldly feel. It was almost like we were standing there and floating in those very heavens at the same time. The walkways that wrapped around the pond were lined with tall gilded pillars and archways. Potted palm plants were placed sporadically through the halls, vibrant and green. The high ceilings were painted with illustrations of dragons and clouds, Draconian and Wingless alike. The paintings looked ancient, in a style of art I'd seen in museums from thousands of years ago. The whole palace felt ethereal, otherworldly, like any minute someone would pinch me and I'd wake up from it.

But it was real—the cold chill in the air that froze my blood, the way my heart pounded against my chest, the feeling that I was standing in the very relic of K'sundi's past—it was all very real.

Kahmel broke me out of my reverie when he nudged my shoulder, pointing to something on the west side of the palace. Two sconces lit with dancing flames flanked the entrance to another hall. Looking around, I realized they were the only sconces or torches in the entire pavilion.

"Let's go that way," he said.

I agreed.

Our footsteps sounded against the tile as we made our way to the west end of the pavilion. It felt like we could drop a pin and it would sound like a boulder.

Or maybe that was just my nerves.

The hall we followed led straight forward with no branching paths to confuse us. More torches lit the way, giving the dragons painted on the ceiling an eerie look in the crimson light. Eventually, we reached a door that was four times the size of anything humans used. Kahmel approached the double doors and tested throwing his weight against it, stumbling as the doors swung open easily.

With a look at each other, we strode inside.

THRONE ROOM OF THE DRAGON KING

Our footsteps echoed through the hall, the door's swing resounding in tandem as it closed behind us. A chandelier with black iron and old-fashioned candles swayed gently above us, but the illumination it provided wasn't necessary. The light from the stars poured through the windows, casting everything in a blanch light that reminded me of dusk.

And at the center of all of this, resting on the richly colored rolls of silk fabric, was undeniably the Dragon King himself.

His piercing eyes never left us from the moment we stepped in the room, nor did his reptilian features divulge any sense of surprise. The light from the windows hit him from behind, giving his pale blue scales a white halo that engulfed his Draconian form. Long and lithe, the Dragon King occupied most of the space in the enormous hall. One of his claws easily spanned the length of my body, and I didn't want to think about how large his teeth looked from where I stood. Horns spiraled about his head, and bulging muscles churned as he adjusted in his lying position, resting his massive head on the ground in front of him, throwing a lazy look our way.

"Ah, what a surprise. A pair of Half-Dracs looking for something. What has it been, a millennium? Two? I knew you'd be back eventually. Took you a little longer than expected..." He shrugged his scaly shoulders. "But you humans are pathetically predictable. What do you want, Half-Dracs? Some other favor you so desperately need, only to forget about us for another few millennia? Hah! You may as well go back the way you came. The dragons aren't interested in helping K'sundii anymore."

Kahmel frowned. "What are you talking about?"

The Dragon King ignored the question, tucking his head under his arm.

A black vortex opened in the floor before us, a swirling blackness that yawned and groaned. Without lifting his head, the King muttered, *"Unfortunately, the portal to the Dragon Realm summons the dragon of in-between for any two Half-Dracs that activate it, despite how unwelcome they may be. This is the exit. Now leave."*

"Hey!" I snapped. "I don't know where all this attitude is coming from, but we didn't come here for the scenery. We came here to talk."

The sleepy demeanor of the Dragon King vanished. He whipped his head around and leaned into me, throwing me off my feet. I scrambled to distance myself from him, but the dragon was persistent, his fiery eyes boring into me inches from my face, and for the first time did I realize that one of his eyes were gouged out, only a hollowed gash remaining.

"You want to talk? *Insolent girl! Last I remember, the K'sundii weren't interested in talking when we needed you. Why should we care about anything you have to say? Leave before I decide to kill you where you stand and show you why of all of the dragons, I reign as King."*

The dragon retracted himself, leaving me shaking like a leaf on the ground. I couldn't speak or even bring myself to stand.

Kahmel stood in front of me, facing the dragon. "I'm the one who sought out an audience with you. Not her. I am Kahmel Axon Kai of the Omah clan, Faresh of K'sundi. Whatever the K'sundii are guilty of is my responsibility."

The Dragon King narrowed his eyes at him. *"And she is your woman?"*

"I am not—"

"Yes," Kahmel cut me off, giving me a glare that meant now was not the time to contradict him. "She is."

"*Then keep this conversation between the two of us, if you insist upon staying and speaking your piece. The consequences of speaking out of place fall on you, and you alone.*"

Giving me another warning glance, Kahmel said, "Very well. She'll hold her silence from now on."

I huffed, but kept quiet, fully convinced that the Dragon King would make good on his promise if I didn't. It appeared the Trembling One was from a time before women's rights. The jerk.

"*So, a Half-Drac Faresh. How long has it been since that's happened? Quite a while, I'm sure, even to me. Regardless, this way is much easier. Now I don't have to rely on a messenger to inform the Faresh that his people*"—his tail slammed into the floor, which caused Kahmel to stumble, barely maintaining his footing—"*are no longer welcome in this realm. Half-Dracs or not.*"

"Why? What wrong have we done? Whatever happened was so long ago, our people have forgotten it even happened."

"*I'm sure you have. Why would you want to remember your own folly? You betrayed the dragons just before the Great War, and then wondered how it is you lost.*"

"Please, tell me what happened."

"*Your people betrayed the dragons! As far as I'm concerned, whatever transpired after that is just what you deserve. So you can forget whatever it is you came here for, because we're no longer interested in helping you.*"

Kahmel paused. "I want to make amends for whatever we did. Please, perhaps if—"

"*You want to make amends, you say?*" The vortex in the floor closed, and the Dragon King darted across the floor quicker than I could react. In one swipe, he had me in his clutches, pulling me along with him to his silken sheets.

"Jashi!"

I screamed as the dragon set me on the ground in a puddle of fabric, then pressed a single claw against my throat, pricking my skin. His pressure was steady, but with a single flinch, it would be over. My heart thrummed against my chest, and sweat beaded down my temple. I didn't even dare call out for fear of moving that enormous claw even a centimeter.

"Let's make a deal, then, Faresh. Your people took something of mine. I want something of yours. Let me kill your woman and I'll give you anything you wish."

I couldn't look at Kahmel, so I was left with the piercing glare of the Dragon King as tears collected in my eyes.

"No, please. You said you'd leave Jashi out of this."

"But if you want to truly make amends, there must be a recompense for what your people have done. In comparison, it's a small price to pay, I would say. Besides, she is only a woman. You could easily replace her."

I flinched as I heard Kahmel's voice crack. "No! There must be another way. I would give you anything else you want, just let her go."

The Dragon King lifted me off the ground so I was facing Kahmel, but he replaced the claw at my neck while the other hand squeezed at my ribcage. "*You have the audacity to come here, in my palace, in my realm, and demand things, just as your people always have. And then you tell me what I can and cannot ask for. I could have killed you both just for the insult. Now that I ask for reparations, you refuse to meet my requirements! Your people may have been foolish enough to forget your mistakes, but I can assure you that you don't differ much from your ancestors. Too blinded by your own pride for any room for humility!*"

Kahmel fell on his face in a deep bow, his voice shaking. "I apologize, Your Majesty. Let the folly be on me. Jashi has done nothing wrong. I'm the one who brought her here so I could have an audience with you, but I humbly ask that you don't make her suffer for my mistake in getting her involved."

A snarl emitted from the dragon's throat. *"Then what shall I take as reparation for the crimes of your people if not this woman?"*

The Faresh didn't look up. "Oh, great Dragon King, what value would taking my wife's life serve to you? Surely a more profitable offer would appease your justified anger. But I would not deprive you your right to a life in atonement for what we've done. I don't know what our crimes were, but I assume it has to do with the broken agreement between the Half-Dracs and the dragons." He paused, but the dragon responded with a growl. Kahmel continued, "In ancient times, when a man owed his debtor, he was allowed to offer himself as a servant until the debt was repaid. Instead of taking her life, take mine in servitude. It's worth more to you than hers, and the debt is more perfectly paid. The people of K'sundi have done you wrong. Accepting the life of their Faresh is equivalent to the penance for the entire nation. Her life is only her own. You wouldn't get the justice you're looking for, and the dragons would never get what they're owed from the K'sundii." He looked to me, his gaze boring into me. "Take me instead."

"Kahmel..." I started, my eyes blurry with tears. But I stopped as I felt the pressure of the Dragon King's claw push against my flesh.

"*Silence,*" he snarled. "*I like the Faresh's offer.*" The snarl then turned to a laugh. "*I quite like his offer a lot. Come here, Faresh of the Omah clan.*"

Kahmel approached the Dragon King, his head bowed. He knelt once he reached the dragon.

I was placed to the side, and the King opened his hand to Kahmel. *"Place your hand in mine."*

Kahmel wordlessly obeyed.

"No!" I screamed, but Kahmel's piercing stare silenced me.

"It has to be done," he said.

With Kahmel's hand in his palm, the Dragon King instructed, *"Ignite your flames."*

Kahmel obeyed, lighting a fire across his palm, then crying out as it turned an icy blue, crawling up both his arms. The fire...burned him? My gut clenched, confusion mingling with anxiety as I had no other option but to watch as Kahmel wailed in agony. Finally, the Dragon King removed his hand, and the flames died out.

When the process was finished, I was breathing out embers just to contain myself.

The Dragon King lifted me up again, then placed me next to Kahmel. I took his hands to examine the damage, but there were no burn marks. Instead, there were now black tattoos of a Wingless dragon that traced all the way up his arms. His arms trembled as though he were still in pain.

"They are the marks of Promise. Within them, I have written the terms of our agreement. Dragons will know it when they see it, and will hold you to your promise."

Kahmel nodded solemnly, taking his hands from me. He kept his head bowed.

Then the dragon sighed, leaning back wearily. *"The Great Spirits know the dragons need someone to protect them, lest they die off completely."*

"I will do what I can," Kahmel said.

The King huffed. *"From what I can tell, you already do."*

At this, Kahmel finally looked up. "Your Majesty?"

Rather than answer, the dragon gestured to the left, and another vortex opened, but in the air. This time, it showed images instead of blackness, flickering between people throughout K'sundi. Strangely, they were all young. Most were children, but a few were teenagers, hardly any of them older than me.

"I keep an eye on all of the Half-Dracs of your world. Even if only partly, they are still dragons, and therefore still under my domain."

"Then you know why I'm here."

"Yes. But I had to be sure you were dedicated to what you say you wish to do. And to make sure you knew your place," the dragon added with a snarl. *"You seem dedicated enough, though. From what I can tell, not many K'sundii nowadays are so well versed in the ancient*

laws. A nice touch." The vortex disappeared. "*You may ask whatever you wish.*"

Kahmel said, "I want to know what happened to the K'sundii. And how did the Zendaalans come to control Hemorah?"

The dragon sighed again. "*Foolishness. Greed. The lust for control. When the dragons first approached me about the fiery-eyed warriors of K'sundi, your people were a good deal more humble and honest. I made an agreement with them that was supposed to stay between me and those whom I made it with and the generations that followed their lineage, along with the Ethereal Fire. I could sense that humanity was going in a dangerous direction, and they were making new advancements and inventions every day. I knew that eventually, despite the power my dragons had, the humans would find a way to overcome them and abuse their power. So I made an agreement with your people, the people most similar to mine in Hemorah. If the dragons looked out for you, then you would look out for them. The agreement went well for many centuries after that. K'sundi became one of the most powerful nations on the planet through the power and prosperity my dragons provided. And you became one of the wisest nations, as well. No other race on Hemorah knew of the power of the Dragon Kings.*"

"Dragon *Kings*? Plural?" I asked, remembering only when the words left my mouth that I wasn't supposed to speak.

But while I clamped my mouth shut and froze, the Dragon King chuckled, now making me feel very awkward and confused. "*It's all right. You can speak. The Faresh has cleared the air for the both of you. I am not the only Dragon King in Hemorah. I am one of four. My name—or rather, the name you humans found easiest to pronounce—was Aithel. The other three Dragon Kings reside in their hidden places with similar access in three other locations. We normally have the power to protect this land from the harsh environment Hemorah naturally creates.*"

"Normally?" Kahmel asked, grimacing as he stroked his arms.

"*Yes. Since Hemorah's beginning, before the eventual habitation of humans, it has been a land of desolation. It produced no life, no foliage, no habitable environment. The other three Dragon Kings and I split the planet into four domains, and Hemorah blossomed into the colorful world it is today. Vibrant and full of life, trees, rain, and rich soil, it was an idyllic place for our dragons to frolic freely. But the more that forms of life took to the environment, however, the more problems it created. Mankind did not know how to cherish this land and took its bounty for granted. Some of my brethren evacuated their dragons, no longer interested in benefiting a people that refused to show gratitude for what they had. But then the K'sundii came along, a race with whom we forged a sort of friendship, a bond. Suddenly, through the Half-Dracs, we had a way to communicate to the humans their folly. And for a time, everything went well. But then the K'sundii got cocky. They didn't want to need the dragons anymore. They were tired of our gifts being the only source of their success, and they felt the need to prove their mettle without us. And then they sold us out."*

FORGOTTEN HISTORY

Aithel paused, turning away from us. *"The Zendaalans became jealous of the connection the K'sundii had with the dragons. They were a people obsessed with extending their lifespans and spent lifetimes researching it. So when they promised a Half-Drac warrior that they had the secret to eternal life, the warrior believed them. From him, the Zendaalans learned of our agreement with the Half-Dracs, and so began the fall of the K'sundii. They asked the treacherous warrior to enter the Dragon Realm"*—the dragon stopped, his voice strained—*"and extract the power from the Dragon Kings. The task wasn't hard. The warrior merely had to enter our realm under the pretense of carrying out business as usual and strike us unaware. From there, he could have taken anything to extract our power from us."* Aithel touched the hole where his eye used to be. *"He chose to take part of my sight. My brothers have lost other things. A horn here, a claw there. We've all been defiled by the greed of this vile warrior. After it happened, the Zendaalans assumed the power from the things the warrior took, and they used it to control Hemorah's prosperity. They chose whom to bless and whom to curse with a whim. When nations were left to deprivation and squander without vegetation or life to sustain them, they were easily overtaken by the conquerors.*

"The dragons might have forgiven the K'sundii for what happened, but when we warned you of what was to come, you

wouldn't listen. You refused to accept the help of the dragons, insisting upon winning the Great War against the Zendaalans without us. When K'sundi and the rest of the world inevitably lost, and the Zendaalans then sought to enslave the dragons so that we would never come to your aid again, you abandoned us and let it happen. The other Dragon Kings and I have had to sit back and watch as our kind slowly lost their intelligent and peaceful ways, converted into murderous beasts by their torment. The treacherous warrior may have acted on his own, but he only brought to fruition what was in all of your hearts, so eager to be rid of us that you leaped upon the first opportunity to prove yourselves mighty without us.

"*The Zendaalans have perverted Hemorah into a far uglier creature than it was before, with areas of extreme desolation and extreme prosperity, with no medium in between. My brothers and I have chosen to leave Hemorah to the Zendaalans. You and your people have left your agreement with us, so we have left you to the consequences of your betrayal. It was your foolishness that underestimated the will of the Zendaalans and doomed the whole world because of it.*

"*After their conquest, the Zendaalans renamed the Great War the Equalization and forced every nation under their rule to erase all of their history from before the war, or alter it. Your speech was very well worded, Faresh, maybe even moving. But you could never atone for everything your people have done. And the Dragon Kings will not help you be rid of the Zendaalans.*"

Tears slid down my cheeks, shame enveloping me. Nana always tried to raise me to believe more in our people's traditions, and I, too, wanted to distance myself as far away from our traditions as possible. Were my ancestors really so different from myself?

I looked to Kahmel for his answer, and watched as his jaw clenched, his gaze lowered. "You're right, I can't make atonement for the sins of an entire nation in just one day. There's no way any of my soft words can heal the wounds we've inflicted." Kahmel looked the

Dragon King in the eye. "But what if I convinced the nation itself to make reparations for what we've done?"

"Bah! Impossible. *Your people have forgotten us completely. How would you convince a nation to go back to a past they don't even remember?*"

"I'm the Faresh of K'sundi. I will change this nation. Already, I have a strong following of people to support me. The rebels will be behind me, and so will the other Half-Dracs, when we find them."

"*They will be stubborn. The K'sundii try to distance themselves from their past, but they are the same people they were a millennia ago. They won't want our help.*"

"I won't leave them any choice. I'm going to put a stop to the slaughtering of the Half-Dracs and let them finally know who they are, as I did with Jashi. And then the dragons will have a friend in the nation of K'sundi, a place where they can be safe from the Zendaalans. I'll enlist the help of other nations." He stopped, looking to me, and I knew he was filling me in on the other part of his plans that he didn't tell me about. "Rebel nations."

Aithel paused, then chuckled, more heartily this time. "*You're either a genius or a madman. But once again, I cannot deny the veracity of your words. Tell me what you have in mind.*"

Kahmel looked back to the King. "I want to unite the world against the Zendaalans and set us all free from their reign. But I need the support of the dragons to do it. I need to restore them to the way they were before the Equ—no. Before the Great War. The Zendaalans aren't rooted to the beginnings that brought them to their conquest in the first place and have forgotten the power of a dragon with his mind intact. This is the only chance the world has at being free again."

"Hmm..." Aithel hummed, his eye dancing with intrigue. "*You know the Zendaalans won't tolerate what you're proposing to do.*"

Kahmel nodded. "I know." He met my gaze and slipped his hand in mine.

My throat went dry at what I realized he was implying, but I knew what he was asking without him saying a word. He wanted me to be behind him on this, but I didn't know if I could do that. If he was thinking what I suspected, this was even riskier than I first assumed.

"Very well, Half-Drac. Some advice that will help you on your altruistic, albeit near-futile mission—enlist the help of dragons all over Hemorah and beyond. Many years have passed since the Great War, and technology has interpreted the battlefield in a totally new way. But the dragons have shifted and changed since then as well. They will never trust you or show you their true power unless they sense you have gained approval from their respective Dragon Kings. In other words, you have three more to go," Aithel said with a wink. "Next, I recommend learning all you can about the dragons. You already have a very extensive knowledge on how to train them, but you will need more than that to face your opponent. You need to find out what the Drake Bond is. Last, stop the slaughter of the Half-Dracs. You and Jashi aren't enough. Half-Dracs once numbered in the hundreds of thousands, but now your numbers barely make a few hundred. You need to save as many Half-Dracs as you can. In this, I will help."

The Dragon King gestured to the left again, opening the vortex that functioned like a viewing screen again. I recognized the image in the swirling window in space, whimpering to himself in his sleep in a small room. "Kahmel, isn't that the boy you introduced me to?"

"T'shan," Kahmel muttered, his eyes wide.

"Yes. He's done his best to hide it, just as all of the Half-Dracs in Hemorah now, but he is one of you."

As we watched the image, T'shan's hands ignited into flames, waking him out of his sleep. Quickly, he got out of bed, grunting in anguish as he forced the flames to die. When they did, he quickly took a pitcher of water from his desk and threw it on his sheets, extinguishing the flames. Then he went to work replacing the sheets, stuffing the burnt material under his bed and fitting new ones over the mattress.

My eyes started stinging again. "Well, this is great. We already have three of us."

Kahmel was shaking his head, his expression grave. "No, this is bad."

I frowned, and Aithel explained, *"The lad is seventeen. He hasn't much time before he, too, is discovered."*

Suddenly I understood Kahmel's solemnity. I'd already forgotten that the only reason I was still alive was because Kahmel married me before the Zedaalans could get to me. Now he had to figure out a way to change the laws the Zendaalans set in place before they got to T'shan, too. All of those faces in the vortex. All so young.

They were Half-Dracs. Any that were older than me were already dead.

"I don't envy your position," the dragon yawned, settling himself in his silk throne. *"I will leave you to your dilemma. Goodbye."*

The floor beneath us turned into the black abyss we saw before, and fell into a world of darkness. A claw grabbed my waist, and I looked up to see a glowing white entity carrying Kahmel and me away, back to the realm from which we came.

PROMISES

Two weeks passed after Kahmel and I talked with the Dragon King. After leaving his cave, we agreed not to speak about it until the time was right. We didn't even tell Nana what we'd found yet. Kahmel said it was best for us to wait for his next secret meeting with the rebels.

But there was one thing Kahmel did explain to me on our way back to K'sundi.

"I want you to understand the importance of what the Dragon King said," he'd said in hushed tones as we sat together on his private plane. "About how the Dragon Kings give life and growth to Hemorah."

"Yeah..." I said slowly, wondering what he was getting at.

"And he said the Zendaalans made a Half-Drac steal something from each of the Dragons so the Zendaalans could assume control over Hemorah's vegetation." He took out his eWatch, tapping and swiping through multiple screens, entering numerous passwords to access certain files. "The public isn't allowed to see these images, and I always wondered why. It makes sense. These are pictures of the landscape of rebel countries."

My breath caught. The images hovering on the screen in front of me showed miles and miles of dry expanse, not a living thing to be seen. There were other, more grotesque images that Kahmel flipped through more quickly, but I still saw the people captured in the photos—thin and hungry, living in tattered remains of anything gave shelter: old homes, cars, caves, abandoned buildings. This wasn't like K'sundi's desert. Even in the desert, there were plants native to the environment and animals accustomed to living there. But the few plants that did appear in the photos were withered and dying, the odd animal here and there looking muted and depleted. I hit the off button on the screen, unable to take anymore.

"Sorry," Kahmel apologized. "The Zendaalans only show these images to world leaders, not to the public, as a way to reinforce the Equalized Law. Leaders of the world already know not to ask questions, but the public isn't so obedient. We were told that this was what rebel countries drove themselves to after separating themselves from the Equalization. No one believes that Zendaal didn't lend a hand in sending these countries to this point, but we've never had any proof."

"And now we do?"

"No," he said. "I can't go around telling the world that Zendaal has a bunch of dragon parts they use to control the world's environment and climate changes. Apart from impeaching me, they'd send me to an asylum."

"Then what can we do?" I snapped, more than a little perturbed and frustrated by it all.

"We wait. I have a meeting with the rebels coming up now that the war is over. Until then, we don't mention this to anyone, not even each other. Understand?"

I crossed my arms, slumping into my seat. "Fine."

Scratching his chin, Kahmel added, "I'll be busy for the next few days, so I won't have the opportunity to research that term Aithel mentioned, the Drake Bond. But you can."

"How?"

"The books in the library of the palace might have it. Maybe you'd enjoy the reading."

I had the feeling Kahmel was trying to set me on a fetch quest to keep me busy. But as much as I hated to admit it, the idea of being in that library again did enthrall me.

Not that I wanted Kahmel to know that. I sniffed. "I suppose it's one way to pass the time."

Kahmel smiled. "Good. And I will handle the Courts. The Zendaalans are inevitably going to oppose my conquest of Omani. But it's not like—" he caught himself. "It's not like it's anything I haven't handled before."

I sniffed again, turning to the window. I caught that. It sounded like he was going to say, *"It's not like it matters."*

Once we returned home to Hashir, a change came over Kahmel—one that racked my nerves and set me on edge. It was like he didn't care what anyone had to say anymore. He assured me everything was fine when I asked, but I wasn't buying it. There was a steel determination in his eyes, one that scared me. It was the kind someone had when they'd already decided their fate. And I was too afraid of what Kahmel had decided on to even materialize my fears into thought.

So I just did as he asked and researched the Drake Bond.

Kahmel assured me he would handle the situation with Attican and Sokir. And to be sure, I never saw Sokir again, not even by chance in the palace—or any members of his family, for that matter, which was odd, because they were supposed to at least have the right to visit the grounds as they wished, like Rand did. But it seemed like whatever Kahmel did worked for the time being, and I wasn't complaining.

I saw Kahmel on the HoloScreen making speeches more often than I did at home, and I couldn't understand why that bothered me. Rather than dwell on it, I took him up on his offer when he suggested I visit Lora and even see Talad in Kohpal, albeit with heavily armed escort, and I had to bring Arusi with me. But I didn't resent the protection anymore. Knowing what I did, I was grateful for it. It was nice to feel protected around so many people all the time. Arusi and Lora became quick friends, and it ended up being a lot of fun. And

Talad couldn't keep his eyes off the petite woman, an interesting fact I reserved in the back of my mind to quiz him on later. I also saw Nana. It was strange now that I knew she was a rebel but not being able to talk about it.

After I got back from my visit in Kohpal, Rand informed me that Kahmel would be gone for a few days, handling talks with Omani about the new shift in territory, and when he got back, he wanted to talk with me. Then Rand pulled me aside and told me in a lower voice that the rebel meeting was soon and that Kahmel hadn't given him details, but I would know what it meant when he said he wanted to talk.

I was left with nothing but to wait for Kahmel to get back. I spent most of my time in the library or strolling through the palace with a book, keen on fulfilling the research task he'd had given me. At first, it was difficult to understand the ancient vernacular, but I was slowly getting used to it. To my surprise, there were a quite a few instances where the Drake Bond was mentioned, but without a full comprehension of the surrounding text, it was hard to tell what it was, exactly, from the context. Not only that, but there wasn't much description, as if at the time it was written it was such common knowledge it needed no explanation. In many cases, it was even a descriptor.

> *"Thine heart, so entwined with mine, our love even surpassed the might of a Drake Bond."*
> *"Twas truth that the Faresh was Drake Bound to his word."*
> *"Not even a Drake Bond could separate me from mine oath, nay, not even death."*

Lines like that filled many of the books I read. I still didn't understand what a Drake Bond was, but the ancient tales themselves had captured my interest most of all, romantic, elegant and beautiful.

One night in bed, I found myself immersed in the pages of such a novel. Why I began reading it, I couldn't remember. It must have mentioned the Drake Bond somewhere. All I knew was, I couldn't stop. It was a romance full of deceit and trickery, and though I was a slow reader given the style of language, there was no separating me from the book.

I only realized that Kahmel had entered the room when he'd called my name for the third time. "Jashi," he said, exasperatedly.

I snapped the book shut. "Kahmel! When did you get back?"

"A couple hours ago. I've been standing here forever and you didn't even notice. I take it you're enjoying your research."

"Yeah..." I said, remembering that I was supposed to be concerned with other things than if Matelo would ever get over his wife, Allara's cheating. "It's going well, actually."

He took off his glasses and raised an eyebrow, amusement glittering in his eyes. "Oh? What have you learned so far?"

I considered the question. "That 'thou' means 'you' and that 'trust broken stings worse than a broken Drake's Bond, and burns three score times hotter,' which apparently, is a lot."

"I thought so."

Kahmel started putting away the bags he was carrying, going into his closet and coming back out with the mattress and retractable bed frame he used to create a second sleeping space in our room next to my bed. It was a hassle to do every night, but this way there were no questions about us not sleeping together. I'd offered to take the smaller bed, since the larger one was his bed to begin with, but Kahmel wouldn't have it, so I gave up. I wasn't sure what he was planning to do for the rest of our marriage, because I wasn't going to sleep with him. But that was his problem.

When Kahmel finished making his bed, he sat down and leaned forward, looking at me. "How was Kohpal?"

"Very different, coming back as the mysterious Faresha that no one knows much about. I'm not used to being famous."

He chuckled. "Yeah, I think the press is eager to meet you. I saw articles talking about your visit. They wouldn't be right about you going to meet a secret lover, would they?"

I scoffed, setting my book aside. "I saw Nana. It was so different talking to her knowing what I do now, pretending everything was the same as it's always been. I don't know how you people do it, leading two lives at the same time."

"Speaking of which," Kahmel said, taking a deep breath, then continuing in a lower voice, "it's time for you to meet the rest of the rebels. We won't be sharing the majority of what the Dragon King shared with us. The meeting is simply to update the rest of the resistance on the progress of our movements, take orders from the rebel leader, things like that."

"Who's the rebel leader?"

Kahmel frowned, as though it was supposed to be obvious. "Me, of course."

I rolled my eyes. "Of course."

With a smirk, he added, "I have been since it became apparent that I could assume the throne. Wouldn't make sense for the Faresh to have a leader to report to, now does it?"

"Just continue."

"Well, I'll be introducing your inclusion to the resistance." Kahmel took off his glasses and set them on the nightstand we shared. "It's normally a more lengthy process, but as leader, I can introduce whomever I please."

"Don't I feel lucky?" I smiled and crossed my legs, leaning over and resting my head in my hands.

"Do you want to be a rebel or don't you?"

I laughed. "Yes, yes. Go on."

"I'll instruct them to direct their efforts toward finding the Fire Bugs. No mention of Half-Dracs, though."

I frowned. "But don't you trust them?"

"I do," Kahmel said, nodding. He got up and sat down next to me. "But they're not ready for all of this. They have a lot to handle as it is, sending support to rebel nations and working to cover their tracks. For the moment, everything about the Half-Dracs will stay between you, me, Taias, and my team—Rand, Arusi, Khes, and Asan."

I leaned over and pulled out a silk cap from the nightstand. Now that I'd settled in a little better, I had more of my things in the room. I slipped the cap on. "And not the kids who joined you? What about T'shan?"

Kahmel pursed his lips, and I realized T'shan probably never left his thoughts from the moment he found out about it. "His birthday is in seven months. I had some people dig up his history and I set some people from the rebels to keep an eye on him. We have until then to have to tell him. But the problem with him is the same problem I had with you. He may be loyal to me now, but what would he do when he finds out I'm against the Equalizers? And if he told anything to the Zendaalan officials, or even K'sundii ones..."

"It would be a catastrophe," I finished for him, shuddering as I imagined what I would have done with that same kind of information had Kahmel told me at the wrong moment. He was right. Everyone who lived in an Equalized nation generally approved of the Equalizers. The likelihood T'shan thought any differently was small.

"Then what will you do?"

Kahmel sighed. "I was hoping you could help me with that. T'shan is learning how to train dragons, and from what I can tell, he's a quick study. I want him and his friends to learn dragon training from myself and Rand. I'm working on getting permission from their parents to allow it. But if they approve, I'd like T'shan to hang around you."

"Me? Why me?"

"Because he'll relax more around you. If you get to know him, he's more likely to trust you as a friend, rather than look to you as his superior. You may not have noticed, but not a lot of people find me very approachable."

I made a face. "No, I never would have guessed."

He chuckled. "Anyway, the more he trusts us, the less likely he'll be to sell out our secrets when we tell him the truth. In the meantime, I'm going to be spending a lot of time with Asan on the political end, working to change those laws about the eighteenth year blood test.

Not to mention *this*," he said, pulling up his sleeves to show the tattoos that now trailed up his arms. "I have to get the policies on dragons changed, too."

I cringed at seeing the marks again. "How are you on that, anyway?"

He stroked his arms. "Fine, most of the time. Every now and then they throb, some days worse than others."

"You mean the pain hasn't stopped yet? Isn't there anything you can do about it?"

"I don't think I'm supposed to. Not until I fulfill my word. I have to make the K'sundii own up to their past crimes and go back to fulfilling *their* word to protect the dragons."

"But Kahmel," I started, biting my lip, "aren't you scared?"

He stopped, the hard look I'd seen in his eyes softening at me. Taking his sleeves down, he got up and sat at my side. "Are you?"

I exhaled. "A little. I mean, what if..."

"K'sundi gets declared a rebel country?"

Blinking tears out of my eyes, I nodded. I felt guilty for not being as brave as he and Nana were, unafraid of the risks that faced them if they were found out. But I was terrified of our nation being turned into a skeleton of what it used to be.

He cupped my cheek in his hand. "It's going to be okay." A pause lapsed between us before he added, "Regardless of what I do, Zendaal might do it anyway."

Just like that, my blood had frozen over. "What do you mean?"

"They never wanted me in power in the first place. I think they thought I'd be dead by now. But now everything they've tried to get rid of me has failed, and they're limited by K'sundii law to eradicate me from the throne. They'll most likely try to force the Courts to impeach me by threatening with the declaration of rebellion on K'sundi."

I could barely see him through the tears that blinded my eyes. "If they wanted you dead, why haven't they done it already? They have all the power in the world; why punish all of K'sundi?"

His eyes were like fire now, bright and dazzling with heated passion. "The Zendaalans killed the Faresh before me for supporting the rebels. Doing it a second time would make them too obvious. That's why they'll have to resort to other means to quash the rebellion. But we'll be fine."

"How, Kahmel?" I snapped, jerking my head away from him. "What you do doesn't just affect you, it affects everyone. We're talking about an entire country being driven to ruin! How can you tell me we'll be *fine* after that?"

"I don't plan to leave K'sundi in ruin. Being declared a rebel country will work in our favor."

Now I was confused. "What are you talking about?"

"Equalized countries cannot maintain talks with rebel countries. The system doesn't allow it, and I'd have no backing if I tried. But rebel countries can do as they please."

"Are you saying what I think you're saying?"

He nodded. "When and if Zendaal declares K'sundi a rebel country, the rebels already have contacts in other rebel nations that can help support us. I plan to form an alliance against Zendaal with *all* rebel nations. K'sundi will survive, and so will the others, if I can help it. And if all goes well, we won't be under those conditions for long. All I need is enough dragons on my side, like Aithel suggested, and we'll be able to go to war. Just promise me one thing, Jashi."

He reached into my hair and pulled out the hair clip I didn't even realize I'd forgotten to take out. "No matter what happens, take this with you, and I'll be able to find you again."

As I realized what he meant by that, I felt so stupid for not figuring out sooner how he always managed to find me when I disappeared somewhere.

But more than that, I finally understood what Kahmel's intentions were, and that of the rebels.

They were going to start the Great War II.

But this time, with dragons on their side.

EPILOGUE

Kahmel Axon Kai, of the Omah Clan

I remained calm the entire way to the penitentiary.

As I stepped out of the car and passed through security to cell block number 832, I maintained a perfectly still visage. Being Faresh for two years, and before that a rebel on the run, I had plenty of practice.

But as soon as I saw my brother sitting there in his cell, something blew a fuse. I managed to keep it from showing outwardly.

Just barely.

The guard left the room and I was left with the vile creature I was forced to call brother.

"You'll never get away with this," Sokir said, standing, putting his arms through the bars and leaning on them. "The Zendaalan government won't stand for it."

I looked around, still maintaining my composure. "I don't see any of them here, do you?"

Sokir sneered. "What, does it feel good to play a king, Kahmel? You've lived like a rat your whole life and now you get to pretend you have some sort of power. The Zendaalans want you to know you're a king on a leash, and your power only goes as far as *they* say it goes. I'm still a royal clan member. When they're through with you, they'll have me released and possibly even give me your throne."

"If they find you."

The sneer fell from Sokir's face. "What are you talking about?"

"Oh, you didn't hear? You're being transferred. These men will take you to another holding cell in another prison." I rapped on the door, and the rebels I'd sent for came in. "I hope nothing happens on your way there, though. I hear the rebel activity these days has been getting out of hand. Government officials being kidnapped and taken to parts unknown..." Reveling in the fear that eclipsed his eyes, I smiled. "It's a jungle out there."

"How can you do this to me? I'm your family, Kahmel. Your own brother!"

"Oh, please," I scoffed. "Family? I wish I could pin crimes on the whole lot of you. You'll have to do, I suppose." In one quick movement, I'd grasped his neck from between the bars and was pulling his skull as far as it could reach between the rods. The "guards" beside me didn't even flinch.

I liked these guys.

"You listen here," I seethed. "I can tolerate a lot of bull from you people, the people you call 'family.' I have already. Abandonment, rejection—you name it. But there's one thing I couldn't stand. You tried to take advantage of my wife. Made her feel like a criminal." I clenched my hand harder against his neck, hearing the short, gagging noises he made as I did. "The way I see it, the only hope you have of ever getting any mercy out of these guys," I pointed to the rebels, cool as cucumbers, "is to tell them what they want to hear."

"Which is—ah!" Sokir choked out, stopping as I squeezed harder for a moment, then loosened the pressure, if only a little. "Which is what, exactly?"

"How many others like me and Jashi do you know of? And where can I find them?"

Sokir laughed, the noise sounding high-pitched and off-key with my hand around his throat. "I'll never tell you."

I grinned. "Good. That means we get to do this the hard way."

Tossing him back, I walked away as my men detained him.

Addressing the man that stood outside the door, I said pointed to the camera in the corner of the room, supposedly hidden. "I want those tapes deleted and every trace of our being here, as well. As far as anyone's concerned, this was just an ordinary transfer."

"Yes, sir," the man responded.

I was immensely satisfied at knowing Sokir would be detached from his many connections, but I knew he was only the tip of an iceberg of problems. How many more of my family were plotting against me with my enemies? Waiting for the perfect moment to strike? The Courts were more than willing to find a way to get rid of me. And the Zendaalans desperately needed me out of the way. I thought about what Arusi told me her investigators found, the pictures they brought back.

The dragons that went wild near the city limits were spurred on, just as I thought. Dead dragons were strategically placed within the borders. The smell of dragon corpses sent dragons on a vengeful frenzy. Ancient documents told of dragons willing to go hundreds of miles just to avenge their dead.

Following a hunch, I had her broaden her investigation, and we found that, as I suspected, it was being done everywhere I was trying to maintain dragon caves. It was the reason every time I thought the dragons were getting better, they would go on a rampage that forced my men to put them down.

I had problems on more fronts than I could count, but I was sure this was road I was destined to tread. I'd come this far despite the odds. If I didn't start a change in this nation, who would?

A notification on my eWatch drew my attention away. Jashi had sent me a message.

I'm with you.

They were only three words, but they meant a thousand. It was almost enough to make me forget the heap of trash being "transferred" behind me. I smiled. Matron Taias knew what she was doing when she arranged our marriage. We were both natural-born fighters.

After all, the dragons didn't call us Half-Dracs for nothing.

Acknowledgments

There's so many people that have helped Conquest become one of the projects I'm most proud of. My mom, who has always been an inspiration to me, and has always listened to my stories since I was little and showing her every small accomplishment I achieved and expecting her to rave about it, even when it was a doodle with a line and two dots, or a story three pages long done exquisitely in crayon. My dad, who taught me not to be ashamed of pursuing something I love doing. My brother, who helped me spur on my love of telling stories by asking me to tell them when we were kids, right before bed.

I want to thank my wonderful friends from across the globe, Gladys and Katerina, who helped me develop my characters with crazy scenario-creating antics in long threads on Twitter. Not to mention just being generally amazing and supportive of everything I do. I love you guys so much!

I'm also so very grateful to the acquisitions director, Beth, the editor, Melissa, and all of the amazing people that work at Immortal Works! Thank you all so much for believing in my genre-mashing story and crazy characters, and for helping me polish it to shine as much as it does!

About the Author

Celeste Harte is an African-American writer living in Spain. She loves reading and writing sci-fi and fantasy, and is obsessed with all things mermaids and dragons.

When she's not building worlds and getting lost in her own fantasies, she's probably dancing to random music or watching (yet another) Korean drama. In addition to her native language, she speaks Spanish and Catalan almost fluently, some French, and would love to learn Korean.